Someone Special

Joy Taylor

For Lea, Lois and Sophie

Prologue

6 years ago

The girl lifted her head from the book she was reading. Her heart banged hard against her chest. She moved quickly, putting the book aside, swinging her legs over the bed, kneeling on the floor, brushing aside her damp sandy runners. She pulled at the rough carpet beneath her fingers, scraping the top of her head as she squeezed her body into the dark space beneath the bed.

It was the sound of something breaking in the kitchen, a plate, a glass, shattering against the wall. She knew what came next and there was nothing she could do but hide. She pressed her cheek against the carpet waiting for the screaming and the deep throated roaring of the man she hated. She knew what that sound meant. She held her breath, the dust pricked her nose. She was surprised to hear her heart beating. She screwed her eyes tight and thought of the boy. She whispered his name over and over, anything to block out the punches, the slaps, those hands, those fingers like fat sausages around her mother's throat, her head bouncing against the wall.

She tried to reach up and block her ears but the space under the bed was too small. Her face was turned towards the door, her back against the wall, her nose pressed into the carpet that held the sweet sickly smell of the glass of wine her mother had thrown at her just three nights ago.

"I know you're under there. Come on out. He's really sorry. He didn't mean it."

She had heard the slur in her mother's voice. The words sounding as though they were made of jelly. She saw her mother's bare feet; the candy pink chipped painted toenails. The feet moved, a glass placed on the carpet beside two shadowed knees. Her mother's face peering under the bed, blocking out the light. It was too dark to see what damage the man had done to her face. The girl knew she would see it in the morning. if her mother hadn't tried to disguise the bruises with make-up.

How she hated him.

She wanted to scream.

But she had learnt to disappear, stay still and silent.

Her mother stretched out her hand and the girl froze. Fingers closed around a handful of the school t-shirt she slept in. The girl didn't speak, she hardly breathed, she arched her back to the underside of the bed, anchoring herself against the pull of her mother's fingers.

'Fuck! You broke my fingernail. There, take that.' The girl gasped as the ice-cold wine caught the side of her face. 'You can stay there all night.' The door of her bedroom slammed shut. The girl hadn't moved as the wine dripped from her face and onto the carpet.

Tonight, she waited for the shouting and the high screams of her mother to begin. This time there was nothing. She tried to remember what she had heard, glass breaking? Her mother's high-pitched scream that stopped suddenly as though a hand had forced the sound back.

The girl could see the man; short and overweight, his stomach bulging through his shirt, leaning over her mother, one arm across her throat, a hand across her mouth.

The girl stayed under the bed for a long time, listening to the sounds of someone moving, doors opening and shutting. She heard her mother's voice pleading for him to stay and his silence as he moved around the house. She heard a car start up and pull away. He would be back. He always came back. She lay listening to her own breathing until the pain in her bladder forced her out from under the bed.

She didn't flush the toilet. She splashed water on her toothbrush, and scrubbed at her teeth. She tried not to look at herself in the soap splattered mirror, but she couldn't help seeing the girl looking back at her, with the tufted, shorn hair that made her look wild. She touched her head, running her fingers over it, feeling the places where her mother had cut it down to her scalp.

The next morning his car still wasn't there. She felt safe to use the bathroom. She showered and put on her school uniform. It was crumpled and grubby. She was hungry.

She opened her mother's bedroom door. She could see the familiar shape of her lying on her side, the covers pulled over her head. Light filtered through the cheap curtains. A sweet smell that you couldn't eat hung in the air. The girl knew that smell, it permeated the house, it permeated her mother like cheap perfume but worse.

She took a step towards the bed, "Mum?" She barely touched the shape where a shoulder might be and took a step back and then another until she was out of the room. She got her school bag from her bedroom and went to the kitchen.

She opened the pantry door; empty except for a handful of cornflakes in the bottom of their torn box, and a large packet of five-minute noodles. Nothing to take to school and no money to buy anything. She ate the last of the cereal. There was no milk in the fridge only a beer that belonged to the man. Her mother's bag was in the lounge room. She searched for loose coins to buy something from the school canteen but found none. She drank a glass of water and left for school.

As usual after the school bell rang, she stayed at school for as long as she could and then walked to the park a block away from her house. Sitting at the picnic table under the peppermint trees, she took out her schoolbooks and waited until the sun was low in the sky. Then she went home.

She pushed open the back door. The dishes from the morning were on the kitchen bench. The torn cornflakes box on the small Ikea table.

Her breathing was ragged as though she had been running.

She put her school bag down and stood still, listening.

The house felt full of menace.

Something waiting for her.

His car wasn't in the driveway. He hadn't come back. She had been fooled once before when she had thought he wasn't home and then his large, tattooed arms had snaked around her waist and her feet were off the floor, her body pressed against his fat stomach. He had held her without speaking until her mother had come in from the garden and saw them. "What are you doing?" she said in a voice the girl didn't recognise. How the girl hated him.

The girl stood listening. She didn't call out. She knew better than that. "Let me sleep can't you. You're old enough to look after yourself." She had been looking after herself for as long as she could remember. There must have been a time when her mother looked after her, but she couldn't remember that. She rubbed her hand over her head, feeling the rough tufts of hair under her bitten fingernails. She had told the case worker from the Department for Child Protection that she had cut it herself. That was a lie. "Do you want to go in a foster home and get sexually abused? No, I didn't think so. It's going to grow back and now you don't have nits, do you."

The girl had thought she might like foster care but not the other thing.

The girl pushed open the door in the lounge room. The curtains were still closed blocking out the bright afternoon sun. The dark familiar shape of the sofa and the single armchair looked small in the sparsely furnished room. The stains on the beige carpet were dark ugly shapes threatening to grab at her ankles. In the half-light, she could see an empty packet of corn chips on the floor. She bent and picked it up, licked her finger and pressed it into the crumbs at the bottom of the packet. She sucked at the salty taste.

She was hungry. All she had eaten that day was the dry cereal and a sausage roll and apple she had found in her desk. She knew who had left them there. She hadn't wanted him to see her with her hair like this. He had stared at her like the rest of the class but he hadn't laughed. She thought about the way he had looked at her, his grey eyes glittering before he turned his head away. She loved that boy.

Her mother's bedroom door was shut. She put her ear against it and waited with her fingers touching the door handle. She half turned the knob and then changed her mind. She didn't know what she would find. It wasn't the first time she had come home to an empty house. She preferred to think of her mother in bed sleeping. She didn't like being in the house on her own at night.

She knew what to do. She went into her bedroom and took off her school uniform and went into the bathroom in her underwear with her tracksuit bottoms and the t-shirt under her arm. She locked the door.

She made herself noodles for dinner in the microwave and then went to her bedroom, took out her homework and sat cross legged on the bed, her back against the wall. A teacher in fifth grade had told her that she was a very clever girl and that if she kept up her schoolwork, she could do anything, be anything. It drove her. She knew what she wanted.

When it got dark and her mother still hadn't come home, the girl took her blanket and pillow into the bathroom, locked the door, got in the bath and went to sleep with the light on.

The next morning, she opened her mother's bedroom door and the smell hit her with a force that sent her running from the room, out of the house and across the road to a neighbour.

Chapter One

Jack Charles, sports hero of St Jude's school for boys, parked his shiny silver new Audi hatchback outside the school grounds. He took one look at himself in the little mirror on the back of the sun visor. His grey eyes looked back at him. Fuck, lipstick, bright pink on the corner of his mouth. Did she kiss him? He couldn't remember. He hadn't kissed her. He would remember that. Fuck no. He rubbed the back of his hand across his mouth until the pink smear had gone.

He grabbed his sports bag from the boot and threw it over his shoulder and sprinted across the manicured front lawns to the school bus that was taking the team for the last football game he was ever going to play for St Jude's.

The sun was an acid orange hovering at three o'clock in a cloudless eye watering blue sky. The trees surrounding the car park were mirrored in the dark shapes that lay across the playing field that bordered the east side of the school. He had spent his time out of class playing on the white marked footy oval with his mates, honing his footy skills and kicking goals for St Jude's. Five years at St Jude's all boys school and now it was ending. The last time he would play for the school. The last time he had to front up to the school coach, Johnson. Jack could tell him more about Australian rules football than he would ever know. Rumour was that Johnson got the job because he was related to the principal's wife.

"

Excuse me Mr. Johnson did you ever play AFL or WAFL? Injured your back sir, that's a shame sir.

Sam Williams and Me sir.

What sir?

Sam and I, (Yeh more of an English teacher than a coach).

Sam and I sir played in City Beach Juniors since we were 12 and then Claremont Development Squad and into the Colts and now Sam and me, oops, Sam and I are going to the Draft Camp, then onto the National draft to get picked to play for the West Coast Eagles and fuck you Johnson.

He was late… again, and Johnson was going to give him hell… again. *What time do you call this Charles? Your teammates Charles, they're all here on time. They didn't have to do their make up before fronting up.* Guffaws of laughter all round at that little jab. *Get your gear on and show us why we should wait around for you princess.* But he had showed them why they waited for him, kicked eight goals for his team against Finbar College.

That was six weeks ago and Johnson had demoted him to the seconds for the next two games. *Change your attitude Charles, it's a team. Know what a team is? And I've been hearing stories about you; out of school stories and you should stay away from the girls. Plenty of time for that later. Focus!*

Jack hadn't wanted to ask him what stories. He didn't want to hear Johnson's answer. He guessed all the teachers knew about the trouble he had got into with the law. But he was through that.

He didn't admit anything to Johnson. He didn't owe Johnson anything, but Sam, his best mate, he owed him. He should have listened to him. Sam had been right, had warned him to stay away from Hughie, the biggest drug fiend in the school. He hadn't seen Hughie since the day the police had shown up at the house.

He'd promised to stop the drinking and the drugs after the eight hours he had spent with his mother, Felicity, at the police station. He had heard his mother cry before, but not the way she cried when she saw the CCTV footage. When she told him she had to tell his father he had pleaded with her. "He's never been interested in me until the paper did that article on me and he read it. Now he's calling all the time."

Felicity knew that was true. Ross had been living in New York with his new wife for the last seven years, he'd been back to Perth three times and barely had time to catch up with Jack, "Business trip, flying visit. Next time I'll stay longer." He never stayed and Jack was glad. Ross could drop dead for all he cared.

In the past Ross had called sporadically and usually began the call with a complaint, "Why haven't you called. It's a two-way street you know. You need to call me mate." *Yeh whatever, Yeh sorry, homework. Yeh sorry exams. Yeh sorry blah blah.* If he missed a call and Ross left a voice message, Jack would put off listening to it for as long as he could, and when he had no choice and he had to take a call he endured it, only half listening to Ross talking about himself, *yeh fucking hot shot.* Then the call a few weeks ago, "You're a dark horse. Kept that to yourself. When were you going to tell me you were going to be in the Draft?" Ross didn't wait for an answer, the anger wasn't even disguised, "Had to hear about it from the paper. Good job I still read the local news. You need to keep me in the loop. I'm still your father." Jack had tried to play it down, "Nah, just going for the try outs. Didn't want to bother you." Now he wanted to tell Jack how to run his life. "Listen Jack don't agree to anything until they've talked to me. Okay, got it?" He got it, he got that Ross, his father, who had never shown any interest in him wanted in on his football career.

Pleading with Felicity hadn't worked, "You're under eighteen Jack. I had to tell him and it's better coming from me." She didn't want to tell Ross but she knew he would find out. He had too many connections in Perth not to know and it had been in the papers.

Jack had screamed at her then, "You don't have to tell him. You don't have to tell him anything." He'd taken a step towards her and she had held her hands out.

"Don't Jack, don't, don't… you sound…" She dropped her hands to her sides. She thought she was doing the right thing. "If he finds out from someone else, or reads about it, he'll…" she shrugged her shoulders in a gesture of helpless surrender.

The blood pounded in his head. You sound *like your father.* That's what she was going to say. Didn't she get it, he despised Ross. He was nothing like his father.

It was a FaceTime call, he hated those. His father's face not quite filling up the screen so that Jack could see where he was calling from - his office. *It's in downtown Manhattan.* The polished glass and gleaming chrome furniture, the modern abstract art on the wall, all black and red squiggles as though someone had ridden a bike over puddles of paint. But it wasn't what he had expected. No lecture, he hardly mentioned it, "*Your mum says you got into some trouble, but it's sorted.*" And then he had raised his eyebrows and winked at him. Really winked.

He didn't get it. It was worse than getting a lecture. He could have dealt with that, pretended to take it on the chin; he deserved it but not from him. What he had done was bad but instead of disappointment his dad had winked at him, as though he was proud of him.

Not Felicity though, she had let him know what she thought of him, given him the lecture, "You're not a bad person but what you did was bad. You did nothing when you should have done something. That is not who you are. You have never stood on the sidelines when something wrong was happening. Even when you were at primary school and you were one of the little kids. This is what happens when you take drugs and you drink, it clouds your judgement and you make decisions you can't undo."

She had twisted and squeezed her fingers and then clasped her hands as if in prayer. "No more Jack, promise me, promise me."

She was right, he knew that. He was an idiot and he was lucky his football career wasn't over before it had started. He had stood on the brink of losing it and the life he had dreamed of unfolding before him like the opening credits of "Star Wars", his career stretching out to infinity had nearly been like the sandcastles he had built at Cottesloe beach disappearing with the incoming tide.

Felicity had insisted he saw a counsellor. "Jack, you have to, you agreed with the Magistrate that you would."

He had argued with her, he'd been to counselling before. He didn't need a counsellor. He had seen a counsellor just after Ross had left. It had been the topic of the last argument he had heard between his parents. Just a short time before Ross walked out of the house to his new life. His mother's voice almost pleading, "He needs to get some help Ross, he's having difficulty regulating his emotions. He's anxious a lot of the time. I've found a counsellor who…".

His mother didn't get to finish the sentence, Ross had cut

in, his voice loud enough for the neighbours to hear. "He doesn't need a fucking counsellor. Regulate his feelings! You need to stop hovering over him. He cries like a baby. That's your doing."

He went to see a counsellor four times, an old guy. He was good. He asked Jack a few questions and then gave him some strategies and suggested he put an App on his phone with more ideas that might help him when he felt anxious.

Jack gave up the drugs, that was easy, but the alcohol was harder. It made him feel okay when everything wasn't. He was making an effort, he had stopped for the first month. His mother had breathalysed him every day for the first couple of weeks. She had grounded him. He hadn't protested, he had got off light. He had been lucky, another three months and he would have been tried as an adult. He had written the guy a letter of apology. He was sorry, really sorry. Hughie had picked the fight, an older guy but smaller than him, and Jack had watched while Hughie beat the guy until someone had stepped in and called the police. He felt bad when he thought about what had happened and then the drink helped and the panic got pushed deep down inside his chest until he couldn't feel anything.

Stay away from the girls. Did Johnson think he was going to become a Monk! No way, girls were going to be the last thing he gave up. He had been getting a lot of attention from that quarter since he had grown from a scrawny 5ft nothing to 6ft 4, and he had put on bulk. His picture had been in the local paper, on the back page, but it had got him noticed, and he had become something of a star in the private school circles, girls' school circles, and he made the most of it. He liked girls and he really liked what they did with him.

He started to run, he hoped Johnson had waited the school bus for him. He grinned, he was going somewhere. He and Sam had got a place in the AFL Draft Camp. He was going to kill the draft. His scores for the tests they put the hopefuls through were more than decent. He was going to get picked by the National draft. He had to, and then, *West Coast Eagles, I'll be playing for my team.* The team he had supported since he could kick a ball.

He turned the corner and stopped. The bus was pulling out of the school gates. Johnson was a prick. They must have seen him running. Johnson thought it was some kind of punishment not letting him travel with the team. The guys were alright. They gave him shit, but on the field, he played as one of them. It was the last game playing for St Jude's, a friendly with a team from South of the river. He would get to the game late, he had his own set of wheels, a present from the arse, his father.

When the car had been delivered to the house on his eighteenth birthday, Jack had stood at the gate staring at the silver car parked outside. The sun bouncing off the black sun visor, the windows tinted a matching shade of black. Felicity was staring too. She pulled on her bottom lip. What was Ross thinking? Jack felt a confusing mixture of excitement and dread. He knew what the car really was. It was Ross's free pass to sweep aside everything he had done to him and jump back in his life as though he had never left and tell him how to run it and… "What the fuck," Jack felt the beating wings in his chest as he stared at the car. He thought he saw a movement behind the darkened window, his father hidden inside like Darth Vadar.

"Oh, my goodness Jack, that's an amazing present." Felicity held her hand to her throat. She had received an email that morning from Ross telling her he had bought something special and it was being delivered in time for Jack's birthday. He also wrote that he had paid her the last of the child allowance *'that I'm legally obliged to pay you'* into her bank account and she should think about selling the house.

The house, the only thing she had got out of twenty years of marriage… and Jack, she had got Jack but she had to share parental rights even though Ross had moved to New York, the other side of the world to live with his girlfriend. It had always been easier to give into Ross and it was the price she had to pay to keep the house. She knew he would never make the trip back to see Jack and he'd taken little interest in him not even asking for Jack's school reports. His son was a disappointment to him. Sensitive like a girl, *a mummy's boy. 'He'd better toughen up before he goes to St Jude's. He needs to develop a thicker skin, stop crying at the drop of a hat.'*

Jack had been sitting at the top of the stairs listening to Ross telling his mother he was leaving. The raised voices had brought him out of his bedroom. He heard it all. His father was leaving. Jack had cried then, and he didn't care if Ross saw him. It was the best news ever. A weight as big as the house was lifting off his chest. He heard too what his father thought of him but it wasn't news, he knew exactly what Ross Charles thought about his son, his only child.

Jack stared at the car, was this supposed to make up for everything? Everything Ross had put him through. The bullying, the relentless teasing.

"I don't want it. He can keep his fucking guilt present. He thinks he can come back into my life now. Well, I don't want to see him. I don't need his approval. I've never had it and I don't need it. He can fuck off."

The anger was like a freight train and he was driving it,

smashing it into his father. He clenched his fists. His mouth suddenly filled with saliva and he had to breath hard through his nose to stop throwing up.

"Jack," Felicity touched him on the shoulder. She heard the anger. "You're eighteen tomorrow. You choose how much contact you want with him."

If only it had been that easy. Nothing was easy with Ross. You didn't choose anything. He did the choosing. What had his mum chosen? She never left him, he had left her. *Yeh mum just like you chose, even when you knew he was cheating on you, even when... don't remember that.* But the image came unbidden, his father, one hand balancing his weight on the table as he leant across the dinner plates and struck Felicity across the face. He'd been ten at the time but the image of that blow was as fresh as if it had been yesterday.

The slap sudden and sharp like a firecracker and the startled cry from his mother. The red mark staining her cheek like a sudden blush. Jack had cried out too as though he had taken the slap. "It's okay Jack," she said as Jack stood up, his knife and fork in his fists.

Ross was still balancing his body over the table, caught between standing and sitting. "Sit down, eat your dinner," said Ross as he lowered his body back into his chair.

Jack hadn't sat down, he'd run from the table, warm urine running down his leg. Felicity found him in his bedroom, his head under the covers. He didn't want to hear her excuses.

He told Sam he wished his father hadn't bought the car for him. Sam stared at the car and at Jack with a jaw that nearly hit the floor.

"What? What the fuck? Are you complaining your dad bought you a car? It's a fucking, new fucking Audi hatchback. My dad would never buy me any kind of car, for fuck's sake Jack. I've got to save for my first car the way his father made him. Get a job after school, work in the salt mines. I told him I thought I would make more money as a male escort."

"TikTok. OnlyFans," said Jack.

It was a brilliant car, he had to admit that, and the girls loved it.

"Look at the seats, they go right down, and the windows are dark, no one can see inside. You should call it the fuck wagon," Sam said as he slid the sunroof back to reveal a perfect blue square of sky.

Jack shook his head, "No. I'm calling it 'the car.'"

***

Jack smiled to himself; he would let Sam drive the car back from the game. Nothing Johnson could do about that. He turned the corner of the school, heading towards the road where he had parked the car. *Going to kick your arse, Johnson.* Jack lifted his foot high and kicked an imaginary Johnson arse through the goal posts and stopped dead. A girl was standing next to his car watching him.

She was wearing a school uniform he recognized. St Helen's, black blazer, pale green pleated skirt. She had her hands in her pockets. He looked at her and then at his car as he covered the distance between them. He glanced up. She hadn't moved. *Fuck.* She was waiting for him. *Not another one!* He frowned as he felt for the keys in his pocket. He had to get to his car and she was standing in his way, he couldn't avoid her. He hitched his bag over his shoulder, it felt heavier than before. He flicked his head as though he was acknowledging her. She didn't move. He had to look at her now. She was waiting for him to speak, her eyes asking a question.

Whatever. He raised his eyebrows and the question in her eyes was gone and now she was looking at him as though she was about to swallow a cyanide pill.

He noticed her eyes then, blue like? He bit the back of his hand. The blue eyes, the black curly hair. She seemed vaguely familiar but he didn't have time to search the memory banks even if he wanted to. He was late. He looked over her head at the row of lamp posts stretching down the street. He fumbled for his keys, the car responded with a sharp burp and the girl stepped away. He wasn't going to look at her again.

"You want something?" he said in a voice full of irritation.

She made a sound as though she was going to speak. It made him stop. He flung his bag on the passenger seat and turned his head and glared at her. He saw her flinch, as though he had hit her. His irritation was growing. He had been stalked by girls before. They wanted more of him. He was eighteen, did they think he was going to marry them? He had no time for anything serious. He was focused on his career.

He took his tone down a notch, he didn't really want to sound like a prick but the way she was looking at him, all hurt, *for fuck's sake.* He was supposed to remember her and he didn't. Too many girls in the last year. He had stopped counting when it got into double figures. Ross wanted to know about the girls, "Take after me mate, the Charles charm."

Jack opened the car door and studied the interior as though he might find an unexpected passenger there.

"I'm in a hurry," he said and glanced back at the girl.

Her head wobbled as if he had hit her. He drew his eyebrows into a sharp 'v' and turned away. He had to go. He slid behind the wheel, his hand about to pull the door closed. He glanced at her again, he wished he hadn't. Her eyes were glittering like blue sapphires. *Yeh sapphires.* The girl swiped her hand across her face, and clenched her jaw. She suddenly kicked at the wheel of his car.

"I waited," she said.

He jerked his head at the sound. He thought he should recognize her, say her name, then he wouldn't feel such a bastard. It made him angry, those tears, that look. He held the door ajar and started the engine. "Look I'm… I don't know who… I'm late…" He tilted his head at the bag lying on the seat beside him, "got a game, I'm late." He was repeating himself. He felt a panic settling over him like a heavy coat.

Something about the haunted way she was looking at him. Her eyes going wide as though he was a shape shifter. *I waited.* He couldn't begin to think what that meant. He shut the door hard and clenched his teeth. The car lurched away from the kerb and he swore. He glanced in the rear-view mirror and swore again. The girl was holding her hand across her eyes. *What the fuck?*

He swung the car hard out into the moving traffic. Was he supposed to feel bad? *Who the fuck?* He was late, he had to get to the field before the game started. *Fuck, fuck, fuck.*

Miranda bit her lip hard. She wasn't going to cry. 'I don't know who you are', that was what he was going to say. What did she expect? He wasn't going to remember her, she was nobody, she was nothing. *Shut up, shut up. You are somebody. You are.* She didn't need anyone. She was on her own, always on her own. He had meant something to her for so long. *You're a stupid idiot.* She brushed at the tears she couldn't stop. She wasn't on her own now. She had Rose. Rose would know what to do.

Chapter Two

THE ACCIDENT

JACK

He got caught in the traffic and the mandatory 40-kilometer speed zone that came into force at the end of the school day. The side roads full of parked cars pulling out ahead of him as the private schools ended the day all at the same time. Three schools in close proximity which forced him to a slow crawl until he was out of the 40-kilometer speed zone, then onto Stirling Highway and heading towards Canning Highway. He shrugged his shoulders, he thought he could make it in time. Ahead on his right, glimpses of the ocean at Leighton beach. The water a dazzling blue. Then his luck was out. He hit every red light.

He was fifteen minutes late when he pulled into the school's car park and got out of the car. He couldn't be sure if the game had started, the playing field was behind the new theatre arts building. Then he heard the familiar sounds of feet pounding on grass, the warbling whistle of the umpire and the straggly boos and cheers of those on the sidelines. He changed into his gear behind his car, scrambling into his shorts, forcing his feet into his football boots, the laces undone, reaching the playing field to hear the umpire's whistle and the bounce down of the ball. Johnson benched him.

"Listen Charles while you are part of this team, you get here on time like everyone else - you're not special here." He pointed to the ground to emphasise the point. "You can sit there and watch."

Jack didn't move, he wasn't going to sit. He put his hands on his hips and scanned the field. He looked for Sam down the wings. He was one of the fastest runners on the field. He couldn't see him. He tugged at his hair. Sam had to be playing. Then he saw him and he groaned aloud. Sam was playing as the full forward, Jack's position. Jack glared at the back of Johnson's head. *Do you know what you're doing you arse? Sam's a runner, a midfielder, you can't put him up the front.* Jack saw the ball kicked to Sam but the trajectory of the ball was intercepted by the full back, a giant of a kid from the other team. *Looks like a sumo wrestler.* Jack watched as Sam bounced off sumo kid and fell onto his back. A jeer went up from the home team supporters standing on the side lines. Jack bit back the insults he wanted to hurl at them.

The ball was travelling fast down to the home team goal. Jack swore, an easy kick put the ball between the posts. The home team were cheering as though they had won the match.

Not over yet you wankers. He visualised the goals he was going to kick. Sumo kid wasn't about to stop him getting goals. The load of McDonald's, he'd run circles around him.

Jack stretched his glutes, clasping one knee after the other, pulling it to his chest. He was letting Johnson know he was ready to run on. *Okay Johnson I've learnt my lesson now let me win this game for you.* Jack moved closer to Johnson, close enough so that when Johnson could smell defeat, he could tap him on the shoulder and send him onto the field and get Sam back in the wings and send off the useless sub playing in Sam's position.

If Johnson could feel the bulk of Jack hovering next to him, he wasn't going to acknowledge it. He kept his face turned away, his eyes scanning the field as though his life depended on it. He wasn't letting Jack play and he didn't care if they lost the game. Bloody upstart. Letting your team down. Too big for his boots. Dodged a bullet because he was under eighteen. Something going on between Charles and that English teacher. If they lost the game they would blame Jack. Johnson knew how the team were feeling about their star player. He had let them down and this wasn't the first time he had rolled up late and expected the team to be so God damned grateful. Well not this time. Johnson turned away and moved down the line shouting out his standard coaching mantra that was supposed to inspire the team to play even harder, "Keep it moving."

"Keep it moving," Jack echoed, making the words come out of his nose. He could do a good imitation of Johnson trying to project his voice. Sounds like a cat with his arse on fire, that's what Sam had said back in their first year of High School.

Jack kicked at the turf, repeatedly digging his toe into the untouched buffalo grass until he had succeeded in wrenching the grass from the soil. It was the first time he had ever been benched. *The last fucking game, and now I've got to watch the team getting thrashed. Fuck you Johnson I could save the game.*

He thought Johnson would bring him on after the first quarter. He didn't think Johnson wanted to lose. He could see Sam, his best mate, was taking a bruising from sumo kid who was blocking Sam like an impenetrable wall. Johnson shielded his eyes and watched the players, he sucked in his thick rubbery lips, a sure sign he was thinking, but he wasn't going to relent. Teach him a lesson.

The whistle sounded for half time. Jack watched his team mates as they approached the benches. He tried to arrange his face in the right expression, anger, frustration. He bit the back of his hand. The team avoided walking anywhere near Jack, resolutely refusing to look at him. One team mate did look at him. Sam, his face a fierce red, his hair plastered to his forehead. He stopped in front of Jack, and shook his head. Jack furrowed his brow as if to say 'what's up' but Sam wasn't about to answer the look. He turned his back on Jack and went and stood next to the team.

What's his problem. I'm the one who's been benched. Jack folded his arms and kept his distance from the team while Johnson gave them the rallying talk. He saw Johnson turn his attention to Sam. Jack walked away, he didn't want to hear what Johnson had to say. Amarto, the son of a night club owner whose father was often in the local paper for his association with Perth's mafia; he wanted Jack to know what the team thought of him. He raised his voice, directing it straight at Jack.

"Well, if the fucking star player had bothered to turn up…" Johnson shut him down with a raised hand, "There are no star players, it's a team effort."

Yeh yeh. You know I can save the game. Fuck you. Fuck you Amarto. Come on Johnson. You want me to grovel.

Jack sat back on the bench as the team dispersed around Johnson. Jack waited. Johnson was walking his way, his head was down. Jack tensed his body to stand up, *about time.* His mood lightened, he was going to play, save the game. Hero, not a villain but then Johnson stopped mid stride as though he'd forgotten something and turned around and walked over to Hudson, the substitute, and patted him on the shoulder. Jack swore, he wasn't so sure that he was going to get on the field now.

Jack dropped his hands between his knees and looked down at his boots. When he looked up, he saw Sam walking towards him. Jack shielded his eyes against the sun that was dropping slowly into the Indian Ocean. The sky looked on fire.

"Where were you?" said Sam. He sat down on the bench next to Jack and took a pull from his water bottle. "You missed the bus." Sam knew where he had been, but he wanted to hear Jack own it. Disappearing at lunch time and not telling Sam where he was going. "Best you don't know," Jack had said with a smug smile that told Sam everything.

"Fuck! You're not serious Jack. She's a frigging teacher. She could get sacked. When are you going to stop fucking up your life."

Jack had shrugged, it was unlikely. He was leaving school at the end of the month and it wasn't as though he was under age, and she wasn't much older than he was… six years at the most.

"Sumo kid is doing a good job." Jack indicated the other team on the far side of the oval. He reached for his own water bottle. It had been a stupid idea. He was a fucking idiot. The text messages were still on his phone. He hadn't told anyone.

"I said, where were you?" Sam tapped his water bottle on his knee. He couldn't keep the contempt out of his voice. Jack was his best mate and he was finding it hard to like him. He was acting like an arrogant wanker. Sam knew about Jack's trouble with the law and he hadn't been sympathetic. Sam had warned him about hanging out with Hughie, the heir to some serious money, who thought he was above the law.

"Christ!" said Jack ignoring Sam's raised eyebrows and the angry look he was throwing at him. *Don't fucking judge me.* "Johnson's not going to let me play. The arse." He pulled his shoulder blades together and blew out a noisy breath through his pursed lips.

He would tell Sam later that nothing happened. He had gone to her apartment. He didn't want to remember that. He brushed his hand over his eyes but it didn't blank out the image of her opening the door and smiling, a strange smile he had never seen before.

He wanted to play, he had to make it right. His last game. It wasn't going to happen. He stood up and took a step towards Johnson. If the prick wasn't going to put him on, he wasn't going to hang around, and he didn't care how it looked. He stood still, his hands hanging limply by his side. He felt his top lip tremble and the familiar stinging in his nose. He had lost something. Something he couldn't name. *Don't be a pussy, not going to cry are you, that's for girls.* He drew in a long shuddering breath and sat down.

Sam wiped a sweaty forearm against his forehead. He could see how mad Jack was, the clenched teeth and the pulse in his cheek gave that away. He wasn't going to help him out of this. He threw his head back and drained his water bottle. Jack needed to apologise to the team. He didn't have an excuse. Everyone knew why he had been late. Everyone had seen the way Miss Grange and Jack had flirted. She should know better. She was a teacher for fuck's sake but Jack didn't know when to stop. Sam had envied the way the girls were all over Jack, but not anymore. It had turned Jack into someone Sam didn't recognise or like much.

The whistle blew and Jack stood up, he turned to leave and then thought better of it. It wouldn't look good, he shouldn't have been late. He brushed his hand across his eyes.

The last ten minutes and Jack had stopped waiting for the nod from Johnson. He made himself watch the game. His team were either playing the worst football or the other team were playing better. Sumo kid was new. Jack had never had to face him. He was good. Sam couldn't get past him. Sumo kid could move despite his build, he had to give him that.

His team were losing. They had lost before but not like this and not to this team. The home team supporters had stopped the jeering, they had grown tired of making up the insults they had been hurling at St Jude's.

Jack studied the tree line beyond the playing field, dark shapes against the grey sky. He pressed his hand against his chest, pressing the bubble he could feel expanding under his sternum. The players were a blur. *When are you going to stop fucking up your life? Sam's right, I'm fucking…* the girl, she knew him, had waited for him. She was just a kid, he didn't think she looked older than fourteen. The possible implications of that. If he had, if they… .He shook his head, *no sixteen, she was at least sixteen, for fuck's sake.* He combed his fingers through his hair. *What did she want?* He didn't want to think about her, but the way she had looked at him. He shook his head, *mistake, gotta be a mistake.* That look, as though he had run her through with a sword.

He remembered the meditation App the counsellor had suggested he put on his phone. It had helped and then he forgot about it. He took a breath and felt his chest rise in response. He tried to put his attention there, where the air was cool on his nostrils. Hold it, slowly, watch the breath all the way in, cool air on his nostrils, warm as he slowly let it out. He rubbed at the feeling that was building in his chest, he didn't want that growing inside him, overtaking him until he had to find a place to hide, lie down, close his eyes and breathe slowly and concentrate on nothing but the air going in and out of his nose, his chest rising and falling, rising and falling. He wanted alcohol, that always made him feel better.

He moved, stamped his feet as though he was getting ready to run onto the field. He wanted to be out there with his team, concentrating on nothing but the game. His one focus on the game, analysing the play, looking for Sam to come up the wing, kick the ball and he'd be there for the mark. Think of nothing but the game.

Jack scanned the field looking for the ball, he saw Sam running up the field, he shielded his eyes as he saw the ball arcing high in the air, and Sam going up for it, his arms out-stretched, the ball between his hands, Sumo kid coming at him, his feet off the ground, his hip against Sam's back, fighting for the ball. They went down together the ball flying in the air, picked up by someone and kicked away. He wasn't watching the ball he was looking at Sam writhing on the ground. They hadn't noticed, they were playing on. Jack started running, shouting, "For fuck's sake, for fuck's sake. Johnson!"

Johnson had seen it all unfolding with horror. The angle of the leg, the weight of the boy. He imagined he heard the sickening crack of the bone breaking. He was there assessing the situation. It was bad. "Take it easy son, don't move your leg. You!" he shouted at Jack, "ambulance. Now!"

Jack felt the blood drain from his face. Sam was scream-ing, bunching his fist into his mouth. Johnson was talking to him quietly, "Don't move, going to get you to hospital."

Jack took his phone from his pocket, and swallowed. The image of Sam's leg and the bone poking through the skin below the knee was burning onto his retina. He had to have imagined it. Can't be that bad. He pushed his way through the players standing in a circle around Sam. Sumo kid held his fist to his chin. "Is he alright?" but he could see he wasn't. "I'm sorry," he said. He looked pale.

"It was an accident," said Johnson sharply.

Sam tried to roll over and bury his face in the grass. "I told you not to move!" Johnson barked. He had his arm under Sam's head.

The ambulance seemed to take forever, and all the time Johnson was talking quietly to Sam. He had shut down any suggestion to move him. He was used to kids getting injured on the field, it was a tough sport, a physical contact sport. But he had never had anything serious happen. This was serious. Sam wouldn't be joining Jack at the Draft Camp in a few weeks. Johnson had the look of a pall bearer.

Sam turned his head into Johnson's shoulder, it hurt like hell and he knew it was bad, the pain was telling him that, and his leg felt strange, he couldn't feel his foot. He couldn't stop the tears that were squeezing out of his eyes.

"Okay you lot, game's over," said Johnson. Johnson nodded to the other coach, "Forfeit, a win for your team." He paused and then added, "you were winning."

The coach for the other team raised his eyebrows. He knew a serious injury when he saw one. He recognised Jack Charles, the boy who was calling the ambulance. The two schools had played in the school league for years. Jack Charles always played the same position. Full Forward, kicked all the goals. He wondered why he wasn't playing. He knew that was the reason his team were ahead on goals.

He walked over to Tamati Brown and put his arm around his shoulder. "You played well Tamati, you did nothing wrong." He turned to the players and held his arms wide, "Come on let's get you all back to the changing room." He herded the players away from the crying boy lying on the grass and the coach kneeling by his side.

***

Jack followed the ambulance in his car. Johnson went with Sam. The traffic was thick on the freeway. Jack sat behind the ambulance, the siren wailing and flashing its lights. Jack tried to keep close, taking advantage of the gaps that were opening up for the green and white ambulance that was ploughing through the traffic like a surf board on a wave. Then he wasn't quick enough and the cars folded back and he was caught in the traffic. He swore as he watched the ambulance pull far ahead until the sound of the wailing ambulance faded to nothing and he was left sitting facing the white van that had cut him off. He read the black cursive handwriting written across the back doors, "Deliah's florist, flowers for every occasion."

It's a funeral thought Jack. He slammed his hands on the steering wheel. "Fuck," he shouted. "Fuck" he slammed his hands again. The traffic stopped, he could see the road curving ahead, traffic backed up to the bridge. Sam wasn't going with him to the Draft Camp that's what this meant. He didn't want to think of Sam never playing again.

"Fuck. Fuck." He choked back a sob. *It's my fault, it wouldn't have happened if I'd played… yeh but you were late… wouldn't have happened if you hadn't gone AWOL after lunch. It wasn't just AWOL though was it.*

He rested his head on the leather steering wheel and cried. Felicity would ask him questions. She'd try to keep the anxiety out of her voice but he would see it in her face, the frightened look in her eyes hoping she was wrong. *Why were you late for the game?* And he would give her some answer, not the truth, he could never tell her that. She would know he was lying. He would know what she was thinking. *Just like him. Like his father Charlie, Ross Charles, the womaniser, the liar.*

"No!" Jack said under his breath. He shook his head. No, I'm not like him, the arsehole. *But you're like him aren't you. Just like him. Narcissistic, trample all over everyone. Missed the game, didn't you. Thought you were a hot shot… fucking your school teacher, something to brag to Ross about. Get his approval, always looking for his… Shut up! Shut the fuck up!*

He turned on the radio, he didn't want to hear that voice in his head, but he couldn't erase that other voice. It was silky and smooth, nothing like the acerbic tone she used in class. She hadn't bothered with hello, they both knew why he was standing in her hallway staring over her head at the gilt framed mirror at the end of the hall. When he saw her reflection move, he felt her hand on his arm and he looked at her pink painted nails and let her lead him into the bedroom. He had given an embarrassed snort that made him sound like a pig. He remembered that and he bit his lip. She sat on the bed and laughed as she patted the floral doona cover, "Come Charlie," she said, as though he was a dog, as though that was his real name. It wasn't his name, no one called him Charlie. It was his arse of a father, Ross Charles, 'Charlie'. He was Jack or JC. Not Charlie. It was that name. It had somehow brought him to his senses.

Fuck, fuck, fuck, and then he ran from the room shouting something he didn't want to remember, "I won't tell. Sorry."

He groaned and slapped the steering wheel and shouted, "Stop fucking up your life, you're not Ross fucking Charles."

He should be grateful she had called him Charlie. It was that name. His father's name. He never wanted to be like him. The thought of what he could have done with her flashed across his mind.

Jack turned up the music, but it didn't erase the image of his teacher, her face a mixture of anger and embarrassment as he had turned and run from her bedroom and the worst image of all, Sam's face crumpled in pain and the look he gave Jack when he was lifted on the stretcher and Jack had said, "I've got your gear."

"Won't need that anymore," Sam had said his face white with pain.

Jack wiped his hands across his wet eyes. He should have been playing, it wouldn't have happened. The whole game would have played differently. Sam wouldn't have… he shut off the music. The car behind honked. Deliah's florist van had pulled away. He drove in silence, his thoughts jostling for attention. He forgot about the girl waiting at his car.

It took forty minutes to cross the freeway back into the city and Royal Perth Hospital. He parked his car and found the parking meter. He swore. It was out of order. He found one on the other side of the visitors parking area.

He ran all the way to the Emergency entrance. The waiting room was full with people waiting to be seen. He stopped before two large doors adjacent to the reception area with the words in blood red lettering, 'Emergency Ward'. A nurse stopped him from entering the doors, she told him he had to wait in the waiting room.

He turned from the doors and saw Johnson sitting in the front row, an empty seat next to him. Johnson had seen him;

Jack couldn't avoid taking the seat. Johnson didn't acknowledge him; he was talking on the phone. Jack heard the name Williams and he guessed he was talking to Sam's father. Jack didn't want to listen; he didn't want it confirmed that it was as bad as it looked. He kept seeing Sam's leg, the weird shape and the bone and red bit of flesh on the tip, just like meat.

Jack looked up as the doors to the waiting room slid open. It was Sam's parents, Richard and Marylyn Williams. Jack gritted his teeth; he wasn't a fan of Richard Williams. He could see he was going to be in for a grilling. Richard Williams was the helicopter parent in the family, but his piloting was about hovering around Sam to make sure he turned out just the way he wanted him. Sam was to be the footballer that he had aspired to be. Sam thought Jack should be thankful that his father lived in New York with his new family. "And you get a fucking guilt present."

Jack stood up at the same time Johnson did. "So, what happened? How did this happen?" Sam's father looked grim, "Where is he?" He glared at Johnson. He liked to ask questions, that's what he did as a prosecutor with the Director of Public Prosecutions. Sam's mother touched her husband on the arm to get him to lower his voice. He shook off her hand, he didn't give a damn who heard him.

"Is he alright?" she spoke to Johnson and gave a bleak look at Jack. "You okay Jack?" Jack's eyes looked red, she wondered if he had been crying. She knew how much it meant to both of them that they were going together for the Football try outs.

"His leg," Jack blinked, "It's… not good." It was bad, fucking bad, but he didn't know just how bad. It wasn't going to be alright in two weeks or even two months.

"What happened Jack?" Williams's tone was demanding.

What happened? Jack pressed his hand to his chest. "I…"

Johnson stopped Jack before he could answer, "He wasn't playing." He thrust his chin in Jack's direction. Behind those words were accusation and anger. Johnson blamed him too. He didn't want Jack Charles giving his account of what happened.

Jack felt a sharp pain in his chest. Marilyn looked puzzled; she heard Johnson's tone.

"I saw it happen," said Jack weakly. He wished he hadn't. He bit the back of his hand hard and tasted blood.

"It was an accident," Johnson said curtly. He could read 'liability' and 'compensation' in Williams's tone. He stepped in between Jack and Williams and thrust his hand at Williams. Williams ignored the hand and put his hands on his hips.

"So, what happened?"

"Is he alright?" said Marilyn.

Johnson chose to answer Marilyn. Williams wasn't going to intimidate him. "He's okay. It looks like a fracture to his right leg."

Looks like! Fuck it's a smashed leg with the bone poking out. Jack felt his breath going out of him. He took a step back, feeling for the chair and fell onto it. Marilyn looked at Jack. His hands were resting on his bare knees. He took a breath and lifted his head. Marilyn saw how pale he was. He was still wearing his football gear. She frowned and wondered why he hadn't played.

"Unfortunately, fractures are very common in contact sports." Johnson said averting his eyes from the glare Williams was giving him. "The school's fully insured for accidents. That's all I can tell you at this stage. He's in emergency. Best wait until the doctor has seen him."

Williams gritted his teeth, "Well, that's it then," he said throwing his arms in the air, "his career is over. He won't be going to Melbourne."

Johnson pursed his lips; the boy's life wasn't over. He would recover and there was every chance he could play but not right now and probably not at professional level. Not that he had a chance, not like Charles, cocky bastard, bound to get picked in the Draft, talented player.

Jack had been listening with dismay, any moment Williams was going to ask him why he wasn't playing and why Sam had been playing in his position. But just when Williams had narrowed his eyes, his hand raised as though he was about to make submissions to a judge, *Jack Charles guilty by omission. A wanker who let his team mates down. He should have played and taken the blow your honour,* the doors to the emergency ward swung open.

"Who's here for Sam Williams?" A nurse in a dark blue uniform looked around the waiting room.

"I am, we are, we're his parents," Williams said.

She smiled, "Good come through, he's being seen by the doctor. Marilyn put her hand on Jack's bare arm," He's a friend."

Williams snorted, "He can wait. I want to talk to Sam."

Johnson lifted his head like a deer who had heard the crack of the undergrowth under foot and was waiting for the bullet to whistle through the air. *Alone, he wanted to talk to him alone.* Williams was gathering evidence.

Twenty minutes later Jack was standing next to Sam's bed. His parents were talking to the doctor in the corridor. Williams gave Jack a penetrating look as Jack passed. *You did this, you fucker!*

Jack swallowed. Sam was white faced. He didn't want to look at Jack. He needed a minute on his own. He wasn't going to cry, he just wanted to swear his head off and kick something with his good leg but he couldn't move. He was lying on top of the bed still in his footy gear. They had taken off his boots and socks and had put a sterile dressing over the break.

Jack stared at the white patch covering the white piece of bone with the scrap of red flesh on it. He could still see it. He wanted to throw up. "What did the…" his voice trailed off, he knew the answer was going to be bad.

Sam closed his eyes, "Compound fracture, getting x-rayed." His voice was monotone.

Jack sucked in his lips. It was a total disaster. Sam might play again but he doubted it. He had missed the best chance of his life and it was his fault. Jack shook his head, "Fuck," he said softly.

"Yeh," said Sam, "Dad's making sure I get the best ortho surgeon to do it. Melbourne's out. I won't be playing anymore."

Jack shook his head, "Fuck, I'm sorry," he turned towards the window and tilted his head to the ceiling, "I'm sorry Sam it's my fault… I let everyone down. I shouldn't have left school. This wouldn't have happened… everything would have played differently."

Sam didn't look at Jack and he didn't answer him. It was his fault. Jack was an arsehole.

Jack wiped his arm across his face.

"Well, I hope she was worth it."

Jack had been his best mate since the first day of High School but he didn't get a free pass on this.

"That was it, wasn't it, why you skipped class? Jack Charles the great stud, chip off the old block." He sounded bitter and he was.

Jack spun around to face Sam, "That's not… shit don't compare me to that arsehole. Fuck, I'm sorry, okay I get you're mad at me."

Sam flicked his hand at Jack, "Do what you like. It's your business. Treat girls like shit but stay away from my sister!"

"What? What are you talking about?" He couldn't stop the heat rising in his face. He looked down at his feet. "Are you talking about me and Daisy in the pool last week. Man, I was just being friendly. What the, she's just a kid … I would never… you know me better than that."

"Do I?" Sam leant back against the pillows, his face ashen. "Leave it." He closed his eyes, trying to block out the pain. The painkiller the nurse had given him was only just beginning to take effect. He could feel the tension falling away from his body, his body sinking into the bed. He raised himself on one elbow, he didn't care what he said. "I don't get it. Why? You're in enough trouble already." He stopped, he was having difficulty getting his thoughts together.

"That's sorted," Jack cut the space between them with a flick of his hand. He didn't want Sam reminding him that he could have blown his career.

"I told you… you didn't listen. You never do. Told you to keep away from that drop kick. Told you." Sam gave a gasp as he moved his body and the pain broke through again.

Jack bit his lip, he could see the pain etched on Sam's white face. He could see he had been crying. He had no right to get angry at Sam. Sam could say whatever he liked and he should take it.

"Sorry, I'm really…" he could feel his voice cracking, he pressed his hand to his forehead. *I'll make it up to you somehow, I don't know how.*

A nurse came into the room, "Taking you down for x-rays," she leant over Sam, and put her hand on his forehead and brushed his hair back. "The pain killer working?" she said, she could see it was, he was struggling to keep his eyes open. "Lie back," she said pulling up the sides of the bed and unlocking the wheels, "we don't want you falling out."

Sam struggled to open his eyes. It felt as though a great white veil was covering his head. He tried to push himself up on one elbow as the bed was maneuvered out of the room.

"Wait," he turned his head towards Jack. "I don't have my phone. I was going to see Rose tomorrow. Tell her I can't make it. I'll…" he didn't know what he was going to do, "tell her I'll call her."

"Okay, yeh sure." Jack knew who Rose was. Sam's first serious girlfriend. Sam had seen Rose a couple of times since the party where they had met. Jack hadn't met her but he'd seen plenty of photos. Yeh he could call Rose. It felt like a reprieve from something really bad happening, like losing his best friend forever. Sam had asked him to call Rose. *That must mean something.* Jack rubbed at the angry spot on the back of his hand. *I'll make it up to him, I'll… .fuck it, fuck it.*

Jack found Sam's phone in his sports bag. He spoke quickly when Rose answered the phone. "Oh no, oh no," Rose kept repeating. He could hear someone in the background saying, "What's happened?" He heard Rose say, "Sam's in hospital, he's done something to his leg."

Jack waited in the empty hospital room. He sat down on the only chair in the room, an ugly oversized upright chair. He stared at the space where the bed had been, where Sam had been lying with his smashed-up leg and his smashed-up football career. The room had grown dark, Jack stood up and walked across the pale green vinyl covered floor to the night covered windows that faced out to the evening sky and the dark silhouetted buildings. He pressed his forehead against the cold glass, he had to shut out the punishing image of Sam's injured leg. He wanted a drink, he needed a drink to shut out the images and to stop the voice in his head, to forget everything.

"Hi everything okay?" a man's voice said. Jack brushed at his wet eyes and looked over his shoulder at a blue clad nurse standing in the doorway with a clip board in his hand.

"Yeh, just waiting for someone, he's gone for an x-ray." Jack cleared his throat.

The nurse nodded, he could see what Jack was wearing. "Oh, the guy who fractured his leg playing footy?" said the nurse stepping into the room and turning on the lights at the wall.

Jack didn't want to talk, he wanted to keep staring out of the window but the nurse was hovering waiting for any answer. Jack folded his arms, "Yeh," he said.

"You were playing too?"

Jack shook his head, *don't ask me anymore questions please.* His phone vibrated in his pocket, he glanced at the text message, where are you? It was from Felicity. He held the phone to his ear and looked across at the nurse, "Hi, yeh I'm here at the hospital." He waited until the nurse walked away and slid his phone back in his pocket.

It was nearly an hour before Sam returned from the x-ray department. Jack thought he was asleep when they wheeled his bed back into place. Marilyn Williams followed the bed into the room. "You're still here Jack?"

Jack rested his hands on the back of the chair. "Yeh," he looked at Sam and swallowed. "Is he going to be okay?"

Sam opened his eyes and looked at Jack. "What do you think?" he said quietly.

Marilyn looked from Sam to Jack and back again at Sam, his white face, the defeated look in his eyes. "He's going to be okay," she said, "it's just going to take time."

Sam sucked in his breath and closed his eyes, he wasn't sure if the pain had come back or it was the memory of it like a fire in his leg. "Mum, can you get me some sparkling water, and where's dad?"

"Your dad is talking to the specialist. We are getting you transferred to St John of God, it's private. Do you want anything else?"

Sam shook his head, he waited until she had left the room, "Did you call Rose?"

Sam stepped round from behind the chair and gave Sam his phone. "Told her you'd call." He couldn't recall what he'd said exactly.

Jack thrust his hands in his pockets and stared at the floor, he felt a weight like a boulder crushing his chest. His eyes stung. "I'm sorry. You were right. I shouldn't have… I'm a fucking idiot. I don't know why I'm being such a dick."

Sam closed his eyes. "Are you still drinking?"

He wanted to lie and say no. "I'm cutting down. I didn't drink today. I didn't do… nothing happened. I left." He wiped his arm across his eyes. "She called me Charlie," he mumbled.

Sam frowned and Jack waved his hand, "That's his name… Ross… my father."

"The father you despise but…" he let the words hang between them. Jack knew what came after the but, *but you're behaving just like him.* Sam had said that to him before and he had denied it. "Your dad still coming over for the draft?" said Sam.

Jack frowned, he didn't want to talk about it.

"Is he?" said Sam again.

"Yeh, yeh, guess so." Ross was flying from New York and meeting him in Melbourne. Nothing Jack said could persuade him not to come.

Sam knew that Jack didn't want Ross anywhere near his football career. Jack shrugged, "Can't stop him. I tried. Flying from New York. Spoken to me more in the last couple of months than he has since he left… he…"

Sam winced, his leg was throbbing, the painkiller was wearing off. "Yeh but he did buy you a fancy car." He didn't want to feel sorry for Jack.

Yeh thought Jack and I have to be so damn grateful as though that makes up for never being around and treating mum like a piece of shit. He didn't want to talk about Ross, he was dreading seeing him. It was awkward enough talking to him on FaceTime. Ross was calling every week, grilling Jack about his performance and telling him what he was doing wrong, criticizing his appearance, "Cut your hair Jack, you look like a girl."

The last conversation had been more uncomfortable than usual. Ross had told him that he and his second wife had split up, "It's all amicable mate. That's life, just didn't work out, we wanted different things. But the good news is I've got more free time." Jack dreaded what that meant.

"Yeh, he did buy me a car."

"Could be worse," said Sam looking down at his leg.

Jack shook the thought of Ross Charles out of his head. Just saying his name sucked the oxygen out of the room. Jack took a breath and sat down in the green hospital chair. "Yeh, I know." He thought he could never complain again to Sam about anything.

Jack's nose was stinging, he could feel the pressure in his chest. He leant forward, his elbows on his knees. He stared at his feet, he couldn't remember putting on his school shoes. The laces were undone. He bent down to tie them and when he looked up a tall girl with blonde hair, wearing blue jeans and a green t-shirt was standing at the foot of the bed, her hands in her pockets. She didn't look at Jack.

"You okay then?" She tilted her head to one side as though she was making an assessment of the situation.

Sam tried to push himself up. He frowned at her. "Rose, what are you doing here?" He didn't want her to see him like this, flat on his back in hospital.

Rose pushed back her hair, "I wanted to see if you were okay. The message I got didn't make sense."

Sam looked across at Jack. Jack shook his head, he didn't know what she was talking about. He knew how to give a message.

"Well, I'm not, okay. Compound fracture and my football career is over." He said it as if he was ordering a McDonald's meal. He gave Rose a twisted smile and leant back against the three hospital pillows stacked behind him like a small snow-covered mountain. He sucked in the air between his teeth.

Rose put her hands on the rail at the foot of the bed. For one moment Sam thought she was going to pick up the chart that was clipped on the rail and read it.

Jack stood up, the frown still plastered on his forehead. He knew he had told her not to come. Rose ignored Jack as if he was a cardboard cutout.

Sam closed his eyes again, he was finding it difficult to concentrate. Rose licked her lips, she shouldn't have come but it was the way Jack Charles had spoken to her, abruptly, as though he was giving her an order. "Don't come. Alright?" No one told her what to do unless that person answered to 'mum' and sometimes not even then.

She liked Sam, but she hardly knew him, they had only been out a couple of times, but she could see the possibility. He was the nicest boy she had met. He was nice and he was funny, that was number one on her list, although being as tall as she was came a close second.

"Okay, call me some time," she said and turned towards the door.

"Wait," Sam struggled to push himself up and then remembered not to move and fell back against the pillows.

"Thanks," Sam said. He gave her a crooked smile. "It could be worse. Ross Charles could be my father." He looked at Jack, one eyebrow raised.

Jack clenched his jaw. He couldn't believe Sam was making a joke when his football career was over. He thought that if he was lying in the bed with a fucking compound fracture, he would be crying his eyes out and he wouldn't care who saw him.

"Yeh fuck that," said Jack, "give me a compound fracture any day over Ross Charles."

Rose looked at Sam for an explanation.

"You don't know Jack's dad," Sam said, closing his eyes and wincing as the hot pain ground into his leg.

"I'll try to avoid him then. Okay, bye." She paused at the door and raised her hand.

Sam lifted his hand from the bed, "I'll talk later okay. Gotta deal with this now." He nodded at his leg.

Jack spoke to her retreating back, "I called you," he said.

Rose turned around and looked at Jack for the first time since she had entered the room. "Yeh, I know who you are." It sounded like an accusation. Rose registered the startled look in Jack's eyes before she turned away and left the room. "You're famous or something," she said over her shoulder.

Jack raised his eyebrows at Sam. *What's her problem?* He didn't think he'd met her before, perhaps he had and she didn't like the fact that he hadn't recognised her.

"Now I've met Rose," said Jack.

"I like her," said Sam defensively.

Jack nodded, "That's good." He hoped it was. Now that Sam would be staying in Perth, she would be a distraction, that had to be a good thing. If it was him, he didn't know what he would do.

A nurse came into the room to take Sam's blood pressure. "I think they've arranged for your surgery this evening." She looked at Jack, and smiled at him as though she knew him. She had dark hair pulled back in a ponytail. She reminded him of the girl who had waited for him that afternoon. The girl with the blue eyes who had said something about... *wanting to be a doctor.* He stood up, he had to get out of the room, a memory was coming at him like a torpedo.

"I've got to go Sam. I'll call," Jack said.

∗∗∗

Jack sat in his car, with the engine running. He pressed his fingers into his eyes. "Fuck," he whispered. He remembered. It was the party, his party, weeks ago. A memory like a movie was unfolding. He had drunk too much. He had broken his promise to his mum and left his own party and gone to his bedroom to lie down. "Fuck," he said again. He thumped his forehead with his fist. He remembered the girl, he remembered the party.

Chapter Three

NIGHT OF THE PARTY

JACK

"Excuse me, that's my jacket." Someone was tugging at the pillow beneath his head. He opened one eye and stared at the ceiling. His mouth felt dry and the room seemed to be spinning, or perhaps he was.

"What?" he mumbled. He pushed himself up onto his elbows and squinted sideways at the girl standing next to him. She looked familiar.

He saw her take a step back as though he might be dangerous.

"Do I know you?" He could feel the words sliding around his mouth. He made an effort. He flopped back onto the jacket beneath his head. He turned sideways and stared at her legs. They were okay, no athlete he thought, as his eyes travelled up over her short red shiny skirt and stopped at her bare midriff. He closed his eyes, the effort was too much.

He rolled onto his back, "Yeh, I know you." He held his arm across his eyes. "You're Snow White. Seen the cartoon, that's you." He waved his hand at her, "black curls, blue eyes." He struggled to get off the bed. He was going to throw up. She jumped out of the way as he lurched for the bathroom and made it in time to vomit into the toilet bowl. He thought he might give himself a hernia, he couldn't stop throwing up. When he finally stopped, he felt exhausted, his head was still spinning. He wiped the back of his hand over his mouth. He didn't expect to see her still there, standing at the bathroom door with a wet towel. She gave him a look that seemed full of disappointment, he almost expected her to say something about drinking too much. She held the towel out to him and waited while he cleaned his teeth vigorously. He took the towel from her and wiped it across his face. He gave her a crooked smile.

"More like an angel," he said.

"What?" she frowned.

He didn't answer, he was staring at her. He drew his eyebrows together in a deep 'v.' He was trying to place that face and those blue eyes that seemed too big for her face. She turned her head away. There was a glass on the bedside table. It was half full of an amber liquid that smelt sickly and sweet. He moved away as she carried it into the bathroom and tipped the contents into the wash basin. He couldn't look at it and he certainly didn't want to smell it, he wanted to lie down again. He threw himself back on the bed. The girl came back with a glass of water. She made him sit up and drink it.

"Thanks, you'll make a good nurse," he mumbled.

She took the empty glass and put it on the bedside table. She folded her arms, "Doctor. I'll make a good doctor."

He couldn't figure out if she was serious or not. She looked serious with her arms folded and the small crease between her dark eyebrows.

"Doctor, yeh, sorry, you'll make a brilliant doctor." He closed his eyes again. The room had stopped spinning.

He felt her tug at the jacket under his head. "My jacket," she reminded him.

"Brilliant doctor," he mumbled. He couldn't seem to focus. He was feeling better but not much better, he shouldn't have drunk so much. He pulled her jacket from behind his head and held it out to her and then snatched it back. He held it behind his back as he pushed himself up from the bed. She stepped back, her hand was waiting for her jacket. He grabbed her hand and threw the jacket back on the bed and pulled her down next to him.

He stared at his fingers curled around the leather steering wheel. *And then what? And then what?* He tried to remember, and then what?

He closed his eyes, *think, think you idiot. What did you do?* He wiped the perspiration from his forehead and rubbed his palms over his knees. His heart was speeding up, he could feel it trying to jump out of his chest. *Come on, breathe, your party, what did you do?* He remembered Sam. *Sam, yeh Sam was at the party early. He was nervous about… .yeh, he was meeting the girl he'd been texting for weeks and… I started drinking, and… and… .the girl and…*He fumbled for the door handle and got out of the car. The sky spun in a great circle over his head and he vomited onto the dark asphalt.

He couldn't remember anything else. He was a fucking idiot. He banged his fists on the bonnet of his car. The rest of that night was a black hole, as though part of his memory had been deleted like the other black hole. He'd been made to remember that black hole when the police had shown him the CCTV footage.

Just that small fragment of the evening that's all he could remember and this time there was no CCTV camera to show him what he had done. He'd done something, but what?

He got back into the car and watched the traffic sliding past the windows. *Sex, it had to be that. That's okay, she would have wanted it. I didn't force her. Didn't have to did I?* "You treat girls like shit." Sam had said that to him back in the hospital. *Stay away from his sister. For fuck's sake.* He tried to remember the girls he'd hooked up with. He hadn't been out with any of them for longer than a couple of weeks. He closed his eyes and tried to remember their faces but the only face he could see was the girl with black hair and blue eyes waiting by his car and the look she'd given him, her eyes glittering as though she was about to cry.

He started the car as his mobile phone rang. It was Felicity. "I'm on my way. Yeh sorry, Sam got injured at the game. Tell you about it when I get home." She sounded worried. He knew why. She didn't trust him anymore. Monitored his every movement. She'd been furious with him the morning after the party. He pulled his car into the traffic.

He remembered the morning after, yeh, he remembered that.

Chapter Four

MORNING AFTER THE PARTY

JACK

His mother is banging on his bedroom door and she's shouting as she walks in, shouting something he doesn't want to hear. He tries to pull the covers over his head but she grabs hold of them and flings them back.

"Mum," he growls at her pulling the sheet back over his naked body.

"It smells like a fucking brewery in here."

He knew it was bad. She never swore. She walked over to the curtains and yanked hard on the cord until the sun was flooding the room like the flash of an atomic bomb.

Jack threw his arm across his closed eyes. His tongue felt too big for his mouth. He needed water.

"There," she thumped a bottle of cold water onto his side table. "Drink that!"

Jack didn't move. His head was about to explode.

"You were drinking last night. After everything that's happened. You promised me Jack." She moved closer to the bed. He didn't want to see her face. "Jack, you promised me." Her voice dropped to a whisper, "What else did you do?" He could hear desperation in her voice and then silence just hanging in the air. Her ragged breathing as though she was crying. He didn't move. His head throbbed like a time bomb.

"Answer me Jack! Answer me! Drugs, did you do drugs?" She was angry now, shouting at him to open his eyes. "Look at me, look at me!"

He moved his arm and held his hand over his chest. He tried to open his eyes. Felicity moved and her shadow fell across him. He saw her through half opened eyes. She looked terrible, almost as bad as when she'd seen the police CCTV footage. She bit her lip and looked up at the ceiling, he saw the light reflected in her eyes. He lifted himself onto one elbow.

"Mum, I didn't do drugs." He knew that was true. His head was pounding.

She took an audible breath in and then another. She turned her head to look at him. His hair was tousled, his eyes bloodshot. She turned her eyes away from his. He knew that look, she'd been looking at him like that ever since that night, the night the police had come knocking at the door. "You're just like your father," she said after the police had left. He couldn't help looking like Ross, it was genetics. But he knew she hadn't meant that.

"Are you telling the truth?"

He frowned at her, she was calling him a liar. Anger surged in him, was she calling him a liar? "Yes mum. I promised you I wouldn't after…" he swallowed, he didn't want to be reminded of what he'd done.

"But you drank didn't you and you promised that too… you were drunk." She didn't know if that was true but when she had asked Sam where he was Sam had been evasive and she had thought the worst.

"I didn't promise not to drink on my birthday." He sat up and ran both hands through his hair. "Everyone drinks when they turn eighteen, it's what you do!."

"For fuck's sake!" She was back to being angry again and she had sworn again. "You did that way before you were eighteen. You promised you wouldn't do this again." She swiped her hand across his body. "This. You promised no more this." She turned away from him and opened the window.

"I'm sorry. Okay." He threw one leg out of the bed, "I'm getting up." He didn't have an excuse, not really. He knew why he'd drunk, he didn't forget that. Ross phoned, that's why. *My fucking father phoned and then I drank. That's not an excuse, not an excuse.*

His head felt as though it was filled with porridge. He'd had a hangover before and swore each time he would never do it again. He showered and staggered downstairs to the kitchen. Felicity looked up from wiping the kitchen bench. It had taken her all morning to clean up the kitchen. The caterers had removed all the hired party equipment hours ago.

Jack opened the fridge and was hit by a smell of something meaty and spicy. A chicken carcass covered in cling wrap sat on a plate. He swallowed and grabbed at the bottle of water in the fridge. He unscrewed the lid and drank quickly, fighting down the nausea that hit him.

"Who was she?" said Felicity.

He put down the bottle on the bench, harder than he had meant to. "What?"

"The girl, in your room." Felicity turned towards the sink and the water gushed out in a blast. "I saw her leaving your room last night."

Jack picked up the bottle again and didn't answer. Felicity turned off the tap and gripped onto the sink with her blue rubber gloves. He had changed, the last six months, she didn't recognise him. She didn't want to believe that he was becoming like his father.

"You don't know who she was, do you?" Her voice sounded flat as if she didn't expect an answer.

"It's none of your business, is it?" Jack said slamming the fridge door. He couldn't remember anyone in his room. The evening was a blank. He felt a rising panic. Not again. Another chunk of his memory wiped out. He pushed the thought away.

He stayed out in the garden most of the day, swimming laps of the pool, hundreds of them, trying to clear his head. Felicity didn't talk to him again. She left the house and didn't return until late. He was lying on a recliner, his eyes closed. He had drunk enough water to fill a swimming pool and his head was clearer but he still couldn't remember anything about the evening. He had tried to conjure up the girl but the effort was too much. What did it matter anyway? Plenty of girls had hooked up with him. He had lost count over the last year. He had never forced anyone. He was sure of that.

Felicity sat in the lounge room, she could see Jack through the glass sliding doors. Jack stood up and went to the edge of the pool and slid in. She watched his arms looping through the water. He didn't look like a boy anymore. He had a man's body, a footballer's body. He was just eighteen but looked so much older. He was still a boy. Making stupid choices. She twisted her fingers in her lap and then pulled them apart and placed one hand over the other the way she did when she was counselling a client. *Hold your hands in neutral, in your lap, relax your shoulders. He's not like his father.* He looked like his father and she knew where those good looks had got her ex-husband. And now she could see Jack going down that same narcissistic path. Treating women as though they meant nothing. He wasn't the boy she remembered. The boy who wanted to bring home every stray dog. Who had too much empathy for other kids. The sensitive boy who cared too much, who cried often.

Ross had teased Jack mercilessly, had been determined to mould him into his idea of a man. *For fuck's sake Fliss, he's even started walking like a girl. Cries at the drop of a hat… boo hoo. It's for his own good. You think the world is going to be kind, it's a dog-eat-dog world.*

Since Ross had left Australia to live in New York he had made little effort to maintain his relationship with Jack or shown interest in him but that changed when Jack had started to get noticed for his football skills and had been in the local newspaper, and now Ross was edging back into their lives.

Chapter Five

NIGHT OF THE PARTY

MIRANDA

Rose didn't bother to knock on Miranda's door, she never did. There was no privacy at St Helen's boarding school. If you wanted that you had to lock yourself in the toilet.

"Milly," she cooed, "Milly, please, please."

Miranda stopped reading and put her hands over her ears. She didn't look up from the books she was reading. Rose was on a campaign and evoking the nickname Rose had given her when Miranda enrolled at St Helen's was part of the campaign.

"Miranda, you've got to come. And…" Rose slapped her hand on Miranda's desk, "you've studied enough!" She grabbed the open textbook before Miranda could stop her. Rose held it behind her back.

Miranda frowned, she was trying to look serious but it made Rose laugh. "You know you want to come. You might meet your next boyfriend!"

"My next boyfriend?" Miranda raised her eyebrows and shook her head at Rose.

"A boyfriend, a real boyfriend. You know the opposite sex. Lose your virginity!" Rose balanced the textbook on her head and caught it as it fell and looked at the cover, "Boring…'Introduction to Organic chemistry'." She opened the book, lowered her voice and read, "Studies have shown that sitting down for long periods of time…," she paused and raised an eyebrow at Miranda, "like studying."

"Like studying? Really?" said Miranda, standing up and advancing on Rose. Rose took a step back which was difficult in the boarding school bedroom, hardly bigger than a cupboard. Her back hit the door. She held the book above her head and Miranda reached out for it. Miranda sighed and folded her arms. "Okay, let's hear it." She smiled, Rose was incorrigible.

Rose gave a quick triumphant smile as she lowered the book. "Yes," Rose stabbed the opened page with one finger. She tried to look serious but the laugh she was trying to hold back was making it difficult, "Studying," repeated Rose raising both her eyebrows. She made her voice deeper as she read, "for prolonged periods of time can lead to… can lead to," she started to laugh as Miranda reached for the book and Rose snapped it shut as she spluttered, "an impenetrable hymen!"

Miranda took the book from Rose and held the book at the base of her stomach, "Any boy who wants my hymen has to get past this." She swung the book like a pendulum, "Not just any boy, he has to be very special." She made a dreamy face and closed her eyes.

"Yeh the fantasy boyfriend… and his dick's got to be made of steel!" said Rose lunging for the book as Miranda swung around.

"A fantasy boyfriend is the best kind," said Miranda.

Rose stopped smiling, "That would be funny, if you weren't serious. And you can't save yourself for a fantasy, because that's what it is. In your head. And." She emphasized the 'and' by putting both hands on her hips. "No boyfriend will ever live up to the fantasy you've created. Let's see what's on your list." Rose looked up at the ceiling and then at Miranda. She held her thumb up, "One, he's got to be drop dead gorgeous."

"I never said that," Miranda interrupted her.

"You implied it," said Rose.

Miranda shook her head, there was no point arguing with Rose. Rose held up her index finger, "Two, he's got to be ripped."

Miranda held her hands in the air and gave Rose a withering look. *Never said that.*

"Three…" said Rose and gave a smile that lit up her eyes and Miranda just knew what she was going to say.

"He's got to have – "

"He's got to be kind, funny and smart," said Miranda. "The rest is a bonus." And she meant it. *Kind, that's the most important and he is, he was, the kindest boy she had ever known.*

"Good luck with all that," said Rose.

Miranda didn't answer, she pulled a face that said, 'want to bet.' She hadn't told Rose about the real boy who had been her fantasy boyfriend since she was eleven. When she thought about a boy, it was him. When she thought about her future, it was with him. The rational part of her mind told her to grow up and get real but she didn't want real, she wanted fantasy.

"Come on Milly, please, come with me. I need back up. I might need to escape if I don't like him." Rose held her palms together and pushed out her bottom lip.

Miranda gave an exaggerated sigh and held her chemistry book to her chest. She didn't really need to study any more, but she hated parties, she always had. She had nothing against having fun but she didn't like the parties Rose enjoyed. Parties with a lot of kids you didn't know, who were keen to experience everything that was barely legal. Drugs, alcohol and sex. She didn't drink and drugs terrified her. She knew what they could do.

Sex for Miranda was on the agenda one day. In the fantasy she played in her head, it was with one person, her hero and she hadn't seen him since grade six primary school. She knew what he looked like she had seen his photo in the paper and he was ripped and gorgeous. She didn't imagine she would ever see him again. But she was good at fantasies, they were better than reality. Fantasy had saved her, had been her escape.

"We won't know anyone. Correction, I won't know anyone," Miranda said. Rose seemed to know the entire private school fraternity.

"My boyfriend will introduce us," Rose said quickly. She could see an opening, Miranda was going to cave.

"Oh, he's already your boyfriend and you haven't even met him… well not in person."

Rose grinned, "Seen plenty of pictures of him."

Miranda groaned, "Me too and I wish I hadn't. What is it with all the dick pics? If I see him, I won't be able to look him in the face without laughing, and going red!"

"I'll make sure you don't. Anyhoo, he's going to be my boyfriend, it's written in the stars. And we've talked heaps."

"Yeh tell me about it." Miranda sat down on the edge of her bed still clutching her text book as though it was a hot water bottle. "You could be speaking fluent French by now. All those hours wasted getting acquainted with a boyfriend." She shook her head and smiled.

"Yeh!" Rose sat down on the bed and pulled Miranda down with her. She knew what the smile and the shake of the head meant. Milly never let her down. *"Merci mon best ami."* She licked Miranda's neck.

Miranda turned her head, "Stop that, save that for Biff-head or whatever he calls himself."

Rose snorted, and turned on her back, stretching out her arms and said in whisper, "Legolas, it's from Lord of the Rings, I looked it up."

Miranda propped herself on one elbow and looked at her friend. Rose's eyes were closed and she was smiling. "You know he's an elf then, don't you?" Miranda said.

Rose popped her eyes open, "Shut up Milly. You're coming. I love you."

"Stop kissing me, save that for the elf." Miranda struggled to push Rose off. Miranda was no match for Rose, she stopped struggling.

"Okay," Rose stood up and caught her long blonde hair back and twisted it into a bun and walked over to Miranda's wardrobe.

"Mm something sexy but not slutty. Not much to choose from in that department, just this." She pulled a red taffeta skirt off its hanger. Miranda put her text book back on her desk, she knew what Rose had found in her wardrobe, the red taffeta skirt she had bought at Rose's insistence from a recycling shop. It was just the sort of thing Rose would wear.

"Jeans," Miranda said, "I'm wearing jeans and a long-sleeved t-shirt. I'll get cold." She would too, she always felt the cold. When everyone else was throwing off their clothes and complaining of the heat, Miranda's lips would be blue and she'd have goosebumps.

"No, you're not. You're wearing this and my black crop top. Yes, stop shaking your head. You've got a great figure, great legs, that's it I've decided." She held the skirt against herself and shook her hips, "Fashion over comfort, you have to suffer to look fantastic."

"That's not a maxim I adhere to," said Miranda, "and neither should you. You don't see boys suffering."

"Don't care what Max thinks. Show those legs and more skin." She poked Miranda in the midriff.

Miranda looked down at her legs, they were slender. She didn't think she had much of a figure. "Come on Rose, this," she made a chopping motion with her hands against her hips, "I'm not complaining but this is not a great figure. I look sixteen on a good day. I'm always getting asked for my ID even though I'm older than you by three months.

Rose ignored her with a wave of her hand, she threw the skirt on Miranda's bed, "I'll be back with the crop top."

Rose's bedroom was next to Miranda's in the boarding school dormitory at St Helen's. They had been dorm buddies since Miranda had been enrolled at the private school that was home for five years to the girls of parents who could afford to send their daughters to one of the top private schools in Western Australia.

***

The dress rustled when she walked, Miranda liked the sound, like leaves blowing along the grass. Rose had insisted she wear eye make-up. "You've got amazing eyes, Milly, you know you have amazing blue eyes and with your black hair and just a bit of mascara… ." Miranda refused to wear lipstick, she didn't care if it made her look older. No gloss either, she hated the sticky feel of it. She wore her only pair of non-school shoes, black flats. The soles were so thin she felt as though she was walking bare foot.

Rose had organised the Uber and the pass from the boarding school. They were to be back by twelve. The boarding house mistress had their GPS on her phone. It was a rule for any girl leaving the boarding house.

The party was in one of the suburbs that skirted the Swan River. The Uber stopped in front of a house with a high black wrought iron fence in front of a hedge of white roses. The house was at the end of a small side street that ran down to a grassed reserve of gum trees. The house beyond the fence was all angles of dark glass and white walls. Fairy lights artfully decorated the trees and lit up the garden. Music was banging against the dark starlit sky. A group of girls had bundled out of a car ahead of them and were already pressing the intercom.

Rose got out of the Uber and hooked her bag over her shoulder. She heard one of the girls say, "Lillian Jarvis with two friends." Rose hoped that Legalos had made sure her name was on the guest list. She hadn't realised that it was invitation only. She turned to say as much to Miranda but stopped when she saw what Miranda was wearing. She hadn't noticed that Miranda had brought a jacket with her and not just any jacket. Miranda was slipping it on, she had felt the cold wind blowing off the river as soon as she had got out of the car. She had one arm through the sleeve when Rose stopped her.

"Get that off Milly. You are definitely not going into this house wearing your school blazer!"

Miranda hugged her arms around her body, "It's cold, the sun has gone down. You know I feel the cold. I can turn it inside out, look no one will know." She took her arm out of her blazer and began pulling the sleeves inside out.

"No Milly everyone will know. It looks rubbish." Rose bit her lip, she had a jacket she could have loaned Milly. She knew Milly received youth allowance as a ward of the state and she managed that carefully, always refusing to go out with Rose and the other girls if she could avoid it. She claimed she had to maintain her marks to keep her scholarship. She consistently got straight 'A's but she worked for them, worked harder than anyone she knew. She wasn't some genius as most of her year thought. Even some of her teachers had said she had a gift. She let them think that. It made her special. No one knew that her studies had been her escape. When she had discovered books and learnt to read a whole different world had become possible. A world that was light years away from her real life.

It was no secret that Miranda had had a tough life but what that meant was only known to the principal and some of her teachers. Her fellow students only knew that Miranda was an orphan, had won a scholarship to the school and been awarded a generous bursary. On each prize night for the past four years, she was the consistent prize winner and everyone expected that in her final year she would be dux of the school.

"Rose, no, look feel the goose bumps. When I get inside, I promise," said Miranda wrapping her arms across her bare midriff as she followed Rose around the side of the house to the wrought iron gates. Rose's phone pinged, "Shirt! Look at this, it's Horrible Horry, she's reminding us we have to be back at twelve, for fuck's sake she told me that an hour ago. It's eight thirty, just minutes of freedom." She stuck her jaw out and made a face.

"And then you lose your glass slipper," said Miranda.

"Two more months and we're done with school Milly."

Miranda was silent. She was dreading leaving school. St Helen's had been the best thing that had ever happened to her. It was a place where she felt safe. It was home, where she had her own room, her own things and she never had to go hungry. It was where she had felt safe for the first time. Horry knew about her life before she won a full scholarship to St Helen's. Jane Horrigan, the principal, Miranda never thought of her as Horrible Horry, all the other girls did but to Miranda she was her saviour. In the first few months at the school, she had helped Miranda to fit in.

Miranda didn't know what it was to have regular meals, or bath time, or clean clothes. She never knew her father, she wasn't even sure that her mother knew who he was. Her mother had a succession of boyfriends each one abusive and supplying her with drugs. The police were called out by neighbours and then the Department sent the social workers to work with her mother to help her get off the drugs, but that didn't last. Miranda had to get herself to school, the only place where for a few hours she could forget about her home life.

She wasn't aware that she thought differently to the other kids in her primary school. She just assumed that learning was what you did at school. It was her escape. She had no one at home who helped her with her homework or who was interested in what she was doing. She did well at school despite her life at home. So many primary schools, so many different houses, so many men that came in and out of her mother's life. She stayed away from them spending hours in her bedroom.

Sometimes her home life would improve after a concerned teacher or neighbour would notify the Department that Miranda was being neglected, missing school and when she did attend it was often without lunch, and then there was the constant nits in her hair. Her mother would swear and curse after they had left and blame Miranda. "Well, there's one way to fix the nits in your hair." She had dragged her into the bathroom and cut it. Miranda didn't cry when she saw herself in the mirror. Her great blue eyes looking back at her, her mother standing behind her, waving the scissors at the mirror. Her own hair a brittle bleach blonde, pulled back in a wispy ponytail.

Miranda had been eleven when her mother had cut her hair. Her mother made her tell anyone who asked that she had cut it herself. They believed her too because it was cut the way an eleven-year-old might cut their own hair, close to the skull, ragged and uneven.

For the short time the Department worked with her mother, life was marginally better. Her mother would buy food and Miranda would make herself lunch for school but then things would go back to the way they were before, and Miranda would have to get herself up for school and come home to an empty house. Then her mother would come back late and Miranda knew to stay out of her way.

Miranda's hair grew back and by the time she had sat the entrance exam for a scholarship to St Helen's her hair was almost three centimetres. Miranda was worried each day that her mother was going to cut it again, she had been threatening she would and then her mother had died.

Ms Horrigan had paired Miranda with Rose. She knew that Rose would look after Miranda. Rose had been a boarder at the school since year five. Jane Horrigan had seen how she looked after the younger girls. Rose came from a big family on a cattle station 2000 kilometers north of Perth. She was the eldest of five children, all girls. Her mother had been a boarder at the school too.

Miranda hugged her arms around herself. "Whose party is it?" she asked.

"Don't know his name but he's the best friend of my… potential boyfriend."

"The elf lives here?"

"No, the best friend and stop calling him that."

"Is he expecting you?" Miranda could see the back yard of the house was crowded with young people. She wanted to leave.

"Yes, and I know what he looks like he's not an elf. I just don't know his real name. He told me to send a message when I got here. I just did that. OMG, it's scary and exciting." She wiggled her hips at Miranda.

Miranda sighed, she just hoped he lived up to the photo. She waited until Rose had turned away and threw the blazer around her shoulders.

"Come on, and don't think you're leaving me." She turned and grabbed at Miranda's hand. "I'm not letting you go and… I said to take that off." She plucked at Miranda blazer.

Miranda scanned the crowd of girls standing on the lawn, a breeze was blowing off the river. The garden was large, she couldn't see the back fence, just dark shaped trees, patches of light where the lights were hung. Music was playing somewhere outside. It was cold, she was going to freeze. She shrugged out of her blazer and hugged it against her stomach. She envied all the girls with bare legs and "barely there" clothes. They weren't feeling their lips go blue. Her feet were freezing.

Rose saw her shiver. She felt bad, "We can stay inside, alright?" She thought of Miranda like a sister, a younger one. She had four of those at home, younger sisters. She knew how to be an older sister – always right but kind.

Miranda followed Rose into the house and through a living room full of pale sofas and modern art. They went up the carpeted stairs and along a corridor of closed doors that ended with a door with a yellow Post-it note that read, 'Bathroom'.

Miranda stepped back when the door opened and three girls came out. They could have been triplets, with their identical long blonde, highlighted hair. She held the door open.

"S'okay. We're looking for a room to put our things." Rose said.

The girl waved her hand at the end of the landing, a door was open. "Down there, you can leave your… jacket." She looked at the bundle Miranda was hugging to her chest as though it was a loved pet.

There were three doors at the end of the carpeted landing. Rose pushed open the first. Light from the garden illuminated the room. It was large with a huge bed in the middle. There were no clothes on the bed. Miranda noticed the window seat. That would be her dream bedroom to have a window seat and to pull the curtains around it.

Rose sniffed the air and pointed at the posters and the sport's equipment falling out of a partially closed door. "Boy's room," she said. A stuffed chair in the corner of the room supported an assortment of clothes, a pair of huge navy runners that had been kicked off in haste, one next to the chair, the other next to an open door to the ensuite.

Rose pulled the folded blazer out of Miranda's arms and threw it onto the bed.

"Leave it here," she said pulling Miranda out of the room. "We don't want anyone to see it." Miranda made a face, she didn't want to argue with Rose. Rose had been the one who had made sure she fitted in. Rose had made her join every social club including the drama club – 'it's such fun Miranda, you are going to love it.' She had been terrified at first but once she got over feeling self-conscious, she had enjoyed a place where you could pretend to be someone or something else.

The room for the guests' jackets and coats was behind the next door. Miranda sat at the end of the bed next to an apricot teddy bear jacket. She absently stroked it while Rose consulted her phone for what seemed like the hundredth time.

"Shit! He's in the garden waiting for me!" She squeaked out the last word. "He said, what took me so long!" Rose spun around, "Bathroom, I need the bathroom."

The white marble bench and the towels looked new and the basin shone. Rose brushed her hair furiously. It fell like a curtain down her back. She sometimes wished she had curls like Miranda, who never had to do anything with her hair.

Miranda sat on the bed and rubbed the teddy bear jacket over her face. It smelled of something that reminded her of summer. "This smells like your mother's garden," she said to Rose. Miranda had spent every holiday with Rose's family since she had started at St Helen's.

Rose dabbed more gloss on her pink lips, and waved her mascara across her long eyelashes. "How do I look?" she turned and gave a nervous smile.

Miranda held the jacket under her chin. She tilted her head on one side and considered the question. Rose took a deep breath and then another one. This wasn't the first boy she had met blind but this was the first one she had felt connected to.

Miranda knew Rose, the deep breathing. The tip of her tongue exploring the inside of her bottom lip.

"Well?" said Rose.

Miranda grinned at her, "Will drop dead gorgeous and he's dead in the water do?"

"Dead in the water! What does that even mean Milly? Don't answer, no time, I have to find him? Come on… and your boyfriend!" She threw an arm around Miranda's shoulder, "The one who is going to penetrate…"

"Eww… stop please," Miranda said.

"He's in the garden," said Rose. Miranda put her hand on the door jam, "You said I could stay inside, I'm not going in the garden without my jacket. I don't care if it's my school blazer."

"No time to argue. You're coming with me. Wear this," Rose plucked the teddy bear jacket off the bed.

"I can't do that. It's stealing." Miranda backed away.

"No, it's borrowing. It will only be for a few minutes. I promise."

Rose threw it around Miranda's shoulders, "Now look as though you own it." She hustled Miranda down the stairs. She leant her head close, "Keep a look out for your boyfriend, he's here somewhere, I just know it." Rose's large gold hooped earring pressed against Miranda's cheek.

Miranda held the jacket around her chin. She looked straight ahead as she descended the last step. Any minute she expected someone to touch her on the shoulder but she made it into the fairy lit garden without anyone noticing her.

A glitter ball spun shards of bright light across the heads of the dancers who were fighting for space on the dance floor erected in the middle of the garden. Rose studied her phone. "He said he's over by the drinks table." She stopped and stepped behind a tree pulling Miranda with her. "You look Milly, is he there?"

Miranda scanned the garden, "I can see the drinks table but there are too many people standing in the way. You'll have to get closer."

"You do it Milly."

Miranda slipped the jacket off her shoulders, she was feeling bad about wearing it, she was still waiting for that hand on her shoulder and the accusation of 'thief' in her ear.

"Hold this," she stepped out of the shadow of the tree and walked past the group blocking her view. He was there, she recognised him from his photo. Legalos, and he wasn't an elf. He was standing at the side of the table one hand in his pocket the other staring at the lit screen of his phone. She saw the back of a guy appear from the far side of the garden. He walked out of the shadows into the light. She couldn't see his face, just his back. He staggered and then reached out to steady himself on the arm of Legalos. He was drunk and loud.

"Where is she then, the girl that looks like a giraffe?" He draped his arm around Legalos and grabbed at the phone.

"Fuck off man, she's here. It's not even late and you're pissed."

He sounded angry and disappointed as he shrugged the other guy's arm from around him.

"Shit, you sound like my mother."

"Yeh well, you better make yourself scarce your mum is heading this way now!"

Miranda saw the other guy hunch his shoulders and stagger towards the back of the garden and the deep shadows.

"Well, did you see him?" said Rose, her hands clasped as though she was praying.

"He's there, he's not an elf, but his ears are pointed," said Miranda. "And he looks tall at least as tall you."

"Yay, to being at least as tall as me and pointy ears are in."

"What like square chins?" Miranda said.

"Okay come with me, you're my wing man… girl."

"No, you go, I'm going to return this jacket and I'm wearing my blazer. It's dark and no one will notice it and if they do, I don't care. I'll find you."

Rose pouted her lips, "We agreed you'd stay… just in case." Rose poked her head from around the tree. She snapped her head back. "Agh! He's seen me, I look an idiot." Rose took a step away from the tree and he was there running one hand across his scalp. His hair was cut close to his head, it made him look menacing thought Miranda until he gave an embarrassed smile that turned into a grin.

"Are you …?" he looked from Rose to Miranda and then back at Rose. "Stardust?" Rose nodded, he looked brilliant in the half light. He wasn't an elf and he was taller than she was.

He waved his phone and laughed, "I know so much about you already except your real name. Mine's Sam."

"Rose," she tossed her blonde hair in Miranda's direction, "This is Miranda, we're at school together." She saw the look Sam gave Miranda, the furrowed brow. A slightly worried look.

"She's eighteen, she's just short," said Rose.

Miranda shrugged. She didn't think 158cm required all this attention.

"Hi," Miranda waved her fingers at him.

"Hi Miranda," said Sam. "Well, a few minutes earlier and I could have introduced you to my mate, Jack Charles. This is his party, and he's hiding in the house from his mother because he's drunk too much." He jerked his head towards the drinks table, "Drink? Only if you're eighteen of course."

"We're all eighteen. Miranda doesn't drink," Rose said. She could have added, 'Miranda doesn't break the rules.'

"Okay walk over with me Rose, great view of the water." said Sam.

Miranda had stopped listening after she heard whose party it was. *Jack Charles.* Miranda looked towards the house, she thought she might catch a glimpse of him. "You two go ahead, I'll come and find you," said Miranda walking towards the house.

She hadn't seen Jack Charles for six years. She wanted it to be the same Jack Charles. She knew she would recognise him, but she doubted he would recognise her. She went straight to the bedroom to return the jacket. She had taken it off as soon as she left Rose and held it bundled to her chest, her head down until she reached the bedroom with all the coats and jackets piled on the bed. She opened the door and threw the jacket onto the bed and then went to retrieve her blazer from the bedroom down the hall.

He was there on the bed. He lay on his back, his arms outspread as though he'd been shot. His head on one side facing the door. Miranda stood at the foot of the bed. She felt as if all the air in the room was thrumming. It was him. He hadn't changed that much. She knew who he was, he was her Jack Charles. Greenfield primary school, year six. Her last year at primary school before she won the scholarship to St Helen's College, before… before everything bad had ended.

She walked around and studied his profile. It was him, the same thick dark hair, the straight nose. She wouldn't, couldn't forget the boy who had seen her take food out of the rubbish bin at school.

It was after lunch, the playground was empty and Jack Charles and another boy, Luke Somers were on their way back to class when they saw her. She dropped the half-eaten sandwich back into the bin and ran into the toilet block. She wanted to stay there and never come out. She was late getting back into the classroom. She knew her eyes were red from crying.

She tried to slip into the classroom without anyone seeing her but Luke Somers saw her and called out, "Where you bin? Bin anywhere good Bin Girl?"

Some of the kids laughed, they all knew that she had been seen scavenging in the bin. It wasn't the first time she had looked for half eaten lunches. She had been careful, waiting until the school yard was empty and everyone was in class. She wanted to run from the classroom.

Miss Simms the classroom teacher looked up from her desk and scanned the room. She could see heads turned in Miranda's direction. Miranda was staring ahead, her face blank. The poor kid, she had a hard time fitting in with these kids. They talked about her in the staff room. How bright she was, so eager to learn. Her written work told them that but it was hard to get her to speak in class. One of the teachers had thought she had a hearing problem but she heard alright, followed instructions.

Miranda didn't fit in with the students whose parents lived in the expensive suburbs that boasted the state's most expensive private schools. Miranda's filthy school uniform and dirty trainers brought her the attention she didn't want. The school principal had shared some of the notes she had received from Miranda's previous school. Confirmed the straight 'As in every subject except sport that she routinely went missing from, or didn't turn up at school on the day. There was the record too of the times the school had made a mandatory report of neglect to the Department.

Kids could be unkind and kids could be cruel. Miss Simms stood up to quieten the class. She would try to find out later what that was about but it was unlikely Miranda would tell her. She had tried before when Miranda had come to school with her hair butchered. She had found Miranda alone in the school yard. She'd kept her tone light, kept the horror out of her voice, "You had your hair cut Miranda?" Her beautiful curls were gone and the hair cut so short. She had gone to the principal at lunch to report it, "Her mother did it, hacked at it, it looks terrible." The principal contacted the Department. She heard later that Miranda had insisted to the social worker that she cut it herself so she didn't get nits.

Some of the class were still laughing at Luke Somers' reference to 'bin girl,' he seemed to be the ring leader. Miss Simms glared at him. Then Jack Charles shouted, "Shut up Luke. It's not funny." He slammed his fists onto his desk. The class fell silent.

Miranda held her hands across her stomach as the memories of those last months at Greenfield Primary school surfaced as she looked at the sleeping face of Jack Charles.

He couldn't stop all the kids calling her names and it stuck for the rest of the year until she left the school. Jack had never called her that, he didn't speak to her and neither did his friends. She kept her head down in the class. She tried to be invisible. She both loved and hated the school. She loved the school work, it seemed harder than any government school she had been to before. She had to work hard to catch up and she loved the challenge. She had something to prove to the kids in her class who looked down on her and moved away when she got near them. Most of the children in her class would be going onto one of the prestigious private high schools in the area. Greenfield Primary was a government school, with an excellent reputation and it was free.

Miranda had attended six primary schools, always moving from house to house. Couch surfing with her mother's 'friends,' that Miranda had never met before. In the final year of her primary school, Miranda's mother had been housed in a government block of flats that stood on the wrong side of the affluent suburb and in the catchment for Greenfield Primary school. Miranda didn't fit in, but she showed everyone that she was smarter.

After she had been caught looking for food in the bin, she found food in her school desk and once in her school bag. She knew it was Jack Charles. He never let anyone see him doing it but once she saw him walk away from her desk and she found the lunch he had left for her.

She saw him looking at her when Miss Simms had handed back their final exam results. She had held onto Miranda's until last. The teacher had made a speech about her marks, she scored near perfect marks for every subject. The class was silent and Miranda had kept her head down. Jack Charles had given a hoot and started clapping, and then a few others clapped. Everyone looked up to Jack, he was the sports star of the school. She felt her cheeks burn and when she looked up, he was smiling at her as though he really thought she was amazing. That's when she had begun to dream about him. He was her personal secret fantasy and now he was real.

She didn't want him to remember that girl, 'Bin Girl.' The girl who sat on her own and had no friends, whose hair was cut to her scalp because her mother couldn't be bothered to get the lice out of her hair. Every school she had attended the girls had got lice. It wasn't her fault. She didn't want him to remember that girl whose mother had turned up at the school in bare feet. The one who talked too loudly and made trouble with the other parents. The girl whose mother had been a drug addict and had died from an overdose.

It had been a blessing really. Everyone was sorry for her but then she had won a scholarship to St Helen's and became a boarder. She tried not think of it as a blessing, it made her feel bad as though she had wished it.

She stared at the sleeping figure of Jack for a long time. She could still see the boy from primary school. He was more angles now, sharp cheek bones and square jaw. His head was on her blazer. He smelled of alcohol, sweet and sickly. She felt a sudden rush of disappointment. She wanted him to be perfect, like the fantasy model in her head. Her nose was stinging. *Don't cry you idiot.* She bit hard on her lips. *Get real, it was a fantasy. Rose was right.*

She reached for the part of the sleeve of her blazer that poked from beneath his hair. She touched it with two fingers and pulled, he didn't move and neither did her blazer. She held it with both hands and pulled harder. He moaned and turned his head. She stepped back and he opened his eyes and swore. He stared at her skirt and then turned his head back and looked up at her. She watched him furrow his brow, he didn't recognise her. "Did you…" he mumbled and then closed his eyes. He held his arm over his eyes, "I know you." He mumbled a name she didn't want to hear.

No *don't remember me please.* She had left that life, that girl behind her.

He pulled his arm away and looked at her again. "Yeh, know you, fairy story." He closed his eyes again, "You're snow white… saw the cartoon." He pulled up his t-shirt as though he was going to take it off. He groaned and turned over, "Get…" he didn't the finish sentence, he pushed her to one side and stumbled to the bathroom.

She helped him clean up, gave him a glass of water. She was used to someone vomiting. She had lived with a mother who had thrown up and not always in the toilet bowl. She knew the trick was to hold her breath when she had cleaned it up.

He looked much better after he had thrown up. She handed him a wet towel and gave him a glass of water. She thought he might recognise her the way he kept looking at her. But he hadn't and then he wouldn't give her back her blazer and had locked the door and pulled her onto the bed.

Chapter Six

MORNING AFTER THE PARTY

MIRANDA

"Hey, where did you get to last night? I came looking for you, I was worried. How did you get home? Where were you? You should have sent me a text."

Miranda was lying on her bed. She looked up from the book she was reading. Typical Rose, asking endless questions. "I sent you a text, I said I was catching an Uber."

Rose tapped on the open book. "Why are you studying and when did you get the Uber App?"

"I'm not studying, I'm just reading," Miranda closed the book. "I don't have the Uber App… someone called it for me."

Miranda swung her legs off the bed and stood up. She didn't look at Rose, she closed her book and put it on her desk that faced the window to the school playing field. One of the gardeners was seated on a ride on mower carving out pale corridors of green. Miranda kept her back to Rose, she didn't want to answer.

"Who called the Uber?"

If she answered that question there would be more questions and she knew Rose and her relentless grilling. She should be a barrister thought Miranda.

"It was a boy wasn't it. It was… who Milly?"

Miranda smoothed her hand across the book on her desk. Rose was her best friend, the closest person in her life but she hadn't told Rose anything about her old life and Rose had never asked. She turned to face Rose. Rose wasn't smiling.

"Don't do that fake puzzled look, I can see right through that." Rose looked fierce, "Who called the Uber?"

Rose reached in her jeans pocket for her phone. She scrolled through her messages. There was a text from Miranda.

"Sorry, I missed it. I had my phone on silent," Rose said.

"Would you have heard it?" Miranda raised her eyebrows. Rose ignored the unspoken question. Miranda wasn't going to throw her off the scent. But it was true she wouldn't have heard it she had spent the night with Sam on the dance floor when they weren't making out.

"Okay, sorry I missed your text. You sent it at eleven o'clock." She looked at Miranda waiting for an explanation.

Miranda could feel the heat rising in her face.

Rose turned and closed the door behind her. She knew Miranda, something had happened. "Okay out with it. Who was he?"

Miranda pressed her fingers to her lips and shook her head.

"Don't shake your head, Milly. That blush is giving you away."

"Tell me about Sam, do you like him? Is he as nice as you hoped?" said Miranda.

Rose held up her hand, "Stop. That's not going to work. Not changing the subject. The answer is yes and yes. Okay, Milly, I can see you in there." Rose took hold of Miranda's shoulders and stared into her eyes.

"Far out! It was him. Shit! It was. Fantasy boy. Tell me."
She pushed Miranda onto the bed. "Tell me everything Milly.
Start at the beginning and don't leave anything out."

Miranda rolled onto her back and stared at the ceiling.
Rose flopped down beside her, propped herself on one elbow and waited for Miranda to give her the details. That was
only fair thought Rose, she gave Miranda the details whether
she wanted to hear them or not.

*Too much information Rose, I don't need all the details. Is nothing
sacred?*

*I'm educating you Milly. You need to know what you want and how
a boy can give it to you. You do know they shoot their load in seconds
and you're left hanging?*

She didn't want to lie to Rose, the only friend she had
ever had. Rose made her feel normal just like the other girls.
She turned her head to face Rose. "It was him. The fantasy
boy." She smiled, a smile full of disappointment, and sat up.
She ran her fingers through her hair, shaking out the curls.
Rose hadn't moved, this wasn't going to be a good story, Miranda didn't sound happy.

Miranda looked over her shoulder at Rose. "Greenfield
Primary. I went there for seven months. It wasn't a good
time." She shook her head at the memory of it. "It was the
worst school. I didn't fit in. Lot of bullying. He was at the
school. I think he felt sorry for me… he was nice, the only
one. I didn't want him to recognise me."

"Did he recognise you?"

Miranda shook her head. "No, he was drunk. It was his
party and he was drunk. Very drunk."

Rose sat up. Sam had said it was his best mate's birthday.
Jack something. "Jack?"

"Yeh, Jack Charles."

"He's the fantasy boyfriend?"

"He was, past tense now. Not a fantasy." Miranda walked over to her wardrobe and took out her runners. "Sunday morning Rose and our quest to stay fit. You can tell me all about Sam."

Rose could be a force to be reckoned with, she could be loud and brash but she knew when to stop asking questions.

Chapter Seven

ONE YEAR AFTER THE PARTY

JACK

Jack dropped his head into his hands, every muscle in his body felt on fire, he had run until his legs felt like lead and every breath was searing his lungs. He had missed two shots at goal and just managed to get one through the sticks. He knew no one in the Swans was looking to blame him but he felt responsible. Those two missed goals would have put them in front and ensured the Swans finished in the top eight teams with a chance of competing in the Grand Final.

Jack glanced at the player sitting to his left. His flat mate, Ryley Short. He was 6ft 3 and everyone called him 'shorty.'

Jack and Ryley had been drafted to the Swans at the same time. Jack had been the number seven pick in the National Draft. Ryley was two years older than Jack and had played for his local footy club in Queensland until he had been spotted by a scout for the Swans.

"That was fucked," said Jack not lifting his head.

"Yeh, but could have been worse. Your dad could have been on the side lines." He gave a grin and punched Jack on the shoulder.

Ryley wasn't interested in talking about the game and definitely not about the goals Jack had missed. He knew there was a lot of pressure on Jack. He was seen as some whizz kicking star. Being picked at number seven had put a lot of pressure on Jack, he felt for him.

Jack still had his head in his hands. His shirt was dark with sweat. Ryley frowned, he wasn't Jack's minder but he was his flat mate and he knew the way Jack would beat himself up. He had never met anyone who was so hard on themselves.

"Come on mate, put it out of your mind. Leave the post mortem to the coach. He can give you a tongue lashing if that's what you want."

Jack lifted his head quickly, "What?"

"Forget it come on – we're meeting everyone at Piccolos. Let's get into the torture bath, get it over with."

Jack knew Mick Grisby would analyse the game with the team minute by minute at the next players meeting. Replaying the game while they sat through all their missed opportunities, fumbled hand balls, missed goals. He also knew Grisby wouldn't humiliate him over the missed goals. Ryley was right he was beating himself up. They were such easy goals, *they were easy goals Jack what were you thinking? You were kicking like a girl.* He shook his head to mentally shut down the voice of Ross Charles.

"I said forget it JC," Ryley flicked his towel at Jack's head.

Jack didn't mind the torture bath. It would shut Ross Charles up. You couldn't think about anything in the freezing water while you were just shivering and turning blue waiting out the fifteen minutes before you could jump under the hot shower.

They were in the car park when Jack got the call. He looked at the name on the incoming call, his father. He shifted his back pack to his other shoulder and winced. *And now for the post mortem with Ross Charles who has never played a professional game of AFL in his life. Fuck off Ross.*

Jack held the phone out to Ryley. "Ross, and he's waited nearly an hour before he's called that must have killed him."

Ryley shook his head, "Don't answer it." He held his middle finger up, "Tell him to go fuck himself."

Ryley didn't get it. You would think Ross Charles would be proud of his son. Not criticising him all the time. He was glad his father wasn't like Ross. His dad only had praise for him even when he didn't deserve it, like today's game with the Bulldogs. His dad had sent a gif telling him how proud he was. Ryley had shown it to Jack.

"Your dad was even proud of your new haircut" Jack said.

"Yeh and what's wrong with it?" Ryley said rubbing his hand over his buzz cut.

"Dad," said Jack. The very word caught in his throat. He switched the phone to his other ear and felt in his pocket for his keys. His temple throbbed, his thumb felt for the button on the phone to turn it off. He had done that before and got away with it. *Sorry dad, battery flat.*

Ross was building up steam, Jack imagined him taking notes during the game. He zoned out. He had got good at that over the years. He couldn't remember a time when his dad wasn't finding some fault. It had been a relief when he had finally left and now it was as though he had never left.

You let him get on top of you, you rushed the kick, you're taking your eye off the ball…

Jack held the phone away from his ear and took a breath. Ryley put his hand on Jack's shoulder and whispered, "Arsehole," he could hear every word Ross was bellowing down the phone. He didn't understand why Jack didn't tell him to fuck off.

"You there son?" The voice was angry and demanding.

Fuck you, fuck you. Don't call me son.

"Yeh, I heard, I've got to go, team meeting. Thanks for the call."

"Well okay, it wasn't all bad," said Ross, his voice dropped an octave. "Don't let the team down."

"Yeh, okay, bye." He slipped the phone into his pocket and wiped the back of his hand across his mouth. His heart was pumping. He squeezed his eyes tight and when he opened them Ryley was looking at him from the other side of the car.

Jack shook his head and raised his eyebrows in a gesture of surrender. He didn't have to explain himself to anyone.

He slid behind the wheel and started the car. He leant across Ryley and opened the glove box and took out a silver hip flask.

"Need this after talking to that arsehole." Jack unscrewed the lid and took two gulps of vodka. He held the flask out to Ryley. Ryley shook his head. Alcohol wasn't the answer.

"Why don't you just tell him to fuck off, or don't answer his calls. Block him."

"Yeh, I know. I will one day." He screwed back the cap and put the flask back. He hadn't drunk much, the flask was still half full. The alcohol helped, it always had.

Ryley threw his bag on the back seat and studied Jack's profile as he pulled on the seat belt. He saw Jack's hands, the knuckles white around the leather steering wheel. Jack dropped his hands and ran his fingers through his hair. Ryley could see Jack was sweating despite the cold interior of the car.

"You know he's an arsehole," said Ryley. He had heard enough of the telephone conversations between Jack and Ross, and witnessed the impact it had on Jack to be confident that his judgement of Ross Charles was in the ball park. Ryley didn't get it, why was Jack so polite to his dad, was he afraid of him?

He wondered what kind of father he had been to Jack before he had separated from Jack's mother. Jack had once admitted to him that he was relieved when he had left, "I just wished he had fucked off when I was a baby."

"You okay mate?" said Ryley.

Jack was hanging onto the steering wheel as though he or the car was about to tip over. "Here, have a drink of water." He held out his own water bottle to Jack.

"Thanks," Jack took hold of the water bottle with shaking hands, he unscrewed the lid and gulped down the water, spilling it down his neck and on to his shirt.

Breathe, breathe, it's just a panic attack, you know what to do. Close your eyes, count your breath, in one, two, three, four, out, five, six, seven, eight. Open your eyes focus on something, that distant tree.

Jack turned to Ryley and handed back his water bottle. He could see concern written all over Ryley's face, "I'm okay, think it was the ice bath. It's happened before, weird reaction."

"Yeh having to get into an ice bath is pretty weird," Ryley said. He didn't believe Jack for one second. He had seen one of his sisters have a panic attack, he knew what they looked like.

Jack blew out his breath, "Yeh." He shrugged his shoulders and started the car.

They drove in silence, while Jack negotiated the steady stream of traffic. The sky had turned into a dirty sheet hung between the high-rise office buildings. It was going to rain and the traffic was even slower than usual. *Don't let the team down, keep your eye on the ball.*

"Fuck," said Jack, "should have stayed at the club." He braked hard as a pedestrian stepped off the kerb and onto the cross walk.

"Shit," said Ryley pulling on the seat belt as it tightened across his shoulders. He looked at Jack and wondered what he was thinking about. He hoped it wasn't what Ross Charles had said.

"Sorry, didn't see him," Jack said. He pulled away slowly and released the iron grip on the steering wheel.

***

Piccolos was crowded. Jack had to shout to make himself heard. "I booked a table," said Ryley leaning across Jack, "under the name Stevenson. The waiter glanced up at Ryley and nodded, he knew who they were but he wasn't about to give them the satisfaction of thinking they were famous or something.

They followed the waiter to the back of the restaurant. Someone at a nearby table recognised them both. They ignored the derogatory comments. "Bulldogs supporters," Ryley said out of the side of his mouth.

After they had ordered Jack hunched his shoulders to the noise behind him, he was facing a bright wall of coloured glass separating a bar area from the restaurant. He welcomed the noise, you could hardly hear yourself talk and the noise shut down the voice in his head.

"Don't look now," said Ryley, "but I think someone is coming over to our table… and yes, they are." Ryley lifted his head and smiled at the girl standing behind Jack.

Jack heard the breathless, "Excuse me but you're Jack Charles, aren't you?"

Jack didn't move, he stared down at the table. Attention had brought Jack sponsorship and a manager. He hated the attention, feeling like a gold fish in a fish bowl but it meant money. "Yes, he is," said Ryley and he gave Jack a wide-eyed look that was telling him he should turn around.

She was beautiful, a model, no an actor, she could have been either. Long blonde hair down to her waist, and cool grey eyes looking at him with the confidence of someone used to being admired.

He hadn't answered her but the look he gave her confirmed that she was right.

"I thought it was you. I saw you come in. I'm Emily Hogan. You might know me from Instagram." She tossed her head in a gesture she had made a thousand times before and her hair swung forward and back behind one bare artificially bronzed shoulder.

Ryley pointed to the empty seat beside Jack. Jack needed a distraction and Emily looked perfect.

"Yeh," said Ryley, "I've heard of you," that was a lie but he could just tell she was going to tell them why she was on Instagram.

Emily shook her head at the empty seat and frowned at Jack. He didn't know who she was and nothing annoyed her more than being invisible. Emily placed the small card she was holding on the table next to Jack and tapped it with her finger. "I'm raising money for charity," she paused to let her good deed sink in, "and I was hoping I might persuade you to…" she smiled, showing perfect orthodontically manipulated whiter than white teeth. Her lips shone as though they'd been buttered.

Jack found himself smiling back at her, his spine unlocking slowly, "Donate," said Jack, "sure." Numbers flitted through his mind, what was an amount that was just right.

Ryley watched from across the table, he could see the effect she was having on Jack. Men were just putty around gorgeous women but not him. He had Nina, and no girl even come close to her in his eyes. Jack needed a girlfriend thought Ryley, someone who could get him out of his head. Jack was living like a monk. Ryley had seen Jack's Instagram account and the 264 thousand followers weren't all football fans, they were Jack Charles fans.

"No," she dragged the word out smiling all the time, "I was wondering if you would come with me to the event. It would help raise money for a really, really worthy cause."

He said he would think about it and took her details. He didn't want any distractions in his life, he was focused on his career. He was giving girls a rest, but Ryley persuaded him to go, "Do you good JC, have some fun." And he reluctantly took the advice.

***

"Hey Sam, how's life?" said Jack. He hadn't spoken to Sam for almost a month and he was feeling bad about it. He had missed a call after the Bulldogs defeat and had forgotten to call back. Sam was his hair shirt, the ever-present reminder to Jack that if he had played that last game for St Jude's, things might have turned out differently for Sam. Sam had never said a word to blame Jack. The dominos had lined up on that day and Jack had set them in motion when he had missed the game that had sent Sam's future in a different direction.

I can still walk yeh great but no more glittering career in Football. But on the plus side I've got dad off my back.

And that was it, Sam had never mentioned his injury again. *"Going to Uni, carving out some illustrious career and gaining fame and a shit load of money."*

Sam was Jack's biggest fan and he could always rely on him to give him honest feedback about the match and his performance.

"Okay, I've been busy with Uni stuff. Saw your last game. Bastards are making sure you don't get your golden boot on the ball. You must have been exhausted. Good goal. You'll show them why you were number seven."

"Thanks," said Jack. "That's a better review than I got from Ross,"

"God, is he still doing that shit. Could you imagine what my dad would have done after every game, if I'd ever played."

It didn't take much imagination to hear Sam's father droning on about the game but he wouldn't have slammed Sam's performance.

"How's the studies going?"

"Well… good."

Jack heard the confidence in his voice. It was more than good. "Yeh how good?"

"Won a prize in Sports Health and…" he paused.

"And?" said Jack.

"I'm going to do Medicine, swapping my undergraduate degree and doing Molecular Biology. I've got some catching up to do, so overloading this semester."

"Wow, medicine, that's fantastic. When did you decide that?"

"Had it at the back of my mind for a while but didn't want to say anything because wasn't sure I could do it. But been out of action for a while… leg's okay, thanks for asking… just no more footy. Lot of time to study my navel but decided to study the books instead."

"Sorry I meant to ask about the leg but… you know…"

"I know you thought it was a no go subject but it's okay. I'm over it just gonna bask in some reflected glory, you know best friend and all that."

"Ha, what glory. Have you read the papers lately! I'm getting hammered. Anyway, tell me about the prize for science, what was it, a great big silver shield."

"Nah, nothing shiny or glittery something better – money. $500.00 and my name on some board in an obscure part of the University. Be able to point it out to the old man and my kids, if I have any. The prize made me realise I'm not the dummy my dad thinks I am. Got a tutor too. Friend of Rose."

"Rose?"

"Yeh, you know the one I met at your eighteenth, we went out a couple of times before I did the leg in. Bumped into her at the awards night. She was with the girl who's going to tutor me. She just won some prize."

"So, you and Rose?" said Jack, his voice holding an unseen smile.

"Yeh well… what about you… your pic has been on every post on Emily Hogan's Instagram."

"You follow her?" Jack asked.

"No, not me, you idiot, Rose."

Jack gave an embarrassed laugh, "Yeh," he hated the pictures she posted.

"I follow your Instagram though. All those pictures with your shirt off."

Jack groaned. There were a lot of photos with his shirt off.

"I don't envy you the work to keep those abs in shape," Sam said.

It was a punishing routine, but he wasn't alone in the gym, all the team was working out. "Yeh, it goes with the territory, you know that." Jack liked being in the gym, it was like meditation, nothing to think about but your form and the weights. As a kid he had always been wiry and small. Ross hadn't teased him but had made a point of telling him he took after his mother's side of the family. "Average, that's okay, you'll be average too."

He thought that he would never grow and then at thirteen his voice broke and he had a growth spurt and was 5ft 11in by sixteen and then added more inches over the next two years.

"So, give us the details. She's got half a million followers for fucks sake."

"Yeh, she's an influencer, whatever that is."

He knew what it was. Emily got paid to promote products on her Instagram page.

He had learned in the first few weeks of dating her that it meant everywhere they went, whatever they were doing she was posting photos and uploading videos on Instagram. He had drawn the line at her posting a near naked photo of him in her bed.

The charity function he had agreed to attend with her on the first date was sponsored by a hair product and he had difficultly working out what the charity was.

"I told you the money goes to a good cause… lots of different causes." She had shaken back her long blonde hair and taken a selfie with a large poster for shampoo in the background.

He never did find out what the charity causes were but by then he wasn't bothered about checking out the details, he couldn't think straight around Emily, he was the envy of everyone. Even his father had sent him a text message asking who she was, 'she's an absolute stunner, don't let her get away, she makes you look good!' He had put an exclamation mark at the end. Jack had puzzled over the message for hours before that ear worm had finally died.

"So, make some time to see me when you're next in Perth," said Sam.

"Yeh will do."

***

Jack was dreaming, drums were playing somewhere and he was standing in an empty football stadium, a football in his hands, no one on the field but him and a man in a suit standing between the goal posts. A man who looked like Ross Charles, and he was gesticulating and shouting at him but the drums were drowning out the words. The drums were getting louder, he wanted them to stop. He kicked the ball straight at Ross Charles' head and the drumming stopped and Ryley was standing at the foot of the bed shouting at him.

He tried to push himself up but his body didn't want him to move. "What?" he tried to focus.

"Come on mate, get up. I've been hammering on your door for the past five minutes. You don't want to be late for training again. Grisby will slaughter you." Ryley couldn't keep the exasperation out of his voice.

Ryley drove them to the training ground. He didn't speak for the first five minutes. He glanced sideways at Jack. Jack had his eyes closed, his head back. A silver water bottle between his legs.

"You okay mate?" said Ryley.

Jack grunted, he couldn't get the words out, his tongue felt like sandpaper.

"Drink more water." It sounded like an order and Jack lifted the water bottle and did as he was told.

"Didn't hear you come in last night." Ryley didn't wait for an answer. He regarded Jack as a younger brother, he liked him and he could see he was in trouble. You didn't have to be a psychologist to work that out. Jack drank and he drank too much. He'd discussed it with Nina, "He's using alcohol to self-medicate. He needs help," she said.

"Didn't hear you all the other nights either," said Ryley.

Jack tried to laugh but it made his eyeballs hurt. He was having fun, or he thought he was. Emily liked to party and he liked to party with Emily.

"Got myself home though." Jack thought that was an achievement. Yeh, he stayed late but he knew he had training, didn't stay the night in Emily's bed, although he wanted to.

"Got home," he repeated.

Ryley sighed, he'd been right that Emily was going to be a distraction but not like this. Now Jack's career was going to be on the line if he didn't get help. Ryley pulled the car into the car park. They weren't late yet. Jack had Ryley to thank for that.

"Wait," said Ryley. He knew he would never forgive himself if he didn't say something. "I know you don't want to hear this but you're drinking too much Jack. You've been hung over the last two training sessions." Ryley knew that was true and anyone looking at Jack on those mornings would have read the signs. None of the guys were saints, they knew what a hangover looked like and they knew Grisby wouldn't tolerate it, he was no fool.

Jack turned away, one hand opening the car door. He couldn't meet Ryley's eyes. He felt the heat rising in his face, *who the fuck does he think he is?* He ran his tongue over his lips, he took a breath. He could feel a pulse beating in his temple. He stepped out of the car, the gravel snapping and grinding beneath his feet. He pulled his shoulders back, and drew in the air through his nose, filling up his lungs hoping it was the cure for the fog in his head. He walked around to the boot of the car, took out his bag and slung it over his shoulder and walked ahead of Ryley.

Grisby was waiting for him as soon as he entered the building.

Chapter Eight

ONE YEAR AFTER THE PARTY

PERTH
MIRANDA

"You're sure you don't mind Milly. Sam said he'll pay more than the going rate."

Miranda changed the screen on her laptop. She knew Rose had seen the screen. She couldn't hide anything from Rose. Rose touched her on the shoulder as she walked around the small table that took up most of the space in the townhouse kitchen. Rose raised one eyebrow but Miranda ignored the silent question.

"No, that's fine. I told you it was okay. He doesn't have to pay more. I saw him yesterday at Uni. I told him I can only give him two hours a week in the Uni library." She shrugged her shoulders, "and we'll just see how he goes. I don't want to waste my time and I don't want to commit to a long period."

At first Miranda had agreed to tutor because she needed the money but then she found that it helped her with her studies. If there had been a good fairy around at her birth then that was the one thing that had been bestowed on her – an almost photographic memory and tutoring meant she hardly had to study.

She didn't mind tutoring Sam, she had seen more of him since Sam and Rose had got back together a few months ago. After Sam's accident the surgery to his leg had not gone smoothly, followed by months of pain and then physio. Sam had broken off their early relationship before it had started.

They met again at the end of year prize giving when Rose had gone with Miranda to see her receive a prize and Sam had been there too. After the ceremony Sam had approached Miranda and they got chatting about doing medicine. Rose had recognised him despite his long curly hair. He seemed thinner and he was wearing glasses. They had hit it off straight away and had been together ever since.

Rose smiled and pulled gently at one of Miranda's curls. "You okay, you seem … I saw what you were looking at." She nodded her head at Miranda's laptop. "Everything okay?"

Miranda brushed at Rose's hand that was hovering over her head ready to tug at another curl. "Leave off the hair straightening Rose."

"I want curls," said Rose pushing out her bottom lip.

"No, you don't you'd hate them like every other person who has curly hair."

Miranda didn't know how many times she had this conversation with Rose. Rose had perfect hair, long, naturally blonde and straight. She didn't wake up in the morning with her hair looking like a bush.

"Okay, but tell me what's wrong and don't say nothing. I know you."

Miranda smiled at Rose, "I'm okay, just tired. Too much tutoring and now your annoying boyfriend."

"He's cute though, isn't he and he's funny," Rose said. "He's also got curls just like these ones." She reached forward but Miranda turned her head away, her curls bouncing as though they were taking flight.

"Yeh he's not funny and he's annoying." Miranda picked up her laptop. "I've got to get changed for work. Full house at the restaurant."

Rose made a face of sympathy. She was lucky she didn't have to work to support herself, her parents gave her a generous allowance and she lived rent free in the townhouse her parents owned.

Miranda slipped on her work shoes. She was tired, that hadn't been a lie but it was the disappointment she hadn't been able to disguise. She had been searching the ancestry website hoping to see a message that told her that she had matched with her biological father. The desire to find out who her biological father was had only got more of an urgency about it as she had got older.

She had thought about trying to locate her biological father since high school when it had been discussed in a biology class. She had saved up the fee as soon as she got herself a job, and sent off her DNA sample to the ancestry website two years ago and had learned that her ancestry was predominately Italian.

It had always been a no-go zone with her mother when Miranda had tried to broach the subject. *He's an arsehole, a fuckwit, okay, a loser* and once when the drugs were taking her to some other place, she had said, *one night stand. I can't remember.*

"Any luck with the Ancestry thing?" said Rose quietly. Miranda hadn't heard her come into her bedroom.

"Nope. I guess it's never going to happen." Miranda sounded resigned as though she couldn't care less but Rose knew Miranda was good at disguising her feelings.

"I was talking to mum the other day and she wondered whether you had thought of asking to see your file, you know the one the Department must have kept. You said they had been involved in your life for as long as you could remember."

Miranda nodded her head. The Department for Child Protection, *some child protection*. "I hadn't thought of that." *And why would I?* She smiled at Rose. Rose was looking worried as she always did if anything about Miranda's past was mentioned. Rose knew that there were things that had happened to Miranda that were really bad. Her mother had dropped hints to her about the domestic violence Miranda had witnessed and there was something about the way Miranda's mother had died that made Rose's mother tear up.

"Come here chooky and give me a hug" she threw her arms around Miranda. "You're not alone, okay. I'll come with you if you want."

"It's okay Rose. It's a good idea. I'll get onto it." She didn't want Rose going with her. She never wanted anyone to read about her life before her mother died.

Miranda closed the laptop. She had an image in her head of who her father was. He was tall and dark, with eyes the same as hers. She wanted him to be the one-night stand who didn't know she existed, and that when he found out he had a daughter he would be shocked and sad that he hadn't been in her life. She didn't want him to be one of the men who had come into her mother's life for days or weeks and then left. She couldn't remember their faces except for the last one and she didn't want to remember him ever.

The morning light was intense with the heat of the sun that hung like a fireball in the blue sheet of sky. Miranda stood beneath the shade of a eucalyptus tree that stood in the grounds of the government building that held the files of the Department for Child Protection. Her file was in there amongst all the thousands of stories about other children and their lives of neglect and misery.

Miranda studied the shadows thrown on the grass. She might find out who her father was but she was going to have to live through parts of her life she never wanted to remember. She wanted to know more about where she came from. She didn't look like her mother she knew that. Her mother had been fair skinned and blonde. There had been no aunts, uncles or grandparents that she could ever remember seeing.

There had been men in her mother's life, an endless line up of men who pushed her out of the bed she shared with her mother when she was small. She remembered the evenings driving down dark streets to houses she had never been to before, waiting in the car while her mother went inside, "I won't be long, just stay in the car. Keep the doors locked and don't open the windows for anyone except me." Often, she had fallen asleep in the back seat and woken up when she was being carried out of the car in the morning.

She hadn't told Rose, she hadn't told anyone. Her mother had drummed it into her, she was to tell no one what happened at home. If she was absent from school, she was to say she was sick even if she wasn't. *You don't want to go into foster care do you.* It was a part of her life she never wanted to discuss with anyone. After her mother had died, they had sent Miranda to a counsellor who specialised in grief and children but Miranda had said nothing but shook her head or nodded to the questions that the counsellor put to her. After three sessions the counsellor said that she thought the counselling was doing more harm than good and perhaps it would be better to see how Miranda progressed.

The desire to know who her father was had grown with each passing year. Over the years she had been asked if she was Italian, Spanish, and even Mexican. She brushed her hand across her face, she didn't know if she was ready to open the door onto the misery her life had been.

A fluttering above her head made her look up. A black crow, as large as a cat had landed on a branch at her eye level. It was close enough for her to reach out and touch it.

What do you think bird should I go and dig up the skeletons and relive my past?

The crow blinked its yellow eyes.

Once for no huh?

The crow blinked again.

Ok I'm going… thanks. Miranda waited for a break in the traffic and ran across the road towards the glass fronted doors flashing glimpses of the passing traffic. *Are you losing your mind, communicating with the birds?*

Miranda noticed for the first time the adjacent shop, a McDonald's. She paused in the middle of the road. The traffic swept past her, trapping her on either side. She hadn't seen it before, how had she not noticed it with its garish red and the yellow arches? She could smell the mixture of sweet cooked meat hanging in the air. If any smell could take her back to her childhood it was this. The familiar smell of a McDonald's hamburger. It made her want to keep running past the government building and the McDonald's, running away from that life. She stood still, she tried to push the memory away, *think of something else, think of something else.* She turned to run back and away from the memory but she was trapped between the traffic.

She couldn't eat it, the smell of it made her stomach hurt. It was the cheese all gooey and sliding over the meat and the green slimy pickle things.

"Eat it. Uncle Bobby bought it for you."

Uncle Bobby, who wasn't her uncle, was staring at her from over the top of the Big Mac he had stuck in his mouth. He was always staring at her as though he had never seen a ten-year-old girl before. She tried never to look at him. He had a tattoo poking out of the neck of his black t-shirt. The head of a snake, the eyes blood red, the blue-black forked tongue resting in the hollow of his neck. She could imagine its body coiled somewhere on his body. He had a fat stomach that seemed to move on its own.

"Eat it, don't waste food." Uncle Bobby spoke with his cheeks bulging. He leant across the table. Miranda saw the snake's head move towards her.

She had a headache and her eyes were hurting. She picked up the burger, it was so big. She put it against her lips and pretended to take a bite when Uncle Bobby reached out and pressed the palm of one hand against her fingers and pushed the burger towards her face. As she leaned away from him, the top of the bun fell onto the table and the burger and the cheese fell into her lap.

"You're going to eat that," Uncle Bobby said.

"We can take it home Bobby. She's not hungry are you. That's my fault." Her mother re-assembled the bun and began to re-wrap it.

Bobby slapped his hand hard on her mother's hand pressing the bun into the table. "I said, she's going to eat it."

A break in the traffic, she turned and ran back and stood beneath the tree. She looked for the crow but it had gone. She pressed her head against the trunk of the tree. Behind her somewhere on the pavement, she heard someone laughing. A raucous high-pitched laugh, as though they were caught between laughing and crying.

Miranda stood away from the tree and brushed her hands down the front of her jeans. She squeezed her eyes shut, *you can do this. You have to do this Miranda, you have to open this door so you can close it. Yes, open the door so you can close it.*

She repeated the words like a mantra as she stood at the kerb, waited for a break in the traffic and ran across the road and into the building.

They took her to the records inspection room. A small room purposely built for inspection of documents. There was a table and chair in the room and on the table were three large manilla files.

She had made sure her phone was charged. She had been told she could take copies of the files. Some names had been redacted, blacked out so that they couldn't be identified. Miranda knew that they were the names of people who had reported her mother to the Department. She knew some of them had been neighbours who had called the police when the screaming started.

She brushed her hands down her jeans. The room felt suffocatingly hot. She stood up and opened the door. She sat down again and pulled the first file in front of her and opened it.

She found what she was looking for on the opening page that documented the first time her mother had come to the attention of the Department. The date was six months after her own birth date. It was a doctor who had made the initial contact to the Department. Just three words next to her name gave the reason *failure to thrive.*

The Department had threatened to make a formal application to court if her mother had not worked with them. Miranda skimmed down the page and she found what she was looking for,

Father unknown

Miranda closed the folder, she didn't want to read the rest of the files and be reminded of everything that had happened to her. She had never really believed her mother when she had told her she didn't know who her father was, but it had been true. She had to accept that she would never know who he was. The fantasy that she had built in her head about her father was over.

Chapter Nine

MELBOURNE
JACK

Jack paused in the tunnel to the Melbourne Cricket Ground 'the 'G' as it was known. They were playing an important game, an elimination final that they needed to win to progress to the finals. His team, the Sydney Swans, had been knocked out in the elimination finals in his first season playing for the club. They were knocked out by the Melbourne team, the Geelong Cats, that they were facing today.

The coach, Mark Grisby, had patted every player on the shoulder as they left the clubhouse with the standard words of encouragement, 'go get em', 'good lad' or something similar that no one really listened to. It was the Grisby touch, the lucky tap that was going to make all the difference to winning or losing.

Grisby was an ex-Swans player who had the look of a university professor, it was the gold rimmed glasses, tall, neat greying hair cut in the style he had worn for the last twenty odd years, *You can keep your sheep shorn look, you look like a bunch of convicts,* he said in response to the ever-decreasing amount of hair the players were wearing. But behind that look of academic civility was a man capable of bringing a fully grown man to tears with a few well-chosen words, punctuated with a few expletives. He'd rip into them after the game and they would dread the post mortem as though they were facing the firing squad. Didn't he get it, they felt rotten enough without him tearing into them.

He left the ripping into them for during the game or after not before. He was all Mr Positive in the clubroom. Trying out the latest psychological pep talk the club's psychologist, Ron Barber, had drilled into him.

"Okay, you know what you've got to do to win this, look for the gaps, don't let them edge you out. Ryley you had a fantastic game last week, I want to see that again."

He named every player and put the pressure on. "Winning this is in your head. Forget last year, this isn't going to be a repeat. We beat them six weeks ago and we can do it today. You're the better team. Charlie?" He'd swept the circle of players looking for Jack. It didn't matter how many times he got called Charlie, it felt wrong but once one of the senior players had called him that it had stuck. He didn't like it. It was Ross's name not his. He was just grateful that no one called him princess in the changing room. The older players would rough his hair or punch him on the arm, 'great work Charlie,' 'fuckin' amazing goal' 'yer a little wizard.' He kept his head down, he was among some of the greats of the game and he was on the bottom rung and he didn't forget it.

Grisby looked hard at Jack. "Forget what the paper called you. You don't get that title until you've kicked a ton in a season and you're doing great but… not there yet and…" he paused and gripped Jack by the shoulder and squeezed it hard.

Someone had heard Grisby mention the paper. Everyone knew what they had called Jack. "King of the Kicks," someone shouted out above the chatter. 'King of the kicks,' the

Sydney Morning Herald had splashed it on the back page, at the end of his first season. He had made a name for himself after a rocky start when he couldn't kick straight. Now, he was on target, kicking goals at every game. Grisby had started him off as a midfielder but he was playing as a full forward now, and he was expected to get the goals.

Jack tried not to think about goal kicking, he just thought of the game, the plays that Grisby and the assistant coach had drilled into them with the precision of a brain surgeon.

"And Charlie," Grisby had added, "Stokes, he'll be on you like a leach, don't let him provoke you into a fight but don't let him push you around either. He's always got something to prove and he's looking for a transfer back to Queensland."

Stokes had built up a reputation over the last two seasons. He was a few years older than Jack and was considered one of the best full backs in the game, but he was never in contention for the Brownlow medal, he played hard and he played dirty.

It wasn't the first time he'd been up against Jedd Stokes and experienced him hanging onto his arm, pushing and shoving at every opportunity. The last game they had played against the Cats, Stokes had jumper punched him. Grabbed Jack's jumper and tried to give him an upper cut to the chin but Jack had twisted away and had gone onto score a goal.

Stokes had been suspended for two weeks last season for the same offence after it had been caught on camera. Stokes' fist and the handful of jumper he had been holding onto when he struck the player with a blow to the chin that sent him reeling.

Jack felt a push behind him, he looked over his shoulder, Ryley was standing just behind him. He played midfield, fast on his feet and a flyer in the air. Ryley raised his eyebrows as if to say 'can you believe it?'

Jack lifted his chin, turned away, took a breath and then another, as he heard the noise in the stadium suddenly erupt in a roar and felt a surge of adrenalin as his heartbeat sped up and the blood rushed to the muscles in his legs and he had to move.

Come on move Smithy. The players paused waiting for the Captain, Sean Smith to lead them onto the field. Jack could see Smithy hold up his hand. *What the fuck Smithy get going.* Then he heard the loud speaker call out the name of their team and the booing of the Geelong Cats supporters overwhelm the Sydney fans as they began to move out of the tunnel and onto the ground. The noise was like a physical thing, a swarm of something thick and heavy. Jack lifted his chest and sucked in the warm air that had settled over the field like a sauna.

He hated the humidity of the eastern states. He had grown up in Perth, and was used to playing in the dry crackling heat that didn't cool down until well into the season. And then the cold, colder than Sydney and the rain, bucket loads of it turned the field into a mud pit that made your legs feel like lead, slipping and sliding, trying to get a grip on the turf with the ball a heavy soggy mess of slimy leather that was unpredictable in its trajectory.

***

It was three quarter time and they were trailing by 7 points. They needed two goals to win. Grisby had them in a huddle, he was trying to keep the angry frustration from exploding. He knew the cameras were on him trying to read his lips. But his team could see the heat that lit up his neck like a red scarf, a sure sign that he was as mad as hell.

"Okay," he said quietly, ducking his head low, and then he let them have it. "You stop all that fucking fancy stuff, get on your man, stop thinking about what you're going do and do it. We pay you to kick goals not kick em out of bounds, stop thinking of yourselves on telly, you know what you have to do. You're the better team, you know that. So, what the fucking hell are you doing out there? You…" He paused and clenched his jaw. Jack could see he was looking straight at him. He had missed an easy goal. He had seen the way Smithy who had been standing metres away had clutched his hands to his head in disbelief. He had run over and tapped Jack on the shoulder as if to say it was okay, don't think about it, get the next goal.

"You…," Grisby said again and paused, as though he was seeking for just the right adjective to describe the miserable pathetic sitter of a goal Jack had bungled, "Fucking earn that title."

He was as hard on Jack as he was on all the players. Jack thought he'd been even harder since he'd ordered Jack to see the club psychologist. That was a meeting Jack was never going to forget. "Get sorted or you're out. You're going to see Wilson every god damn week, twice a week if he says so. And you ever turn up to training or… don't even think about coming to a game looking like this, your fucking career is over. Now get out on the field and fucking train."

Kings of the Kicks is that it. Jack ground his teeth, he had played a good game, he knew that. Yes, he had fucked the kick but what about the disposals, getting rid of the ball cleanly and to one of the team, not like the sloppy handball Smith had just executed. *For fuck's sake.*

"But some good disposals Charlie," he seemed to have read Jack's mind. "Frost, Giles, Ryley, good defence, no, brilliant defence. Keep it up. These guys are doing the work. You forwards do yours." Spit flew out of his mouth. His face was a worrying shade of red heart attack territory. Grisby spat onto the ground between his blue and white sneakers, he was running out of steam, "Okay, okay, we're 7 points down that's 8 points from winning. And you know what that means. You're playing well, getting the ball down, we've got to convert that play into goals."

Jack took another gulp of water and shifted his feet. He didn't want to play another quarter, he wanted to get in a hot bath and soak his aching body. But if they didn't win this game they were out of finals, the Big Dance, and the cup and the ticker tape homecoming.

"Okay you know you can do it. Kick some goals and let's nail this. I don't want to see another wasted goal, get it!"

Jack looked down at the ground. He felt as though every eye was on him. His first opportunity in the game for a goal and he'd blown it, just ten metres out from the sticks, a sitter, he couldn't miss, the two white big posts like arms waiting to take the ball from him *so fucking easy you could have thrown it between the posts,* and he had missed it. He didn't know how. Stokes had been shouting at him, waving his arms, calling out, trying to throw his concentration and then his boot had connected with the side of the ball and it shanked to the left, a wobbling mess that missed everything and then bounced out of bounds. It was a terrible kick, the worst he had ever done in a game. It was the goal that would have put them just one point behind and left them with the final quarter to win the game.

The siren went and the huddle broke up and they jogged back on the field. Ryley was beside him, "You weren't the only one to miss a goal mate," Ryley said.

Yeh but I haven't scored a goal either. Jack gave Ryley a withering look and shook his head.

Ryley watched Jack pick up his pace and run to the 50-metre zone in front of the Cats' goal. He knew that Jack would beat himself up over the missed goal and his team mates wouldn't. They knew what it felt like when you screwed up and let the team down. All the passing, tackling and just brute strength to get the ball up to goal and then a stupid pass, a missed mark or a missed goal that you could have kicked with your eyes shut.

Jack rolled his shoulders and stretched his back. It hurt like hell. He felt battered, he'd taken an elbow in the back that had felt like a sledge hammer. He knew who had landed it, Jedd Stokes. A tattoo covered powerhouse of bulging muscles who was gaining a reputation that had seen him before the tribunal twice already and the season wasn't over. He had been tagging Jack so closely the entire game, breathing down his neck, tugging at his jumper, elbowing him at every opportunity.

The noise was deafening. The Cats supporters were anticipating the kill, and they would be on their way to the next final.

Jack tried not to look at the sea of blue and white scarves that were waving in the stadium. He focused on the centre square and the players jostling each other while the umpire walked to his position, holding the ball in front of him as if he was about to sacrifice it to the gods. A sudden hush and then the Cats supporters began singing the club song. A few bars were bellowed out and then the singing was replaced with "Go Cats, Go Cats," at a fever pitch, as though the more they sang the more they could guarantee a victory. They couldn't let up until the final siren and the game was theirs. Everyone in the stadium knew that defeat was just two goals away for both teams.

The Swans supporters held their breath, knuckles pressed hard against their mouths. They looked like mourners at a funeral. Jack glanced across the field, the Cats were gathering in defence determined that they wouldn't let a goal through. The umpire slammed the ball into the turf for the bounce down for the last quarter. Brad, the Swans 201cm ruck launched himself high in the air and batted the ball to Kyle a midfielder he fumbled, twisted away from a Cats player, ran and kicked the ball, a mighty kick down towards the Cats end of the ground. Ryley was there, running into a space. Jack pivoted away from Stokes and shrugged off the hand that held onto his shirt. Ryley had the ball, he bounced it once, twice, dodged a Cats player and kicked it from an angle towards goal. A bellow of triumph went up from the Swans supporters as they watched the ball spin and miss the goal and sail through the behind posts for a point.

Stokes leant into Jack bringing his elbow hard into Jack's bicep, "Know who your girlfriend's fucking?" he shouted above the roar of the crowd.

Jack barely heard the words. He shoved Stokes away with both hands. He couldn't let himself hear anything, he had to maintain focus, they had to win this, he had to redeem himself, had to score. He had to prove to Ross he could do it and he didn't know why that seemed more important than anything.

He pivoted away from Stokes, reading the play, the ball arcing towards an empty space. His lungs were burning.

Stokes was glued to his side. The ball ahead of them, Jack propelled himself high, Stokes went up with him, Jack reached for the ball as Stokes threw his hands up, a fist slammed Jack high in the cheek and Stokes' arm snaked around Jack's neck. Jack stumbled, reeling back from the force of the blow. The piercing whistle of the umpire cut through the cheering. The Swans were awarded a free kick for Stokes' high tackle but it was too far to kick for goal. Jack took the ball and kicked it quickly to Riley but the ball was intercepted and sent back towards the Cats goal.

The Swans seemed to be playing harder than they had the first quarter, as tired and exhausted as they were, they were doing everything they could to get the ball through the goal post. Three more missed kicks, two from Smithy and Rainford, both on the run and at impossible angles and then a hand ball from Smithy to Ryley in the dying minutes of the game and he kicked it straight through the posts and they were looking at a draw. The crowd was suddenly silent as though they had stopped breathing. The Swans needed to score a goal to win.

The umpire moved to the centre, the rucks moved around the ball. Grisby had bitten through his cheek and a bright red spot of blood leaked from the corner of his mouth.

The clock registered 2 minutes to full time. Jack sucked in the warm air through his teeth. The team had run themselves into the ground but they needed to find something more.

The ball bounced high in the air, it was batted once, twice and then again. A Cats player picked it up and kicked it in a panic and the ball sailed out of bounds. Jack watched the throw in from the side lines. He pivoted and took a step when he felt a burning pain down his calf. He had been kicked hard and he knew who was behind him but no time to think about it. On the other side of the field Ryley was handballing the ball to Foster. Foster looked for a Swans player and kicked the ball high into the middle of the ground.

Jack was running, estimating and tracking the trajectory of the ball, scanning the field as the ball arced just ahead of him, sixty metres out of the Swans goal. He launched himself in the air, found purchase with his knee on the back of some other player, reached high above the other outstretched hands. He had it, he took the mark, the ball held tight against his chest as his feet hit the turf.

Stokes was behind him, his hands on the ball trying to wrench it from Jack. But the other players had stepped back, they didn't argue with a clean mark. And then the siren for full time whined across the stadium.

The whole of the stadium fell silent. The rules were clear. If you take a mark before the siren, you can kick for goal. The umpire walked forward and marked the spot where Jack had to take the kick. Jack wiped his hand across his forehead. He looked at the distant white goal posts. He estimated the distance at 60 metres. It was impossible. *No. fuck that. You can do it, you've kicked this before, but not in a preliminary when the match depended on you. Stop thinking, just fucking do it.*

Stokes stood in front of him, waving his arms, trying to distract him, break his concentration. He shouted something into the silence but Jack wasn't listening, he was blocking out every sound, all he could see was the distant goal posts. He knew the kick he had to give to the ball to get it high in the air and cover that distance.

He took three steps back, he looked past the waving arms of Stokes. He ignored the ugly look plastered on Stokes' face.

Stokes knew the punch he landed on Jack would probably get him a fine or worse, a suspension.

Jack held the ball at an angle across his body, turning it so he could see the lace, right hand slightly forward, the left behind the lace. He dropped his shoulders drew in a long breath through his parted lips, took two long strides, the ball angled across his kicking leg, *no time to think, just kick it with everything you've got left.*

"I fucked your girlfriend," Stokes shouted out as Jack's boot connected to the ball. It spun high in the air like a heat seeking missile, a torpedo, a fucking brilliant winning kick, on target, and clean through the goal posts.

***

"Fucking brilliant goal," said Grisby. He stared into Jack's eyes as though he would find something there. He squeezed Jack's shoulder, "Good Jack, keep it up." He wasn't talking about the football.

They were back in the clubroom, and Grisby and the rest of the team hadn't stopped telling him what a brilliant goal. Now Grisby was all Mr Nice guy singing their prowess on the field, "Full of heart, this is what you can do when you want it bad enough," and they had, they had wanted it and now were exhausted and elated at the same time.

They had no thought for the Cats, even though they understood what it was like to have victory snatched from you in the final minutes of a game. It was gutting.

After the handshaking and the commiserations, they headed back to the clubroom. Ryley had seen Stokes ignore Jack's outstretched hand, he'd turned away and shook Ryley's. Jack wasn't noticing anything. He was on cloud nine, for the first time in weeks the dagger of fear he had felt in his sternum had gone. He had proved himself to the team and maybe, just maybe, Ross would back off.

Smith grabbed Jack in a head lock and rubbed his knuckles across his head, "Fuckin king of the fuckin kicks Charlie. We're playing in the preliminary finals next week in Perth – we're going to smash the Eagles."

Someone shouted above the din of the clubroom, "That'll be on YouTube for the rest of your life, and beyond."

The call he expected from Ross never came and when Ross called him a week later, he didn't mention it and neither did Jack. But his mum phoned, as she did after every game, she never missed, she was Jack's number one fan and he knew it. She made him grin the way she went on about his amazing goal. It was on YouTube and she had watched it more than once.

A week after the game she phoned again. He could tell as soon as she spoke that something was wrong, just the tone of her voice always so light and upbeat had a falsity about it, too upbeat too cheerful.

"Hi Jack is it a good time to talk?" she said.

"Yeh mum, I'm at home, just chilling before the game tomorrow. Everything okay?" He paused the image on the flat screen.

"Yes, everything's good. Now I don't want you to worry. I'm going to be fine. I'm starting chemo on Monday," she paused, she heard the sharp intake of Jack's breath.

"What?" Jack felt his stomach collide with his heart.

"Jack, listen they've got it early, a small lump in my breast. I'm going to be fine. I have six weeks of chemo and then re-assess if I need surgery."

"When did this happen? When did you find out?" He didn't know what questions to ask but he felt as though the ceiling had just fallen in on him.

"Just my regular check three weeks ago. I'm on top of it. You don't have to worry about me. It's going to be fine."

Jack held his hand over his chest, *cancer, she's got cancer. Fuck fuck.*

"Jack did you hear me? I said I'm going to be fine. The specialist is confident, I'm confident." She made her voice light, "the whole world's confident."

He tried to sound okay but he wasn't. Felicity was the only person on the whole planet that he loved. "Mum don't die, promise me you won't die." His voice was breaking, he couldn't stop it.

"Jack, Jack, honey. It's going to be alright. I promise you this is not going to kill me. Now just take a breath." She laughed. "I can't promise I won't die one day but I'm planning on babysitting my grandchildren and living until I get great grandchildren!"

Jack wiped his hand across his wet eyes. He pressed his lips together hard. He couldn't trust himself to speak.

"Okay, okay," he said.

As soon as he said goodbye to Felicity, he phoned his manager and told him he wanted a transfer back home on compassionate grounds. He knew his mum and he didn't trust her to tell him the truth. She had always protected him, tried to shield him from his bullying father. He could hear it in her voice, trying to make light of it, laughing, *for fuck's sake mum no one laughs at cancer.*

Chapter Ten

MIRANDA

Sam checked his watch; he was five minutes early. He had found a study table free in the corner of the library where Miranda said she would meet him. Rose had told him not to be late. "She's in demand and she works, and she's doing this as a favour."

He checked his emails while he waited. A short one from Jack telling him he had applied for a transfer on compassionate grounds. Jack had confided in him about Felicity and he knew that Jack was worried about her and wanted to give her support.

He searched for Emily's Instagram account. He didn't follow her but he had seen it. It was full of photos and videos of her at various venues throughout the day. From the moment she got up until the moment she went to sleep. He glanced at a few photos of Jack looking awkward and some he obviously didn't know she was taking. Jack sitting on the edge of the pool with the caption *'Lazy day with JC'*

What a poser. I'll give him shit.

"Hi."

Miranda was looking over her shoulder at the library. Most of the long tables had someone sitting at them and students were walking in and out of the rows of library shelves.

"Uh huh. Do you mind if I sit there?" She pointed to the chair Sam was sitting in. "I don't like my back to the room."

Sam had taken the seat facing into the library and the chair at the adjacent corner faced the wall.

"Sure," he moved to the other seat and Miranda sat next to him. He saw her scanning across the library floor. "Are you expecting someone?"

She shook her head, "No."

"Oh okay, I just thought you were looking for someone."

"Oh, just a habit." Miranda smiled. She always wanted her back against the wall, a habit from childhood and the memory of a man's arms suddenly snaking around her waist, lifting her up, telling her she weighed nothing, she was oh so cute. Her mother's halfhearted protest when she saw the look on Miranda's face, her body stiff and unyielding. *"She doesn't like to be picked up. She's a big girl."* But there was no authority in her voice, and she would be smiling and trying to make the man with his arms around Miranda not get angry.

Miranda opened her laptop and pulled up the notes she had on Molecular Biology.

***

"So how did it go?" Rose asked Miranda. They were both sorting and folding the washing that they took turns to do. The two of them had got on pretty well in getting a routine that they stuck to. Living in the school boarding house had been good for that. Miranda had never had a routine and she loved it. It made her feel secure like invisible walls around her.

"Okay good. Are these yours or mine?" Miranda held up a pair of white cotton pants.

"Are you serious? I couldn't get my arse in those."

"Arses are in?" said Miranda adding the pants to her pile.

"Just good then?" said Rose, she sounded disappointed.

Miranda shook her head, "Rose he's smart and he picks things up quickly. I didn't have to explain anything twice. Okay."

"Okay." Rose threw a long-sleeved t-shirt at Miranda, it landed on her head, "Yours, you can fold it."

Miranda raised her eyebrows but she smiled. Rose was intense, she needed her choice of boyfriend to be endorsed by Miranda.

"He's nice okay. Very polite and yes, he's funny." Although she couldn't actually think of a funny thing he had said.

Rose grinned, he was funny and he was kind. She like that about him more than anything.

"He is, isn't he? He reminds me of Stew," said Rose.

"Your dad, Stew, or beef stew?"

"Dad Stew of course."

"I'm assuming that's a good thing," said Miranda. It was a good thing. Miranda liked Rose's parents. She wished she had a father like Stew, ordinary, and kind. The first time Miranda stayed with the Banks family she had tried to blend into the furniture, pretend she wasn't there but Julia, Rose's mum and Stew treated her as though she was one of the kids and expected her to do chores like the rest of them. On the first day she was in the kitchen helping with the cooking and later that day, cleaning out the chicken run with Rose.

Rose felt bad, she tried not to mention her dad too much although Miranda didn't seem to mind.

It had been six months since Miranda had found out that she was unlikely to ever find out who her father was. When she had returned from reading her file at the Department, Rose hadn't asked Miranda anything. She knew that if she had found a name, she would have told her. She could see it in her face, that dream had gone.

Rose wasn't so sure that it was a bad thing, she had wondered what impact it would have on Miranda if she discovered her father was a criminal and not some upright citizen, a great dad like Stew.

Chapter Eleven

JACK

"What's up?" said Ryley throwing his wet towel onto the bench. They had just finished a killer of a training session that had left them both several kilos lighter. Jack sat with a towel across his lap, staring into the distance, his hair dripping with sweat onto his shoulders. He turned his head towards Ryley and frowned. Why did anything have to be up just because he was quiet.

Ryley seemed to possess a sixth sense for working out when something was bothering Jack. Ryley claimed it was because he had four sisters and he had been the only male in the house most of the time when his dad was in the army. "It's my feminine side – it's more developed than your average Neanderthal male."

No one but the management knew that Jack had asked for a transfer. Felicity had tried to persuade Jack that it wasn't necessary and he wasn't to feel responsible for her but he wanted to get back to Perth. Emily had distracted him for a while and it had been exciting but not anymore and the counselling that Grisby had made him do seemed to have increased the panic attacks and now he couldn't rely on alcohol – he hadn't drunk for months.

Jack didn't mind Dr Wilson, the team's psychologist, he thought he was a lot smarter than the counsellor his mother had made him see. After the second session he had dreaded seeing Wilson again. The panic attacks had increased. It had begun innocuously enough with Wilson asking him how his mum was doing and when he had told him that his auntie was there and it seemed to be going according to plan, Wilson had nodded and said,

"That's good news. Okay, so when you first came to see me, you asked me not to call you Charlie, is that what your dad is called?"

"Yeh," Jack swallowed. He could sense where Wilson was going with his questions and he didn't want to go there.

Wilson already had a pretty good picture in his head of Jack's father and what his bullying had caused. He had counselled enough young men to know that alcohol was Jack's attempt to self-medicate his anxiety.

"So, when you hear yourself being called Charlie tell me about that."

Jack rubbed at his forehead, as if to rub away the thought of Ross. "Him, it makes me think of him. Puts him in my head," *and makes me fucking anxious.*

Wilson nodded, "Okay and how does that make you feel?"

"Shit, anxious, not good."

"Last week we were talking about the anxiety and the panic attacks and you were trying to remember when they began." He looked down at his notes, "Primary School, when you were in Grade 4."

Jack bit at the callous at the back of his hand. His eyes pricked, he squeezed them tight. Grade 4, he remembered.

Wilson leant forward, "It's okay Jack, tell me what you can."

Jack took a breath; he didn't want to dredge up that memory. "I was nine, playing in the Junior Match programme for Auskick. I'd been playing for as long as I can remember. He only ever came to a few of my games. Ross… my dad." Jack stared at the floor between his feet. "He played golf most weekends, but then…" Jack felt the sudden fluttering in his chest. He squeezed his eyes shut and pressed the back of his hand to his mouth.

Wilson waited, he was comfortable with silence, his steady breathing infusing the room with calm.

Jack lifted his head and gave Wilson a bleak look, "I got good. Won fairest and best a few times and kicked a lot of goals, and then he stepped in."

Wilson nodded, history repeating itself, the father back on the scene trying to take control.

"When he watched I couldn't play. I just lost confidence. He'd criticise me in front of the team, say I'd let them down, that kind of shit. Some of the parents told him off and that made it worse because he would wait until we were in the car and start again. Mum tried to shut him down but then he'd get stuck into her."

Jack stretched his back; he knew the exact moment of the first panic attack. "I was sitting in the back of the car; it was after a game. Ross was saying shit."

"About you?" said Wilson.

"Yeh about me. Mum told him to shut up. She shouted at him." Jack closed his eyes, he was that nine-year-old boy watching his father raise his arm and bring his elbow into hard contact with his mother's head. Her body slumping to the side, her head hitting the passenger window, Ross reaching out and pulling her upright. He'd stopped the car, claimed it was an accident, said he was sorry and then Felicity had seen Jack in the back seat struggling to breathe.

"After that, if I knew he was coming to watch I'd get stomach cramps, throw up, and he stopped coming and played golf."

Wilson had told him the anxiety might increase but he was giving Jack strategies to face conflict. "It's going to be a challenge Jack, but alcohol is not the long-term solution. It's going to take time, but you've got football. Just focus on that."

He was right about the mental challenge but physically he was feeling better than he had in a long time.

"I said what's bothering you?" Ryley said.

Jack rubbed a towel across his head and ran his fingers through his hair. He didn't want to talk about what was bothering him.

"Come on mate, I know something's bothering you. You have hardly said a word for the last two days and I know it's not about the game next week in Perth, is it?"

Jack shook his head, "Do you read your wife like this? I bet she loves that?"

"She does mate. I'm sensitive to all her needs. It's a skill worth developing." Ryley grinned. "Nina adores me."

Ryley and Nina had met three years ago and married within six months. They had been living in separate states because Nina hadn't wanted to give up her job as a permanent primary school teacher at the school she was at in Queensland. But now she was pregnant she was planning on moving to Sydney and then Ryley would be moving out of the apartment he shared with Jack.

"So, I'm guessing it's Emily, your girlfriend. Things not going well." Ryley wasn't guessing, he knew that Jack had pulled back from Emily. He had heard the excuses when she called. He couldn't imagine anyone finding Emily interesting. Ryley thought she was a dead bore; he didn't know what Jack saw in her but he wasn't about to criticise his choice. He didn't mention that he had heard Jack on the phone the other night. They had both been in the kitchen and he couldn't help hearing Emily's raised voice. He knew Jack had told her that he wasn't going to some so-called fundraising event.

"I've bought a dress."

"I'll give you the money for it." Jack said, "To be fair Em, I never said I was going. I told you I wasn't keen on going."

"You never said you weren't going! I've told my FB followers that I was going and I've got my Insta account. I have to go!"

Jack was spared from telling Ryley what was on his mind. Smithy came over and invited them both to his place for dinner that night. Smithy's wife was a great cook and Ryley never missed an opportunity for a meal but Jack said he had plans. Jack was grateful for the interruption. As much as he liked Ryley he didn't want to talk about Emily. It felt like a betrayal to bad mouth her.

Jack left the clubhouse and walked to his car. He heard his phone ping and he saw that Emily had sent a photo of herself wearing a figure-hugging flame red dress. He pressed the Instagram icon on his phone.

"Fuck, fuck." The photo was there with the tag line 'this is what I'm wearing to the 'Stay Hold' promotion with JC.'

Hair spray, another fucking promotion, not a fund-raiser. Knew it.

He got in the car and started the engine. "Fuck, fuck." He slapped at the stirring wheel. He was an idiot. When he had first met her at Piccolo's he hadn't been able to see past her looks, the blonde hair, blue eyes, pouting lips, and long legs that went on forever. For the first few times they had been out together, she was quiet and he had the impression that she was really smart. She told him that she had wanted to study philosophy "but then I won a modelling contract and it was a no brainer."

He should have ended the relationship months ago and he knew why he hadn't. He didn't want to hurt Emily, hurt her pride. She had done nothing wrong; she had just been herself. That was the excuse he was giving himself but there was another reason he didn't want to examine and it had something to do with Ross Charles.

He started the car and pulled out of the car park into the traffic. *Going to end it, it's my life not his.* His heart sped up at the thought of a confrontation with her. He was not good at confrontation. He wiped a finger across his top lip and sucked in the air. He wanted to run away, but he couldn't run away from Emily. She had an intensity about her that was scary. He had tried to pull away, hinted that it wasn't a good time for him now as he was trying to concentrate on his career. She had cut him off with a wave of her hand. "We're good together." She said with the finality of a judge sentencing him to ten years hard labour.

He tried distancing himself, stumbling through lame excuses that she brushed aside, or worse, ignored and then turned up on his doorstep with a meal that she had ordered.

He had hinted to Emily that his plan was to get back to Perth but he knew that there was no guarantee and if it did happen, it would be at the end of the season. He had been in Emily's bed at the time he had mentioned Perth. Not the ideal time to raise the issue. Emily had pressed her naked body against his and said, "You're not leaving this, are you?"

He confided to Sam that he had tried to break up with Emily but she just wouldn't listen. "Get rid of her man. Dump her before she starts boiling rabbits in your kitchen," he had said.

"What? Rabbits... what the hell?"

"Old movie, scary stalker women breaks into this guy's home and boils up the pet rabbit."

"Well, that's okay, I don't have a rabbit."

"This is what you do, okay. You just look her in the eye and rip the band aid off."

"Yeh and what do I say?"

"Just let me think..." Silence and then, "Okay, tell her you don't love her anymore... she can't argue with your feelings."

"Never loved..."

"The break up conversation will be scary." He paused. "Use I statements."

"I statements?"

"Yeh, hang on, I've got some here."

"What! Are you reading that advice off the internet?"

"Yeh, some good stuff here. It says you shouldn't delay..."

"Okay, okay. I'll read it myself."

Jack didn't drive straight back to the apartment, he drove down to Manly beach, parked his car and sat looking out at the water. He had told Sam he didn't love Emily and the truth was he didn't even like her. She was obsessed with her looks and nearly every conversation they had, she turned it back to a promotion event, or some praise she had received on her Instagram account. *So sweet, Jack look at this, she said I looked like Elsa from Frozen.* He didn't have a clue who Elsa was.

It had been eight months of hating himself for not ending it and letting the relationship become a habit that wasn't good for either of them.

He got out of the car and walked along the path that skirted the beach. He pulled the hood of his sweatshirt over his head and held his hands under his armpits. He felt his phone buzz in his pocket. He knew it was Emily, she had already sent a string of messages, each one more demanding.

He took the phone out of his pocket and called her, he didn't wait for her to speak. If she spoke first, she wouldn't stop and his resolve would evaporate.

"I'm sorry Emily, this isn't working for me. *An I statement.* I just don't need a girlfriend at this point in my life. I can't give you the attention you… y*ou demand you want…* you deserve and I'm sorry but I think it's best if we end it now." He spoke quickly hardly taking a pause but she had to have got the message. He felt lighter, he had said it, it was done.

"What, sorry what did you say? I couldn't hear you; you were breaking up."

"Yes, that's it, I said it's best if we break up." She had heard, he knew she had.

"You can't. I won't let you… you. Say it to my face… you coward. I want you to say it to my face."

He felt the sudden jump in his heart rate, the beating in his throat. He took a breath and said slowly, "Okay. If that's what you want."

"Yes, it is. Say it to my face Jack Charles you fucking bastard."

"Okay," *rip the band aid off.* "Where do you want to meet?"

"You can come here! To my place." She was angry and wasn't hiding the fact.

"No let's meet somewhere nearby, the park at the bottom of your units. Now." He named the park.

"Well, I can't," she shouted down the phone, "I'll meet you in an hour."

She made him wait, he knew she would. It was dark when her car pulled up alongside his in the small car park adjacent to the park. Jack got out of his car and leant against the bonnet. The lights of her car illuminated the dark park, the trees glowed in the gloom. She didn't get out of the car, or turn to look at him. He could see her profile. The light on her phone lit up her face. She was texting, no calling someone. He stood up and walked away from his car and stood with his back to the park. He wasn't looking forward to this. He had never actually broken up with a girl to her face. He had never gone out with a girl longer than a couple of weeks, a month at the most. *Ross is going to find out.* He rubbed at the spot in the middle of his chest, and took a slow breath, counting slowly as the air went in, holding his breath while he counted four and then he heard her car door slam shut. He turned towards her.

She was out of the car pushing her arms into her faux fur jacket awkwardly as she tried to hold the phone to her ear. "Okay, gotta go but catch up soon. Okay tomorrow."

Jack turned towards her, she was smiling as she tossed her hair back and swung her bag onto her shoulder, she was going to make him squirm. She lifted her chin at him as though she was inviting him to land a punch to her jaw.

Jack had seen the smile on her lips when she put the phone in her pocket. He couldn't guess what that meant.

"Well Em, like I said to you on the phone," he began but she held her hand up and curled her lip and then laughed.

"I'm breaking up with YOU CHARLIE," she pointed a finger at his chest. She had never called him that before after he told her to call him Jack. "I was going to do it after the fund-raiser but as you're not going, I'm doing it now." She pointedly looked at his groin and made a face he couldn't read. "I'm going with Jedd…" she squeezed her mouth in a simpering way, her eyes glittering like a snake about to strike, "Stokesy," she said and she lifted her chin as if to say, "so there!"

Jack stared at her but he wasn't seeing her, he was seeing Stokes waving his arms at the game and calling out and he could hear the words above the booing of the Geelong supporters, "I fucked your girlfriend," his concentration blocking it out and he was amazed at himself.

"Did you hear me?" she demanded. This wasn't the reaction she wanted, she wanted outrage, she was Emily Hogan, she had more than two hundred thousand Instagram followers, she was an influencer, she was somebody.

Jack raised his eyebrows, he was still remembering. He guessed he should feel angry or something but he felt relief, he almost smiled but instead he nodded his head as though he was thinking this bit of news over.

"Stokesy?" he said and shrugged.

Emily clenched her teeth and he saw the narrowing of her eyes and immediately saw his mistake. "Fucking great!" he said with as much anger as he could fake, "fucking great!" he repeated, flaring his nostrils in what he hoped was an angry look. *Fucking great!*

She turned and cat walked her hips back to her car, her right hand held over her head in a one finger salute.

Three days later Ross Charles called Jack. His father didn't wait for Jack to say hello. He bellowed down the phone, "Get back on the horse."

"What?" Jack pressed the remote control on the flat screen and the screen froze, a player in a purple shirt poised midair as though defying gravity.

Ryley was in the bedroom face timing Nina.

"I said, get back on the horse."

Jack was silent, he knew it had something to do with breaking up with Emily.

"Son, I saw on her Facebook and Instagram, she's going out with Jedd Stokes he's taking her to some fucking function. How did that happen? Mate you need her. When did she dump you?"

Jack heard Ryley laughing in the other room, he pressed play on the flat screen and turned the sound down.

"You follow her on Facebook and Instagram?" He couldn't keep the contempt out of his voice.

There was a pause at the other end of the phone, then a sound like a choked laugh. "No mate, not me. Mel, she showed me the post. She's saying some shit about you."

Mel?

Jack watched a player punt a ball in a high arc across the emerald green turf. He wasn't listening anymore, he was following the trajectory of the ball, the smooth exchange from player to player and then a kick and the blur of purple and white shirts and the player with the ponytail leaping high for the mark.

"You should read what she's saying. You should get a lawyer."

"Yeh?" Jack wasn't listening.

"Yeh mate, you paying attention? She's saying a lot of defamatory stuff. Mate, you've got to fight back. Get a lawyer."

"A lawyer? What, get a lawyer and give credibility to whatever shit she's saying. It was mutual." *Mate* "The break up…"

"That's not what she's saying," Ross interrupted.

Jack was silent, he paused the screen and froze the action as a tangle of players wrestled on the grass for possession of the ball.

"Did you hear me?"

Jack clenched his jaw, he could imagine Ross's face, the nostrils flared, that look that told him what was coming. *Fuck you, fuck you.* He took a breath. The bedroom door opened and Ryley had his iPad facing Jack.

"Nina wants to say…" he glanced at the frozen screen and the phone in Jack's hand.

"Sorry," Ryley said.

Jack saw the face of Nina, she was smiling and waving.

"Gotta go dad, important call coming in."

"Wait, you have to take someone else to this thing she's going to… It's important for your profile."

Your profile you mean.

Yeh, *I hear you and I don't give a fuck about what she's saying or my fucking profile.* "Gotta go," he repeated and ended the call. His hands were shaking when he turned to Ryley and the outstretched iPad. Nina wasn't smiling she was chewing on her lip wondering what she should say.

"Sorry Nina," said Jack, he tried to get the anger out of his voice. He couldn't breathe, his heart was hammering but he felt alright. He was alright.

"I'm sorry," said Nina. "I was following Emily so I could track what you and Ryley were up to as you two never post anything." She didn't mention that she had read the posts that Emily had posted. She didn't understand why anyone would post intimate details of their private life for public consumption and the stuff she had said about Jack said more about her. She hoped Jack never read it.

"Don't worry Ryley," said Jack later in the evening. "I honestly don't care what Em has said. Before I found out she had been seeing Stokes I was feeling bad but now…" he shrugged, "It's worked out. I feel relieved."

Chapter Twelve

ONE WEEK LATER

PERTH
MIRANDA
EWAN

Ewan peeled off his leather jacket, wiping the sweat off his forehead with the back of his hand as he walked through the restaurant door. The gesture made him wince. His knuckles were still bloody and swollen from the door he had punched a hole in the night before.

"Fuckin Bitch," he mumbled. The anger was still in him, waiting to hijack him at an instant. *Who the hell did she think she was? Putting out and then...* How was he meant to read the signals? That was the fuckin problem. Now a girl could take you right to the point and then say, *Sorry don't feel like it.*

But he'd stopped like a good boy. Zipped up his trousers and felt the heat of it simmering in him, like a pot about to boil. He'd had to drive her home from the park. But he showed her, gave her a scare made her hang on tight, had bent the bike low when he took a corner.

"You're mad," she said when he squealed to a stop at the train station and she almost fell off the bike. She was lucky he didn't know where she lived, he could make her pay. When he got home to the rented house he shared with fellow Scottish travellers, he remembered the way she had pushed

131

him away and jumped up from the grass quickly adjusting her clothes and almost running out of the bushes and onto a path in the park. Kings Park they called it, although as far as he knew they had never had a King. Bloody joke. He could see she was on her phone when he was adjusting his clothes and trying hard to hide his anger.

"Just texting my dad. He wants to know where I am." Her smile hadn't seemed genuine. He felt the anger creeping up his spine.

"Oh yeh," he tried to relax his shoulders, he could feel his muscles tense, the heat in his chest. What a bitch. She knew what she was doing. He didn't say anything, stuck his chin out at her.

"He's a policeman, a sergeant." she said pulling her jacket around her.

He stopped then and jerked his head up, was he supposed to be afraid. "Well, ya better not let him know ya went to off to a park with a guy ya met in a bar," He stopped and looked at his watch in a pointed way, "not even an hour ago." *Fuckin bitch.*

It was dark in the park even with the lights from the road. She looked afraid, her face white. He'd never want to be a woman. If there was an afterlife he'd sooner come back as a rat.

His bike was in the car park, he could see it from where they were standing. She could be lying about her father, but he couldn't take the chance. He didn't want any trouble; he couldn't afford that.

He flexed his fist. He couldn't remember any of the strategies he had been forced to learn in prison. The anger management course they made him do in the UK. Had to do it, or no parole. Some programme to change men's behaviour. No frigging way. What about changing their behaviour? But he wanted parole, he had been given two years for assault occasioning bodily harm. It was an accident, he'd only given her a push, hardly touched her and she had fallen backwards through the shop window. The Judge had told him he was lucky that a nurse had been close by and stopped the bleeding or he could have been facing a manslaughter charge. A fuckin accident and he had been given two years.

He was already thinking up an explanation when he walked into the employee's cloakroom at the restaurant. He put his gear in the locker and took out his white coat.

He heard someone behind him. He shrugged a shoulder into his uniform and turned around. He hadn't seen her before, but then he had only been at the restaurant a week and the wait staff seemed to be different every day.

She was putting her bag in the locker opposite his, her back to him. He watched her tie up her dark glossy curls. She was small, he thought he could pick her up with one arm. He leant back against his metal locker and the door made a loud metallic screech but she didn't move. He brought his elbow back on the metal door and still she didn't turn around.

"Sorry," he said, and then she turned around. "The noise, sorry for the noise."

She frowned, she hadn't really heard it she had been somewhere else, in her head, shutting out the world. She was good at that. He was new, she took in the white coat and the apron. She had heard they had advertised for someone in the kitchen. 'A chef de tournant'. She googled it. A relief chef.

He hadn't seen her before. He thought he had met all the wait staff in the last week. He gave her a lazy smile that lit up his grey eyes. "Hi, I'm the new dogsbody in the kitchen."

She smiled, she liked that. He hadn't made out that he was someone important, and she liked his accent. Irish, Scottish, she wasn't sure, she wasn't good with accents.

"Hi, I'm Miranda. Just a waitress, another dogsbody."

"Something in common already," Ewan said.

The way he said it made her face go warm, and she didn't know why. He didn't say anything, just looked at her with one dark eyebrow raised and the lazy smile leaving his lips. Miranda looked away and twisted the apron between her hands.

He pulled his cheeks in and the smile disappeared. It was that easy. "M'name's Ewan," he said, "like the actor, only I'm younger and better looking."

She wasn't sure who he meant. "Hi," she said and waited for him to move away, he was blocking the door.

"I haven't seen you before are ya just working the weekend shifts?"

She shook her head, "No had exams, last week. I do week shifts too."

"Ah well I'll be seeing a lot of ya then." He planned on that.

"Uh, guess so. I have to get to work," she said abruptly.

He frowned, he'd heard the sharp tone, "Yeh sure," he stood back and waved her through.

He watched her walk away, he thought she might be Italian with the dark curls and the blue eyes. He'd made her blush. He liked that.

He wiped the back of his hand across his forehead, "Fuck," he'd forgotten his bloody knuckles. He would have to cover them with a bandage and wear a waterproof glove. *Jeez ya fuckin idiot.*

He found the first aid kit and quickly applied a dressing and took a sterile glove from the half-filled box. He could feel the sweat in his armpits. He didn't think he would ever get used to the Australian heat. He couldn't wait to push onto New Zealand and the cooler weather in the South Island. A bit of skiing in the cold more like Scotland. He had arrived in Perth two weeks ago and just his luck right in the middle of a heat wave.

"It's not a heat wave mate," said the Chef on Ewan's first day in the kitchen. "This is an Aussie summer; you better get used to it." The air conditioner was wafting cool air through the kitchen, providing little relief from the bank of stainless-steel ovens throwing out a constant blast of heat.

"Get yourself down to the beach," the Chef said, "best beaches in the world."

Yeh and the sharks. Ewan had said nothing. No way was he hanging around getting used to the heat. He had told the manager that he had a working visa for two years and would be staying around. Wasn't a good idea to say he just wanted a couple of months, enough work to make some money so he could move on.

He'd landed a job within days. It was the same in every country so far. His destination was New Zealand, he had a cousin living there.

'The Bay Restaurant' was a decent restaurant, as far as he could tell from the menu and the frantic rush every night. He could take the rush, he had trained in some of the busiest London restaurants, even did a stint with Jamie Oliver. But he didn't tell anyone that just in case someone checked up on him and found out why he had to leave. He didn't have to worry, you could have no experience and a new restaurant would give you a try out, get the Chef to ask you a few questions and you were in. Chefing was a tough job but a great portable job, and he needed to leave Scotland after he had got out of prison.

The Restaurant had been fully booked all day. He made up an excuse to the Chef to explain the gloved hand. He hadn't thought about the girl he had taken to the park since arriving at the restaurant. Miranda had taken his mind off that. She had been in and out of the kitchen all through lunch. No time to talk to her but now the lunch crowd was dispersing and there were just a few diners left in the restaurant.

He was up to speed with the orders, nothing left to do. He was doing the desserts. "Do you think you can handle that?" the Chef had asked him.

Arrogant wanker, but he had kept his temper. There wasn't anything he couldn't do in the kitchen. He had made fifty sticky date puddings, and countless lemon meringues. The meringues were fiddly with his gloved hand.

He took a break and found the restrooms at the back of the restaurant, off the verandah that looked out onto the river. As he left the restrooms he saw Miranda, standing at the far end talking to someone on her phone.

The sun was blazing and the river was still, not a breeze anywhere. He walked silently behind her. She was talking quietly, he couldn't hear the tone of her voice. Boyfriend? He took another step and she turned around as she was pulling the phone away from her ear.

Ewan stopped and leant back on the wooden railing, spreading his elbows wide. He put his head back, "Good to get a break, eh?"

Miranda turned away and spoke into the phone and then put it back in her pocket.

Ewan had caught the words, "I'll call you back." Could be anyone but he wasn't going to waste his time if she had a boyfriend.

"Boyfriend?" he said.

The phone felt warm in her pocket, she had turned it off when she was working and saw she had missed a call from one of the students she tutored.

"Sorry?"

He heard the puzzlement in her voice. He bet she had heard. He hated it when girls did that. They made you repeat everything when you were just being friendly. It wasn't a quiz show.

She was moving away from him, he filled up all the space. He was like some great polar bear in his white outfit. She glanced at his hand but said nothing.

"This," he held up his gloved fingers, "don't tell anyone but I got into a bit of a fight. Some wanker, last night rough- ing up his girlfriend I just… should have minded my own business." He gave a snort of a laugh.

"Really, that's terrible… where?"

"Car park back of the pub."

Ewan flexed his fingers, "Thought I'd broken my hand, he ducked and I hit the wall. And then she told me to mind my business." He gave a wry laugh and met the startled look in Miranda's eyes. Every girl loved a hero.

Chapter Thirteen

JACK

No one on the coach was talking. The moment they had left the airport and passed the stadium where the game was to be played the talking stopped. The mood was somber as though they had already lost the qualifying game for the last eight. The tight playing schedule and the long flight to Perth left them just a day to prepare before they walked out onto the ground. The players felt the tension creeping into muscles that still held the memory of the last match they had played against the Tigers.

Jack sent a text to Felicity as soon as they landed and told her he wouldn't be able to see her until after the game. He had been phoning her every day until she told him to concentrate on his football and wait to talk to her when he got home. "I'm doing fine Jack. We'll be able to have dinner after the game."

Jack leant his head back against the cushioned headrest, selected the eighties music on his phone, adjusted his ear buds and closed his eyes. Violent Femmes was playing in his ears, his dad's favourite band. He changed the music to Post Malone, he didn't want to think about Ross and the text he had sent him the night before. He tried to avoid his calls if he could and when he took a call, he said little, letting Ross do all the talking. Each interaction with Ross left him wanting to drink. The text was just three words,

back in Perth.

Ross had told him just a few days ago he was moving back to Perth. Jack had felt the sweat break out on his forehead.

"Good news huh?" said Ross. "Can do my job anywhere with the technology we have now." Jack hadn't been able to speak, his heart pounding in his chest. "Hello, you there? Did you hear me?" Ross couldn't keep the edge of irritation out of his voice.

"Yeh, I heard you. Yeh great, can't talk now." It wasn't great, it was the worst news. Just when he had asked for a transfer back to his home town. The thought of Ross in his life was unbearable and Felicity didn't need him adding stress to her life. He knew that Felicity would worry about him and he was right, she had called him as soon as she heard the news from Ross.

"It's okay mum, don't worry about it. Chill, I can take care of him." He'd tried to sound confident, he'd even laughed, "I'm bigger than he is." He hoped he'd reassured her. *Yeh I can take care of him.*

Ryley nudged him in the ribs. "Hey Jack, there it is." The bus was passing the Perth Optus football Stadium. It stood under the night sky like a giant bird's nest. The stadium where he would be playing in front of the home team. He had played Perth's home teams the Eagles and the Dockers three times in the past year but never on their home ground. It felt odd, a betrayal somehow to be playing for another State. Felicity had swapped her allegiance to his team, the Swans. Ross was an Eagles supporter, he hated the Swans and he'd made his views known.

Jack knew that his father was going to be at the game. He had moved back to Perth the day after he had sent the text, he had been planning it for weeks. Felicity was going to be there on Saturday, shouting herself silly, and Sam, he would be there and the guilt would re-surface. He envied Sam his ability to remain positive. "What's the point, only got one life. Told you, long after you've hung up your footie boots and your body's broken, I'll be the famous one. Doctor to the stars and you'll be a 'has been.'"

Jack knew that Sam's father had been furious that Sam hadn't chosen to do law. "Fuck that. I told dad, no way. Could you imagine it Jack, the rest of my life having him breathing down my neck."

If Sam was disappointed, he had hidden it well. He was an optimist. He had told Jack that the loss of any football career he might have had was more of a loss to his dad. "I told him, I didn't want him to go on about it. That it was more of a disaster for him than me. I got the compensation, I'm not in a wheelchair. I've got a life and a career ahead of me, so dad shut the fuck up and he did, hasn't mentioned it again."

Jack wished he could be like Sam. *Go fuck yourself Ross, go fuck yourself.* The bus slowed at the traffic lights, a small group of people wearing the Swans colours of red and white started shouting and waving. Jack looked out of the window, one of the guys pointed to the red and white Swans striped scarf he was wearing and mouthed something at him but Jack's attention was caught by the girl with the dark curly hair standing next to him. She was looking in her back pack and then she looked up at him and her expression froze as though she'd been caught doing something wrong. He knew her, it hit him in the chest like a fast pitched ball.

As the coach pulled away from the lights, he twisted in his seat to see her. It was the same girl who had waited for him. That girl, her hair was longer but it was her. Her face had haunted him for weeks after he'd driven off and left her standing there with her hand to her eyes. He hadn't wanted to think of her... *I waited for you.* That's what she said. Why? He'd thought the worst. He'd had sex with her, he thought he had but it was vague like a dream as though it had happened to someone else. He couldn't be sure. And then he'd banished it from his mind. He was careful, his mother had made sure of that. His father's advice was crude and too late, "Never ride bareback son." He'd been twelve, he didn't need a lesson from his distant father about the birds and the fucking bees. "Don't get stung son, that's why it's called the bees." He thought it might be for another reason but he'd said nothing. He knew what 'bareback' meant and he didn't need that lesson from his dad. His mum had got in before his father had the awkward conversation over FaceTime with his second wife giggling in the background.

But what if the condom had broken, what if someone at the factory had put holes in a batch just for the fun of it. What if he hadn't worn a condom. He couldn't fucking remember. But then he'd reasoned girls didn't have babies they had terminations. Shit, he hoped it hadn't been that. And then he forgot all about her until the coach pulled up at the lights.

He closed his eyes, he was pretty sure he'd had sex with that girl and if he was right, that girl was Miranda, Miranda... Miranda... no he couldn't remember her last name, she hadn't been at the school long, just the last term of year 6. She was the girl who had eaten food out of the waste bin. He pinched the bridge of his nose. He hadn't recognised her, who would? Her hair had been cut like a boy then. She was short and skinny, she looked younger than the rest of the class.

He'd told Felicity about her, he remembered that and how horrified she'd been. Perhaps she'd lost something, his mum had said, thrown something away by mistake. No, it was a half-eaten sandwich and when she saw him watching her, she'd thrown it back. He'd ignored her but he'd left food for her in her desk. He didn't want anyone to know that he'd felt sorry for the girl no one wanted to sit near. She was like a small, abandoned dog, hunting in the bins for food. He squeezed his eyes shut, he could see that girl, the look she gave him scared but ashamed. He had said nothing, just turned and walked the other way as if he hadn't seen her. But Luke Somers, he had seen her and he said something, called her the Bin Girl, what an arse. He stared out of the window but all he could see was that face turning towards him, the eyes wide and the look of shame. He turned up the music. *I waited for you.* He turned the music up louder.

***

Everything went wrong from the moment the ball was in his hands. He thought the crowd were booing every time he touched the ball. Usually, he could shut out everything but the play. He felt sluggish as though his boots were made of lead. He kicked the ball to Ryley, an easy kick but he didn't see the Eagles player running to intercept the ball. *For fuck's sake.* A roar of approval went up from the crowd. Jack ran hard chasing down the play but it was too late, the ball was down the other end and the Eagles had kicked a goal.

He played as though he had a weight in his stomach. An uneasy feeling that he tried to ignore. Focus, *for fuck's sake focus.* The Eagles were already 20 points ahead. It was never a good feeling to come from behind. Putting points on the board was a psychological lift, all the players knew that.

The second quarter of the game and the Swans chance to fight back. It was an easy goal. Jack had taken the mark in front of the goals just thirty metres back. He heard the roar from the crowd, a straggling cry of boos. He ignored the sound, the Eagles midfielder standing in front of him waving his arms halfheartedly, no chance of stopping this goal. Jack took three steps back, held the ball in front of his body, stepped forward and kicked. At that moment, the moment his foot touched the ball, his focus broke. The noise of the crowd washed over him, and he saw her, her face swimming before him. He watched the ball skewering off his foot, arcing in the air away from the goals. He felt as though he'd been punched.

A roar of triumph from the home crowd. Some might have felt sorry for him standing on his own, staring blindly at the white posts. Jack Charles had missed an easy one. He knew the cameras were on him, but he couldn't help the look of disbelief that flickered across his face as he put his head down, his lips moving so that everyone who saw it wondered what he'd said.

Miranda.

Smithy ran past him and touched him on the shoulder. 'Get over it', that's what the touch said. He gritted his teeth and tried to focus on the game, just the game.

Two attempts at goal in the last quarter both at impossible angles and he'd watched with the bile rising in his throat as the ball just skimmed past the goals.

When the final siren sounded the Swans were out of the competition, a humiliating defeat, the worst of the season. The worst of his career and in front of his home town.

Back in the changing room Ryley patted Jack on the back. He had heard the booing when Jack touched the ball. It was what the crowd did, he hoped Jack wasn't taking it personally.

"You played a good game, that goal was a scorcher," Jack said to Ryley, stripping off his sweat-soaked jersey. He couldn't wait to get under the shower.

Ryley nodded, it wasn't a bad goal but nothing made up for losing and not getting in the top eight and the chance of playing in a grand final. Ryley sat down on the bench and studied his mud-stained boots.

Jack glanced around the changing room, no one was talking. The disappointment was etched on everyone's face. Jack caught the eye of Smithy, he shook his head. They were all feeling gutted.

Jack sat down next to Ryley and let his hands hang over his knees. He bowed his head as though he was praying.

"You, okay?" said Ryley. He knew Jack was off his game, something was bothering him, he could tell.

Jack turned his head, he knew Ryley wasn't asking him about the game. He raised his eyebrows in answer.

"Yeh well I know something's bothering you Jack," Ryley said and then he stopped talking as Grisby came into the room.

"Okay," said Grisby standing in the middle of the room. He stuck his hands in the pockets of his trousers and rocked back on his heels. "Well," he scanned the room and took in every bleak exhausted look. "Now is not the time for a post mortem. I know you all did your best." His eyes found

Smithy and he nodded back at Grisby. He didn't want Grisby cutting into the guys like an electric hedge cutter. They didn't need that now.

"Some good play out there. Strong crowd support. Not easy playing an away with so much hanging on it. We'll learn from this."

He looked over to Jack as though he was going to say something and then cleared his throat. "Okay get yourselves cleaned up, I'll see you back at the hotel." He paused, "most of you."

Jack wasn't meeting up with the team. Grisby had already okayed him catching up with his parents. He had tried to get out of it, tried not to sound angry with Felicity for agreeing to it but in the end, he had said okay for her sake. He wasn't looking forward to it. Playing happy families. Ross's idea. He didn't know why Felicity had agreed to it. Didn't she have enough on her plate without having to put up with Ross? She knew what Ross was capable of. She knew what a bully he was, a controlling arse. She hadn't been able to make a move without his permission. He had heard the arguments when he was younger. His father's voice always sarcastic, "I'm not stopping you, you want to make a fool of yourself, it's your funeral. Go ahead, apply for the job, you won't get it, you haven't worked for years." And when she got the job, part-time counselling at a government centre he had put her down. Fuck he didn't want to witness it. He wanted an excuse to pull out. Too late, he had wanted to bring Sam along but Felicity had said, "Better not, you know your dad hasn't seen you for a while."

He should have stood up to him, called him and told him he would catch up with him some other time. Why hadn't he? Why didn't he just tell him to fuck off?

Jack was heading out of the building when Grisby pulled him aside and walked with him out of the building. Grisby knew what it was to play a bad game in front of your home crowd, when nothing you did went right and you couldn't pull a rabbit out of the hat. You felt like crap. He put his hand on Jack's shoulder, "We all have at least one horror game in our career." He gave Jack a one-sided smile, and narrowed his eyes, "I actually had three, or maybe it was four." He waved the memory away with his hand. "Put it behind you. You've had a great season, Jack. The club wants to keep you but you've asked for a transfer." He gave Jack a sympathetic smile. "I understand. I hope everything goes well for your mum. Go and see her and we'll see you in the morning at the airport, don't be late, 7.00am."

He gave Jack a pat on the shoulder. He got all the players to check in regularly with the team psychologist to see how they were travelling. He'd seen enough players with anxiety disorders to know something wasn't right with Jack. Jack had been under a lot of pressure for a young bloke and he had forgotten that at times. Spoken too harshly to him in front of the team. He should have known better. If anyone knew what the pressures of playing top football could do to your psyche and your relationships, he did. Jack Charles wasn't the first footballer to use alcohol to manage his anxiety. He had done it himself, but he'd got help and managed to hang onto his marriage. He hadn't been a saint, he just had a forgiving wife.

Chapter Fourteen

JACK AND MIRANDA

The restaurant was fully booked for the night, the lights over the white clothed tables shone a honey coloured light. Miranda tied her apron over her black pants leaving visible the restaurants regulation white t-shirt with 'The Bay' embossed in black gothic lettering. She went outside and stood on the verandah. She loved the view across the Swan River. She leant over the railing and looked at the sail boats cutting across the bay in sharp angles. She listened to the sounds bouncing from the water, voices, the twang of the sail ropes, bird calls, and the water breathing against the sand. The light was fading as the sky turned from brilliant blue to indigo. At the mouth of the river the sun was beginning to set over the Indian Ocean. Soon the lights from the apartments and the million dollar buildings across the river would light up the night sky.

To the west of the river the city skyline of office blocks cut into the sky. Voices floated across the dark water, distant sail boats sucking up the wind. This was her transition time, from quiet study to the noise and pressure of the restaurant. She liked the work and she was good at it. There was the added bonus of eating some of the best food in Perth. She didn't plan on staying behind after the restaurant had closed;

a regular event on a Saturday when the staff ate a very late supper and sat around talking. She didn't feel hungry, her stomach had been in a knot since she'd seen Jack the day before. She thought her heart had stopped.

She knew he was coming to Perth. It had been in the paper, some important game, a home game for the Eagles who were hoping to make the finals. Jack Charles' picture had been on the front page of the local paper. But to see him, his face pressed up against the window, if only for a second had brought back all the feelings she'd managed to suppress for the last two years. He'd looked at her with a blank look. He didn't recognise her, why would he? She didn't want him to ever recognise and remember her and what had happened, because after what had happened, he had forgotten her and she had managed to forget that night until she saw him looking out at her from the bus.

"I thought I'd find ya here."

Miranda jumped. She hadn't heard Ewan walk up behind her. She didn't like it; he had done it before. It made her heart race.

He had told her he was twenty-six, on a working visa travelling around the world on his motorbike with New Zealand planned as his next stop before he crossed over to Asia. He was from Edinburgh, his accent a challenge to understand, like a foreign language. "Sorry. I didn't get that." She felt bad every time he had to repeat himself.

"What! Yer canna understand me." And then he'd make his accent even stronger and use as many Scottish words as he could and she'd be totally confused.

"Hi Ewan, just taking a breather before the rush. How's things in the kitchen." Miranda stood up and smoothed down her apron.

He lent his elbows back against the verandah rail. He looked sideways at her, the last of the bright sunlight illuminated the red in his hair. He made his eyes warm when he looked at her. He was good at that. She looked away.

"Ay as usual, Chef is working himself up to a fair heart attack."

Miranda nodded, "Yeh it must get pretty frantic in the kitchen." She wasn't looking at him. There was something about the way he looked at her that made her afraid. Something wolfish when he did that thing with his eyes, as though they were on fire. She moved towards the door.

"Miranda when are y'gonna let me take you out on my bike." He had found out she didn't have a boyfriend. He knew the status of all the girls who worked in the restaurant. He had a practiced charm about him that came from having worked in restaurants in Europe. The girls liked him and Miranda had seen him chatting up the waitresses.

He was smiling, one eyebrow raised, stroking his fingers through his hair. "Never," she said smiling and reaching in her pocket for her hair tie.

"Ah never say never Miranda."

Miranda shook her head. One minute the curls were bouncing around her shoulders and then she was twisting her hair into a pile on the top of her head.

"Cute," Ewan said, "up or down," he flicked at her head, "ye're very cute." Miranda gave him a warning look, she hated being called cute.

"Wait, are ya staying after work for the meal and a drink later… of mineral water." He laughed uneasily. He had asked her before and he knew she didn't drink. He could see she was about to say no. "Stay for a dessert." He said it more loudly than he had meant to, "Your favourite's on the menu."

"That sounds tempting, what is my favourite?" She didn't wait for him to answer. She knew there was no favourite. He was friendly and she could see why the girls liked him. But he wasn't staying and he was really only looking for casual hook ups and she didn't do that. She had made one mistake in her life and she wasn't about to do that again. She wasn't going to let history repeat itself. She wasn't her mother.

People started to drift into the restaurant, some regulars that came early and didn't stay late and then the tables started to fill with the diners who made an evening of it. Just as the light outside darkened, the city skyline came alight and lights flickered over the water. The restaurant was designed to ensure that all the diners had a view through the great wall of glass across the water to the city.

She was waiting on the tables with the first-class view of the river. Fifteen tables in all, four tables for couples they called 'the romance tables' and the other tables that seated up to eight. If it got too busy one of the waiters from a less busy section would be recruited to help.

She'd taken the orders for all the tables except one, a middle-aged couple, a handsome grey-haired man and an attractive blonde woman. They didn't look happy. The man was studying his phone, the woman studying the menu. They ordered drinks from the drinks waiter. Miranda went to the table to take their order and stopped, she could see the table had been set for three people, they were waiting on someone.

"My son," said the woman, "he won't be long."

"Our son," the man hissed through his teeth, "he's my son too."

The woman's mouth trembled. She looked at Miranda and pressed one finger against her lips. Felicity was glad her son didn't have to hear his father lay claim to him now that he had made a name for himself. Ross was so obvious, she wondered what she had ever seen in him. She thought the last three years in therapy had shown her why she stayed. She twisted her fingers in her lap, she thought she could do this for Jack, be here, be some kind of shield. She hadn't been good at that when they had been married. She had tried, tried to deflect the constant teasing and the put downs. She needed a drink but she had stopped drinking since her diagnosis. Not that she had drunk much but she was trying to ensure that she was doing everything that would boost her immune system. She changed her mind when the drinks waiter came for their order.

He was still a handsome man, the grey hair at his temples hadn't made him look older just distinguished. She wasn't surprised when she opened the door to him that evening. Ross Charles was still a striking looking man and he knew it.

She had changed. He saw it too, the way he ran his eyes up and down her figure, taking in the way the black slim fitting dress showed off her new body. She had turned her attention on herself when he had left. Taken control of her life for the first time since she had met and married Ross. Taken control of what she wore, what she ate, what she did and who she saw. She had friends and she had a life.

The look of surprise vanished in a nano second, replaced by the put down look she remembered so well, the arched eyebrow, the half-smile that said 'you've got to be kidding.' He recovered well, took a step back, "Felicity, you lost weight, good for you."

She hadn't invited him into the house, had grabbed her bag as soon as the Uber pulled up. She had choked back the words she wanted to say, "Comfort eating when you're married to a bully." She had been polite.

Felicity looked around the restaurant. It hadn't changed much since the last time she had been here with Ross years ago. It held bad memories. All the work she had done on herself and all the therapy and still she hadn't said no when he told her he had booked the table. "I think Jack will like it. Good for him to see his parents together, getting along." Who was he kidding, Jack hated the idea but Felicity persuaded him. "Just this once, you know how persistent Ross can be."

She was regretting it, why had she agreed. Old habits? She put her hands on the table, she wanted to leave. Jack was doing okay without Ross around. She wondered how he would cope. She had watched the game at home, she wanted to see the close-up shots of Jack. See the whole field. He looked so much older with the rough stubble beard he had grown for the endorsement he had signed up for. "Don't worry mum, I'm not going to keep it. It itches like hell and I have to trim it every day so it doesn't get too long.

Ross was looking at his phone, Felicity could see the screen. He was playing a video on YouTube of Jack missing the goal. Her heart sank, she just prayed he wasn't going to start a post mortem of the game. She knew enough about the game to know that Jack had missed an easy goal – Ross had talked of nothing else and how he wasn't on his mark. She had tuned out and said nothing until they had got out of the car. "Unless Jack brings it up. I think he would probably want to forget the game now that his team are out of the finals."

"For fuck's sake Felicity don't tell me what to do. Do you think I'm an idiot?" The car door had slammed with a force she remembered.

The drinks came. Felicity drank half of it. She needed something to calm her. Ross's words were earworms in her head. *My son, he's my son too. Yes, the son you bullied, you bullied him and I didn't protect him.*

Miranda thought the man at the table seemed agitated. She noticed the clenched jaw, the fingers drumming on the table cloth. As she approached the table, he said something to the woman. She turned her head away and stared blankly across the room. Neither of them seemed to notice when Miranda put the basket of bread rolls on the table, but as she turned to leave the woman picked up her phone from the table and said "Can you set another place please?" She spoke to the man sitting next to her "He's on his way, he's bringing a girl."

Miranda returned with a place setting, the table was round and easily accommodated another seat. She glanced at the woman, she was attractive, pale blue eyes that were concentrating on Miranda as she placed the napkin and the cutlery on the table. The silence was a tangible presence that hovered over the table. Miranda felt awkward, clumsy, a knife slipping from her fingers onto the table.

"He's twenty minutes late. Didn't you tell him we were meeting at eight?"

Miranda glanced at him as she pushed the extra chair under the table. His voice had an edge to it. She felt the small hop of fear inside her chest. She hoped that when the others arrived the tension would lift. She hated serving at a table where there was an air of hostility hanging over everyone. The man picked up a knife and pressed lines into the white table cloth. He muttered something under his breath and glared at the place Miranda had just set.

Jack parked his car and turned to the girl sitting next to him. He hadn't planned to take anyone with him but the thought of having dinner with his father and his mother, no matter how civil they were, was not on his list of things 'to do.' He knew his father; Nicole would be just the distraction. He couldn't face a pseudo family meal. He just wished his father would fuck off.

Jack made the introductions after his father threw an arm around his shoulder. Jack made sure Nicole sat next to Ross. He brushed his lips across his mother's cheek. She slid her eyes across to Ross who was already distracted talking to Nicole.

"Good idea," she said beneath her breath. Jack raised his eyebrows and tried to look innocent and then turned to the girl waiting to take his order.

Miranda hadn't seen him come in, her heart beat in her throat. She couldn't speak. She dropped her pen onto the floor and watched it roll under the table. She bent down to pick it up and heard Nicole say, "Someone's recognised you. Must be a footy fan."

Jack studied the menu. He didn't look at her, he couldn't. He knew he would see those wide blue eyes, and he would feel like a shit and he didn't know why. He asked for the first thing he saw on the menu.

"Since when did you like liver?" said Felicity.

"Liver? No, I meant the chicken." He raised his eyes from the menu, he felt the heat in his face as he looked at Miranda. He was acting like an idiot. Miranda wasn't looking at him she was concentrating on writing his order, slowly, as though she was writing it in Chinese.

"The chicken fricassee?" she said so quietly that he could hardly hear her.

"Yep, that's the one." He leant across the table to his father, "How's the business plan dad?" Anything to signal the end of needing to look at Miranda. His father wasn't listening, he had already started quizzing Nicole.

Miranda walked back to the kitchen without stopping to take further orders. She had to get out of the restaurant. Get her game face back on so that when she faced Jack Charles again, she would be okay. She could do it. *You can do it, he's nobody, he's nobody.*

She handed the order to the wheel man and collected meals from the kitchen. She concentrated on the table she was walking towards, her eyes fixed on that and nothing else. She didn't look at him, although she couldn't help catching a glimpse of him out of the corner of her eye.

He seemed larger than life, dominating the restaurant in the same way she had felt his presence at school. There had been a time when she couldn't wait to get to school, to be in the same classroom space. Just knowing he was in the school, her hero, the boy who stood up for her when others treated her like a pariah. She had never made it obvious, stayed back in the shadows, but she thought about him a lot. Created private conversations with him in which he would tell her she wasn't to worry he would hit anyone who said a bad thing about her.

A hero, what a joke. She paused at the kitchen doors and retied the strings on her apron. She thought he might have recognised her, she couldn't be sure, and then she had dropped her pen and heard his girlfriend say something about Miranda having recognised him. *The football star.* As if

she knew anything about football or wanted to know anything about it.

She bit her lip. She could see the way he looked at her, he
was flustered that's why he had ordered liver. *Don't recognise
me* please. *I don't want to know you.*

"Yer say something?"

Miranda looked up and shook her head at Ewan. She had
spoken aloud. Ewan put three plates on the bench in front
of her.

"Talking to yerself are ya?"

She shook her head again and gave a weary look that she
hoped conveyed that she was run off her feet.

"Table seven," she said as she picked up the three plates
and backed through the kitchen door. *I won't look at him, no
I'll look through him as though he isn't there.*

She carried the plates to table seven, the table next to Jack
Charles. She thought she could feel his eyes tracking her but
she didn't look, she kept her face turned away from him, de-
void of any expression until she reached table seven and put
the plates down. The plate balancing on the top of her hand
began to tilt, the food sliding from one side to the other. She
gave a small gasp, but it was alright, it hadn't slid off the plate.
A curl escaped from the tie on the top of her head, it fell
across her eye. She lifted her head and brushed it away and
saw him staring at her. She looked away quickly. Her face felt
hot. Her heart was racing in a frightening way.

Jack felt the pressure of Nicole's arm against his and then
it was gone and she was leaning towards Ross. He was old
enough to be her father. Jack gritted his teeth. Nicole knew
power and money when she saw it, she was so fascinated

with hearing about the penthouse in New York and the chateau in France and the villa in Italy *and whatever other fucking real estate he's got.*

Jack pushed his chicken around his plate. He had a knot in his stomach and it wouldn't go. He wished Sam had come but his father wanted it just to be a family dinner. "Aren't you spending weeks with your mate after the season finishes, cycling in Europe or something. I arranged to be in Perth so I could see you." *What a lie. You came so you could be seen with me. Tell everyone you're my father.*

Nicole left the table, she had to use the bathroom. "She's a delicious morsel," said Ross. He gave Jack a grin. *What a creep.* But he was glad he had asked her to dinner, his father hadn't directed one question at him or given him his version of how he should have played.

"You're a dark horse," he said, "did you know about Nicole?" he directed the question to Jack's mother. He didn't wait for an answer, he excused himself from the table, "Got to use the boy's room," he said.

Jack almost laughed aloud, *shit he's so obvious.* The cloakrooms were outside the restaurant on the covered verandah that ran around the building. Good luck with that thought Jack and he meant it. Jack watched the retreating back of his father as he strode across the restaurant floor. He was a commanding figure and he knew it.

Felicity held the napkin to her lips. Her mouth was wobbling, it felt like a de ja vu moment watching Ross chasing after a young girl. But she didn't want to laugh, she wanted to cry. What father competes with his son for a young woman. Her wonderful son who had never missed calling her every week and now almost every day, even if it was just to say good night.

She squeezed the napkin into a ball and put it on her plate. "He's still a prick," she said. Jack looked at her eyes, they were full of concern for him. "Don't mind him Jack, he's pathetic," she said, resting her hand on his arm.

"It's okay mum. I really don't care. I don't even know her, I met her last night in the hotel, a few of us stayed on after dinner, just sitting in the lounge. Ryley was talking to her. She's an executive in some real estate business. I brought her along to keep Ross off my back."

Felicity gave a hoot of laughter that made the people at the next table look across at her. Then she looked worried, she didn't think it was the sort of thing Jack would do. "That wasn't very kind to Nicole though."

"Mum, she can take care of herself. She's thirty-five. She's just got divorced. I said I would introduce her to Ross, that's why she's here."

"She's thirty-five!" Felicity said.

"After tonight I won't see her again… but I think Ross will." He raised his eyebrows.

Miranda was over the other side of the room when she saw Nicole leave the table and then his father, she guessed that's who he was. You could see the resemblance, the same eyes, straight nose and square chin. Classic hero looks that's what she'd thought when she had seen Jack lying on the bed, some Greek god that had come to earth.

She heard the hoot of laughter that Jack's mother gave. She didn't seem to care that her husband was chasing after Jack's girlfriend. Miranda had worked in the restaurant long enough to pick up the subtle and not so subtle vibes between the diners.

Miranda turned to the nearest table and began to pick up empty plates. *Don't look at his table. Do your job.* But she couldn't help noticing that Jack's girlfriend seemed more interested in Jack's dad and neither Jack or his mother seemed to care. *Think of something else.* The thoughts were coming unbidden and she knew the more she tried to stop them the more insistent they became.

His mother isn't wearing a wedding ring. She noticed that as she picked up the plates. She had left the empty plates as long as she could until she saw Roger, the front manager scanning the room. She licked her dry lips and walked to the table. She couldn't help hearing the tail end of the conversation.

After tonight I won't see her again.

Miranda bit down hard on her lip. Her hand was shaking as she reached for the plates. Jack pushed the plate towards her. He had hardly eaten anything. The curl had escaped again. He felt the urge to pull at it, it was like a tightly coiled spring. He looked down at her hands, they were small but he could see how strong her fingers were, gathering the plates, balancing them on her arm.

"Thank you," said Felicity.

She was supposed to ask if everything was alright when someone didn't eat their meal. She looked awkward the way she had turned her shoulder at him, her head twisted in an odd way as she picked up his plate.

His stomach was in a knot and it was because of her, this girl who, two years ago, had waited for him. He had done nothing wrong, he was sure of that. Yeh, he'd drunk too much but he wouldn't do anything like force a girl to have sex with him. He was sure of that too. He just wished he didn't have a blank in his memory, he couldn't remember anything after she'd fallen into his arms, or had he pulled her into his arms? She was turning away, her back to the table.

"I know you," he said. He had to speak to her, sort this out. She didn't stop walking.

"What?" his mother said frowning at him. He had an angry look around his eyes. His statement had sounded like an accusation. "Who do you know?"

Jack jerked his head at Miranda, "That girl, the waitress. I know her. She went to Greenfield, year six."

Miranda lowered her head and kept walking, she had heard him. She didn't need him to know her. It was alright. She didn't care. She pretended she hadn't heard. She had work to do. The front manager was watching, as she walked past, he stopped her.

"What's this?" He pointed to the plate with the half-eaten food.

"Fasting." She said the first thing she could think of and rushed into the kitchen.

"How's it going out there?" said Ewan. He looked up and smiled at her as he continued piping cream into miniature lemon meringues. She wasn't smiling, he noticed that.

"What's up?" He held the piping bag in the air and looked at her. She tried to smile but tears were threatening.

"Nothing, just tired. I had a lab at Uni yesterday and didn't sleep. Dead bodies."

"Ugh, don't tell me. Jeez I don't know how you do it." He went back to piping the lemon meringues, "Here, I'll save you one of these." He squeezed a final swirl on one and straightened his back. "Table six," he said.

"Thanks." She picked up the plates.

Ewan called her name as she backed out of the swinging kitchen door, her hands carefully holding the plates. He rolled the 'r' in her name, his Scottish accent thick. It

sounded foreign to her ears, like something exotic, "Murr –
ander."

She didn't wait to hear what he was going to say, the mo-
mentum of her body and the doors opening took her
through into the small space before she stepped back into
the restaurant. She knew what he was going to say, he had
been saying it for the last month.

"I'll give you a lift home," "Come on I'll go slow," "I've
got a helmet."

He had a motorbike and she had no intention of ever getting on it. No protection if you came off it. And she didn't
want him to get the wrong idea. She was focused on her studies. She didn't want a boyfriend and if she did, it wouldn't be
Ewan. He made her feel uneasy, like the feeling she got when
the house was empty when she got home.

Miranda served the desserts to table six. She noticed
Jack's father and the girlfriend had returned. No one was
talking at the table. She paused, she hadn't given them the
dessert menu. Roger would notice, he was like a drill sergeant.

Roger was holding them out to her, making a point, letting her know he had noticed. He didn't speak, he shook
them at her as though they were on fire. He bent his head
close to her ear, his voice low, "You do know who's at that
table, don't you?"

She tried to pull the menus out of his hand but he wasn't
letting them go until she answered.

"Yes," she said.

She pulled at the menus. Roger gave her a look.

"I know," she said, she didn't want to say his name, have those words on her lips. Remember his mouth on hers, remember, remember. "Jack Charles," she said almost in a whisper.

He hadn't expected her to answer. He had recognised him as soon as he came in the restaurant. He gave her a patronising smile, "Well that explains it."

Miranda gave him a puzzled look.

"The way you're behaving this evening. In a daze."

"A daze?" She pulled hard at the menus in his hand, practically snatching them from him. "I'm not." She spoke fiercely, she had never spoken to the front manager like that, she had been afraid of him, he could sack you in an instance if he didn't like you. She could see by the look on Roger's face, the pinched mouth and the eyes wide as though they were about to fall out of his head that he didn't like the way she had spoken to him. She tried to smile but she couldn't.

She was a pretty girl. He had noticed her blue eyes the first time she came into the restaurant looking for a job. You couldn't help but notice them, ice blue, the riot of black curly hair. He tried not to stare; he didn't want any accusations coming his way. He thought she was too young and too fragile to do the work. He had told her she needed to be at least sixteen. He was surprised when she told him she was eighteen. He said he would give her a trial, "You won't get paid."

She had surprised him at how quickly she learned the work, and she was good with the diners. She had just the manner the owner liked, deferential without being obsequious. And she hadn't missed a weekend shift. He had to send her home one day when she came to work with flushed cheeks, and a red nose. He heard the cold in her voice when she said she was perfectly fine. He liked the fact she was studying at university and someone had told him she had won prizes at school.

Daze, no way! "Okay," she opened her eyes wide and pulled her shoulders back. "Is this better Roger?"

Roger stared back at her wide-eyed astonished face, "Don't overdo it Miranda," he said. "Go," he almost smiled as he nodded towards Jack Charles' table. "Poker face," he said. She knew what a poker face was, the look as though you weren't there, you were somewhere else behind your eyes. She was good at that. But not tonight. Not around him. She didn't want to go back to that table not after she heard him say, *"I know you."* He didn't know her, not really know her. He hadn't wanted to know her, not that girl, the Bin Girl.

She couldn't explain what he had meant to her that last semester at Greenfield. He had been kind to her. It had meant nothing to him, an inconsequential time in his life. But in her life of misery, it had been a rocket exploding in the sky.

Sometimes she wished she had never gone to the party, that party, but she had gone and it was pointless regretting things. She had learned that at St Helen's on her first day. The principal had taken her into her office and spoken to her before she introduced her to Ms Horrigan, the boarding mistress.

"You have your life ahead of you Miranda. Bad things happen to people but that doesn't have to define you. You have a gift. Your mind. That's what's going to make you a wonderful future. You scored the highest score we've ever had on a scholarship application and that tells me what you're capable of. The staff here at the school only know that you're an orphan."

It wasn't a gift. It was an escape and she had worked hard at school Anyone could have got the marks she had if study was all they did. And she wanted to show the school that they hadn't made a mistake. She had won the prizes and got into university on a bursar. Her fees were paid for but she needed to maintain good grades. It didn't matter how often Rose would tell her she didn't need to work so hard. Rose had never had to bother about failure, her parents were there with open arms ready to support her whatever happened. All they wanted for Rose was for her to be happy.

She walked towards the table her eyes fixed on the older woman, it had to be his mother, the way she was looking at him. He was staring at Miranda, she tried not to look at his face. She saw him put his hands on the table as though he was going to stand.

Miranda couldn't stop her lips from trembling. She pinched in her cheeks to hold them tight and the smile got wider. *Too much, smile less.* She bit her lip as though she was concentrating on a puzzling thought. Jack's mother was looking at her. *He's told her, she knows who I am.*

Felicity Charles hadn't really noticed the waitress who was serving at their table. She had been too worried about her ex-husband flirting with Jack's girlfriend but after Jack had explained who she was, she tried to relax and just enjoy Jack's company.

When she saw Jack enter the restaurant with the blonde-haired woman, her heart had sunk. She didn't know he was bringing anyone, he hadn't said he had a girlfriend. She looked too old for him, she had a worldliness about her, but now she knew she wasn't his girlfriend she felt relieved. Ross had a weakness for blondes, Felicity had been that blonde once, before he moved on, and left her and Jack. His contact with his son had been sporadic, sometimes weeks and then months went by before Ross contacted Jack, and now he was trying to be a father. She squeezed her fingers together, why was she here, why had she made Jack come, why couldn't she say no to Ross?

Felicity smiled at Miranda, the young waitress with the blue eyes, who was walking towards their table. Jack hadn't said anything more about her, only that he knew her in primary school. Felicity smoothed the tablecloth in front of her. Jack was alright, he wasn't dating the woman leaning against her ex-husband's shoulder. They're probably touching feet under the table, she didn't care and she could see Jack didn't.

Felicity could feel some tension in Jack as though he was ready to leave, his body tensed, his hands pressed on the table.

"You want to leave. Skip dessert?" she said.

He sat back in his seat, relaxed his shoulders. He didn't answer, he was looking at the blue-eyed girl standing at their table. Felicity felt some relief that Jack had remembered an old school friend.

She worried how much he had changed. The attention he had received since he was sixteen had fixed the trajectory of his life. She had found it difficult to remember the boy he had been. He had kept in touch with her every week but he had made it clear that his personal life was none of her business. Hearing him call out to an old school friend had somehow reassured her that he was at heart the boy she knew, kind and thoughtful. She didn't want him to get arrogant the way some of the other young footballers had. Too much fame and too much money when they were so young.

Miranda handed the dessert menus out quickly as though she was a croupier dealing out cards. Jack took it and placed it on the table. He wasn't hungry. He had a thought in his head that he pushed deep into wherever forgotten memories went and it was resurfacing like a deep-sea diver coming up with treasures but this wasn't a treasure, it felt like an unexploded rusty bomb. He knew her and it made his skin prickle, because whatever had happened between them, he was afraid it wasn't what she had wanted. The black hole that refused to let the light in was growing paler and although he had tried hard to remember what had happened on that night, he didn't want the hole to open up here when she was standing in front of him. No one seemed to notice that he was staring at the waitress. The rest of the table were studying the dessert menu trying to decipher the exotic descriptions of the choices laid out before them in copper plate script.

Nicole seemed to realise that Jack hadn't spoken to her for most of the evening and she had been focusing too much attention on his distinguished and uber wealthy father. She shouldn't be too obvious. She leaned away from Ross Charles.

"What do you want Jack?" She said it in a husky voice as though she was offering him a different kind of dessert that she might provide later.

He didn't answer. He didn't want anything from her. He kept looking at Miranda. She seemed to be looking right through him. A blank look in her glittering blue eyes, as though she wasn't here standing in front of him but out there, behind the darkened restaurant window.

Ross looked sideways at Nicole and touched her foot with his just a quick tap it could have been an accident. "I know what I want," he said studying the menu. Felicity almost burst out laughing he was so obvious.

"And what's that?" Felicity said raising her eyebrows.

Ross ignored his ex-wife. He paused and said to the table in general, "Chocolate Mousse." He slapped the menu down on the table as though he was placing a bet.

"I'll have the same," said Nicole, she ran her tongue around her lips and looked at Ross.

Felicity wanted the evening over. She was never doing this again, playing happy families with Ross. Jack had been quiet the whole evening, something was bothering him and it wasn't his father and it wasn't the game. It was something else, a worrying thing. He had hardly said two words since he came into the restaurant. She brushed her hand across his bare arm and felt the swell of muscle under her finger tips. He wasn't a boy anymore. She gave his arm a pat.

"Okay?" she said softly and glanced at his profile. The muscle in his jaw was working. He was staring at the waitress. Felicity glanced at her and saw her blink and a single tear roll down her cheek. At the same time Miranda was turning away and almost running to the kitchen. Jack pushed away from the table.

"Excuse me," he said and followed after Miranda.

He didn't know what his plan was, he had seen that tear and before that a look that gutted him. He headed for the rest rooms on the far side of the restaurant. He kept his head down, someone had recognised him and he saw heads turn to look at him and heard a whispered "that's Jack Charles." He had never got used to it in nearly two years. He thought he would love the fame but he hated it. It made him a stranger to himself.

He thought he was going to vomit. The word *rape* swam across his mind. He leant his hands on the washbasin and then turned on the cold tap and let the water slip through his fingers. He held his wet palms to his face and stared at his face in the mirror. *Shit, shit, shit.*

"What's up mate?"

His father stood next to him and spoke to his image in the mirror. "Why'd you dash off like that?"

"Like what?" said Jack. He was buying time, standing tall, taller than his father. He walked over to the urinal.

"Okay… I thought… you were, you know pissed at something."

"Like what?" Jack repeated. He zipped up his fly and washed his hands. The hand dryer drowned out whatever his father was saying but he caught the words, *"she said she wasn't your girlfriend."*

"Oh yeh, and when was that?" He didn't want an answer. He walked past Ross and put his hand on his shoulder. "It's fine, she's too old for me but evidently not too young for you."

"Okay, I was just checking, your mother was looking daggers at me." He laughed "I think she'd like to throw a few."

Jack could see himself throwing a few daggers in his father's direction too.

"Go ahead, I'm going out on the verandah to call Sam, I'm catching up with him later." The calling Sam was a lie, he had already made an arrangement to see him. He didn't want to go back to the table. He could see the effect he was having on Miranda and it was making him feel sick.

He took the steps from the verandah down to the grassed area that separated the restaurant from the foreshore. Lights from the restaurant lit up the trees and threw dark shadows down to the water. Jack walked to the edge of the grass where the sand met the water. He sat on his heels and traced the letter 'M' in the sand and next to it a '?'. He stood up and twisted his heel into the sand. He turned and looked back to the restaurant. The light inside was the colour of honey.

He found her straight away amongst the tables and the diners. She was collecting dessert plates. He could see his dad drinking coffee. He reckoned another thirty minutes and the restaurant would be empty. He wasn't going back in. He sent his mother a text to say he was leaving and one to Ross, telling him he had gone to Sam's and could he get the bill and take mum and Nicole home. He didn't care what Ross thought of him and he would explain it to Felicity. He leant his back against a giant Morton Bay Fig tree and waited.

She had to go back and take the orders. She told Roger she had a sudden stomach cramp and had rushed to the toilet. She couldn't afford to lose her job. When she got back to his table he was gone. She felt relief flood over her.

As soon as the last diner had left the restaurant Miranda headed for the staff room. Ewan had seen her enter. He put his head around the door Miranda was hanging up her apron in her locker.

"Ya going already? Come on stay." He could see she was leaving, her bag was on her shoulder. "What about the dessert I saved for ya?"

She could hear an edge to his voice, was he angry? "I'm sorry, I have to get home. I need to get up early, exam on Monday... anatomy."

"Didn't you have that exam last Monday?" Ewan frowned at her. She had given him that excuse before.

She looked in her bag for her keys. Did she say that last week? She looked up, "Yeh it's in two parts."

"Okay, wait while I put the dessert in a box for ya. Take it with ya." He went to leave and then popped his head back in the door. "I could give you a lift ya know. You'd be home quicker, more time to study."

She took the hair tie out of her hair and ran her hands through it loosening the curls. "No, I'm fine Ewan, I've told you I catch the bus outside the restaurant and it drops me across the road from my place." She liked the short ride on the bus it was like a bridge between her working world and her life at home and by the time she got home she had left the restaurant and the frantic rush behind her.

She carried the white box with the lemon meringue carefully, she was taking it home for Rose. She didn't know how her life would have turned out if Rose hadn't said she had to live with her because she didn't like living on her own and she would never get through university without her help. Rose's parents paid the rent for the unit and Miranda insisted she make a contribution. And it was true she did help Rose with her studies and she was glad she could.

She pulled the door behind her and gasped out loud. He was standing by the door, he had suddenly appeared from nowhere and he was there. "I waited for you," Jack said.

The dessert box fell from her hands and he tried to catch it but it fell onto the wooden floorboards. He bent and picked it up. "Sorry," he said. She took it and put it in her bag, it was ruined so now she didn't have to keep it upright.

"It was a lemon meringue pie," she said absently. "I was taking it home." She started walking away from him, she didn't want to miss her bus.

"Wait… look. Can we talk?"

Miranda pressed the pad of her finger into the sharp corner of the dessert box. She shrugged, "There's nothing to say."

Jack held his hand at the back of his neck. "Okay, I just wanted to say I was sorry. I didn't remember you back... the party... you know Greenfield."

"That's okay, it doesn't matter," she didn't want him to talk about what had happened at the party. She wanted to get away. "It doesn't matter," she said again, her voice barely above a whisper. The not remembering who she was had mattered for a long time and then it didn't because it had been a silly fantasy in her head and now it was gone and he wasn't a hero any more.

"So..." he felt his heart speeding up the way it did when he was about to kick for goal. He followed her down the steps of the restaurant and onto the white gravel path that led from the road to the shiny glass doors of the restaurant. The bus stop was across the road.

"Well, look I don't know how to make it right." He wasn't a bad guy, he needed her to know that.

Miranda's hair shone under the street lights. Jack stared at the top of her head, he had stepped closer without realising it and now he was too close, standing over her. Miranda felt wings beating in her chest. She saw the door of the restaurant open and Ewan came out, his bike helmet under his arm. He was talking to someone on his mobile. He started to turn towards the car park when Miranda called out, "Ewan." He turned and looked at her. She didn't let Jack finish what he was struggling to say. "I've got to go... my boyfriend," she said and almost ran to Ewan.

Ewan looked up as Miranda ran towards him, "Gotta go talk later," he said quickly into the phone. "Did ya change your mind?" He looked over at Jack who hadn't moved but was watching them. "D'ya know him?" he said. He knew who he was, he had heard the Chef say some football player was in the restaurant. He wasn't interested in Australian football, it was a rubbish game, his game was English football that the idiots called soccer in Australia. "Ya kick it with your foot, ya don't touch it with ya hands that's why it's called football ya fucking idiots."

"Can I get a lift?" she said.

Jack watched the two of them walk through the car park. He saw how Ewan put the helmet on Miranda's head and fastened the clip. She seemed awkward the way she got on the back as though she had never done it before. She was hanging onto the back of Ewan's leather jacket when he reached behind and pulled her arms around him.

She hadn't let him talk but it was okay he had tried and now he was going to forget Miranda and the night he couldn't remember. He ordered an Uber and headed over to see Sam.

***

Ewan tried to drive slowly, he didn't want to scare her off. Her arms around his waist. The first step in touching and it was so easy. He liked it when the girl sitting behind him held onto him as though her life depended on it. Miranda's body pressed against his, her fingers gripping onto his leather jacket. Just a few layers of clothes separating their naked bodies. He felt the familiar surge of desire in his groin. Too soon, she wasn't ready yet. He could wait.

Ewan pulled the bike to a halt when Miranda shouted in his ear. It had taken less than 5 minutes and now she was getting off. He needed more time. Time to get past the solid wall she had built around herself. She never looked him in the eye, never smiled. She'd do well at a funeral – she should hire herself out. She wasn't his type really, he liked girls a bit more solid. Thighs you could sink your fingers into and breasts. As far as he could see she didn't have any. Flat as a pancake. He smiled to himself. He'd find out soon.

Miranda struggled with the clip. "Well, what did you think of it," he said, "the ride?" He pushed up his visor and took off his helmet, he was hoping she'd invite him in but it was late.

Miranda had felt the cold wind rip through her black cotton trousers and the thin jacket she was wearing. It was a mistake, she knew it straight away, she hadn't been thinking straight, she just had to get away. She couldn't talk to Jack, she could never tell him what had happened. Ewan was looking at her in a way that made her stomach clench. *Mistake, mistake, mistake.*

She rubbed her hands, "Cold," she said. Her fingers were numb she had been holding on so tight. "Thanks," she said, she wanted to get away from him, what had she been thinking, she was an idiot. He took a step closer and she felt her insides dissolve in a familiar way. She moved away but he grabbed hold of her hand.

"I'll give you a lift tomorrow." It wasn't a question. He looked at the row of town houses he'd stopped in front of. "Is this your one?" He said jerking his head towards the house behind him.

"No, uh yes, but it's not mine. I share it with a girlfriend. She tried to pull her hand away, he had taken off his gloves and his fingers felt hot. He tightened his grip, he wasn't letting her go just yet.

The double storey modern house with gleaming windows and a wrought iron gate confirmed what he thought about Miranda. He knew she was studying at university, someone in the kitchen had told him she was a genius, but all he saw was a snob and she had money.

"Lucky you," he said.

"Thanks… for the lift… thanks," she tried to smile and pull her hand away but he increased the pressure in his grip. It was so easy to hold her there.

"Is that it eh? Thanks, what about…" He suddenly leant forward and pulled her hard against him and kissed her on the lips. She pulled back but he had already let his hand drop and was turning away and putting on his helmet. He curled his lip in a mockery of a smile.

Miranda gasped and wiped her arm across her lips. She didn't care if he saw her rubbing at her mouth. Ewan was getting back on his bike, pulling on his gloves. He started up the engine and roared away as though he was in a race. When she shut the door behind her she leant back against it, her legs were shaking, she wiped her arm across her lips again.

He had seen her, "Fuckin bitch," he shouted above the noise of the traffic. The traffic was in two lanes heading towards the turn off for the freeway. Ewan slipped in between the two cars ahead. He didn't bother to glance at his speedometer. He knew both cars ahead were travelling at the speed limit, 70 kilometres. He knew the road rules, he couldn't filter between the cars. He twisted the throttle and roared past the inside car. The driver swerved towards the kerb, and then the sound of the car's horn blared out in protest. He increased his speed and slipped in front of the car and then slowed down and raised his gloved hand in a one finger salute before he roared away.

Chapter Fifteen

NIGHT AT THE RESTAURANT

PERTH
JACK

Jack sat in the back of the Uber, the driver hadn't recognised him and he was grateful for that, there was only so much talk about the game he could stomach. He took out his phone and sent Sam a message that he was bailing out and would see him tomorrow. He scrolled through the messages, one from Ross, he didn't bother to read and deleted it. A text from his mum, he sent her an emoji.

He should be feeling better now that he had spoken to Miranda but her face was haunting him. The look on her face, her eyes wide and her trembling mouth as though she was scared of him, of what he might do to her. He shook his head, that wasn't her boyfriend he could see that. She had to get away from him. He thought the worst.

"Drop me off here mate," he said to the driver. He needed to run off this feeling of doom that kept grabbing hold of him. His rational mind told him he was being ridiculous but his intuition said something else. He had done something wrong and it was hanging over him like a black cloud.

The porch light was on when he got home. Felicity called out to him from the lounge room. She was lying on the sofa with an open book on the floor. "You didn't wait up for me, did you?" Jack said.

She sat up and pushed back her hair. "No, I needed to put some distance between your dad and sleep." She picked up the book and held up the cover. "Romance, trashy romance. Anything to… hey you alright. What's up?"

Felicity could read Jack like the book she was reading. Jack put his hands in his pockets and shook his head. She patted the seat next to her, "Your dad get to you? He's not worth it." She should be telling herself that but it was the way he treated Jack that got to her. She had married the biggest narcissist, but out of the disaster of a marriage she had Jack and even if it meant she had to have a relationship with Ross for the rest of her life, Jack was worth it.

Jack didn't answer. He took his jacket off and threw it on the back of the sofa and sat down. He stretched out his legs and kicked his shoes off. He didn't look at her. He was going to tell her what was bothering him.

"That girl, the one I told you I knew from Greenfield, the waitress tonight. I waited for her." He leant his head back and closed his eyes. Felicity said nothing.

"I had to find out," he said. He opened his eyes and rubbed at his chest. Felicity felt alarm. She held her breath.

"Find out what?"

"Whether I," he didn't want to say the word. He shrugged. "I met her here, on my eighteenth. I didn't recognise her." He bit his lip, "I'd been drinking."

Felicity nodded at him, she remembered that night, the girl and the drinking.

"There's a black hole… I can't remember. I just remember." He swallowed, "I just remember pulling her onto the bed. That's it."

"And you don't know whether you what?" Her heart sank, she didn't think she wanted to hear his answer.

"She came to find me at school a couple of months after the party, waited for me." He ran his fingers through his hair. "I didn't recognise her… I hadn't seen her again after that night. She said she'd waited for me but I was going to a game and I was… in a rush." He didn't want to think about that day and what had happened to Sam because he was late.

Felicity looked at her son, there was more to it, she knew him. Felicity could see Miranda at their table that night. She had thought she might be a new waitress, not confident about serving customers. She had noticed the way Miranda's hands had trembled, and how she had tried to avoid looking at anyone at the table.

"You spoke to her?" she said.

"Yeh… no not really. She, she said it didn't matter."

"What didn't matter?" said Felicity.

Jack shrugged, "I don't know mum. I don't know," he was trying to remember what he had said. "I just said I was sorry."

"What were you sorry about Jack?"

"Everything." He leant forward, "Everything mum. The way it happened, not finding out what she wanted to say to me… and because she was Miranda Miranda…Millington." He remembered her name at that moment. It came to him as though it was waiting to hijack him, to make her more real.

"That girl mum, her mother was a drug addict. She died. She was that kid who ate out of the bin. The kids called her names." He didn't want to repeat the names they called her. "Her mother cut her hair." He remembered that, "Shit, down to the scalp." He could see her trying to hide from everyone, so small, her hair in tufts like something out of a horror story. "I treated her like trash," he said quietly.

Felicity remembered that girl. Who could forget seeing her at a school that had never had a child who had been so neglected. She had stood out in the worst possible way. Miranda's life had been terrible for at least the first twelve years but she hoped it was better now.

"Didn't she win a scholarship to St Helen's," Felicity said. She thought she remembered reading that in the Greenfield school newsletter. Felicity closed her eyes, "Yes, she scored the highest score out of all the students who sat the entrance exam for the scholarship to St Helen's." She remembered talking to the other mothers about her.

"She's a very bright girl," Felicity said. She wanted to add I'm sure she was smart enough not to get pregnant but that wasn't what was worrying her and she wasn't going to ask him the question that was sitting like a time bomb between them.

"What did she say Jack?" Felicity leant forward and stroked Jack's hand.

"It doesn't matter," he said.

"Tell me."

He lifted his head from his hands and looked at Felicity, "That's what she said, it doesn't matter. And then she pretended some guy who works at the restaurant was her boyfriend and got on his bike and left. She didn't even know how to put on the helmet." He could see her holding her head up while the guy in the leather jacket adjusted the clip.

Felicity let the silence fill the room until Jack spoke again, "She thought I was ... I don't know... some kind of..." He didn't want to say hero. He was no hero. "Back at Greenfield. I took extra food to school. I felt so bad for her. You wouldn't treat an animal the way she… I left it in her desk. I didn't want her to know it was me…" He shook his head remembering her. "I know she knew it was me the way she'd look at me like I was some big fucking hero. None of the kids went near her…" He stopped and bit his lip. "I never went near her," he said, his voice a whisper.

"Fuck mum. She had the shittiest life. I treated her …" He shook his head. "I shouldn't have… I should have… fuck I wish I could remember." He put his head in his hands. Felicity could see the tension in his shoulders. She stood up and stroked her hand across his head. She patted his back.

"Okay tell me everything you can remember, perhaps it will help," she said.

"I don't remember much, not the important bit. I just remember throwing up." He rubbed his hand over his head, "She said she wanted to be a doctor, I pulled her onto the bed… and that's it. I fell asleep and, in the morning,…" He felt the heat rise in his face.

Felicity inclined her head, telling him to go on. He could tell her anything he knew that.

"Blood…" he glanced down at the floor and away from his mother's eyes. "On the sheet in the morning when I got up. I can't remember anything else, what I did, we did."

"And the blood, that wasn't from you. A cut…?"

"No… it… I had a smear on my leg." He dropped his hand onto his lap.

Felicity was parsing the statement, the implications. She let out the breath she had been holding and felt the tension fall away. *Her period no pregnancy.*

"Her period most likely," said Felicity. "That's not unusual."

"Yeh," said Jack. He wanted that to be true but he just knew it wasn't. He held his hands out, "That's it and when I woke up, she was gone. I didn't see her again until she came to find me at the school the day Sam busted his leg."

"And you didn't see her before that?"

"I'd been away mum. You remember Sam and I were in camp for four weeks training for the try outs. I left straight after the party."

"Okay, well why think the worst Jack. I don't like to ask you this but have you ever pressured a girl to sleep with you… can you remember?"

Jack glared at his mum, he looked angry and then he took a breath before he said something he would regret. "No never. This has never happened before I promise. The girls were pressuring me… well making it clear that's what they wanted."

Felicity shook her head. She hated to hear Jack talk like that as though he was full of himself, just like Ross.

"Mum, I… don't… I've not been…" *sleeping around.* Sam's accident had been his wakeup call. He hadn't stopped the drinking but he had stopped the girls, avoided them. He felt it was his penance for what had happened. "I haven't okay? Just Emily, and I told you I've been sober now for weeks since the counselling. I've been trying to remember what happened with Miranda, I just can't be sure… it's a blank and I don't know if I'm making this up mum because I need to think it was okay, she …" he shrugged his shoulders.

"She?" Felicity said softly.

"I don't know," he kneaded his forehead with his fingers, pressing hard as if it would help. "I thought she said…" He didn't want to say the words he thought he heard Miranda say in the fog of that night, it was something a dick would say when he was boasting to his friends. He stared at the floor, "I thought she said something about being glad it was me." He gave a frustrated sigh," Or maybe she said she was glad she found me. Fuck, it's a black hole."

Felicity stood up, she looked at her phone, "It's late Jack, let's talk more tomorrow. We'll think about how we can make this right if you need to." She didn't think he could ever make it right and there was real danger in making any admissions. He definitely shouldn't do that she thought. She didn't want to see her son ruin his life. And he might have got it wrong. He sounded confused about what had happened.

The next morning Jack slept in. He'd felt relieved as though he'd left a huge weight in the kitchen when he'd told Felicity what had happened. But he wasn't an idiot he knew you didn't go around admitting a criminal offence if you didn't want to end up with police record or worse.

Felicity made herself a coffee and waited until it was nine o'clock before she called one of her university colleagues, a school counsellor at St Catherine's a private girls' school.

Jack stumbled into the kitchen when it was nearly noon and he was hungry. "I'm starving," he said, "what have you got to eat?"

Felicity was making herself a salad. "I've got a cooked chicken. Sandwich or a salad?"

"Salad, not rocket."

"Sleep, okay?

"Yeh good."

"That's good." She felt relieved. She didn't tell him that she had hardly slept at all. She opened the fridge and assembled the salad ingredients on the bench. "Here, you cut off as much chicken as you want." She pushed the plate towards him, and glanced at him. He looked better than he had the night before.

"I made a few enquiries this morning," she said as she opened the fridge and put a bottle of orange juice in front of Jack.

"What sort of enquiries?"

Felicity stopped moving around and leant her hands on the bench. "Miranda is studying at UWA, she wants to do medicine and she's doing well."

Jack stopped pulling the chicken apart. "She is? That's good." Actually, it was great. She was at Uni she was studying for something prestigious. Her life wasn't shitty any more.

"You know what that means," said Felicity.

Jack frowned, "Yeh, she's going to be a doctor one day."

"Yes, and her life's going to be okay."

Jack nodded, he hoped that was what it meant.

"Yes, so put it behind you and stop worrying Jack." She didn't think he would. She pushed the plate of salad across the bench, "Dressing?" she said. "Jack, I said do you want dressing?"

He took the bottle and shook it. He wanted to put it behind him, if only he hadn't seen her, if only he hadn't.

Felicity watched Jack walk out onto the terrace. She frowned, it was cold outside, the wind was whipping the leaves off the trees. She watched him put his plate down on the glass table of the outdoor setting. He walked to the end of the garden and looked out across the river to the distant houses and the iconic red roofed 'Bay' restaurant where Miranda worked. He didn't move for a long time, the sun glinting off the water, the clouds racing overhead. Felicity stood in the kitchen watching, she could hear the fridge humming, she was more troubled than Jack.

Chapter Sixteen

THE NIGHT AT THE RESTAURANT

PERTH
MIRANDA

Miranda walked into the lounge room where Rose was watching something on the flat screen. One look and Miranda knew it was another South Korean romance series. Miranda didn't mind because when she was trying to study in the lounge room instead of her bedroom, Rose turned the sound off and just read the subtitles. Rose paused the tv, "Hey I heard a motorbike. Did you let the Scots Kilt bring you home?"

"Yes, I did," said Miranda, she flopped down on the settee next to Rose and leant her head on her shoulder. "A mistake. I shouldn't have done it." She closed her eyes, the memory of the evening was too raw. Why had Jack waited for her? He sounded sorry and he'd said sorry twice.

Rose read the look on Miranda's face. "What did he do?" said Rose her voice sharp. Miranda frowned. "The Kilt, did he do something?" said Rose.

Miranda shook her head, she didn't want to mention the kiss, she wanted to forget that so it wasn't real.

"You okay chooky," said Rose.

"Yeh," she sat up and yawned, "Jack Charles came into the restaurant tonight. I served his table." She spoke as though it meant nothing.

"Oh," said Rose. She turned off the television. It meant something. "How was that?"

"He said he was sorry," Miranda said reaching for the remote control and turning on the television.

Rose took the remote from Miranda and switched the tv off again.

"He said he was sorry two years later. Well, that was nice of him."

"I guess." Miranda smiled.

"I was being sarcastic," said Rose. "Did he say anything else? No, answer that later, where were you when he spoke to you, who else was there?"

"He was with his parents and a girl. She seemed older."

"Did he..." she was going to say recognise you this time but changed it at the last minute, "So did he say this in front of everyone?"

"No. He waited outside after all the diners had left, including his parents and the girl. He was outside. That's why I got a lift with Ewan."

Rose raised her eyebrows in a question.

"Because..." Miranda tried to speak, she shook her head, she didn't want to cry. "I can't explain it. It..." she brushed at her eyes. Rose put her arm around her shoulders. "I know," she whispered against Miranda's hair, "he was the nicest boy you'd ever met and then he wasn't."

Miranda nodded her head and pressed the back of her hand against her face. She tried to smile, "Yeh something like that." She pushed herself up from the sofa, "I'm going to bed now, I've got another shift tomorrow and an exam next week."

"Miranda, you ace everything. You're never going to lose the bursary. Don't push yourself so hard, have some fun with the Scots kilt… OMG you might end up having sex." Rose threw her arms wide.

Miranda shook her head, she didn't want that conversation. "Never," she said firmly.

"Never Milly? You're twenty, you never know, you might like what he's got on offer," said Rose. They'd had this conversation before and it always ended the same way.

"Rose not again please. I just want it to be with someone I care about and who cares about me and forget the kilt, that is never going to happen. He's probably slept with half of Perth and all the available girls from Scotland, France, Spain… ah all that geography in his penis."

"Yes, but just think how good he'd be though, he must have learned a few creative moves," said Rose thrusting her hips at Miranda.

"Yeh and how formulaic too," said Miranda. "I would hate that."

"You wouldn't know what you'd hate in that department."

"Night, going to bed," said Miranda.

"Does he play the bagpipes?" Rose said to Miranda's retreating back.

After Miranda left the room Rose didn't turn the tv back on, she sat thinking about Miranda. They had been boarders at St Helen's for five years and now flat mates. Rose knew Miranda better than she knew her sisters. She had never asked Miranda questions about her childhood she knew it had been terrible. Rose's mother had received information from the school principal and she had shared some of that with Rose because she knew that the school had put Miranda in with Rose for a reason. Miranda had been bullied at primary school and the principal of the school was determined that wouldn't happen at St Helen's. Rose was popular at the school and hadn't been brought up in a hot house environment like the majority of the girls from the Western Suburbs. Rose's parents were farmers, practical and down to earth and they made sure Rose didn't come home in the holidays with any fancy ideas about who she was.

When Rose had heard about Miranda's childhood, the number of schools she had been to, the neglect, the poverty and the family violence she had experienced, Rose had wanted her mother to adopt Miranda. They had fostered Miranda as it was the simplest and quickest way to bring her into the family. At the end of each term, she went home with Rose. Miranda loved the farm, and she loved Rose's sisters. She never spoke about her childhood.

Chapter Seventeen

JACK

The airport lounge was full of Australians heading back home. The holiday was over and Jack hadn't thought about Miranda once, no one knew him in Europe and that had been the best thing about the holiday. He'd been able to walk down the streets of Vienna and not a single person recognised him. He had wanted to cancel the holiday but Felicity wouldn't hear of it. "Jack, you need this holiday, some time away from training. You'll have a fun time, you always do. Aunt Lucy is here, she is staying until after the surgery." Felicity was having surgery while Jack was away. She didn't want Jack around, she knew his anxiety was causing him problems. She was more worried about Jack than she was about herself. She was feeling confident that the chemo and the surgery would give her the all clear.

Jack knew he had been spotted as soon as he sat down. He had waited until the last minute before walking to the Departure lounge. He didn't often get asked for his autograph, it was usually a selfie, but if he did, he always felt awkward about his signature. He wondered if he ever signed it the same way twice.

Sam watched Jack scrawl his signature on a scrap of paper and hand it back to an acne covered boy and then he let the boy take a selfie with him. Sam tried not to laugh.

"Fuck that kid will delete that photo and terrible signature mate," said Sam, "more like a doctor. I might copy it when I qualify… if I qualify." Sam stretched out his legs and Jack glanced down and saw the scars beneath his shorts. Red and angry marks, like a shark's bite around his knee, the pins holding his femur together. It didn't matter how many times Jack saw the scars, he felt the old guilt each time.

"Nah mate, he will treasure that pic, probably have it printed and sleep with it under his pillow." He punched Sam on the arm. "I thought you were doing ok at Uni?"

"Yeh, I am. But it's tough. I'm doing okay."

"More than okay. I'm proud of you mate." Jack put his sunglasses on, folded his arms and put his head down. "Not looking forward to going back to Sydney," he said.

"You think you can get a transfer back to Perth?" said Sam.

Jack sighed, he hadn't wanted to ask for the transfer. He liked playing for the Swans and being away from Perth had felt like a fresh start although he missed his old friends, especially Sam, but supporting Felicity was more important.

"Yeh the management are doing everything they can… so it's on the cards."

"How's your mum doing?"

"She said she's doing okay." That's all Felicity had said to him when he asked her. Every inquiry he made she would tell him not to worry, that it was going according to plan. He didn't want to talk about it with Sam, it made it real.

Jack raised his sunglasses and looked at Sam. "How's things with you and Rose, did you get it sorted?"

"No, not yet. But I think she's going to forgive me."

"You told her that nothing happened? That was true, wasn't it?"

'Yeh, no, nothing much happened. No skin on skin. But she said trust was broken and I didn't get a second chance."

"Excuse me, are you Jack Charles?" Two girls had walked past and one of them had turned back and was now standing in front of him. Jack nodded. "I'm a Tigers supporter," the girl said.

"Good team," said Jack.

"Can we get a photo with you? We follow you on Instagram."

"Yeh," the other girl said, "you should put more photos up without your shirt."

Sam gave a snort of laughter.

Jack didn't answer, he knew he was blushing like a fifteen-year-old.

After the girls had left Sam noticed more people looking over at them. "Think there's going to be a stampede any moment. They don't know who you are but they want a photo just in case."

At that moment the loud speaker announced that they were boarding. "Saved from the stampeding crowd," said Sam.

"When do you go back to Sydney," said Sam putting his bag in the overhead locker.

"I've got two more weeks in Perth."

Jack adjusted the seat belt and leant back. It was a long flight, he hoped there were some good movies to kill the time. "So, what's this about Rose forgiving you. I thought she was never going to forgive you?"

"Yeh, man I tried everything. I was a frigging idiot." He shook his head he didn't want to go back and see himself being that idiot.

"It's been a month, nearly two and Miranda, her flat mate, had been tutoring me the whole year and then Miranda broke up with me too. Said she couldn't tutor me out of loyalty to Rose. I got that, but I saw Miranda in the library before we left and practically went down on my knees and begged her to get Rose to give me another chance. I wrote Rose a letter and Miranda said she'd give it to her." He grinned, "The Williams charm – taking Rose to dinner, in…" he looked at his phone, "36 hours."

"Miranda?" said Jack. It had to be the same Miranda. He knew Rose had gone to St Helen's.

"I said I'm having dinner with Rose," said Sam.

"Yeh heard that, I was just wondering who Miranda is. Haven't heard you mention her before."

Sam frowned, he wasn't supposed to mention Miranda to Jack. He'd thought it was silly but Rose had said that Miranda would only help him if he didn't mention it to Jack. He'd asked why and Rose had said it was something about Jack knowing her when she was at primary school. "She got bullied," said Rose, "the kids were horrible to her."

Sam didn't answer, he was fiddling with the tv screen on the back of the seat in front. "Who's Miranda?" Jack said again.

Sam pulled off his earphones, "Yeh, you know her, Rose said you went to the same primary school." He hoped Jack wasn't one of the bullies.

Jack pulled a magazine from the pocket in front of him, he tried to sound casual, he shrugged his shoulders, "Lot of kids at the primary school. Could have been in another class."

"She's a genius. Rose said she won every prize at St Helen's. But you wouldn't know it, she's pretty modest about her success. I couldn't have got through the year without her. Rose is very protective of her wouldn't let me set up a date for her with Matt Gordon."

"Matt Gordon, the dropkick with a pony tail?" Jack turned the pages of the magazine, "She going out with anyone?"

"She's too smart for you."

Jack didn't answer, he was thinking about Miranda with her arms around a guy on a bike. He turned the pages of the magazine without looking at the glossy photos.

"It was a joke," Sam said. "Anyway, you live in another state."

"I've got a girlfriend," said Jack, anything to shut him up.

"Emily? I thought you broke up. I'd know if you had a girlfriend."

"We did, weeks ago. Alright, I don't have a girlfriend and I don't want one, okay, give it a rest."

Jack pulled his iPad out of his bag and put in his EarPods. He searched through his downloads and watched back-to-back comedy shows until they brought lunch and the uneasy feeling that had resurfaced had gone.

Chapter Eighteen

ROSE AND SAM

"What do you think?" Rose said, "the t-shirt or the blouse." She held the garments up for Miranda's inspection. The t-shirt was plain white and the blouse was blue silk.

Miranda looked up from the book she was reading, "You decide." She wasn't sure Rose was doing the right thing. Rose had been angry but mostly hurt when Sam had confessed to her what he had done in Sydney.

"I'm not going to be one of those girls who is going to be treated like a doormat. He's said he's sorry, and I've told him what's not negotiable. I've got to make compromises but, the old Rose has retired, no more dropping my plans to fit in with him. My friends are just as important as his."

Miranda had watched Rose pace up and down their small living room as she listed off the non-negotiables. Having a relationship looked like hard work and it came with the potential for a lot of heartache and self-doubt. She had spent hours listening to Rose dissecting her relationship with Sam. What had she done? Was it her fault? Should she be more understanding? The list of self-recriminations seemed endless.

Miranda had heard some of the details from Rose. She knew Sam had gone to Sydney to watch Jack play and she couldn't help but think Jack was responsible somehow.

Miranda listened as Rose had argued with herself over the degree of betrayal. Rose wanted to forgive him. They had been going out for more than a year, had met each other's parents and then Sam told her what had happened in Sydney.

Miranda tried not to influence Rose's thinking, Rose had to make up her own mind. Miranda liked Sam; she had got to know him over the months she had been tutoring him. He was serious about his studies and always turned up on time.

Sam had wanted Miranda to hear what had happened but she had stopped him. She didn't need to hear the details and she didn't want to. Rose was her friend and she had told him that when he had tracked her down in the library. She had sent him a text to say she wasn't tutoring him any longer, her loyalty was with Rose.

He made Miranda listen, following her out of the library telling Miranda that he kissed the girl and he didn't have an excuse. He had been drinking but he knew what he was doing and he stopped himself. He loved Rose and he was a fucking idiot. He begged Miranda to give Rose a letter.

When Miranda had got home, she had thrown it on the table and told Rose she was sorry she took the letter to shut him up. She would tear it up for her if she wanted. But Rose had read the letter.

"I'm not going to stay long," said Rose. "I'll just hear what he has to say." Rose slung her bag over her shoulder, "I don't think I will ever trust him again."

"Okay," Miranda could hear the anger in Rose's voice but she also knew that Rose wanted to forgive Sam.

"Yeh trust is at the heart of every relationship, I guess. If you don't have that, well, not much of a relationship." Miranda gave a weak smile. "What would I know. But I guess he could have said nothing, just kept quiet. Perhaps that's a good sign." She raised her shoulders.

Rose was biting her lip wondering if she was doing the right thing. Miranda didn't know. She didn't think she would forgive someone who had betrayed her trust, but maybe she should. She hadn't had Rose's life.

Rose paused at the door, "You think I should forgive him Milly?"

"No, no." Miranda held her hands up. "I'm not saying that, it's for you to decide. You have to decide whether…"

"What? I have to decide what Milly?" Rose sounded frantic as though Miranda's answer would free her of her indecision.

Miranda loved Rose. It had taken her a year at the school with Rose as her constant companion before she had begun to trust that Rose wouldn't disappear. That the life she was living with Rose and her family wasn't going away and she could trust that Rose would always have her back.

Miranda smiled and said softly, "Rose, only you can decide whether he's worth forgiving."

Chapter Nineteen

JACK AND MIRANDA

Jack had been home a week since the holiday with Sam, spending most of the time lying around the pool with Felicity who seemed happy to do nothing but read and sleep. Jack scrutinised her every move, looking for signs that she wasn't as okay as she claimed.

He had three more days before his holidays were officially over and he had to be back in Sydney for training. He heard his phone buzz, Sam had sent him a text saying he was heading for the beach did he want to join him.

Jack borrowed Felicity's car and drove around the beach front trying to find a parking spot. It was late in the after-noon, the sun had lost its intensity as it began to sink into the ocean.

Jack hung his towel around his neck and pulled his hat down over his eyes. He scanned the beach looking for the spot where Sam said he would find him. The beach was crowded with families, little kids everywhere running in and out of the surf. Sam had told him to look for the blue and white striped umbrella. Then he saw Sam waving his hat in the air. Jack walked over and glanced at the other towels spread out next to Sam. "Who's here?" he said.

"Couple of girls," said Sam grinning. "They're in the water."

Jack groaned, "No really. Sam, tell me they don't know I'm coming please. Even better tell me they don't follow footy." He kicked his shoes off. "Fuck, if I'd have known I wouldn't have come."

"Settle. And that's why I didn't tell you. No, they don't know you're coming and as far as I know neither of them follow footy… and Jack, I never talk about you to anyone." He wanted to say 'get over yourself' but he was feeling generous. Dinner with Rose hadn't eventuated. Rose was only prepared to talk and hear him out and then she said she would think about it.

He'd waited two days to hear from Rose and then he'd sent her a gif of a man on his knees and it made her laugh and she agreed to meet him at the beach. He hadn't expected her to bring along Miranda but he could live with that. Rose was sending him a message, Miranda was there for a reason, he was still on probation - he got that.

Jack dropped his towel on the sand, kicked off his shoes. He looked out at the swimmers, he could see a few close to the beach and then nothing beyond. He threw his hat and sunglasses on his towel and jogged towards the water. Sam watched him disappear under a wave and then resurface and start swimming out away from the beach.

Rose ducked her head under the water. She had met Sam for a drink at a bar. She had told him she wasn't doing dinner. "I told him I would hear him out but I wasn't staying. He was really trying Miranda, promising me that he would earn my trust. I didn't say yes and I didn't say no." She had told him she would think about it. "I want to forgive him Milly but I don't want to be a pushover, the needy one."

She had been nervous about meeting Sam at the beach. "Barely wearing any clothes and in the water and you know he'll put his arms around me." She had nearly changed her mind but then had decided Miranda had to come. She had begged Miranda to come with her, promising it was the last favour she would ever ask. "I can't meet him on my own Miranda, I'll probably try to drown him."

"You want me to help? is that it," said Miranda. "It will be awkward Rose. He wants to talk to you. How can he do that with me there."

"He knows you Milly, you delivered the letter. You can be the mediator."

"No! Definitely not. You're on your own. Look I'll come for an hour and then I'll leave you two."

Miranda swam towards Rose, "I think I'm going to ditch, okay?"

"You haven't even got your hair wet," said Rose "or your shoulders." Miranda dropped her shoulders under the water.

"They're wet okay and leave the hair alone." She had wound her hair on top of her head, salt water made the curls go mad. "Okay I've done the awkward bit and now you two can sort it out."

"You don't have to, but…" Rose smiled, "Sam didn't seem to mind that I brought you along."

"Well, he was good at masking it," said Miranda. Rose hadn't seen him mouth 'thank you' to Miranda.

"How you getting home?" said Rose. "Do you want to take the car and I'll get a lift with Sam."

Miranda raised an eyebrow, "I could do that for you." She could see where Rose's evening was heading. Miranda looked back towards the beach, Sam had set up a beach umbrella and was lying under it.

"Okay I'm getting out. You stay here," she jerked her head in Sam's direction, "he can join you."

Rose threw her arms around Miranda's shoulders, "And that's why I love you, my bestie." Rose lifted Miranda out of the water.

"Don't throw me Rose!" Miranda screamed in her ear. Too late she was lifted out of the water and then Rose threw her and her head went under. She emerged spluttering, with her wet hair unwinding onto her shoulders. Water had got up her nose and her eyes were stinging.

"Rose! I'm moving out. Stop laughing it's not funny." She pushed water in Rose's face. "No, don't retaliate, you bully."

"Sorry Milly,"

"You're not," Miranda said as she adjusted her bikini top and walked out of the water.

"I saw that," said Sam as Miranda bent down to pick up her towel. "Hope she does that to me." He grinned. He could see Rose wasn't coming out of the water.

"I think I'll have a swim," he said. Rose watched him run down to the water. She could feel sand in her bathers, her hair was dripping salty water onto her face. She picked up her shorts and t-shirt and headed towards the change rooms.

Jack rubbed his towel across his wet hair and then laid it out on the sand under the umbrella. He put on his sunglasses and looked out towards the setting sun where he could see the silhouetted figure of Sam with a girl he knew was Rose. He couldn't see the other girl. He lay back on the damp towel and closed his eyes.

Miranda ran her fingers through her wet hair as she walked back to the blue and white striped umbrella. She stopped, confused, someone was lying under the umbrella, she could see a man's muscular legs and faded blue shorts. It wasn't Sam. There was no other umbrella the same colour

on the beach. She could see her sandals and a towel she recognised as the one Rose had brought.

She walked closer, he was lying on his back, his arm
across his face, his head resting on her beach bag. He moved
his arm away. She was standing with her back to the sun, her
body cast a long shadow across his face. "Hi," he said "are
you with Rose? I'm Jack." He didn't get up. He was waiting
for the girl to answer.

"Uh huh," she turned in a panic towards the water looking for Rose. She knew that Sam and Jack Charles were best
friends, he was that Jack, that Jack Charles.

Jack came up on one elbow, the girl had turned her back
to him and was looking towards the water. He knew who it
was. The unmistakable hair, the slight frame and when she
turned towards him the blue eyes.

Miranda bit her bottom lip, she wouldn't look at him. She
would never forgive Rose, how could she. She had confided
in her told her some of what had happened. Why would she
do it.

Jack saw the frantic look in her eyes, she had been taken
by surprise but so had he, the hammering in his heart was
unexpected. She took a step away and then bent and picked
up her beach bag from behind his back. Her arm brushed his
bare arm and he sat up.

"I didn't know Sam was meeting anyone." He spoke
quickly, watching her as she stepped back and held her bag
against her stomach.

"I'm leaving now, okay," he said. He searched the sand
for his beach shoes. They were full of sand, he picked them
up. She had turned towards the ocean. She was leaving too
but she didn't want to walk back to the car park with him.

"Sam didn't tell me he was meeting Rose." He felt the need to explain himself. He was going to kill Sam. He stood up brushing the sand from his legs.

"I'm sorry," he spoke to her back, he didn't know if she could hear him above the noise of the ocean slapping the sand.

"I thought I was just meeting Sam, he didn't tell me until I got here that he'd asked a couple of girls. I didn't know it was Rose and you." He knew he sounded defensive. Why should he be making apologies?

A seagull screeched overhead.

Jack clenched his jaw. The hammering in his chest was there, it felt like anger. He took a slow breath. He didn't want to sound angry.

He brushed the sand off his damp board shorts as he watched her slip her bag over her shoulder. He could see the weight of the bag, the way she held her body, leaning over to counter balance the weight. He thought she might be carrying books, a fleeting thought amongst all the other confused thoughts flashing through his mind.

"Why am I always saying 'sorry' to you?" His words came out unexpectedly. He was surprised that he had said them aloud.

Miranda held her hand up to her eyes, shielding them from the bright light. If she had remembered to bring a hat, she would have jammed that on her head and pulled the brim over her eyes. She turned back to him and although the sun was behind her she kept her hand over her eyes.

"You tell me," she said and dropped her hand and he couldn't read the look in her blue eyes. Contempt?

"Okay, okay." He took a sudden step towards her, he wanted to close the gap and not have to shout. Miranda jumped back as though he was threatening her. He saw it and the hammering started up again.

"Look I don't know what to say. Miranda, I don't… remember." He shook his head, "I just don't know what happened." *I don't know what I did.*

She lifted her chin and he saw anger in her glittering eyes. He had seen girls cry before, he wasn't good at this. He saw a tear escape and she swiped it away with her fingers and turned her back on him. He stepped up behind her and bent his head close to her.

"I was drunk Miranda, some of it I can remember but," he shook his head, "there's a black hole." He raised his hands.

"How convenient," said Miranda brushing away more tears. "Great defence," she said bitterly.

Defence? Jack heard warning bells ringing loudly telling him to get the hell off the beach. "Do I need a defence?"

Miranda shook her head, "No, it doesn't matter."

"That's twice you've said that to me, but honestly you look at me as if I… you look at me as if I did something that mattered. I'd like to know what I did that night. Because…" he had to take a breath, "not knowing, is making me think the worst of myself." He turned his head and looked over at the water, he couldn't see Sam and Rose.

Miranda rubbed the back of her hand across her forehead. She didn't think he was lying. She shielded her eyes against the glare of the water, she could feel him at her back waiting for her to say something. She turned to face him, he could see her lips were trembling, "You didn't do anything I didn't want, if that's what you want to know."

He let out the breath he'd been holding, he pressed his hand against his chest. It was good, he could stop worrying but why didn't he feel better. He could see Sam and Rose stepping out of the water, "Miranda can we talk please. Let me drive you home." He jerked his head towards Sam and Rose. "I'm leaving those two to sort out whatever needs to be sorted."

Miranda saw Rose pull on Sam's arm.

Sam had just told Rose that he'd brought his mate along to meet Miranda just as they were walking out of the water.

"Your mate, not Jack Charles?" She sounded horrified. "I told you that they went to the same school, she got bullied."

"Yeh but he didn't bully her, he's not the type. All the girls want to meet him," said Sam.

"Not Miranda," said Rose. She could see their body language, she thought she saw Miranda wipe her hand across her eyes.

"What? She hates football players? This will be a first for Jack."

Rose didn't answer, she slowed her pace and pulled Sam back. "Wait, let them talk. She knows him," she said.

"Yeh, you said primary school?" Sam put his arm around Rose's shoulder and turned her towards the ocean. He didn't leave his arm there; he wasn't going to assume anything. He was glad he had written Rose a full confession, he had tried to answer every question he thought she would want to know. Some of the questions he didn't know the answer to himself. But it had made it easier when they met. He knew that Rose was special. She was kind, unpretentious and she had integrity, something he had discovered he was lacking. She didn't have to point that out to him, he had worked that out for himself. Even his stupid father didn't have a bad thing to say about her.

Rose glanced over her shoulder, "Yeh, primary school, year six." It wasn't her story to tell. She glanced towards Miranda and Jack and started to walk in their direction, "I think we can go now," she said to Sam.

Miranda and Jack watched them approach. They didn't speak. Miranda clutched her beach bag to her chest as though it was a life jacket. Jack shielded his eyes although his sunglasses were perfectly adequate.

"I see you've met," said Sam uneasily. He thought the least said the better. Neither Jack nor Miranda were looking particularly relaxed.

"I'm giving Miranda a lift home," said Jack, jamming his cap on his head. Rose looked at Miranda to see if she was okay about that, Miranda gave a small nod in her direction.

"Okay then," Rose said cautiously.

Chapter Twenty

JACK AND MIRANDA

They walked in silence to the car, he felt lighter, as though he had more room in his chest to breathe. He hadn't done anything she didn't want. It was okay he hadn't forced her, done nothing that could get him into trouble. But he had been a bastard, he'd given her the brush off.

"Mum's car," he said stopping beside a black and cream Mini Cooper and pressing the button on the car keys to unlock the doors.

"It's nice," she said. It was hot inside the car. Jack opened the windows. Miranda held her bag on her lap and then dropped it at her feet.

"You can leave the windows open," she said as he pulled the car away from the kerb, "just for a bit, dry my hair."

"Okay," he nearly said, 'amazing hair,' but he'd stopped himself in time. He drove along the coast road. He didn't know where she lived and he hadn't asked her.

He could feel the top of the car roof brush against his hair. He touched his head, "I'm too tall for this car," he said, for something to say.

She was only half listening to him; she was thinking about what she was going to tell him.

He pulled the car into a car park next to a beach side restaurant. "Is this okay. Nice view," he said pointing with his chin to the blazing red sun that was lighting up the water.

"Do you want to get out?" He found it hard to be close to her. There was Miranda the girl with the heart shaped face and a mind as big as a planet that had saved her from following in her mother's trajectory and then there was Bin Girl. That girl had haunted him at school, he couldn't even begin to imagine what her life had been like.

Miranda got out and walked to the front of the car. A grassed area with benches fronted onto low dunes and the ocean. Jack stepped over the pole fencing and turned to help Miranda but she ignored his hand.

They sat with space between them. She folded her arms, it was still warm outside but the wind off the water was cold. He was waiting for her to talk, the silence was getting uncomfortable.

"What do you remember?" she said. She didn't really want to have that night laid out before her for dissection like one of the cadavers in her anatomy classes. But she wanted to know.

He half turned towards her, he needed to be looking at her when he told her that he could only remember some of it and not the most intimate moments that might have meant something to her.

He shrugged, "Lying on the bed, vomiting." He rubbed his hand across his forehead, "we were talking. I think I remembered you from primary school-"

"-You called me Bin Girl."

"No. I never called you that," he sounded indignant.

"No not at school, others did. I meant that night."

"What?" he couldn't believe that he could have done that. "No, really?"

"You didn't recognise me. I guess I'd changed a lot. I had hair for one thing. But when you recognised me, you did, you called me that." She could see the effect it was having on him. "You apologised later," she said. He had, he'd been mortified, kept repeating how sorry he was.

Jack nodded, he hated to think that even if he'd been drunk, he had inflicted that horrible degrading name on her. He knew what it was like to be called names, Ross was an expert at that.

She sighed, what was the point in torturing him, he couldn't remember. She stood up she had her back to him, "I recognised you straight away, you brought food to school for me. I knew it was you." She let the sound of the waves thumping on the sand fill the silence.

He didn't speak. He watched her raise her hands to her hair and fan out the curls. He grabbed a handful of sand and let it fall.

She half turned towards him, "You stuck up for me once… you won't remember…I… thought you were… you were the only one who was nice to me." She didn't want him feeling sorry for her. She held her hair back from her face and turned towards him. She raised her voice, "I hated them and I envied them." She didn't tell him how much she wanted to be one of those other kids with a normal mother.

"You were smart," he remembered that, "smarter than all of us," he said.

"No, I'm not. I just work harder." She couldn't read the look in his eyes, he wasn't smiling. He brushed his hand over his hair. It was a gesture that seemed so familiar to her. She thought she remembered everything about him. He held his hand at the back of his head. He could feel the unwelcome sting in his nose and looked away from her. She wasn't that girl with the shorn head rummaging in the bins for food. He didn't want that memory.

"You were my hero." She gave him an embarrassed smile.

Jack stared at the sand between his shoes. *You were my hero.* The words didn't make sense. He turned his head and met her eyes.

She was going to tell him because it explained that night. It explained why.

"I had a big crush on you at school." She touched her lips. It was more than a crush, she adored him, hero worshipped him.

"I grew out of it," she said quickly. "When I got the scholarship to St Helen's I gradually forgot about you." She wasn't going to tell him that she cut out his photo from the local paper. She sat back on the bench and hugged her arms around herself. The sun had disappeared. He didn't want to interrupt her but he could see she was shivering.

"You're cold," he said, "let's get back in the car. He looked up at the brightly lit restaurant, he didn't want to have this conversation there.

The car was still warm. He started up the engine. "There's fish and chips at Fremantle Harbour, it's sheltered away from the ocean," he said a name, "we can eat there, it will be warm."

He backed the car out of the car park and pulled out onto the road. "Keep talking," he said. "I just saw you were shivering."

She rubbed at the space between her eyebrows. "When I saw you and you didn't recognise me, I was pleased, I didn't want you to remember that girl the one at Greenfield… Bin Girl." She said the name quietly. "I never wanted to be reminded of that life. And you didn't recognise me for a while, you said I was…"

"-Snow White," he said as a flash of memory danced across his mind. "I remember, the black curls blue eyes... like the cartoon," he said apologetically.

"And then, and then... the rest... you don't remember..." her voice trailed off. They drove the rest of the way in silence until he parked the car and bought fish and chips. Miranda stood next to him while he ordered. The girl behind the counter didn't recognise him but the couple in front did.

"Hey aren't you Jack Charles, saw you play." Jack was polite but terse, he didn't leave any room for discussion. As they were leaving someone called out, "When are you going to play for the Eagles?" He shrugged.

Miranda could see that attention was something he didn't like. She didn't like attention either.

They sat at one of the tables overlooking the dark oily water of the Harbour, away from other people and the bright lights that were strung along the boardwalk. Miranda could hear the buzz of his name as people pointed him out.

"Does that happen all the time?" she said.

"A lot. More here and in Sydney. But it goes with the territory." He shrugged, "I'm doing something I love." He opened up the white paper and spread out the fish and chips. He didn't want to talk about himself.

After a while he said, "I'm really sorry I can't remember all of that night. Were you okay?"

She nodded, she had been more than okay, "Mmm..." She tried to make light of it, "I was glad it was you," she said.

"Did you say that?" he said more sharply than he meant.

"Maybe," she knew she had and he'd said, "I'm glad it was me too." But it meant nothing, just words.

"Do you want this," he said holding out a capsule of tomato sauce.

She nodded and pointed to a space next to the chips, he folded the capsule and tomato sauce squirted sideways onto his arm. He held his arm out to her, "Not very hygienic," he wiped it off with a paper napkin and squirted the rest of the sauce onto the paper.

Her hand was trembling when she reached for a chip, this was the part of that night she didn't want to talk about but she was going to tell him. She dropped the chip onto the paper and clasped her hands under her chin.

"I had a termination," she said.

"Termination?" The word wasn't registering. He should know what that meant.

"Mmm," she nodded her head. She could see the way he'd pulled his eyebrows down that he didn't understand.

"An abortion," she said.

He put his hands on the table to steady himself. He knew why she was telling him.

Miranda pressed her hands against her thighs, her legs were shaking. She couldn't believe she had told him. She watched the seagulls swooping at the tables, one came and perched on their table. Jack lifted his head and stared at it. It hopped forward, its black beak open ready to snatch a chip. Miranda saw the wind ruffle its feathers. It snatched a chip and flew off. They both watched it hop onto the ground, the chip dropping from its beak, and another seagull swooped across the boardwalk and snatched it up.

He didn't know what to say. He felt as though a stone had lodged in his sternum.

"An abortion?" He shook his head, he didn't like the image that was forming in his mind.

She nodded, "Yeh," she looked down at the table and half eaten meal spread out on the white paper.

He didn't need to ask if it was him, he knew it was. "I'm so sorry," he said at last.

"Yeh, pretty unlucky I guess the first time and…" she let the words hang in the air. "Rose came with me."

Jack shook his head. He chewed his bottom lip, "That's why you waited for me at the school?"

"You don't remember but we had arranged to meet when you got back from…"

"Training camp."

She folded the paper napkin into a triangle. "I was never going to have… I thought you should know. It was my decision but I…" *thought you should know.*

"I am so, so sorry, Miranda. Really, fuck," he said softly. Another seagull had perched itself on the back of a chair close by and was watching them waiting to make a move. Jack didn't ask Miranda if she wanted anymore, she had hardly touched the food. He folded the leftover food into a parcel.

"Was it… were you okay?" What did you ask someone after you had got them pregnant and left them to have a termination on their own? It was out of his experience but he thought it must have been frightening and lonely.

She was giving him a sad smile, her eyes were brimming with tears. "It feels as though it happened to someone else now. It was nearly two years ago."

"Did Sam know?" he said suddenly.

Miranda shook her head furiously, "No only Rose. She would never betray me."

I betrayed her. She thought I was a hero but I was a bastard. There was nothing he could do to make amends. The thought of offering her money crossed his mind but he dismissed it quickly, he wasn't that much of a fool.

"Shall we go?" Miranda said. There wasn't anything more to say. She could look at him now without feeling like something that had been thrown away.

"Let's go this way," he didn't want to walk past the other tables again. The boardwalk ahead was free of tables and dimly lit. There was no railing between the boardwalk and the inky black water. They walked in single file in silence until they reached the end of the boardwalk where wooden steps led down to a path to the road.

Miranda could hear Jack's steps behind her, heavy on the wooden boards. She couldn't see how many steps led down to the path, the dark shadows and steps were indistinguishable. She thought she had reached the last step and was stepping onto the path but there were two more steps and she cried out as she lunged forwards twisting her ankle as she put her hands out to save herself. It happened quickly.

She tried to stand up, Jack was beside her, holding her by the shoulders. "You, okay?" She touched her head, she had hit it on something. Her hands were stinging. She wanted to cry. It was too dark to see what she had done.

"Bastard steps, my fault. I should have gone first. You, okay? Can you walk?" Jack said.

Miranda put her hand out and held onto his arm, she tried to put her foot down and cried out. "No," she gasped. She grabbed onto his t-shirt. The pain brought tears to her eyes.

Jack didn't ask, he just put his arm under her legs and carried her down the path towards his car. "Get into the light so we can see what's happened," he said.

She felt awkward in his arms. She held herself stiffly. "It's okay I can walk," she struggled to break his hold.

He didn't answer but kept walking. Her ankle was throbbing, she thought it might be broken. He carried her as though she weighed nothing. He could feel her bare arm against his fingers. Her skin was cold. The car park was ahead. A group of youths were walking out of the Harbour just ahead of them. Someone called out, "Hey Jack Charles you loser," he'd learnt to ignore the jibes. "Is your girlfriend drunk?" someone said.

She felt exposed in his arms, as though she was being paraded, she pressed her head into his neck. He saw the flash of a phone; he gritted his teeth. "Great," he muttered. Now they were following him. They followed him to his car making obscene comments. He didn't respond, he knew the type. He tuned out to them he was concentrating on getting Miranda into the car without her face being photographed.

"Okay," he said when he reached his car. The group of boys were now standing behind him calling out names. One of them leant forward and touched his shoulder. He froze.

"Oooh you mustn't touch Mr. Million dollars." It was a girl's voice, high pitched like the squawk of a seagull. Miranda lifted her head, she couldn't avoid hearing what they were saying. They reminded her of all the cowardly bullies she had endured at primary school.

"Miranda" he said softly, "I'm going to put you down while I open the car, keep your head down and face the car. I don't want them to take a photo of you." She put her good leg on the ground and held onto the car while he found his keys and opened the door. He helped her while she hopped on one leg as she maneuvered herself into the passenger seat. At that moment someone kicked him behind his knee and his leg gave way, he turned quickly, he was going to kill the shit.

"Hey what's going on," a man's voice called out. A security guard appeared from nowhere. He waved his torch in the direction of Jack. "Everything okay?" he said. The gang of youths had turned and were running into the dark.

"Thanks," said Jack. He uncurled his balled fists and took a slow breath. He'd never been in a fight before and he was relieved that the security guard had turned up just at the moment.

Miranda tried not to put her foot on the floor of the car. Her hands were shaking when she tried to put the seat belt over her shoulder. Jack slammed the car door and started the car. "You, okay?" Stupid question he thought. She had just told him something pretty bad and then she had fallen head first down those frigging steps.

He heard her give a small gasp of pain. He saw her struggling with the seat belt. He leant over and took it from her hands and fastened it. She didn't say anything. He drove out of the car park and onto the road. He drove fast as though it was an emergency.

"Don't get a speeding ticket," Miranda said. "I think it's a sprain, I don't think it's broken."

He slowed down. He slammed his hand on the steering wheel. "Fuck!" The word came out explosively. He inhaled loudly as though he had been holding his breath. "Sorry, those punks. God I was going to hit that guy. I wanted to smash his head in." He smacked the steering wheel again.

"Sorry," he repeated. He had to calm down. This wasn't about him. He drove silently, the anger he felt was a hot ball in his chest. Miranda was having trouble keeping her foot in the air.

"Ow," she gasped and put her hands either side of the seat. Jack looked across at her, he could see the problem. He pulled the car to stop and grabbed his towel from the back seat. He rolled it up and unclipped her belt and helped her wedge it underneath her leg.

"I'm taking you to the hospital, we need to get that looked at in case it's broken."

She didn't want to go the hospital, "It's not broken."

"You're not a doctor yet," he said tersely. He felt an unexpected anger towards her. He shrugged his shoulders, and said almost apologetically, "Better to get it checked."

He drove to the emergency department of the hospital. She didn't want to be carried. "You can't walk," he said. "Wait, I'll find a wheelchair." He left her sitting in the car for what seemed like ages and came back without one. His hair looked wet, he was sweating. The evening was warm but it had been the running around the hospital that had made him sweat. "Someone's gone off to find one," he said. He pulled at his t-shirt, it was sticking to his body.

While she had been waiting, she had sent Rose a text, she didn't say she was at the hospital, she said, 'All ok, going to be late, talking.' She didn't want Rose coming to the hospital and she would. Sometimes Rose felt more like a mother than a sister.

Jack stood outside the car with the passenger door open. He was in a five minute drop off and pick up bay. Too bad he thought.

Miranda shifted in the seat, she had undone the seat belt. She needed to use the bathroom. She swung both legs out of the car.

Jack stepped back. "What are you doing?"

"I need to use the bathroom."

"They're inside," he said. He helped her out of the car, she took her purse and her phone out of her bag. She tried to put her phone into the pocket of her shorts. The pockets were too small. "Here, give me your bag. I'll carry it." She dropped her phone and purse into her beach bag. He put it over his shoulder. She reached up and put her hand on his arm. He held her with one arm against his hip and kicked the car door shut and locked it. He helped her inside to the waiting room. It was going to be a long wait, there were at least five or six people ahead of them. He expected the photos. Someone had recognised him. He carried her to the rest rooms, one arm around her waist. He looked around for a nurse, there was only the office staff sitting behind the glass windows.

"She needs to go to the bathroom," he said. The woman behind the glass pointed to the corridor behind him. Miranda squeezed his shoulder, she was desperate. He turned and carried her through to the rest room.

"You can't come in," she said. He turned his shoulder to the door and pushed it open. There were three toilets, the doors were open. "It's empty," he took his arm away and Miranda took a step into the closest toilet and he pulled the door behind her. I'll just wait outside. He just hoped that no one had seen him enter the ladies' toilet and that no one came in. He heard the toilet flush. "Okay," he said pushing open the door, he helped her to the wash basin. He stood behind her his hands on her waist. He looked over at her reflection, she glanced up at him, the corner of her mouth went up. Her hair was hanging over her face, she pushed it back and he could see the swelling on her forehead. It had already started to turn purple.

"Shit," he said. "You hurt your head."

"Mmm, I think it was the post on the steps." She looked at her hands, the pads at the base of her thumbs were bright red, one had a scratch. She turned off the tap. He looked towards the door. He didn't wait he just grabbed her around the waist. "Dry your hands on my back," he said as he pushed open the door.

"No, it's okay I can walk. I'll just lean on your arm." She struggled out of his grip and he lowered her to the floor but kept his arm around her shoulders, so that her foot barely touched the floor.

"Fuck," Jack said as though it was the last straw. The waiting room was crowded and he caught a flash from the corner of his eye of a blue and gold jacket. A diehard fan who didn't need a game to wear his Eagles jacket. Jack turned his head down to find Miranda looking at him with a question in her eyes.

"Sorry. We're going to have to wait."

"Oh, you don't have to wait. You can go. Please." She wanted him to go. There was nothing left to talk about.

"Hey you're Jack Charles, aren't you?" A voice from somewhere in his periphery called out to him. He kept his head turned towards hers. She saw something like a mask slip over his face and he wasn't there anymore.

"Please go. I'm alright. You don't have to…" *put up with this*, she was going to say but he stopped her.

"I'm staying." He stood with her in the queue at the reception desk. When they reached the desk, she sat down and he walked over to an empty seat and took out his phone and read his emails.

They waited for nearly two hours before they took Miranda down for an x-ray. Jack muttered something about elevating her foot while they waited. "You need to ice it," he said at least twice.

"Have you done a first aid course?" she asked.

"No, you just learn a lot about the treatment of injuries when you play football." He looked at her ankle, it was swollen and turning purple.

"It's not broken, look," said Miranda and she slowly twisted her ankle. "It's a sprain." She hoped that was all it was, she couldn't afford to take time off from work although Rose would insist that she rest it and not bother with the rent. "For goodness sake Miranda you're part of the family, you don't have to pay rent." Miranda had insisted she pay, she didn't want to depend on anyone ever. She was an adult and no longer a foster child, that had ended when she turned eighteen.

"Don't" said Jack more sharply than he meant to. "Best not to move it, just in case."

The doctor looked away from the computer screen where an x-ray picture of Miranda's ankle was displayed. She smiled at Miranda. "Well, it's not broken. Just a nasty sprain. Stay off it for a week or two." She looked down at the intake sheet. "It says here that you fell down some stairs. You didn't hit your head, did you?"

"Yes," said Jack. Miranda glared at him.

"It's nothing," said Miranda touching the bump on her forehead.

The doctor shone a light in Miranda's eyes and asked her questions, did her head ache, was her vision blurred, and did she feel sleepy? No, no and *yes of course she did it was nearly midnight.*

"Are you her partner?" she asked Jack. Jack could tell he hadn't been recognised. She was a young Indian doctor. She looked as tired as Jack felt.

"Friend," said Jack.

"Do you have anyone at home," she asked Miranda. Miranda nodded; the day had turned into a nightmare. She wouldn't be able to work. She was a casual, they didn't get paid sick leave.

"How long before I can walk on it?" said Miranda.

"Rice," said the nurse. Miranda looked bewildered. The doctor inclined her head towards Jack, "Your football friend knows what that means." She'd recognised him the minute he came into the emergency ward. She knew who he played for. "I'm a Dockers supporter." She smiled. "You can go now. Use a crutch for the first four or five days. You can hire them from the hospital."

Jack paid for the crutches. He insisted. He didn't want to talk about it. He helped her into the car as she managed the crutches as though she had always used them. She hadn't complained once about the pain. She waited outside the emergency entrance while he jogged over to the car park. He had moved his car from the drop off zone while she was getting an x-ray.

He helped her into the car and put the crutches in the back. He hadn't been able to stop looking at her. He felt responsible for her falling down the stairs, he felt responsible for her shitty life. The accident had overshadowed what she had told him. The implications of that were gossamer threads of possibilities that were dangling before him.

Miranda leant her head back on the seat rest and closed her eyes. Jack glanced at her and back to the road. He drove carefully as though she was fragile. He didn't want to bump her ankle. She told him where she lived. He knew the road, it wasn't far from the restaurant she worked at. He thought she wouldn't be able to work. He clenched his jaw. The silence in the car was oppressive.

Miranda opened her eyes, she could see his profile, the pulse in his jaw, the haunted look on his face. "It wasn't your fault," she said quietly.

"It was," he said evenly. "I wanted to avoid getting recognised."

"I meant the other thing."

He didn't answer, *'the other thing'* he knew what that meant. It could have meant a baby. He could have been a frigging father at 18 and all that would have meant. For the rest of his life. He didn't want to think about it.

"The house next to that lamp post," she said. She had meant it. It wasn't all his fault. She had to take responsibility for her part. She wasn't an idiot but she had been one that night.

He stopped the car, she undid her seat belt. "Wait, before you go give me your number." He took out his phone.

"It's okay, you don't need it. I'll be okay. It's just a sprain."

"Please Miranda, give me your number." She had given him her phone number once before but he had never called.

"I said I'll be alright. I'm not your responsibility." He thought she sounded cold as though he had done something really bad.

"I know where you live," he said lightly. She frowned, she told him her number. He punched the numbers into his phone and then her phone rang. "That's me," he said, "you'll have my number."

"Okay," she wouldn't call him, she knew that.

"I've got one day left in Perth and then I go back to Sydney. I'll call you."

He won't, Miranda thought.

Jack got out of the car and handed her the crutches. He carried her beach bag up to the door. She fumbled for her keys. The door opened, it was Rose. "What the fuck!" She glared at Jack.

"It's alright Rose, it was an accident. I fell down some stairs. Jack took me to the hospital." She turned to Jack. "Thanks."

Rose was still glaring at him as though she just knew that he had pushed her down the steps. "I'll call you tomorrow," Jack said.

"What have you done," said Rose as she followed behind Miranda. Miranda flopped into an armchair. "I told you, I fell down the stairs. We were at the fish bar at Freo."

"Okay." Rose sat down. "You know I didn't know he was going to be at the beach, don't you? That was Sam's idea."

"Yes, I know."

Miranda told her what had happened. How Jack had told her he didn't remember some of their meeting.

Rose raised her eyebrows, "That's convenient."

"That's what I thought but he explained it and he's been worried he couldn't remember."

"Did you tell him?" said Rose.

"Yes," Miranda leant her head back and closed her eyes. She didn't want to talk about it, not tonight.

"You've got a lump on your head?" said Rose.

"Mmm, they checked me for concussion. I'm going to bed Rose. Can we talk in the morning? I want to hear all about you and Sam. Was that good?"

"He's not out of jail yet," Rose said.

Chapter Twenty-One

JACK

The following morning Jack tapped on Felicity's bedroom door. "You awake mum?" he said pushing open the door," I brought you tea."

Felicity pulled herself up to a sitting position and reached for her glasses from the side table.

"Did I wake you?" Jack said, handing Felicity the mug of tea.

"No, I was just lying here listening to the birds outside," she lied.

Jack lifted his head, "Funny how you only notice them when you listen for them. They are making a hell of a noise." He stopped smiling and drew his eyebrows together, "You okay?"

Felicity took a sip of the tea. "Yes, perfectly fine Jack, it's all going according to plan." She smiled over the top of her cup. She could see Jack was looking at her pillow and she knew he was seeing the distressing amount of hair she had lost overnight. She sat up higher in the bed and pulled an adjacent pillow behind her back.

"Jack it's just hair, it will grow back and who knows, might be curly."

He touched his own hair and then dropped his hand and rubbed at his chest.

Felicity knew what that gesture meant. It was something he had begun to do when he was six years old when the sleep walking started. She had made enquiries with the school to see if his teacher had noticed anything but his teacher had said Jack was a kind and cheerful boy and well liked and she hadn't seen any evidence of anything worrying Jack.

Felicity had spoken to her doctor who had asked if Jack was anxious about anything at school or home. She had said nothing at school and that Jack was doing really well at sport. He had been doing Auskick since he was five and got on well with the team. She didn't tell the doctor that Ross hardly ever attended any of the games and she was glad of it because when he did, he was short on praise. "So, everything okay at home too?" She had lied about that. She was sure Jack was too young to sense the tension between her and Ross. She was careful to shield Jack from the arguing.

The doctor suggested she take Jack to see a child counsellor. Ross was furious, "For fuck's sake there is nothing wrong with him. You should see a counsellor, it's all in your head. He's not seeing a counsellor. He'll grow out of it. Lock the bedroom door so he can't get out if you're worried about him sleep walking."

She blamed herself for Jack's anxiety. She should have done something about it, got him help, stood up to Ross. She should have left him, the endless what she should have done and didn't.

It was only when Ross had left that she got Jack to see a counsellor and she saw one herself. After years of therapy, she understood the power dynamics of her relationship with Ross and what it meant to be in a relationship with a coercive controlling partner.

When she had met Ross, she had liked that he took charge. He was an alpha male, a leader in the business world. He was going places, making money. He was going to look after her, keep her safe. It meant that he cared for her and even his possessive behaviours were, she thought, evidence of his love for her. She hadn't wanted a quiet, sensitive man, who avoided confrontation. She could have had one of those. Craig, her first boyfriend who she left for Ross. He had become an English teacher. She had seen him in the city with his wife and three daughters. The one big regret in her life.

Jack had seen the counsellor for six months, and then he had refused to go. He was alright, it was boring he would sooner be playing football. The counsellor told Felicity that she shouldn't force Jack. The counsellor had given Jack some strategies and suggested a couple of mindfulness apps to put on Jack's phone.

"I didn't hear you come in last night Jack, were you hanging out with Sam?"

"Sorry I should have sent you a text." He knew she worried about him. He felt bad, she had enough to worry about without him adding to it. "I was at the hospital. Not for me… that girl, Miranda."

"What?" Felicity tried to keep the alarm out of her voice. "What happened? Is she alright?"

"I took her to the hospital, she fell down some steps. Badly sprained ankle and hit her head. She's okay but won't be able to weight bear for couple of weeks."

Jack spoke quickly not looking at his mother. "Tell you about it later."

***

Felicity got up straight away and found Jack in the kitchen. He told her about meeting Sam at the beach and what had followed, how he had left the beach with Miranda and they had gone to Fremantle to eat.

"She filled in the blanks, you know the night of the party, and then when we were leaving, she fell down the steps."

"And you said she's okay?"

Jack nodded, "Yeh, quite a bad sprain and she hit her head... but no concussion."

"That's good and you said she filled in the blanks?" Felicity looked at Jack's back as he moved towards the fridge. He hadn't looked at her once since entering the kitchen. "Do you want to tell me?" she said.

Jack paused with his hand on the white cold refrigerator door. He could feel the life of it humming beneath his fingertips. He turned and looked at Felicity, and shook his head, he wasn't going to tell her. Jack turned away from the blank look on his mother's face. He opened the fridge.

He knew she deserved an explanation but it wasn't something he could bring himself to tell her. "It's okay mum. I've stopped drinking. I'm sorry but you don't have to worry about me." He pulled out a stool from under the bench and sat down. "I was supposed to meet Miranda when I got back from footie camp, a date I guess." He shrugged, "I didn't remember and then she came looking for me. That's why she waited for me at school."

"Is that all?" said Felicity. She knew there was more, there had to be. She knew not to pressure him.

"Yeh," said Jack turning away to the fridge and taking out a carton of orange juice, "But I don't want to think of how I brushed her off." *And left her to deal with it on her own.* He looked for a glass in the cupboard. "She said I'd been her hero at school." He gave a mocking laugh "Yeh a hero, that's me."

"Is she angry at you Jack?"

Jack shook his head, "No I think it's more disappointment. I took her number. I'll just make sure she's alright. It probably wouldn't have happened if I hadn't wanted to sit somewhere where I couldn't be recognised - in the darkest part of the Harbour."

Felicity left him at the kitchen table and went out to the front garden to collect the paper. She tore off the plastic covering and spread the paper out on the table and smoothed out the front page. She turned the page over before it registered. On the front page was a picture of Jack carrying a young woman. She stared at the picture. She guessed it was Miranda, you couldn't see her face, her head was pressed into Jack's neck. Jack looked grim, he wasn't smiling. The headline said, 'Jack Charles rescuing a damsel in distress.'

"You have to see this." She slid the paper across to Jack.

"Fuck," said Jack.

There were more photos inside the paper, someone had taken a photo of Miranda leaving the hospital on crutches. The paper wondered if she was Jack's love interest. It made him want to puke.

"What a load of shit," he read that he'd been seen talking with the unidentified girl in the fish bar at Fremantle Harbour.

Jack closed the paper and rolled it up. "I'm going to see her. Can I borrow your car?"

Chapter Twenty-Two

MIRANDA

Miranda hadn't read the paper. They didn't get it delivered. She got all her news from her phone. Rose answered the door, Miranda was still learning how to use the crutches.

Rose thought he looked angry as though he was about to pick a fight. "I've come to see Miranda," he didn't ask if he could see her, or if she was in.

"I'll see if she's taking callers," said Rose sarcastically. Jack frowned. "She's in, isn't she?" He held the rolled newspaper in his hand. "I've got to talk to her about this," he opened the front page and held it out.

Rose peered at the paper as though she needed glasses. "Is that you and Miranda," Rose said incredulously, "Why are you on the front page of the paper?" She read the headline, "Hero, huh?" Jack felt his face go red. He was hearing her say something else.

Rose held the door open, "Come in." She indicated the lounge room, "Wait in there."

Miranda heard his voice, she was in the laundry putting her washing in the washing machine. "I told you I'd do that," hissed Rose. "He's in the lounge room. You're in the paper."

"He's here? I'm in the paper?" She struggled to get the crutch under her arm. It was hard to walk without knocking into the furniture. He stood up when she came into the room. He took the crutches and helped her sit down.

"How's the ankle?" he said. He could see the lump on her forehead, it was purple and yellow.

"It's good, I've been ricing it this morning."

He looked at the support bandage around her ankle critically as though he was some kind of expert. He held out the paper, "I wanted to talk to you before you saw this."

"Oh no. Is that you? It is, and you're carrying me." She squeezed her eyes shut and then opened them again. "You can't see my face," she said.

He shook his head, "Sorry." He opened the paper to page three and the photo of Miranda walking on crutches out of the hospital. There were two photos, one of her concentrating, not looking at anything but where she was putting the crutches and a photo of Jack looking at her. He had his arm around her and the expression on his face the journalist had called, 'tender concern.' Miranda felt her face go warm.

"How can they do this, make up this- "

"-shit," he said. "They do it all the time. Everyone with a mobile phone is a paparazzi. These and more of them will be on social media."

"I won't look," said Miranda. She studied his face, she could see the small pulse in his cheek, the bleak lost look in his eyes. She gave him a small smile, she could see he was looking anxious.

"It doesn't matter," she said.

He saw the smile, it was a peace offering, it wasn't about the photos or the shit that had been written she was forgiving him really saying it was okay.

He nodded, "Okay," he stood up, "I just wanted to be here when you saw the photos. I'm flying back to Sydney tomorrow. Stay there," he saw her struggling to stand up. She looked up at him, her hair still tousled, her small heart shaped face lost in the tangle of her hair. She wasn't looking scared, or ashamed, or her blue eyes wide with something like fear. She was looking at him telling him it was okay, that she didn't think he was a bastard. He felt grateful for that.

He felt the last thread of tension evaporate, "Okay," he smiled. He stopped at the door, he didn't look at her when he said, "I'll stay in touch." He didn't ask permission, he was going to do it. "Miranda," he added.

"Well, what did he say?" Rose barely waited until Jack had shut the front door before she came running into the room.

"Nothing really. He just wanted to show me the paper himself."

"Is that it?"

"Yep. He feels responsible for that and this," she held her foot up. And the other thing she thought. She'd seen the look on his face when she'd told him. As though he'd heard something truly terrible.

"He's not a bad person." She thought that was true. She didn't want him 'staying in touch' out of some idea that she was his responsibility. She wasn't the Bin Girl. She hoped he wouldn't stay in touch but that was a lie. She knew that the Bin Girl hadn't let the idea of Jack Charles her hero leave her.

A week later and she was back at work. Everyone at work had seen the photos of her and Jack. Ewan looked at her as though she had cheated on him, he barely spoke to her for the first hour, turning his back on her when she went into the kitchen until one of the kitchen hands said, "You kept that a secret, when's the wedding?"

Ewan glanced up at her from the pan he was furiously shaking on the kitchen stove. He didn't say anything, he sucked in his cheeks. He didn't like to be made a fool of. He had been chasing her for weeks, the bitch, she had strung him along. He had worked it all out the week she had been away. They had some kind of lover's quarrel. She had used him when she had got on his bike. He banged the pan hard on the stove. Miranda started back and gave a small gasp. Ewan thrust his chin at her and twisted his mouth into an ugly grimace. Miranda turned away and pressed her trembling lips together.

Roger was all formality when he handed her the dessert menus. He didn't mention Jack Charles, that wasn't his style. He had worked it out too. He remembered how she had run from the table, said she was feeling sick. The girl with the blonde hair that Jack Charles had brought with him to the restaurant. He was playing some kind of game with Miranda. He felt sorry for her. That was a low game he thought. She was a dark horse, hadn't told anyone that Jack Charles was her boyfriend, but he approved of that. Ewan wasn't going to like it. That boy was too full of himself, thought he was a regular Don Juan the way he was working his way through the girls.

Miranda's ankle twinged a bit but it was okay. She was careful where she stepped. Jack had texted her every day, always the same message, "How's the ankle?" She had texted back on the third day that it was 100%. He sent back 'bull shit' 50% possibly, she texted back a smiley face.

It was a few days later when Ewan spoke to her, he waited until she was outside the restaurant on the verandah. She had been looking at her phone. She put it in her pocket when she saw Ewan. He saw her smiling. "Ya boyfriend ay, the famous football player, is it?"

She held the phone tightly in her pocket. He wasn't her boyfriend, he wasn't even a friend really, he was someone she barely knew. She didn't have to explain herself to anyone. She gave him a blank look. "Full house tonight," she said. "You'll be busy." She went to walk past him but he stepped into her path, his hands on his hips.

He wasn't the guy you could fob off like that. She owed him an explanation and he was going to make her squirm. "I said the guy you were talking to when you asked me for a lift, the football player."

Miranda straightened her shoulders, he had an ugly look, it transformed his face. She studied it as though she wasn't sure what she was looking at. He was angry at her. He had made that obvious from the moment she had stepped into the kitchen.

He's looking at me as though I broke up with him. Miranda thought she should tell Ewan that Jack Charles wasn't her boyfriend but it was none of his business. A ride on the back of his bike didn't give him some ownership rights over her. And she hadn't kissed him back!

She had already tried telling some of the waitresses that Jack was an old school friend and had brushed off the photos but they had seen the way he was looking at her in that one photo with his arm around her. She had frowned and shaken her head, 'photoshopped' she said.

"Can't fool us. You two are tight. What does he look like with no clothes on?"

"Shut up, you can't ask her that. He's got a six pack, hasn't he? That's not photo shopped!"

"Have you seen the ad he did for some underwear product Victa. His abs are real. I searched for him on the internet. Hundreds of photos."

Miranda hadn't searched the internet, she wasn't going to

do that. His face had started to haunt her, she could feel herself slipping back into that old Miranda who lived the fantasy
life with Jack Charles in her head. She wasn't going to do that
again, she'd promised herself that.

"Excuse me Ewan I have to get back to work," Miranda
said. She didn't like the way Ewan was refusing to move,
blocking her way back into the restaurant.

He lifted his chin at her, "Ya should have told me," he
said accusingly.

Miranda frowned at him, she was trying to buy some time
before she answered. There was menace about Ewan, a bristling anger that made her afraid. If she said she was sorry
would that be the right answer and make everything okay?
She knew it would never be okay unless she gave him what
she wanted. *I'm not my mother, I'm not my mother.* She said nothing, her vision narrowed as she began to retreat inside
herself, finding the safe place.

"What ya looking at?" His voice stopped her, it was nasty
and demanding. She jerked her head as though she had just
awoken. She pressed her lips together and felt her heart beating hard in her chest.

He prodded her shoulder with one finger, he put weight
behind it. She had to take a step back to keep her balance.

"Ya should have told me," he said again and then stepped
aside and let her pass. She wanted to say something, retaliate
but she had sensed the potential in Ewan to hurt her, the
threat behind the push with one finger to her shoulder. It
said you're weak and vulnerable and I can easily do so much
more. She needed to be careful to manage his anger. She
knew how to do that, she had lots of practice with anger, all
those times when her mother or her boyfriend had descended into a methamphetamine rage. You hid and if there

was nowhere to hide you hid inside yourself. You found the empty quiet place and closed your eyes so they couldn't see the fear. You kept your head down, stayed still, so still, as though you weren't even there.

Roger was walking away from the wall of windows at the front of the restaurant that gave a view of the verandah. He hadn't had a clear view. Ewan had blocked Miranda but he had seen her stumble back as though she had been pushed. He frowned, he wasn't sure what he had seen. There was no need for him to do anything. If she complained then that was a different matter. He didn't look at Miranda, he walked back to the front of the restaurant and stood behind the reception desk. He adjusted the large vase of native flowers a centimetre to the left and did the same with the glass bowl of blue wrapped mints.

He rehearsed in his mind what he would say to Ewan, if he thought it was necessary, and it wasn't yet. But if it was necessary, he would keep it light and casual, nothing too serious. He would tell him that he was the manager in charge of the staff, he had to make sure everything was running smoothly, no issues amongst the staff. 'It's a dangerous time to be a man in the 'Me too' movement you couldn't even say 'boo' to a woman.' Yes, that's how he'd handle it, if he had to. But no, it hadn't come to that.

After the incident on the verandah Miranda tried to avoid being alone with Ewan. It had only been a prod in the shoulder but it meant he had no boundaries. It had been more than a touch, she had felt the pressure of his finger. One finger and she had stumbled back. She knew what he was capable of.

After that she was careful never to be on her own with him. There were always a few kitchen staff in the kitchen so she never had to worry that he would say something but after work she was careful to make sure she left before he did.

Ewan kept up the hostility all that week, slamming dishes down when she was around. Making comments under his breath and then a week later a new waitress, Michelle started working at the restaurant. She was nineteen, blonde and pretty and studying Early Childhood at Edith Cowan University.

Roger asked Miranda to show Michelle around the restaurant and introduce her to the rest of the wait and kitchen staff. Ewan was in the kitchen swearing in his thick Scottish accent when Miranda pushed open the kitchen door and paused, she raised her eyebrows at Michelle. She knew Ewan was in a foul mood. He had been in a foul mood since the weekend when he had read something in the paper about Jack Charles on the trade list hoping to get a transfer to Perth and to play for the Eagles.

He made a point about saying something to Miranda, "See your boyfriend's coming back to Perth. You won't have to work as a waitress then will you."

It wasn't a question and the undisguised contempt in his voice was laced with anger. But as usual no one else heard him. He was careful to keep his constant harassment hidden from the head chef or Roger.

Rose wanted Miranda to make a complaint to Roger but what was the point. They were heading into the summer season and chefs were hard to come by. Ewan knew he was on safe ground. "He would have to do something pretty bad to be fired," Miranda said.

Miranda pretended she hadn't heard Ewan's comment. It was news to her that Jack Charles might be returning to Perth. It made her unsettled as though it was something she was going to have to deal with. She had tried hard not to go back to the fantasy of Jack the hero. She needed to focus on her studies. She wasn't going to think about *Jack Charles, Jack Charles, Jack Charles.* It was an ear worm driving her crazy.

"So this is the kitchen," Miranda said to Michelle in a voice loud enough for the kitchen staff to look her way. Even Ewan glanced away from the pan on the stove and looked over his shoulder.

He had been in a foul mood but it was miraculously disappearing as he locked eyes on Michelle. Miranda felt the tension disappear from her body. It was going to be okay, she didn't have to find another job. Ewan would leave her alone.

But the reprieve didn't last long, Michelle had a boyfriend and he showed up on Michelle's second shift and made sure Ewan saw him and the bullying started up again.

"What's the dick been doing?" said Rose at the end of Miranda's last shift. One look at Miranda's face and she knew it hadn't stopped.

"Oh, nothing really." She didn't want to tell Rose that Ewan was calling her Mrs Charles at every opportunity and even the kitchen staff thought he was being funny but Miranda knew differently. He might smile with his mouth but his eyes said something else.

"No seriously Miranda, tell me what has he done? Can you get a restraining order, or something?"

"Mm not sure how that would work with us both working in the restaurant."

"He would have to leave," said Rose.

"No, I think I would," said Miranda, "and that's what I'll do if it gets worse. Don't worry about me."

Chapter Twenty-Three

JACK

Jack was out having dinner with Ryley when he took the call from his agent Rick Southern. It was the call he had been waiting for.

"Good news Jack, you're going home and you'll be playing for the Eagles. The Swans didn't want to let you go, you know that but they have traded you on compassionate grounds. Swans are going to take Seth Andrews, he wants to get back to Sydney, his family are here and he's got young kids. His wife needs the support of her family. So, it works out well for both of you."

Jack punched the air, he was going to play for the Eagles, this had been his dream, to play for his home team. "Fantastic Rick just great. Thanks." He would be back in Perth and he could support Felicity.

"Don't start packing yet, and remember the away game you've got with the Eagles."

"Yeh, I know that. I'm playing for the Swans until my contract's over. I don't think I need a reminder." He sounded annoyed, what did Rick think? There was no question that he wouldn't play his best he wasn't a dick.

"No, I know that. Listen, you heard of Prada. They want a young sportsman for some spread in Vogue. They want you. They're sending over the contract."

Jack groaned, he hated dressing up and posing, even if he

did get to keep the clothes. It was worse than anything, he would sooner sit in a dentist chair. "Rick. No!"

"Raising your profile Jack, you know that the sponsors are where the big money is. And wait for it, the shoot is in Spain. Alhambra."

"Alhambra?" repeated Jack.

"Yeh it's…" Rick paused and looked at the computer screen in front of him. "Yeh, palace and fortress of the Moorish monarch of Granada."

"When?" He was planning on doing nothing before the season started and if he was back in Perth that meant the beach.

"It's just 8 days at the beginning of your break. You get to see the Alhambra and the money's great." He mentioned a sum that didn't impress Jack. How much money did he need to be okay? He wasn't Ross Charles. No amount of money was ever enough for him.

"I hear you."

"Okay, good … and thanks Rick."

He grinned at Ryley. "You heard? It's done. Being traded for Seth Andrews."

"That's fucking awesome." He punched Jack on the arm. He had moved out of the apartment they shared and was now living with Nina.

Jack hadn't wanted to share with anyone after Ryley had left, he thought it was a bit of a lottery. He had been lucky that Ryley had been so easy going.

"The last game for the Swans and you'll be playing the Eagles. You can't win either way," said Ryley.

Jack remembered the last game he had played against the Eagles. That had gone badly. He just prayed he could do better. He didn't want to come into the team with a bad last game.

Chapter Twenty-Four

MIRANDA

It had been six weeks since she'd fallen down the steps when Jack called. She hadn't expected him to call her or contact her again since she had sent back the last text that said, '100%,' she had added 'good luck with your life.' He didn't owe her anything. She knew he had felt bad about the termination but it was all history now and he was a reminder of that time she wanted to forget.

It had been a bad time, she'd made light of it to Rose, pretended it meant nothing. But after she had woken up from the twilight sleep, she had never cried so much and she didn't know why. She wasn't religious, she didn't think it was wrong. She got over it the way she had got over Jack Charles.

He was nervous when he made the call. He had read the finality in her last text. He couldn't stop thinking about her, little snapshots of her were in his mind and they kept popping into his thoughts. He kept hearing the quiet sadness in her voice saying, "I had a termination." He felt gutted every time. He told himself he wasn't phoning her out of guilt. He liked her, she was smart, smarter than he was but she didn't parade it. She was living on a scholarship and working six nights a week at a restaurant.

He had money now, lots of it. His agent had made him get a financial advisor when he started to get the sponsors.

The last eighteen months he had earnt enough money to buy a house. He was going to do that when he got back to Perth.

Miranda was on the bus when she felt the phone in her pocket vibrate. She hated talking on the bus or in public places. It was Jack. She hesitated for a second, should she ignore the call? Miranda bit at her lip. She didn't want there to be any bad feeling between them. She didn't think of him badly. She just didn't want to be that girl he felt guilty about, like he had when she was at school. The bus was pulling up to her stop.

She spoke quickly, "Hi."

"Hi," he said and then had to clear his throat, "how you going?"

"Good. I'm just getting off the bus, I start work in the restaurant in ten minutes."

"Okay, can you talk for a few minutes?"

She got off the bus and watched it pull away. "Sure," she said as she crossed the road and walked towards the restaurant. He started to talk as she walked around the back of the restaurant and down to the water. She was listening but the words weren't really registering they were getting confused with her moving across the grass, the boats sailing across the water, and getting away from the great glass window of the restaurant. She hid behind a tree and pressed the phone to her ear. He had stopped talking. She didn't know what to say.

The silence stretched down to the river and back, "Is that a no then," said Jack. He knew he shouldn't have asked her. He hardly knew her really. He was an idiot, he didn't owe her anything. He should let her get on with her life.

"Um, sorry. I thought you were telling me something about an award you were getting."

Jack cursed under his breath, he didn't want to have to repeat it all over again, he took a breath, "I'm not getting an award, forget it, it was just a thought." Jack leant his head against the mirror in his bathroom, he was an idiot. He didn't have to take a partner.

"Forget it, okay, it was just an idea."

"Sorry. I didn't hear." But she had. He had asked her to go with him to an award ceremony. She didn't know what to say, but she knew she didn't want to go anywhere with Jack Charles.

He thought he could hear Miranda breathing on the other end of the phone. "Forget it," he said again, "It's just…It's boring as hell and, it's okay, forget it." *Stop fucking repeating yourself.*

He took a breath, "Perhaps we can catch up when I'm back. I'm staying for the awards in Melbourne this weekend and then I'm back in Perth next week, one more game with the Swans and then I'm playing for the Eagles next season." He waited for her response and added, "It's a trade from the Swans."

"Trade?" Miranda furrowed her brow.

"Yeh, they swap me for a player who wants to go back to Melbourne," said Jack.

Oh, I see, I guess your parents will be pleased." She kicked at the grass with her toe.

"Yeh, no, Mum is. They're divorced. He lives in New York. Well, he did, and now he's moving back to Perth."

"Oh," said Miranda. He didn't sound happy about it… She could see the time on her phone, she was going to be late. "Sorry, I'm at work. I've got to go," she said.

"Yeh, I'll call you when I'm back in Perth okay bye." He was speaking fast, he felt awkward for calling her.

"Bye Jack," Miranda turned her phone off and put it in her pocket. She jumped back and let out a cry as Ewan stepped from the other side of the tree.

"Bye Jack," he said in a sing song voice. He put his arm on the tree trunk and blocked her path. Miranda looked towards the restaurant, she couldn't see anyone, the lights weren't on yet.

She felt her face go hot, Ewan brought his face close to hers, "Ya like to tease don't you Miranda."

She swallowed. She could feel the anger flare up in her, *one ride on the back of your bike doesn't give you permission to talk to me like this.* She didn't move, she stared at the yellow stain on his chef jacket. It looked like a small animal, a dog, a poodle. She was blocking out everything he was saying.

"Ya used me to make ya famous football boyfriend, jealous." He leant in again his face an ugly scowl, "and I don't like to be used." He almost spat the words at her. He waited for her reaction, he leant his face closer, "Did y'fuckin hear what I said. I don't like to be used."

She pulled her eyes away from his jacket. She heard what he said. She licked her lips, "Well I'm sorry if it looked like that." She was going to say, he's not my boyfriend but something stopped her. She was afraid of Ewan, she felt as though she was in a snake pit and any wrong move was going to be lethal. She tried to look past him but he blocked her vision. She looked at the top button on his chef's jacket and saw how red his neck was. She couldn't understand the anger that was vibrating between them. She swallowed, her heart seemed to speed up as she remembered another man like Ewan, holding her mother around the throat pushing her backwards into the wall and then holding her there while he spat in her face. She had run from the room looking for a place to hide. When she heard the front door slam, she had crept out from under the bed and found her mother holding a wet cloth to her blackening eye.

That hadn't been the first time, she had lost count of the boyfriends and the beatings she had either heard or witnessed. *You're not your mother, you're not your mother.* She had to get away she could feel her heart beginning to race. She took a breath counting slowly in her head, one, two, three, four, five. She looked up into his half-closed eyes. *Don't show your fear.*

"I'm sorry Ewan if I gave you that impression. That wasn't my intention." She waved her hand and looked past Ewan, "Coming Roger," she called. Ewan didn't turn around he dropped his arm and Miranda ran past him. Her heart was beating hard in her chest. Roger hadn't been on the verandah looking for her. He had been watching Ewan from inside the restaurant wondering what he was doing out on the fore-shore leaning against a tree when he should have been in the kitchen. His shift started an hour before the wait staff.

When Miranda got back to the restaurant, she called Rose and asked her to pick her up from work when her shift finished. She said she would tell her why when she saw her. She had a bad feeling about Ewan. She shouldn't have gone on his bike and he'd kissed her, and she hadn't stopped him, that wasn't her fault, *but she hadn't kissed him back.* She couldn't concentrate. She had forgotten all about the phone call with Jack.

Miranda fell back on the sofa, she was tired and she wanted to go to bed but Rose wanted to talk.

"You should go to the police," said Rose.

"No, he hasn't done anything. He hasn't threatened me or hit me."

"What about stalking?"

Miranda raised her eyebrows, "We work at the same place."

"You need to get yourself a boyfriend."

Miranda looked away, and said "Uh huh."

"I'm serious. You've never had a boyfriend and you're twenty."

"I said Uh huh. Don't want one, don't need one. And, I'll remind you that a month ago you said you were over the opposite sex." Miranda lay back on the sofa and stretched her feet out alongside Rose.

"True," said Rose. "I did mean it at the time," Rose dug her feet into Miranda's ribs. "Sam said Jack has got a trade to Perth, he'll be here in a week… for good."

"Uh huh," said Miranda.

"What's with the Uh huh," said Rose.

"He called me today and told me."

"What!" Rose sat up, "and you never told me that. You didn't say who you were talking to when Ewan was listening."

Miranda pulled her hair back from her face. "I'm sorry. I guess I just felt… I don't know it feels weird. As though he's doing it out of some guilt that he… you know wasn't there. It makes me feel uncomfortable to even talk about it."

Rose didn't know if she was right. Sam had never mentioned him or really talked about him. It was an off-limits subject.

"You don't think it's possible that he really likes you. Because that would really be weird seeing what a troll you are!" Rose tapped her foot on Miranda's thigh.

"Rose, really." She sat up, "It's not about liking me, it's about making himself feel better about what happened and I think he wants to show me the high life or something. Take pity on that girl back at primary school. Rose, I get to make choices about my life and that includes who I want to like and I don't like him that way, I don't even know him." The boy she had thought he was had been the fantasy in her head. She had held onto that idea of who he was for so long, some perfect hero.

"Anyway, I'm concentrating on my studies, that's the most important thing in my life right now, not getting a boyfriend and," Miranda paused at the door, "when I do get one, you Rose Banks will be the first to know."

"You know he's playing tomorrow," Rose shouted as the door shut.

Miranda had never followed football, she had never been any good at sports and she had never bothered to get interested in the national game.

Chapter Twenty-Five

JACK

Jack got the message, he wasn't going to contact Miranda again. He felt relieved, he had not stopped thinking about her since he had got back to Sydney. It was a distraction he didn't want. He remembered back at primary school the few times she had been absent and he had worried about her but at the same time he was glad he didn't have to see her and feel responsible for her. Didn't have to listen to what the other kids said about her and pretend not to hear them. He scrolled through his contacts and deleted Miranda's name.

He was flying back to Perth with the team on Monday for a fund-raising game against the Eagles. Both teams were playing to raise money for the bush fires that had devastated both States. It was his last game with the Swans.

He rubbed his hand across his face, the stubble itched, he didn't see himself ever growing a beard. "Prada mate, they want the assassin look," said Rick. "God in my day we called that the hobo look. You'd better start growing it and don't get your hair cut. They want it girly.

"Very funny Rick."

Jack was due to fly out to Spain two days after the game with the Eagles. He had packed up the few possessions he had acquired, sold his car and his bags were packed. He was going to be sorry to leave the Swans, they had been a great team to play for but he needed to get home for his mum and playing for the Eagles, a home team, was a dream he had when he first started playing football at primary school.

He had left the apartment a week ago and was staying at a hotel close to the Swans' training ground. He took one last look around the room and headed downstairs for the Uber to the clubhouse and the coach for the plane to Perth.

***

He shouldn't be feeling this nervous he told himself. *For fuck's sake. It's a fund-raising game.* The Swans had lost to the Eagles the last time they had played. Both teams were fielding their best players. The Swans had something to prove.

Jack bounced up and down on his toes trying to relax his muscles. He bent his legs one after the other, catching his ankle and pulling it up until he felt the stretch in his quads. He touched the sweat band he'd had to wear to keep his hair out of his eyes. It was itching already and the game hadn't started. *Fuck Prada.*

Jack looked either side of him, he could see the Swans forwards jostling with the Eagles defenders as though the game had already started.

Jordan Saunders, the Full Back for the Eagles was already crowding Jack, leaning against him. Showing just how close he was going to stick to him.

Jack knew Saunders' reputation, he played fair but he played hard. He made the term 'contact sport' mean something. He remembered the last game he played with the Eagles, the ball he kicked wide of goal, a sitter of a goal.

Jordan was the tallest player in the Eagles side. He could have been the Ruck, the one to jump up and tap the ball away but he had proved himself in defence as a brick wall to get past. Jordan said something but the siren went and the words were lost in the noise.

Jack felt the push and he dug his heels into the ground and pushed back against Jordan as he watched the ref slam the ball down on the ground.

Jack saw the Eagles' Ruck jump high into the air and tap the ball but the Swans' Ruck got his fingers to the ball first and punted it to Ryley who was moving like a whippet, bouncing the ball and looking for Jack but he could see Saunders one step behind Jack. Jenks, a Swans player, was in the forward zone and running into a space down the side of the field. Jack feinted to the left and then spinning on his heel he took off. Ryley kicked it high and Jenks was there climbing high on thin air to take the mark. Jenks had taken the mark on the side line, the angle steep, he would have to bend the ball. Jenks looked as though he was going to try for goal, but at the last moment he kicked it high into the air anticipating that a forward would read the play. Jack had already begun his run the moment the ball left Jenks' boot. Three Eagles defenders moved with him. Jordan was practically breathing down his neck. Jack sped up and then ran back as the ball spun high overhead. Jack climbed high, the ball was between his hands, he landed and in one twist of his body he turned and kicked a perfect goal through the white posts. The roar of boos drowned out any cheers.

At three quarter time the Swans were eight points down to the Eagles. Every player on the field looked as though they had run a marathon. Not one player was going to treat this game as just a fund-raising game. Winning mattered as though they were playing in the Grand Finals.

Grisby gathered the team around, sweat was beading his forehead and his face was red as if he had been on the field running himself into the ground. "Okay just eight points, that's two goals and we're home and we showed them we are the better team." Mike was nodding his head, "You can do it, okay." Mike knew enough about sports psychology to know that he had to ignore the missed goals and there had been many on both sides. He had to motivate them to drag their aching bodies back on the field for the last minutes and win the game.

Grisby started to run through players one by one, picking out some piece of play to praise. "Jeff great placement, Banksie beautiful mark of the year material, and the conversion." He continued naming all the players until the siren went and he turned to Jack.

"Two great goals, showed the Eagles why they did the trade for you. Do us proud."

Afterwards Jack thought it was the best game he had played all season. Maybe he had something to prove to the crowd who were booing him every time he touched the ball. Or maybe he wanted to show the Swans that right up until the final siren, he was a Swans player.

"Three goals Charlie. A great way to end your time with the Swans. You did us proud." Grisby was smiling as he usually did after a win. Every face was turned towards Jack and water bottles held high in acknowledgment. He was glad the Swans had won, a 4-point victory. It had been a nail biter of a game.

Despite the elation Jack felt at the prospect of playing for the Eagles, he felt sad to be leaving the Swans. He had learnt a lot playing for them, he had made some good mates and he was sorry to say goodbye, but nothing was going to be better than playing for the Eagles. The next time they played, he would be wearing the blue and gold of the Eagles, and he would be doing his best to make sure the Swans lost.

Chapter Twenty-Six

MIRANDA

Miranda sat on the edge of the bed and watched while Rose packed her suitcase. Rose was going home to her family for a week and she was worried about leaving Miranda in the house on her own.

Miranda sighed and laid back on the bed and closed her eyes, she wished Rose wasn't leaving but she would never tell her that. Rose frowned, Miranda looked tired, she thought she could detect dark circles beneath her eyes.

"What's up Milly, the dickwad getting to you?"

Miranda opened her eyes, "I think I'm going to have to find another job. He just isn't letting up and now that it's the term break and the restaurant has offered me full time work, I'll have to put up with him every day," said Miranda

"That's it, you're coming with us. You can take a week off work, drive up with us. You know everyone would love to see you."

Miranda pushed herself off the bed. "It's not that bad. I can manage, you know I would love to see everyone but …" She let her voice trail off.

Rose put her hands on her hips, "Tell me this is not about money," Rose sounded fierce. They had argued frequently about Miranda's refusal to live rent free in the townhouse. Miranda was determined to pay her way. That wasn't the only reason Miranda wasn't going. She knew that Sam was seeing

Rose's parents for the first time since they had got back together and she thought it was better if they did that without her around.

"I've promised to tutor three of my regulars during the break, I can't let them down." It wasn't a complete lie she had told them she would think about it.

Miranda was doing an 8 hour shift at the restaurant, it was the usual busy Saturday, she had no time to worry about Ewan and he was busy in the kitchen, his mood edgy and nasty and she made sure she had the minimum interaction with him. But when he produced the wrong dessert, she had been forced to speak to him. He blamed her for the mistake and swore at her under his breath, "Fuckin bitch."

The Chef heard him and swung around from the stove, "What did you say?" he said, his face glistening from the heat of the ovens.

"Nothing chef, talkin to meself." Ewan didn't turn around to look at the chef. He knew the Chef was not like the chefs he was used to working under. They wouldn't have cared what he called a waitress."

"Here ya are Miranda," he took a prepared dessert from the row in front of him, "sorry about that." Nothing about his face said sorry, it read hatred. "Fuckin bitch," he mouthed at Miranda as she took the plate from his outstretched hand.

As the day progressed, Miranda became more and more apprehensive when she entered the kitchen. Ewan seemed to be waiting for her, ready for the game he was playing, enjoying making her uncomfortable.

Roger knew something was going on between Ewan and Miranda. He wasn't a fool, he had been managing the front of house for 16 years, he wasn't new to kitchen relationships.

They always ended badly. The atmosphere in the kitchen was tense enough when the restaurant was operating on full capacity. He didn't need more tension. Roger had seen Ewan staring at Miranda as though he would like to run her over with his bike. Roger thought he knew what that was about. Ewan couldn't compete with Jack Charles. He smiled to himself as he checked his watch and then walked over to the restaurant doors and unlocked them. He didn't like Ewan, he was a cocky bag of tripe. He wouldn't have hired him if it had been up to him but he had no say in the hiring of the kitchen staff that was the head chef's domain.

Roger ran his eye down the reservation list. He frowned, it was a Saturday the busiest day for the restaurant and it was only three quarters full. It was the weather; it had been raining all day and the forecast was for high winds. Just the kind of weather that kept the diners at home.

He checked his phone and swore. Two of the waitresses had texted him to say they were sick. *Liars, bloody lazy liars*, and at the last minute. He would have to share the extra tables around. Miranda would have to be on her toes.

He found Miranda in the staff room putting on her uniform, he could always count on her to be on time. He stared at his watch as two of the other wait staff, Chloe and Sally entered the room.

"Hi Roger," they chorused ignoring the look he gave them.

"Sarah and Lucy have called in sick. I've shared out the extra tables. It's on the board." He didn't wait to hear their protests. In his day you got on with it, this generation had it easy.

"Fuck that," groaned Chloe, her voice loud enough to follow Roger down the corridor to the restaurant.

"Language, language," Roger muttered pulling down his jacket sleeves and straightening his tie.

Miranda studied the board, noting the tables she had been given. This wasn't the first time it had happened. It meant working faster and a little pressure on the diners to place their orders.

"Right, on your toes then…" Roger said to the three girls as they walked past him and into the dining area. Their job was to set the tables and they had fifteen minutes to do it before the first diners arrived.

"Fuck this," said Chloe collecting the silverware from the trays. "I've got three extra tables."

Miranda gave Chloe a warning look, she could see Roger standing at the reception desk, and the pursed lips and the furrowed brow were telegraphing that he had heard Chloe and he didn't approve.

Chloe was new to the restaurant and she had made it pretty obvious that she was only staying until she found another job. Ewan soon made Chloe the focus of his attention. Pointedly ignoring Miranda every time she came into the kitchen and trying to give her the wrong order again, for the second time, but Miranda saw the mistake straight away. She was good at keeping the orders in her head.

"That's not my order," she said, that's Chloe's table. "Mine's the fish and the fillet."

"It's the order you took," Ewan said.

Miranda said nothing. Chef had heard, he stepped over bringing his head close to Ewan's head.

"She doesn't make mistakes. Fix it."

When Chef moved away Chloe whispered in her ear, "That was a bitch thing to do. Ewan's really nice and Chef's a bully.

Miranda ignored her, she didn't want to get into more arguments by defending herself.

***

The evening hadn't turned out to be a night of rushing from table to table as the weather forecast of rain turned into a storm with the sky turning black and rain battering the restaurant windows, the wind roaring relentlessly. More than half the bookings for the restaurant were cancelled. Roger deleted each one without emotion, with luck they would all be out of the restaurant early, he knew how to get the stragglers out.

Miranda took the dessert dishes away from the last table. A couple who had braved the weather and arrived late in the evening appeared oblivious to the fact that they were the last in the restaurant and keeping the staff from leaving.

Miranda swiped at the curl that routinely refused to stay behind her ear. It was nine-thirty she could be home before ten. She was glad she had borrowed Rose's car as there was no shelter at the bus stop.

She backed into the kitchen carrying the empty dishes and placed them on the stainless-steel bench. Gerry, one of the kitchen hands snatched them up and scraped the last of the chocolate cake into the bin under the bench.

"We done?" he said as he placed the plates into the dishwasher.

"Yeh, that's the last," said Miranda.

"Chef's gone," said Gerry. Miranda knew that the Chef had a new baby and had left early when he saw the numbers were down. He had told Roger that he was leaving Ewan in charge once the bulk of the main meals had been served.

Ewan was wiping at a bench, his back to Miranda. Miranda glanced up and saw Ewan's body freeze as though he was waiting for something to happen.

Miranda felt a sudden pressure in her chest. "Yes, the last couple now, just waiting for them to finish their coffee. Roger is doing his thing."

Roger's 'thing' was hovering until they got the message that he had a life too and wanted to get home.

"You can go Gerry. I'll finish up," said Ewan without turning his head.

"Great," said Gerry taking off his apron and grinning at Miranda. "I'm off. Hey, I'm going to watch the replay of the game. Your guy, Charlie, did well for the Swans, but next season he'll be wearing the blue and gold and kicking goals for the Eagles!" He thrust a clenched fist in the air to make his point.

Miranda looked blank, she didn't know what the right response was.

"Charlie, your boyfriend," said Gerry, his eyebrows shooting up," kicked three goals for the Swans."

Charlie, Jack Charles? Miranda frowned.

Gerry misread the frown, why couldn't he mention her boyfriend. He didn't want his autograph or anything.

"He's..." Miranda thought she saw Ewan's shoulders stiffen. *Not my boyfriend,* but instead she smiled, "He's good," she said, her face felt hot. She had made Gerry think Jack Charles was her boyfriend and it was a lie. She would tell him the truth later. But not yet.

She glanced across the room at Ewan, he held his body still as though he had made himself into a piece of the kitchen equipment. She wanted to run and get as far away from him as she could.

"Ok see you Monday," said Gerry moving towards the door. Miranda was ahead of him, untying her apron as Ewan began to turn around.

The last two diners were leaving the restaurant and Roger was standing by the front door ready to lock it behind them. There were coffee cups on the table. Roger never helped out that way. She picked them up and took them into the kitchen – it was empty. Ewan's chef's apron was on the bench where he had thrown it. Chef wouldn't like that she thought. No dirty linen was to be left in the kitchen.

Miranda took off her apron as she walked into the staff room. She wanted to get home, curl up and relax, then she remembered Gerry saying he was going to watch the replay of the game. She had never watched football. She didn't even know the rules.

She grabbed her bag from her locker and headed out to the car park where she had parked Rose's car. The rain was sheeting down. The car park was flooded in parts where the ground had subsided. Rose's car stood in the middle of a what looked like a small pond.

She found her umbrella, useless with the wind so furious and in the end, she abandoned it and ran to the car with her bag over her head. She saw Roger's car swing out of the car park and onto the road.

Her shoes were full of water by the time she unlocked the car and pulled the door shut. She had only driven the car a few metres and knew something was wrong. The steering felt heavy and the car was pulling to one side. She drove towards the exit to the restaurant car park. She stopped the car. She knew what was wrong with the car, a flat tyre and if she drove the car any further, she knew she could do serious damage to the wheel.

"Fuck," the word exploded out of her. She was tired, she wanted to get home and out of the howling wind. She twisted around looking for a solution in the empty car park. Ewan stepped out from the shadows and stood under the porch of the restaurant entrance. The light fell on his wet leather jacket, his hair was plastered to his head. He stared at her and then his mouth twisted into a smile before he put his helmet on and ran out into the rain towards his motorbike.

Miranda felt the tension leave her body when she saw Ewan's bike turn out of the car park and onto the road. She bit her lip and pushed open the car door to try to see if she could see the wheels without getting out of the car, but she couldn't, the rain and the wind were pushing back the car door. She got out of the car and saw the front tyre. It was flat.

When she got back in the car the rain was dripping off her and onto the car seat. She pushed her wet hair back off her face and reached into her bag for her phone and searched for Rose's number.

"What's up," said Rose.

"Sorry Rose, I drove your car to work, we've got a storm here, it hasn't stopped raining all day -."

"-That's ok, I told you to use the car."

"It's got a flat tyre. It was okay when I drove it to work."

"What?" Rose sounded puzzled as though she had never heard of a car having a flat tyre. "Okay, flat tyre, sit tight. I'm a member of RAC. I'll give them a call and call you back."

Miranda locked the car doors and pulled her jacket tightly around her. A small branch fell on the bonnet of the car and made her jump as if she had been electrocuted. Miranda stared at her phone, waiting for Rose to call her back. Twenty minutes later she called.

"Sorry I had to wait on the phone. A lot of call outs in Perth. We're in luck there is an RAC man in the area. He said he'd be there in fifteen minutes. Call me back when you get home."

Miranda couldn't stop her teeth chattering and by the time the RAC van pulled into the car park she was finding it hard to stop the convulsive shivering that gripped her.

Miranda almost cried when the mechanic got out of his van and ran over to her car. He was wearing a bright yellow rain coat with a hood that shielded his face. He was carrying a large square light that he shone on the wheels of the car.

Miranda tried to open the door but the RAC man held up his hand and shone the light into the car. "Hi I'm Dan." He shouted above the rain. "Bloody terrible night for a flat tyre." He saw her shiver, "Why haven't you got the heater on? Too late now. Stay there. I'm assuming you've got a spare tyre."

"It's not my car," Miranda shouted back at him and held up her hands. She prayed that Rose had a spare tyre. She would have one, she must.

More than an hour later she pulled into the townhouse driveway and called Rose.

"Poor you Milly. I'm so sorry. I've never had a flat tyre and I've been driving Daisy for three years.

Miranda told her what the RAC mechanic had told her. "He said it was deliberate. The valve on the wheel had been wedged with a matchstick."

Rose sucked in her breath and swore, "There's only one person who would do that. That fucking bastard Ewan, he did it."

Miranda didn't want to rush to that conclusion. She wanted it not to be true. "We can't be certain of that. It could have been a disgruntled diner. Perhaps the last couple that left. They weren't happy Roger was rushing them to finish." As she was speaking, she remembered what she had seen. *He was waiting for me.*

"His hair was wet," Miranda said. She could see Ewan standing under the porch of the restaurant, the water streaming down his face, his wet jacket shining under the light.

"Whose hair?" said Rose.

"Ewan," said Miranda, "He left before me… I don't know how long but he wasn't in the kitchen when I took in the last of the dishes. I saw Ewan when I tried to drive the car, when I knew something was wrong with the tyre. He was sheltering under the porch, out of the rain but he was soaked."

"He did it," said Rose, "not some disgruntled diner. Seriously Miranda, a disgruntled diner is not going to get soaked and risk a tree falling on them to sabotage your car, my car and they wouldn't even know whose car it was."

Miranda didn't want to think it was Ewan because that had consequences for her. Would she ignore him at work, pretend it didn't happen? Confront him? She shook her head at the thought. He would deny it.

"I guess you could be right." *You are right.* "But there's nothing I can do about it. Let's hope the travel bug gets him again soon," said Miranda.

"I am worried… for you. He's already been intimidating. You should have come with me; I shouldn't have left you on your own."

"Rose, I'm okay. I'm freezing, going to have a shower and jump into bed. g'night Rose, I love you."

Miranda was asleep when a noise woke her, she thought it was the wind and the rain beating at her window and then she heard her phone vibrating on the bedside cabinet. It was one thirty in the morning, an unknown number. She pressed 'end' and pulled the covers over her head, and then it rang again, and she sat up and looked at the phone, the same number. She let the phone ring until it went to message. Whoever it was hadn't left a message.

She hadn't given Ewan her phone number but she knew it was him. She blocked the number.

The next evening shift, Miranda arrived later than usual and saw that Ewan was in the staff room hanging up his motorbike jacket and changing his boots for sneakers. Miranda hesitated at the door before she went in, she wanted to turn and run. She didn't want to admit she was afraid of him but she seemed to have stopped breathing the moment he had turned to look at her. His eyes narrowed as though he wasn't sure who she was. She held his gaze, her expression blank. *He's not going to see me, he's not going to see me.*

His expression suddenly changed and he drew his eyebrows together and pushed out his bottom lip as though he was about to cry, "Poor little Miranda, need a shoulder to cry on?" He screwed his fists into his eyes. "Boo hoo," he said.

Miranda's expression didn't change, she could do this, blank him out. She opened her locker and hung up her jacket. As she turned to leave Chloe came in declaring that she'd had a rough night partying after work and had only slept for four hours.

"Ya poor thing," said Ewan. "Come over here Chloe," said Ewan patting his shoulder, "I'm offering my shoulder for a cry. Miranda here doesn't want it. She likes big broad footballer's shoulders to cry on. Don't ya Miranda."

Miranda didn't answer, she left Ewan and Chloe talking in the staff room. She didn't know what this was about but she knew she would find out.

Later, when there was a small break in the restaurant, Chloe came up to her and took a folded piece of newspaper out of her pocket.

"I don't know why but Ewan said to give you this.?"

Miranda opened the page and saw that it was a picture of Jack Charles with some girl. The headline jumped out. THE EAGLES STAR RECRUIT AND HIS GIRLFRIEND, MODEL KIRSTY DAY.

Miranda almost laughed. She wanted to shout after Chloe's swinging pony tail, "He's not my boyfriend, never was." But the thought that was going through her mind was that now Ewan knew that Jack Charles wasn't her boyfriend, would he leave her alone? She didn't understand why he was still so angry at her. She couldn't believe that he hadn't had a girl say no to him before.

Chapter Twenty-Seven

MIRANDA AND EWAN

The corner of the library where Miranda was working with Sam was quiet, and away from the bank of windows that looked across the tree leafed courtyard where students were sitting with their lunch. It was the working zone, nothing to distract her, or in this case Sam, who was staring at the blank screen of his laptop.

Miranda waited, she had shown Sam her methods for recalling facts and now he was trying to visualise the human skeleton. He liked to do it with his eyes open. "I'm seeing it on the screen," he nodded, "Yep, starting with the axial skeleton."

Miranda listened as he named the bones in the skull, closing her eyes and visualising them with him.

"Great," said Miranda. He had a good memory and that's what you needed for human anatomy. She changed the screen on her laptop and as she did, she saw the message in her inbox appear in the corner of the screen. The words jumped out at her and she gasped.

YOU FUCKIN WHORE

"What's that?" said Sam. "Who's that from?"

Miranda couldn't speak, her breath was trapped in her chest. She turned in her chair and scanned the library.

"Who sent that to you?" Sam was scanning the room too, although he didn't have a clue what he was looking for. "Someone here, in the library sent it?" he said.

Miranda swallowed. She knew who it was, there was only one person who would send her a message like that – *Ewan*.

Miranda closed her laptop. She shook her head, "Who knows," she tried to make her voice sound light as though it hadn't sent her heart racing and the hair on the back of her neck prickling.

"What's the email address?" said Sam. "Do you recognise it?"

"No, I'll check it out later and block it." She knew how it had happened. It was Roger, he had everyone's email address. He had sent an email out to everyone a week ago asking for sponsors for his daughter's walk for some charity. He had put everyone's email in the address. She had noticed it but it was too late to complain.

"Okay are you ready for this?" she tapped the book Sam had been resting his elbow on. She didn't want to think about the email sitting silently amongst all her innocuous emails. She wanted to forget it.

"We've already gone over that," said Sam. She wasn't concentrating, her mind was somewhere else and he knew it was the email she was thinking about.

"You worried about that email?" he said. She looked worried. He had seen the reaction when the email had appeared. He couldn't imagine anyone calling Miranda that. She was a nerd, always had her head in a book, never went out much. He knew Rose worried about her. "She studies too much. Never goes out." Once Rose had said that things had been tough for Miranda and when he asked how, she changed the subject.

Miranda looked at the laptop and bit her lip. She couldn't tell Sam who she thought had sent it and why. She knew that would get back to Jack Charles, his best mate.

Miranda frowned, "No, just tired. I worked last night and I'm working tonight. Do you mind if we stop now? I can work with you tomorrow evening, FaceTime for an hour.

"Yeh sure." He grinned, "I'm seeing Rose later today." He raised his eyebrows.

Miranda knew the holiday at the farm had gone well. Sam had been forgiven.

Sam liked Miranda, he knew how busy she was and he was grateful that she had agreed to tutor him. He had only worked with her a few times but it was already making a difference. It made him study harder because he knew Miranda would report back to Rose how he was going. He knew that Rose had forgiven him, she hadn't mentioned it again but he thought he might be on probation for a long time. He could see she held back and didn't make herself as available as she had before. He could live with that.

***

Rose was in the front room when she heard the front gate shut. It was Sam, and he was early. She didn't expect him for another hour. She was waiting for the doorbell to ring and when it didn't, she went to the front door and opened it. There was no one at the door. On the doorstep was a brown paper bag. Rose picked it up carefully by the top of the bag which had been twisted and looked like the touch paper of an explosive. The bag was heavy with something solid. She walked to the front gate and looked both ways down the road. No one was in sight. She turned back towards the house and pulled the top of the bag apart. Rose let out a cry of disgust and screwed the bag tightly. She didn't need to look in the bag, the stench had told her what it was animal or human faeces. She threw it in the rubbish bin and washed her hands under the garden tap.

She thought back to the moment she heard the gate shut and another sound, a motorbike. She could hear the whine loud at first and then nothing. She knew who had left the bag there and who was meant to find it.

Sam pulled up just as Rose was walking back up the path. She waited until he got out of the car, the look of disgust still hovering across her face, the vile smell still lingering in her memory.

"What's up?" said Sam, he didn't think the look was meant for him.

Rose pointed to the rubbish bin, "That," she said, "I just threw the little present that was left on my doorstep in the bin, a bag with shit inside."

"What. That's fucking disgusting. Who? Why would anyone do that?"

"It wasn't meant for me," said Rose pushing open the front door. Sam followed her inside. "It was meant for somebody else."

"Somebody else?"

Rose shrugged, she had said too much and she knew that Miranda wouldn't want her talking to Sam about Ewan because that would mean mentioning Jack.

"Just wait here," said Rose, "I'll just get my jacket."

"Okay," said Rose slipping her arms through her green velvet jacket. Sam had said he was taking her somewhere nice for dinner in the city. A restaurant in the new five-star hotel that overlooked the Swan River.

"You look nice," said Sam, "Green suits you." He walked to the front door and pulled it open. He stood like a doorman holding the door until Rose had walked through.

"Thanks. Where are we going?"

"I thought the new wine bar in Subiaco for drinks, it's the one above 'The Provender's' in Rokeby Road. Have you been there?" He was hoping she hadn't.

Rose turned in her seat, "No, have you been there?"

It was a loaded question and he could hear the ammunition in it. Had he been there with some other girl.

He twisted his hands on the steering wheel. "Rose, I told you everything. It was the one time. I never went anywhere with her… that person. I didn't see anyone after you broke up with me. For three months, I did nothing but study. I never went out. So, the answer is, I haven't been there but Jack told me about it. He thought it was pretty cool, lots of atmosphere and then I thought we could go to the restaurant at the top of the new hotel just down the road. It's got fantastic views…Jack told me… I haven't been there either." He reached for Rose's hand and she hesitated before opening her hand to his.

They found a corner in the wine bar that was decorated with walls of bottles of wines, the bottles tied artfully with string and brown paper labels that declared the name of the wine and the price. They were costly. This was a popular bar with groups of young people talking loudly.

Sam waited until they had ordered before he spoke, he had to raise his voice above the noisy chatter of the group sitting on a well-worn leather chesterfield around a small table that was crowded with glasses and a cheese plate.

"Was it meant for Miranda… the bag on the doorstep?"

Rose sighed and leant back on the stool she was sitting on, her head brushed against the row of wine bottles. What was the point in pretending she didn't know the answer but before she could answer, Sam spoke, "You know someone sent her an email today? I saw it pop up on her laptop, something about her being a whore."

"What!" the word exploded out of Rose. She looked across at the table next to them, they were all looking at her. Rose leaned closer to Sam and whispered, "Fuck. He's a fucking bastard. She's got to go to the police. Get a restraining order."

Sam had never heard Rose this angry, even when she found out what he had done and told him it was over, she hadn't been this angry. She had looked at him as though he had broken her heart. He wished she had been angry. He had thought that when he confessed, she would forgive him but she had told him to leave and she never wanted to see him again.

"Fuck, fuck. She doesn't deserve this, no one deserves this." Rose banged her knee with her fist. We should go back. I need to see if she's alright. Make her go to the police."

"I thought she was going to work, won't she already be there?" said Sam. Rose stood, her bag over her shoulder, she nodded and sat down again.

"Yes, I forgot, she's doing every shift she can. We should go and wait for her, make sure he doesn't do anything again."

"Again?"

Rose told him about the flat tyre and how they were sure it was Ewan.

"Let the tyre down! He let the tyre down. Who is this guy? Did she go out with him?"

Rose shook her head, "No, he gave her a lift home once, she was trying to avoid… she… he gave her a lift and now he thinks… who knows what he thinks." Rose bit her lip. How much should she tell him?

Sam shook his head, it didn't make sense that someone would act like that after one lift home. There was more to it, he could tell by the way Rose was studying the floor.

"So, who was she trying to avoid? Another guy at work?"

Rose held her wine glass to her lips and then put it down. "Ok, it was your mate Jack Charles she was trying to avoid."

"Jack? But…"

"Don't ask me any questions, alright. Miranda made the mistake of getting on the back of Ewan's motorbike, that's his name, he's a chef at the restaurant. He's been there a few months, travelling around the world. Thinks he's hot shit. He saw the photo of Miranda with Jack Charles in the paper and thinks she used him that evening to make Jack jealous. He said as much to Miranda and then he overheard her talking to Jack on the phone."

"They talk on the phone?'" said Sam, it was the first he had heard of it. "He's keeping that to himself," Sam muttered.

"No not anymore, they talked when she sprained her ankle. He called a couple of times to see how she was. He felt responsible, that's what Miranda said." *and she hates for anyone to be responsible for her.*

"So, he's let a tyre down, left shit on the doorstep and sent an email."

"Yes, and been intimidating to her at work."

"Any witnesses? Any evidence?" said Sam.

Rose shook her head. She didn't know if any of it could be proved. "Miranda's worried about making it worse. She's just waiting for him to move on. He's supposed to be going to New Zealand soon."

Sam thought the evening wasn't going the way he had planned. He could see Rose was worried about Miranda. He knew they were close and Rose considered Miranda like a sister.

"What time does she finish work?" said Sam.

"Ten-thirty. She's borrowed my car. I made her take it and if he lets down one more tyre, I will be going to the police." Rose slammed her wine glass down harder than she meant to."

Sam raised an eyebrow, he could see Rose was fired up. "What are you thinking of doing?" he said.

"I think we should go to the restaurant and make sure she gets home okay?"

"Got a better idea. Wait there just going to the men's room," said Sam.

He gave Rose a thumbs up sign as he walked back across the room to her. "All covered, I've got someone escorting her to her car. Finish your drink, we're off for dinner. Our reservation is for seven o'clock."

"Who?"

"Who do you think. The boyfriend." Sam grinned.

"Jack Charles? Oh, I don't think Miranda would like that." Rose was already regretting that she had let Sam into her confidence.

"None other. Let's see what Ewan does when he sees Jack's back in town."

Rose grabbed hold of Sam's arm. "Call him back tell him we'll go. Please, Miranda's going to kill me."

"No, she won't. Look he wasn't doing anything. He's been at training all day and it's just what he needs."

Chapter Twenty-Eight

JACK AND MIRANDA

Jack pulled into the car park and found a spot opposite the entrance to the restaurant. The car park was still half full but people were leaving in a steady flow. It was late, ten o'clock, he had checked with the restaurant before he left home and asked what time they usually closed. They were open until 11pm. He found his EarPods in his pocket, and settled down to listen to music. Over the next hour he watched as the car park slowly emptied.

He sat up and pulled the EarPods from his ears when he saw a man leave the restaurant and pause under the porch lights, zip up his leather jacket and then walk to a motorbike that was parked somewhere out of Jack's view.

Jack got out of the car and stood in the shadows, he wasn't going to do anything unless it was necessary. He waited listening for the sound of the motorbike starting up. Two girls came out of the restaurant and two more cars left the car park. Then he saw her, caught under the lights. Miranda with her dark hair tied back, a red jacket splashed against the doorway. He heard the bike, and saw Miranda press back against the door, her hand in her bag, looking for something.

The bike gave a roar as it seemed to spring out from the darkness. Jack took a step out from the shadows, but the bike kept moving slowly past Miranda. He saw Miranda lift her head. Ewan said something he couldn't hear and then he spun the wheels of his bike as he turned out onto the road. Jack stopped, he saw Miranda was watching Ewan leave, she frowned and then he saw her opening her tote bag, searching in the bag and then feeling in her pockets.

She's looking for her keys, "Hi, can I help?" Jack said as he stepped into the light.

Miranda jerked her head up. "You!" She made it sound like an accusation.

"Yeh in the area, what's the problem."

"In the area? Were you in…" she turned her shoulder to the restaurant. She hadn't seen him there. It had been a busy night and she'd been too worried about avoiding Ewan in the kitchen, not looking directly at him when he spoke, or grunted at her. But he had been careful around the chef and the kitchen had been full with staff. She was definitely going to look for another job.

"No, I wasn't in the restaurant," said Jack.

Miranda frowned, she was tired and he wasn't making sense.

"I heard you were having problems with the motorbike guy." He jerked his head in the direction that Ewan had taken.

Miranda rubbed her hand across her forehead. *Heard from who?* "Rose? You've spoken to Rose." She was the only person who knew anything about what had happened with Ewan.

Jack shook his head, "No. Sam called me. Rose told him about the parcel on the doorstep and Sam told her about the email message he saw… oh and there was something about a tyre being let down."

"Parcel? I don't know anything about a parcel. Rose didn't tell me anything about that." Miranda pulled her phone from her pocket. She saw she had a text message from Rose.

Sam called him, not me.

"Yeh, I heard it was a bag of shit, left on the doorstep today," said Jack.

Miranda felt her nose sting, *You are not going to let that bastard make you cry*. She shook her head. "That's sick."

"You think it's the motorbike guy?"

"Yes, no. I don't know." She pulled at her bottom lip. What was the point in denying it? It had to be Ewan. "Yeh it's him. I don't have any proof, but he's said things to me." She blinked away the tears that she couldn't stop. "Now I can't find my keys, they were in my bag."

Jack noticed the tears. He wasn't good with crying. He felt the familiar sting in his nose and gritted his teeth as he took hold of her arm and led her back to his car. "Did he say something to you just then? I saw him stop and say something."

Miranda nodded; the words he had shouted out to her confirmed it was him.

"He said, shit happens."

"The fucking bastard." Jack clenched his fists and then unclenched them. He notched down the anger in his voice. "Do you have any spare keys at home? A key to get in the front door?"

Miranda nodded, she knew where Rose had blue tacked a spare key behind the rain pipe and Rose had a spare car key somewhere in a drawer in her bedroom.

"Okay, hop in I'll drive you home and then I'll drive you back here."

Jack drove the short distance in silence. He was thinking through various scenarios. The one he liked the best was where he confronted Ewan knocked him to the ground and told him to leave his girlfriend alone. He knew the trouble that would get him into with his career. So, he dismissed that and thought about encouraging Miranda to go to the police.

He waited while Miranda slipped her hand behind the rainwater pipe, sliding her fingers up and down. "I can't find it," she said bending down to where the pipe met the drain.

"Could be higher," he said, "Here let me." He felt along the pipe for the lump of blue tack with the tip of his fingers, he found it but he couldn't get his finger behind the pipe. He looked down at Miranda. Rose had put the key at a height out of Miranda's reach.

"I guess Rose didn't take into account the height differ-ence. I can't get my fingers to it though. I could lift you up?"

"No, it's okay, I can stand on that." She pointed to an empty bucket next to the dustbin.

Jack turned the bucket over and Miranda held onto the pipe as she put one foot on the bucket and reached up to where Jack's hand was and slipped her fingers behind the pipe and pulled the key off.

"Got it," she said.

Jack followed her into the house and waited in the hallway while Miranda went into Rose's bedroom to find the spare key. Jack pushed open the other doors and looked inside. If this mad bastard had her keys who knew what he would do.

"You'll have to change the locks," said Jack as they drove back to the car park. "I hope you don't mind but I've sent a text to Sam and told him about your keys. He's told Rose and I think she's organising for a locksmith to come tomor-row to change all the locks."

"Can you stop the car," said Miranda with one hand on the door ready to open it. "I'm going to…" she didn't finish the sentence. The fear that had been coiled like a waiting serpent came rushing out as Jack pulled the car to a stop.

Jack knew the kind of fear that made you throw up your guts, he'd experienced that many times before a game. He said nothing but waited until she got back in the car.

"Okay? Here…" he held out the bottle of water that had been sitting in the middle consul of his car. "It's probably warm by now." He twisted off the cap.

Miranda took a few sips and then held the bottle to her chest and leant her head back. "I don't know how to make him stop. He's so angry at me," she said as though she was speaking to herself.

"Did you go out-"

"-No, no." she shook her head. "Just the one time, I let him take me home on his bike and now this."

Jack glanced sideways at her. She was clutching the water bottle as though it was a lifeline. He could see she was trembling even in the dim light of the car.

He drove to the restaurant car park and angled his car so that his headlights reflected back from the windscreen of her car. "Okay I'm going to follow you back home and wait until Rose gets home."

Miranda didn't protest, she was feeling scared and she hadn't felt like this since she'd been a child. Then she'd been scared nearly every day. The lights of his car behind her and the shape of him filling up the rear-view mirror was comforting. *Breathe, keep breathing. You're going to be okay.* Miranda forced herself to breathe more slowly, counting the breaths in, filling her lungs and counting to eight as she breathed out.

It always worked. When she parked the car and got out, her hands had stopped trembling.

Jack followed Miranda into the house. "You don't have to stay, I'm sure he's not going to try and get in the house. He's just doing stuff to make me feel uncomfortable," Miranda said pulling at the scrunchy in her top knot and running her fingers through her hair.

Jack took a step into the lounge room and sat on the sofa, "Yeh, you're probably right, but I'll wait anyway. That way I won't worry about you. Do you mind?"

Mind? I don't want him feeling responsible for me. "Rose will be home soon. I'll be fine." She said without conviction. Miranda was still standing; she was tired, she really wanted to go to bed.

"I'd like to wait, okay?" said Jack.

Miranda's eyes felt hot as though she had been crying. She hoped Rose got home soon, the air in the room felt alive, it was making it hard for her to breathe normally. Jack was staring at her as though he was reading her mind. She suddenly turned towards the kitchen.

"Okay, do you want something to drink? I'm not sure what we've got. I could make you tea?" She opened a cupboard above the breakfast bar. She didn't really know what she was looking for. She closed the cupboard and rested her hands on the bench. Jack was looking at her in a way she couldn't read.

Jack wasn't seeing Miranda, he was seeing the girl back at school. The girl who hid away from the other kids. Hiding in the school library or somewhere in the school grounds, hiding until the bell went. He didn't want to remember that girl. It made him feel bad remembering how badly everyone treated her. He didn't know why he knew but he did, she was afraid and not just of the motorbike boy but of him.

He stood up and followed her into the kitchen, "You okay?" he said. "I can wait in my car if you would prefer it."

Miranda shook her head, "No, of course not. I'll make tea." She turned away from him to fill the kettle with water. She felt her face grow hot. She didn't know why. She took two mugs out of the dishwasher and put them next to the boiling kettle. Her voice sounded thin as though air had been sucked out of her lungs. She turned and faced him, he had his hands locked over his head and was looking at her under his arched brows.

"No, I'm really grateful," she said without conviction. Jack dropped his hands and thrust them in his pockets.

"You feel okay?" said Jack.

Miranda spoke as she poured the boiled water into the mugs.

"Yeh, I'm okay. Sorry about throwing up-"

"-Hey, no problem, I do it all the time."

"You do?" she said, she jiggled the tea bags in the hot water. "You haven't got bulimia, have you?"

Jack could hear the smile behind the question. She was joking, that was a good sign.

"Hell no, that anorexia thing? Not me I like food too much."

Miranda held the carton of milk up and Jack nodded. He didn't really like tea, he preferred coffee. Miranda set the mugs down on the coffee table and sat at the end of the sofa.

"Just before a game, not every game, but the important ones. Nerves, fear, call it whatever but that's where it gets me." He held his hand across his stomach. "Lot of guys throw up before a game and sometimes after too."

"Was that the Eagles and Swans game?"

Jack raised his eyebrows, "Fund-raiser game. Did you see it?" He sounded surprised.

Miranda wished she could have said yes and then they could have talked about the game, and the small sofa with the two of them might have felt larger and the tight feeling across her chest might lose its grip.

She shook her head, "Sorry. No, I just saw your picture in the paper. Something about your last game and you got a goal."

He should have said she didn't have to be sorry, he knew not all of Western Australia followed football but he was disappointed.

"Kicked three goals," he said and sipped the tea to hide his smile.

"Is that good? I suppose it is. Sorry, I don't know anything about football. I didn't grow up with it." *No one who hung around long enough.*

"No brothers then?" said Jack.

Miranda shook her head, "Or sisters, only child," she said quietly.

And you weren't spoilt, I know that. Jack had the sudden image of that girl back in his primary school, the eyes too big for her small face.

"Yes, me too, only child," *but my life was so removed from yours. I had everything.*

Jack studied the tea in his mug. "So, the ride on the bastard's motorbike was that when…" he let the words hang in the air.

Miranda felt the heat rise in her face.

"Okay," said Jack, "don't answer that. You didn't want to talk to me then but we've moved on. We can be friends. So, why is this dickwad behaving like this?"

Miranda shrugged, she didn't want to tell him, it didn't put her in a good light and it mattered now what Jack Charles thought of her, it mattered a lot.

"I know it was something about the picture of us in the paper," said Jack.

"Yes, it was that." She held her arms across her body. She didn't want to remember the ugly way Ewan had spoken to her. She didn't want that fear sitting inside her.

"He thought… you and I… it was ridiculous. He was so vicious. He had no right to talk to me the way he did, call me names." She shrugged, "I didn't want him bothering me, so I let him think what he liked."

"Okay, I get it."

"But I never said you were, you know my-"

"That's okay, I can be the pretend boyfriend if it keeps that dick head away." He tried to make his tone light. The words, 'it was ridiculous', were echoing in his head. He nodded his head at how it was making him feel as though she had rejected him. He pursed his lips in a surprised smile, the dimples appearing in his cheeks.

Miranda smiled, she felt herself relax. "But it hasn't. It's made it worse."

"Oh really? What happened?"

Miranda told him everything that had happened since she had sprained her ankle and her photo had been in the paper. She didn't tell him that Ewan had told her about the photo he had seen of Jack and some girl in the paper before he had thrown the paper at her.

Jack rested his elbows on his knees and looked sideways at Miranda, she had curled her feet under her and was leaning back against the arm of the sofa.

"Are you working tomorrow?" said Jack.

"In the evening, it's double time on Sunday."

"Okay. You and me, we'll hang out somewhere. I don't have training tomorrow. I'll pick you up at say 12, we'll go somewhere for lunch. Get a picture of us out in social media."

"What! No. I don't want my picture in the paper." Miranda held her hands out blocking the image that had sprung into the space between them. A photo of Jack carrying her out of the hospital.

"Oh no. I'd hate that. Sorry. I just don't like the attention. And what about your girlfriend, she would have something to say about it."

"Okay. I get that. It's the one thing I hate although getting my picture taken to promote Prada stuff pays a lot. And what girlfriend? I don't have one"

"It was in the paper," said Miranda. She knew she sounded lame.

"Yeh don't believe everything you read in the paper. She was the model in the photo shoot. She's got a boyfriend."

"Okay but really, it's alright." She couldn't think of anything worse than him pretending to be her boyfriend.

"I think he's interested in a girl at work," she said, and it was true, he had been flirting with Chloe and Chloe seemed to like the attention, although she had heard her talking to one of the other girls about her tattoo artist boyfriend.

"But that didn't stop the email and the present on the doorstep," said Jack. Miranda looked at Jack from over the coffee mug. He raised his eyebrows waiting for a response. He knew he was right.

"We don't know for certain that it was him." She knew what she was going to say sounded pathetic. "So far, I haven't reacted to anything that's happened. I think he'll get tired of the game if I do nothing."

Jack couldn't keep the surprised look off his face, "I hope you're right but his behaviour is pretty extreme, considering you never had a date." There was a question behind his statement. *Did you?*

"No, I've never been out with him, just that one time he gave me a lift home." *When he kissed me.*

She could feel her face going red before she even spoke, "Um, he did kiss me… that time he took me home."

Jack jerked his head back as though he had been punched on the chin. "Oh, I see."

Miranda widened her eyes, *there's nothing to see.* Jack was studying her as though he was seeing more than that kiss.

"He kissed me. I didn't kiss him." Miranda said fiercely. "And even if I had, one kiss doesn't give him any rights over me. It's not as though I slept…" She could feel her face burning. *Why did I say that? Idiot.*

Jack nodded his head, "Sorry, yeh right."

Miranda studied the inside of her mug, she was replaying the words, *It's not as though I'd slept with him. Like I slept with you and you can't even remember it.*

"It was just an idea," said Jack. He wished he'd never suggested it. He could see she didn't think it was a good idea. Jack Charles her boyfriend, she hated it, even if it was all pretend.

"Thanks for your help," said Miranda.

The front door opened and Rose called out as she came into the lounge room, Sam was following behind.

"You okay chook?" Rose said, walking over to Miranda and throwing her arms around her. She glanced across at Jack who was standing up looking as though he needed to be somewhere else.

Sam raised his eyebrows at Jack in a question and Jack didn't respond.

"Okay, I'll get going," said Jack, setting his empty mug on the kitchen bench.

Miranda stood up, she had an awkward smile on her face. She wished they had been talking about something else when Rose and Sam had come home. She didn't want to say good-bye to Jack with that awkward conversation as the last one she would have with him.

She walked him to the door, "Thanks for driving me home… and everything."

"Okay, see you around," Jack said over his shoulder. He didn't look back even though he hadn't heard the front door close and knew she was standing there.

Miranda watched him until he got in his car and drove away without looking once in her direction.

Jack hit at the steering wheel. *It's not as though I slept with him.* He felt a knot of anger in his chest and he told himself to calm down, there had been no accusation in her voice. No, she was making the point that there was nothing between her and that chef.

Chapter Twenty-Nine

JACK

Jack spoke to Sam the next day. "Miranda thinks he'll lose interest if she doesn't react. She said she wasn't bothered by it but looked to me as though she was," said Jack.

"Yeh, she was definitely worried when the email popped up, I could tell," said Sam.

"'I'd' definitely be worried if I had a sister who was getting the kind of attention Miranda's been getting," said Jack.

Sam nodded in agreement. He did have a sister a younger sister, she was sixteen but he was pretty confident his parents would have made sure she went straight to the police.

"Miranda told Rose the guy was heading to New Zealand, that she thought he wouldn't be staying much longer. Rose thinks he's a psycho. She's more worried than Miranda," said Sam.

"Yeh, I agree with that. Who puts a bag of shit on someone's doorstep? That's weird as man."

"I spoke to my dad about it. He said he's probably got a criminal record in the UK," said Sam.

"That's a thought. We could google his name," said Jack.

"Good idea, I'll get Rose to get his name from Miranda."

Rose didn't have to ask Miranda Ewan's surname, she remembered Miranda telling her his surname was Smith and she had laughed and said, "Not McGregor then."

***

"Look, read this. I googled his name, it's got to be the same person. He's the right age. Rose said he was about twenty-five and he's from Scotland."

Jack read the article and let out an explosive, "Fuck!" He read the rest in silence. "This is bad," he shook his head, "really bad, the guy's dangerous." He lifted his head from the screen and stood up. "Fuck, he pushed a girl through a glass window. She was his girlfriend. She could have died."

"Yeh," said Sam, closing the laptop. "Bastard tried to say it was an accident but the jury rejected that bullshit."

Jack took a turn around Sam's bedroom. He'd noticed all the posters of footballers had been removed and were replaced with a wall calendar with Sam's neat printing alongside due dates for assignments, and a large poster of a skeleton showing the bones of the body.

He stopped in front of the poster of the skeleton, "The girlfriend gave evidence of previous assaults," said Jack, he turned to face Sam, "and the medical report showed bruising around her neck which corroborated her story that he tried to choke her before he pushed her through the window." He wiped his hand across his eyes to erase the image of Ewan with his hands around Miranda's neck.

"Miranda has got to see this," said Jack, "she's got to take this seriously, he's a fucking…" he searched for the word, "psychopath."

"Yeh, but better to send the article to Rose, and get her to show Miranda, let her talk to her, she's more likely to listen to Rose than you," said Sam.

Jack frowned, "I wasn't suggesting I talk to her."

Sam gave a small nod of his head, he didn't know what was in Jack's head. Sam typed into his laptop.

"Sent it to her phone. Told her to read it now."

The phone rang minutes later.

"This is going to freak Miranda out," Rose said, her voice loud enough for Jack to hear. "It's freaking me out. He's a fucking psychopath. She has to go to the police."

Rose waited until Miranda got home before telling her that she had something she had to see. She ignored Miranda's protest that she needed to wait while she put her Uni bag in her bedroom. Rose followed her into the bedroom, "No this can't wait, this is important."

Miranda read the first few lines, and the words, 'he'd tried to choke her' jumped from the screen. She couldn't read those words without seeing her mother against the wall, the hands of her policeman boyfriend around her throat. She looked up at Rose and shrugged.

Rose stared at Miranda wide eyed. "You have got to be kidding me!" Rose couldn't keep the frustration out of her voice.

Miranda knew Rose would never understand. She kicked off her shoes, took her books out of her bag and placed them on top of the small bookcase next to her bed and lay on the bed and closed her eyes.

Rose waited until she could keep the anger out of her voice, "Milly you will go to the police, won't you?" *You must go to the police.*

Miranda shook her head.

"But why not Milly? He's got a police record. He went to prison," she repeated the details from the article. "It will be your word against his."

Miranda shook her head again, "I've got a headache Rose, can we talk about this later. Had a big day at Uni and I said

I'd cover Mia's shift tonight and tomorrow morning, I owe her. I just want to lie here for thirty minutes."

"I don't believe this!" said Rose. Rose paused at the door and turned back to look at Miranda. She studied her for a few seconds before she spoke. "Miranda, why?"

Miranda flung her arm across her eyes, "I know about men like Ewan…My mum had boyfriends like that… one of them was a policeman. You just stay out of their way."

Rose didn't know much about the details of Miranda's home life, just scraps of information that she had gleaned over the years. She knew that her mother had died of a drug overdose, she thought everyone at the school had known that.

"Just going to stay out of his way," Miranda said softly.

Rose closed the lounge room door and called Sam and told him Miranda's response when she had shown her the article. "That's what she said, going to stay out of his way," Rose said. "I tried to persuade her not to go into work but it was no good. If Miranda makes her mind up about something you can't persuade her otherwise. If it was me, well I know what I would do."

"I think she's scared," said Sam. "She obviously doesn't trust the police. I showed the article to Jack, he's really concerned," he paused, "I think he likes her more than he's letting on."

"Think so? I'm not so sure about that," said Rose, "He'd better not hold his breath, I don't think Miranda is thinking about him that way, not every girl wants to go out with a football jock."

Sam laughed, he wondered what Jack would think if he had heard Rose call him a football jock. He called Jack as soon as Rose had disconnected the call, "Yeh, don't ask me why, I'm just repeating what Rose told me. Rose said something about her not trusting the police because her mum had a police boyfriend."

"Guess you can't force her to go to the police, but someone needs to talk to her," said Jack.

"Not you," said Sam, the words out of his mouth before he could stop them.

"Why d'you say that?" said Jack. He felt a pulse tick in his temple and he pressed his fingers there.

"Oh no reason," said Sam.

"Did Miranda say something?"

"No, I haven't spoken to her. Chill mate, I'll see you later." Sam hung up the phone and smiled. *Yeh, he likes her.*

Jack put his phone in his pocket and started running again. He'd stopped to take the call from Sam and now he was wishing he hadn't because now he couldn't stop thinking about Miranda not taking what had happened seriously. The guy's dangerous, doesn't she see that? *Someone's got to talk to her.*

He was running along the cycle path that ran from the University into the city. He was on his way back running against the steady stream of cyclists heading into the city for work. On his way out he had passed the Bay Restaurant. It was six thirty and the car park was empty. He remembered someone saying that Miranda was going to work in the morning, that she was covering for someone and Rose was trying to dissuade her from going. Didn't she get how dangerous this guy was? *He'd better not hurt her.* The words were in his head before he could stop them and the anger like a force ready to explode in his chest. All the old feelings he had felt towards her when she was that thin beaten girl with the scruffy runners and the blank expressionless face that never

seemed to change. She was hiding in there, somewhere behind those blue eyes that looked right through you until the
day he had told Luke Somers to 'shut up' and the blue eyes
let him in and he saw… s*he loved me. I wasn't just a hero… fuck.*
He remembered other times too, when she had caught his
eye after he had left food in her desk and just the eyes speaking to him. The memories spinning in his head made him
stumble.

He stopped to catch his breath at the "Eliza statue," the
female bronze sculpture of a woman with her arms above
her head ready to dive into the water. She was wearing a tat-
tered wedding dress. Someone had rowed out to the plinth
to dress her up. She looked fearless standing poised ready to
dive into the grey swirling waters of the Swan. He wondered
what the point of the wedding dress was. He'd seen the
statue dressed in army fatigues on Remembrance Day, and
happy birthday signs around her neck were frequent addi-
tions. The statue distracted him from his thoughts of
Miranda until he turned the corner at the traffic lights and
the Bay Restaurant came into view. He glanced at his watch
and turned back to home. He was going out that morning to
look at apartments with Felicity.

A week ago, Felicity had greeted him with good news
when he got home from training and the fear he had been
holding inside for six months disappeared almost instantly.
She had told him that her specialist had just called her to say
that he had received her latest blood test results, the triumphant grin on her face told him that the news was good.

"I'm in the clear, no trace of cancer," she said pumping
both her fists to emphasise the news.

Jack had found it difficult to hide his relief. From the moment Felicity had told him that she had cancer he had felt a

weight on his chest. He covered his face with his hands when she had said the words, "clear of cancer" and gulped in the air as though he had been holding his breath since he had first heard the word, cancer." He cried and he didn't care if the world saw the tears. He pumped his fist in the air and threw his arms around her.

Being around Felicity had made his anxiety worse and when he learnt that she was going to be okay he wondered what she would think about him getting his own place. He had raised it with her a few days ago when they were both in the kitchen cooking together. He had tried to sound casual about it, "I thought you could help me find something. Thinking of an apartment somewhere near the river. Take a few weeks to get it sorted. That's if you are okay about it."

Felicity wasn't okay with it, she wanted him to stay longer so she could keep an eye on him, she was still worried about the pressure that his football career had put on him and the drinking, although he had repeatedly told her he wasn't drinking, she still worried.

"Why don't you take your time, you've only been back a few months. You're training with the Eagles, just focus on settling in and," she touched his arm, "I like having you around."

"I won't be far away and you need space mum so you can bring home your latest boyfriend… what's his name Ben? Bill?" The truth was he needed the space, he'd got used to being independent and he didn't want to worry Felicity. He knew she hadn't been able to sleep the nights he had come home late, and though he had told her he hadn't been drinking he could see the way she looked at him, as if she wasn't sure if he was being honest.

"His name's Ben, and you know it. He's hardly a boyfriend. I've known him for years. He's been overseas and we've just caught up a few times. We're just good friends." She looked affronted but the pink flush on her cheeks told Jack they were more than friends.

"With benefits," Jack said digging his elbow into Felicity's side.

Felicity said nothing but gave him the out of bounds look. She wasn't about to discuss her sex life with Jack. Felicity didn't think it was hypocritical to talk about Jack's sex life, that was reasonable, she was his mother after all.

Felicity followed Jack's Instagram account; all the players had one. And then she had followed Emily's Instagram account and seen the photos of her with Jack, so many photos. It seemed that every moment of their lives was being recorded for Instagram. She'd asked Jack about it in one of their weekly FaceTime chats. He told her that Emily was an influencer and he'd changed the subject and she thought he looked embarrassed.

Felicity found out that Jack and Emily had broken up through the Instagram account. Jack had been replaced by Jed Stokes. Felicity knew who he was. Jed Stokes was the player who had punched Jack and been suspended. The bastard deserved it she told Jack after the tribunal handed down a six-game suspension.

Chapter Thirty

JACK AND MIRANDA

The first apartment Jack and Felicity looked at was in a new high-rise block in Subiaco, with a restaurant and shops on the ground floor. Felicity rejected it before the real estate agent could show them the penthouse apartment with views of the city. "Too noisy," said Felicity.

Jack didn't think he would mind the noise and the numerous restaurants and wine bars just a walk away. He didn't bother to say anything, he couldn't stop thinking about Miranda and why she wasn't going to the police and why she wouldn't let him help her. He thought his proposal to pretend to be her boyfriend was a good one. She'd seemed horrified at the idea; he could still see the look on her face. He was still puzzling over the look; he couldn't read it but whatever it was it was clear the last thing Miranda Millington wanted was to be seen with Jack Charles.

While Felicity was preoccupied with politely telling the real estate agent that they would like to see the other apartment and they had the address and would meet the agent there, Jack looked at his phone, he'd felt it vibrate minutes ago and had hoped it might be Miranda, but it wasn't, it was Sam arranging to meet him in the evening.

Jack had thought about sending Miranda a text that morning but he remembered he didn't have her number, he had deleted it. He sent Sam a message asking him to send him her number.

Sam didn't ask why but he sent two love hearts with Miranda's number.

She doesn't want you involved she made that clear. Jack ignored the voice in his head and sent Miranda a message.

You, ok?

The minutes ticked by and he hoped that he would feel the familiar buzz in his pocket but he didn't get a response.

The last apartment they looked at was a corner apartment on the 10th floor overlooking the Swan River close to the restaurant that Miranda worked at. Felicity vetoed it before they had even been shown around the spacious rooms. "No, it's north facing. You'll get the sun at its hottest and you don't want that in the summer." It was a definite no from her.

"What would I know about real estate," Jack said, he was already bored with the project. "Let's do lunch at the Yacht Club," he said as he turned the car out of the parking bay. The Yacht Club was adjacent to the Bay Restaurant and it gave him the opportunity to check out the car park. He drove past and scanned the car park looking for the blue Hyundai, it was there, parked next to the exit.

He pulled into the Yacht Club and drove towards the parking lot. Felicity glanced at his profile, "Everything okay?" she said, "you seem preoccupied, are you worried about anything?"

"No, only wondering how I'll ever get a place of my own with you finding fault with every apartment we've looked at." He shook his head, and turned the car around.

"Changed my mind, don't fancy lunch here," he mumbled the words as he drove out onto the road and pulled into the Bay Restaurant and parked the car.

"Lunch here then?" said Felicity, stating the obvious.

"Yeh, thought we could look out on the river… and the food's better, he added, realising that the Yacht Club had more of a view of the river." He sounded lame, he knew that.

Felicity glanced sideways at him, "Does… Miranda still work here?"

He pretended he hadn't heard the question as he backed his car into a parking spot.

"You have to book here," said Felicity, "we'll be lucky to get a table."

"Let's see," said Jack. He felt a shift in his mood at the prospect of seeing Miranda, as though a good thing was about to happen.

Felicity didn't repeat her question, she knew the answer, Miranda still worked at the restaurant.

Roger looked up as Jack and Felicity entered the Restaurant. He recognised Jack straight away and then looked down at the restaurant bookings, although he had already scanned the list and knew that Jack Charles hadn't booked. Did he think he could get a table without booking? Who does he think he is?

"I'm sorry we haven't booked, any chance of a table?" said Felicity. Roger glanced at Jack who appeared to be checking out the patrons.

"No booking?" said Roger. *He's looking for Miranda. Ewan won't like that.* "Well, you're in luck, a cancellation and a table near the window."

It was only when they were sitting at the table that Jack had the thought that Miranda might think he was stalking her. *You're an idiot.* He half stood up to leave, he didn't know what excuse he was going to give for changing his mind.

"Oh hello," said Felicity. When Jack looked up Miranda was at their table and was looking at Felicity. A crease across her forehead she looked at Jack, a question behind her eyes.

Jack felt his ears go red. He rested his elbows on the table and said in a voice that was louder than he had meant, "This is my mother," he hesitated, "this is Miranda, uh we went to Primary School."

Felicity smiled at Miranda. She had seen the tips of Jack's ears turn red, she knew what was happening. "Hi," she said. "Jack and I have been looking at apartments close by and I thought it would be nice to have lunch here. Such a lovely spot." She half turned in her chair to take in the view behind the window, the blue river, the white sailing boats. A perfect day.

The frown disappeared from Miranda's forehead.

"Yes, mum's idea," he said. *Not my idea, I'm not stalking you or anything.*

"Yes, it is lovely, all that water… and the boats… on the water… sailing," said Miranda, *I sound like an idiot.*

Felicity noticed the pink in Miranda's cheeks. She leant back in her chair, she wondered what was happening between the two of them. She waited until Miranda had taken their order. She had to help Jack order as he appeared to have lost the power to think coherently.

When Miranda walked past Roger on her way to the kitchen, Roger stared hard at her in an accusing way. Jack Charles in the restaurant and the loud whispers he had already heard from another table. 'That's Jack Charles, new Eagles player.' Really, the least she could have done is let him know, and he should have booked.

Roger watched Miranda walk to the kitchen. The restaurant was almost full. He had seen the tension between Ewan and Miranda. He tapped his pursed lips with the biro he was holding. He didn't know what they got up to outside work hours but when they were in the restaurant, well they had better behave. The sooner the bag of tripe left, no the haggis, yes, he's from Scotland, the sooner the haggis left the better. He's trouble.

Felicity smiled at her son, her eyes were laughing at him.

"What?" he said defensively.

"Mm so that's why we're enjoying this view is it?"

He didn't answer but shook his head at her.

"So have you caught up with her since the accident?" she asked.

He spread his hands on the table and nodded. "Yes, last night." He looked over his shoulder and lowered his voice.

"There's some creep, works in the kitchen has been hassling her. Miranda tutors Sam. I got a call from Sam last night and I came here to make sure she got home okay.

"She's Sam's girlfriend?"

"No." He looked away as a sailing boat flashed a white sail in the distance.

"She's no one's girlfriend," he said.

"Okay, so why are we here?"

"Well, it's my fault about the guy who's hassling her… sort of my fault."

Miranda paused outside the kitchen. She wished Jack Charles wasn't sitting in the restaurant. Ewan would hear about it, one of the wait staff would recognise him and tell everyone in the kitchen. She felt tired and weary. She had argued with Rose after Sam had left in the morning. Sam had supported Rose but he had not pushed the issue like Rose.

"Why Miranda? I don't understand why you won't go and just report it, then they have it on record, just in case, you know…" Rose hadn't wanted to think what the 'just in case' was.

"I'm not going to the police. They won't do anything."

Rose threw her hands up. "It's the police, it's their job. They will, he's got a record, a really bad one with women."

Miranda bit her lip, what did Rose know about the police, had they come to her house when her mother was getting beaten up by her boyfriend? What had the police done to save her mother? They had done nothing but collude with the perpetrator, a policeman.

"Trust me on this Rose. I know what I'm talking about."

Rose sighed; she knew when to stop. She just hoped Miranda saw sense before things got worse.

Miranda had checked her emails before she went to bed. She hadn't checked them since she had seen the anonymous email that she knew was from Ewan. She wasn't going to open it again. She scrolled down until she found it and deleted it.

She saw she had a new email from Ancestry.com. She had been receiving emails from them since she had sent off her DNA. Every time she opened one, she hoped it was something that would help her find her father but they were just news letters that she didn't bother to read. She closed the laptop.

Miranda didn't sleep that night, she lay awake remembering her mother being held against the wall by her throat while she had run from the kitchen and hid under her bed. The police came to the house after a neighbour had called them when she heard the screams. The two policemen who had answered the call knew her mother's boyfriend, he was one of them. They didn't even look at her mother's injuries. They took the boyfriend outside to talk to him and gave him a notice to leave the house for 72 hours but then he came back and it all began again. They called it the circle of violence. Things would be alright for a week or two and then the fighting began again.

But this was different, she wasn't in a relationship with Ewan. He didn't live with her. She thought she could manage the situation. Keep a low profile, stay away from him. Don't interact. Pretend nothing happened. He would get sick of the game and then he would get on his motorbike and leave. She didn't need Jack Charles looking after her. She wasn't like her mother. Jack Charles wasn't a hero.

Miranda felt a knot of anxiety in her chest, she clenched her jaw as she pushed into the kitchen with the orders. The kitchen staff were working furiously, juggling pans, dodging each other as they worked across the stoves. Two of the kitchen staff were plating up the lunch dishes on the long stainless-steel bench at the end of the kitchen. Miranda pushed the new order under the metal clip. Roger had told her they were going digital in a few weeks, all the orders would be taken on an iPad and go straight through to the kitchen. She wished they had installed that now and she wouldn't have to spend so much time in the kitchen.

Ewan had his back to her. She had seen him turn his head as she came into the kitchen.

"Here," he said. "This is one of yours," he turned to face her holding a plate with a chef's cloth. It was a fillet steak on a broccoli mash. He placed it on the bench with her other orders. Plates were heated before they were plated up and if they were very hot the chef would warn the wait staff. Miranda picked up the plate and let out a cry of pain. The plate was on fire. She managed to put it back on the bench without dropping it. She shook her hand, and then pressed her fingers with her other hand.

"What's up? Ewan said, his voice full of false concern.

Miranda didn't answer. Chloe came into the kitchen as Miranda was leaving.

"What's up?" said Chloe. Miranda was holding her hand to her chest and biting her lip.

"Can you look after my tables. Burnt my hand, first aid kit, won't be long," Miranda said.

The pain in her fingers made her eyes smart. Ewan had heated the plate deliberately, she knew that. It had never happened to her before. The chef would always warn you if the plate was hot. *Bastard, bastard.*

Chloe gave a gargled cry of delight, "Ooo sorry about that but Jack Charles. You do know he's at one of your tables. He's a footballer and he's a hottie."

Miranda wished Chloe hadn't said anything. It was going to make Ewan even more angry than he already was.

Miranda was pushing through the swing doors but she saw Ewan thrust his face over the kitchen bench.

"He's got a girlfriend," he sneered. "She's a fucking model. She was in the paper."

Miranda knew the news was meant for her and not Chloe. Jack had told her the model wasn't his girlfriend. She wished Jack had a girlfriend and then perhaps Ewan would stop.

It wasn't Miranda who brought the meals to Jack's table, it was Chloe. Jack thought Miranda must be at another table. He glanced around the restaurant but he couldn't see her.

Chloe delivered the meals in slow motion, waiting for Jack to look at her so she could shatter him with her brilliant smile. It was a pity she thought she couldn't shatter him with her cleavage too but the dress code in the restaurant didn't allow for cleavage or too much thigh.

When she asked Jack if she could get him anything else it was Felicity who had to answer because Jack was distracted by Miranda's absence.

After Chloe had left, Jack told Felicity what he knew about Ewan and what he had been doing and how everyone, Rose, Sam and he were trying to get Miranda to report him to the police.

"He's got a criminal record. We found it on the internet. Pushed his girlfriend through a window. Went to prison."

"This is serious," said Felicity. She looked grave. She had clients who had been victims of domestic violence and she had her own personal experience.

"She should go to the police and report him. Get a restraining order."

"She won't, she says it's his word against hers and she can't prove any of the things."

"Yes, but her word is going to have credibility. He has a record of violent behaviour and Miranda doesn't. That behaviour is treated very seriously." She paused and looked around the room. "Where is Miranda? I don't see her in the restaurant."

Jack sighed, "I think she might be avoiding me."

Felicity jerked her head up, "Why, has something happened between you?"

Jack put his knife and fork down on his plate and pushed it away. He had hardly eaten anything.

"No, nothing's happened."

Felicity didn't know whether he sounded bored or weary of the conversation.

Jack gave his mother a wry smile, "I did suggest that I could pretend to be her boyfriend." He paused and gave a self-deprecating laugh. "I don't think that went down too well. She said no."

Felicity seemed to be considering his suggestion. "Well, I don't think that was a bad idea Jack but there might be other reasons she said no."

He waited for Felicity to tell him what the reasons might be and when she didn't say anything, he said, "Like what?"

"Well don't you think she might have thought you were patronising her." Felicity raised her eyebrows at him.

"No. In what way patronising."

Felicity shrugged, she didn't want to hurt her son. There were other reasons that Miranda might have said no. She might have thought Jack had tickets on himself. Or, she thought their brief history was simmering in the background and Miranda didn't want to get hurt.

"Well, it doesn't matter. It looks as though she's left. We might as well leave." He pushed away from the table and stood up. He had been trying to look as though he wasn't in the restaurant. It had been a mistake. Miranda hadn't answered his text message. She didn't want him involved. He got the message.

"Sit down Jack. Miranda's coming to the table," Felicity said.

Jack remained standing. Miranda looked at the plates. They couldn't be leaving, the plates were hardly touched.

"Oh, what have you done to your hand?" said Felicity.

Jack looked at Miranda. She was wearing a plastic protective glove over her right hand.

"Oh, it's nothing, just a burn. Happens sometimes."

"Really," said Felicity. "How did it happen? I thought burns only happened in the kitchen not to the wait staff."

Jack was still standing. He was studying Miranda's face. She looked as though she had been crying.

"It was an accident. A plate was too hot." But it wasn't an accident and she knew it.

"I don't suppose you want dessert," Miranda indicated the plates.

Jack bent his head close to Miranda's ear and whispered. "I sent you a text earlier. Just checking to see if you were okay."

"Did you?" she looked startled her eyes widening for a moment before she said, "Sorry. I have to leave my phone in the locker. It's a restaurant rule." She gave a tight smile, "I can't talk. Are you leaving?"

"No," said Jack. "Mum wants dessert, I think." He glanced across at Felicity for confirmation but she was studying Miranda with a look of concern.

"Just going to the..." he didn't finish the sentence, and turned awkwardly, aware that he was drawing unwanted attention to himself.

He was washing his hands at the basin when he heard the door open behind him and saw Ewan's face in the mirror above the hand basin.

Ewan recognised him. He curled his lip and walked over to the urinals. Jack felt a sudden tightening in his chest, a ball of anger, waiting to be discharged. *Don't do anything stupid, don't fuck your career.* He washed his hands slowly, waiting for Ewan to stand next to him at the basins. He shook the water off his hand and moved over to the dryer as Ewan turned on the tap. He had his head down concentrating on washing his hands slowly. Jack held his wet hands under the dryer. The noise filled the space between them.

When it stopped, the silence in the room was heavy with expectancy. Jack hadn't moved, he was going to say something but he didn't know what and then Ewan spoke, "You're that footballer. Aren't ya famous or something?"

Jack couldn't miss the sarcastic tone; he was used to it. Strangers often took the opportunity to speak to him, some of them to praise him and some to let him know that they thought he was rubbish or the team was rubbish. He never answered those comments. He let them wash over him as though they had been spoken in some foreign language. But this time he didn't.

"Yeh that's me. Just popped into see my girlfriend, Miranda, she works here."

"Got two girlfriends, have you? The model and her." He jerked his head towards the restaurant dining room.

Jack squared his shoulders. "Nope, just her," he jerked his head in imitation of Ewan.

He didn't wait to see the response, he turned and left Ewan with his hands under the running tap.

He took a long slow breath as he walked back to the table. Miranda wasn't there.

"I ordered for you, not that I can see you're eating much." Felicity arched her eyebrows at him. She waited until he had sat down before she leant across the table and said, "I'm sharing your concerns about Miranda. I don't think it was an accident. She told me it was a dinner plate that burnt her fingers. I've never heard of a plate being that hot. Warm yes but not like that. She should go to the police but perhaps there is a valid reason why she doesn't want to."

Jack frowned, he couldn't think of a valid reason for not going to the police. Felicity knew that the police had been involved in Miranda's life at the time of her mother's death. She wondered whether Miranda had a fear around the police. Past trauma that was triggered by the police. She had clients who were more afraid of the police than the situation with their abusive partners.

Jack leaned on the table and held his fists under his chin. He didn't regret what he had done. He thought it was the right thing to do, that it would make Ewan stop.

"He was in the gents just then. I told him I was her boyfriend." He gave Felicity a crooked smile.

Felicity reached and touched his hand, "Jack." There was reproach in her voice. "After Miranda said she didn't want you to do that."

"I know," he rubbed his fist against his chin. "He's a fucking bully, someone needs to teach him a lesson."

"Shh Jack. Not so loud. Now listen to me. It's not going to be you teaching anyone a lesson. Miranda has to go to the police and report what has happened."

Miranda noticed the change in Ewan's demeaner as soon as she went into the kitchen to collect the desserts. It wasn't anything he said, it was what he didn't say. He put the dessert plates on the bench without speaking. Before he had seemed bristling with anger and now, she couldn't read what was going on in his head.

Miranda was too busy to stop and talk to Jack and she didn't want to. She wanted him to go and get on with his life and leave her alone. She didn't need any distractions, she wanted to focus on getting through university.

Her lost car keys were found at the reception desk. Roger didn't know anything about them. He told Miranda they had been there when he got in that morning. She didn't want to risk losing her new set of keys and kept them in her pocket. She had left her phone hidden in her car. She didn't trust the staff lockers.

Chapter Thirty-One

JACK AND MIRANDA

Ewan swerved in and out of the traffic. He crouched low on his motorbike. He changed gear and opened up the throttle as he drove onto the freeway. The sky was still bright with the late afternoon sun. He swore loudly into his vizor, *fucking bastard, fucking bitch.* It became his mantra as he sped past the cars, delighting in over taking every vehicle ahead. He could hear Jack Charles in his head, see him, the cocky bastard, "Nope just her." She was his girlfriend, not that glamourous blonde model he was photographed with. *"What the fuck,"* he muttered. *"It's no contest."* The blood was pounding in his head. He would get even, no one made a fool of him.

Miranda's shift finished at four, she was tired, she hadn't slept much the night before. She glanced at the empty spot where Ewan parked his motorbike, he had left before her and she felt a small sense of relief wash over her. She wondered what had caused the change in him. The sullen look of undisguised loathing had been replaced with a mask of something else, something that made her feel more alarmed at what he might do.

Miranda had hoped that Chloe might distract Ewan from the vendetta he had launched at her. It seemed to be working for the first week but now Ewan was back with his focus on her.

She unlocked Rose's car; Rose had insisted she borrow it. "We should get you a car. You know dad would buy you one." He already bought them so much, she was saving, she would buy her own car.

Miranda's fingers were stinging. She wondered whether they had blistered. She started the car and rubbed her thumb across the pads of her fingers. *Nothing serious.* She shook her head, *not an accident, I know you did that on purpose.*

She thought about the brief hurried conversation she had with Jack's mother. What did she know? What had Jack said to her? Miranda leant her head on the steering wheel. She hated people talking about her, knowing about her. Felicity had given her a card, she hadn't looked at it, had taken it and put it in her pocket. She felt the sharp edges of the card against her thigh. She read the elegant blue cursive script, Felicity Charles, counsellor and her contact details.

Miranda bent the card in two and threw it on the seat next to her. She didn't need counselling, she never wanted to see a counsellor again. After her mother had died, they had made her go. She hadn't wanted to talk about it she wanted to forget it. Forget the white face, the blue lips, the curled-up body, the bruises around her mother's throat.

She knew what they thought about her at every school she went to. She was the girl who was always late for school. Who never had a school uniform and when she did it was always second hand and either too big or too small.

The teachers looked at her with sad faces. They asked her questions in whispers loud enough for the other children to stare over at her and then tease her in the school yard.

"She's got no lunch. She's poor, she smells, she's got nits. Stay away from her. I hope I don't have to sit next to her."

Every school had been the same. But at every school she had outshone the brightest, the prettiest, the richest child, boy or girl. She tried not to think about her school days but when she did, she thought about him. Jack, she thought about him, and what he had meant to her then, when her life was so bleak. At High School, life had been different, better, and there was hope for her future. He had become her fantasy boyfriend until he wasn't anymore. It was habit, she told herself when the old fantasies she had rehearsed so often popped up again. *I'm over him, I'm over him. I'm going to travel and leave Australia and all the memories behind me.*

Miranda pulled up behind a car parked outside the townhouse. It looked familiar then she dismissed the thought. When she opened the front door, she heard Rose talking to someone. Her voice loud as though she was addressing an audience. "I've always talked loudly. It's all the sheep at home. Have to make myself heard above all that bleating."

Then the other voice, Miranda didn't recognise it and then she remembered the car outside, a cream and black Mini, the car Jack had borrowed from his mother the night of the accident. Miranda paused at the foot of the stairs and took a breath. Miranda could see Felicity sitting in the armchair facing the open door. She looked up and gave a small smile. Rose hadn't heard the door but she saw Felicity look up.

"Hey is that you chook? You've got a visitor." Rose was standing at the door blocking out Felicity and giving Miranda the look that said, nothing to do with me.

Miranda turned on the step, dropping her bag to the floor. She knew why she was here. Jack must have told her where she lived.

"This is Jack's mother." Rose sounded apologetic.

"We've met," said Miranda. She looked hard at Rose.

"I was just telling Felicity what a freak… amazing tutor you are. All the students you help and you still… you're so…I'll…I've …" she stopped talking and slipped past Miranda who had the blank look that Rose knew so well. She squeezed Miranda's shoulder. She hoped Miranda had got the message she hadn't betrayed her and had said nothing about Jack Charles or Ewan.

Felicity smiled and stopped herself from inviting Miranda to sit down. Miranda perched herself on the arm of the sofa. She waited for Felicity to speak, she could handle silence. Somewhere upstairs, a door opened and closed.

Miranda studied Felicity's face, she couldn't see anything of Jack Charles looking back at her. Maybe the grey eyes but that was all. She thought he looked like his father. Felicity was tall. She had seen his father at the restaurant. That's where Jack got his height, two tall parents. She knew from studying genetics that other factors contributed to height, but having two tall parents almost guaranteed their children would be taller than average.

Her own mother had been short and she didn't know how tall her father was or what he looked like. Her mother had resolutely refused to tell her anything about him. "Who knows, I was drunk at the time and I didn't know I was even pregnant until I was four months."

"How's your fingers?" said Felicity nodding at Miranda's bandaged hand.

Miranda looked at her hand as though she was seeing it for the first time.

"It's okay, thanks." She shook her head, "just an accident." She didn't know why she added that. *Why is she here?*

"I hope you don't mind Miranda but Jack did tell me about the young man at the restaurant. A chef, I think." She didn't wait for an answer she was getting the measure of Miranda; she could tell that Miranda wasn't about to offer anything.

"I work with a lot of…" she hesitated to say the word victims. No Miranda didn't want to be classified as that. "A lot of women, old and young who are targeted by violent men. Men mostly, sometimes violent woman. I'm afraid it's unlikely that he will stop without some intervention."

Miranda stared down at Felicity's hands. They looked smooth, the nails unvarnished. The hands of a nun thought Miranda although she didn't think she had ever seen a nun in person.

"Mmm," Miranda nodded as though she was thinking it over. She knew what kind of intervention she was talking about, the police.

"You mean the police?" said Miranda. She didn't deny how Felicity had categorised Ewan as a perpetrator of violence. He was and although she tried to minimise it to Rose, she could see that was the wrong thing to say to Felicity.

"Yes, I definitely think you should report his behaviour."

Felicity saw a pulse beat in Miranda's throat. She suddenly looked scared, more afraid of the police than of Ewan.

"Well, that's one option," said Felicity, "the other is to get someone to speak to him."

Miranda raised her eyebrows. She could imagine how that would play out. She would never hear the end of it from Ewan. She could imagine the taunting that would raise.

"He's leaving soon, going off to New Zealand," Miranda said hoping that would end the conversation.

"And in the meantime?" said Felicity. "How will you stop him from hurting you." Felicity kept the concern out of her voice.

"Hurting me?" said Miranda. She held up her hand, "Do you mean this? This was an accident," said Miranda firmly.

"Mmm. Okay. I'm wondering if the other things that have happened were designed to hurt you in other ways. Make you fearful, afraid to go out. Anxious about what he may do next? What do you think?"

She was fearful, she knew that about herself. She didn't want to be. Didn't want some creep like Ewan making her afraid. But she had felt the old knots of anxiety creeping back. The triggers that made panic attacks overtake her.

She shrugged. "I'm okay." She could read the concern on Felicity's face. "If he doesn't leave in a couple of weeks, I'm going to look for another job."

Felicity didn't want to frighten her but Ewan sounded dangerous and he had a record. She wondered how much Miranda knew about him. Felicity stood up, she could see that Miranda was not going to be easily persuaded.

Felicity smiled, "Okay Miranda, it looks as though you know what you're doing. Just take precautions until he leaves the country." Felicity followed Miranda down to the front door.

Felicity paused at the open door. She turned towards Miranda, closed her eyes and shook her head. "Oh, and I should have said before, and I'm sorry. Jack shouldn't have said anything but I'm afraid he told Ewan that he was your boyfriend."

"What!" Miranda's body went rigid. "He had no right."

"Yes, I'm sorry Miranda. I've told him he shouldn't have. He has some idea in his head that it's all his fault that Ewan has been bothering you. He blames himself."

Miranda pressed her teeth into her bottom lip. She could feel the sting in her nose. It was anger she felt. She didn't want him feeling sorry for her.

Felicity touched her on the shoulder. "I know it's not what you wanted him to do and I hope it makes things better not worse." Felicity wasn't confident that it was going to help.

"If you want to talk to someone, … well you've got my card. Or I can refer you to a colleague."

"Thanks," Miranda waited until Felicity had closed the front gate before she closed the door and fell back against it. Feeling the solid wood against her back. She didn't feel as though her legs could hold her. She slowly slid down onto the floor.

"What's up chook?" said Rose running down the stairs. "You, okay? What did she say?"

"Oh, just about what's been happening. She's a psychologist… a counsellor." She gave Rose a weak smile and leant her head back against the door, "Apparently Jack Charles is my boyfriend now."

Rose held Miranda under her arms and hauled her to her feet. "What? You're going out with him?"

Miranda didn't answer, she shook her head.

Rose held Miranda at arm's length. "Is that a no or a what?"

"It's a no and a what. No, I'm not going out with him and what the fuck." Miranda walked into the kitchen and Rose followed.

Miranda flicked on the kettle and turned and opened the fridge.

"We need to go grocery shopping the fridge is empty."

"Don't change the subject," said Rose.

Miranda kept her back to Rose and moved the contents of the shelves around. She turned around and was holding an opened tub of yoghurt.

"I thought you didn't like passion fruit?" said Miranda.

"Miranda don't make me tip that yoghurt all over you. Take it, and answer me."

Miranda searched in the drawer for a spoon and ran it around the inside of the yogurt tub.

"Jack told Ewan that he was my boyfriend or…" she licked the spoon, "that I was his girlfriend."

"What? When did he do that?"

"Today. He and his mother came to the restaurant for lunch. She just told me."

Miranda pointed the spoon at Rose, "And he told her everything about Ewan."

"Aw that's not my fault. Sam saw your email," Rose said. "Anyway too late now. Look Milly, who knows it might work. JC is pretty impressive."

"Not to me, he isn't," said Miranda sharply.

Rose raised one eyebrow at her. "Okay, wrong word, not impressive but intimidating. He's a fucking giant."

"He's a freak," said Miranda intent on stirring the yoghurt container.

Rose had never heard Miranda describe JC that way. She wondered what was going on in Miranda's head.

"So, what did his mum say, anything useful?"

"No," said Miranda. She rinsed out the empty yogurt tub and put it in the bin and rinsed the spoon under the tap.

"Nothing useful."

She felt her phone buzz in her pocket. It was still on silent. She looked at the message, it was Jack.

Can we talk?

Miranda put her phone back in her pocket. She didn't want to talk. What was there to say.

"I'm going to get changed. You start a list for shopping. Don't forget passion fruit yoghurt for me, not you."

***

Jack lost count of the number of times he pulled his phone from his pocket. He had sent her the text hours ago and she still hadn't responded.

He typed out another message to Miranda, looked at it and deleted it. She would probably never talk to him again. He was an idiot. He wasn't a hero. *I had been her hero and then I wasn't.* But he wasn't that twelve-year-old boy his father had bullied. *Man up princess and stop being a fucking girl.*

Well, he had stopped being a fucking girl. Whatever that had meant, and he'd become something else that he hadn't like much. He wasn't a hero, he knew that, but he could be okay, he could be a decent person.

The year he had taken drugs and drunk himself to oblivion had left him with black holes in his memory. Things he had done that he couldn't remember, people he had hurt and he couldn't even remember what he had done. And Miranda had been one of those people. He knew what had happened between them and it must have meant something to her and he felt bad about it. But that wasn't why he was trying to help.

"You're going to wear out the carpet," said Felicity looking up from the paper she was reading.

Jack stopped mid stride. "I just wanted to make up for…" he swallowed. He shook his head, not remembering suddenly seemed overwhelming.

"Jack?" said Felicity standing up and dropping the paper to the floor. She put her arms around his waist and squeezed him tight. She hadn't seen him cry since the night he'd been brought home by the police and he thought his dream of playing professional football was over.

"It's okay," she stepped back and held her open hands against his chest. Why was he beating himself up so much?

"Did something else happen Jack that you haven't told me."

Jack wiped his arm across his face. "Yeh." He saw the look of concern flare in her eyes.

"Okay, come and sit down and tell me." She pulled him by the arm but he shrugged her hand off.

"I don't need counselling mum." He sounded angry he knew, but he was angry, angry with himself.

"Okay, okay," Felicity took a step back and held her arms across her body. "Tell -,"

"-She got pregnant and had a termination." He said it quickly, the words running into each other like a freight train passing through the room.

"Oh?" said Felicity.

Jack could see the confusion in his mother's face.

"Me, it was me. She didn't just get pregnant. I, we… and, I don't remember. I don't remember any of it." *Not the sex part.*

"And you didn't know?" said Felicity.

"She tried to tell me. She came to find me the day, the game when Sam did his knee in. I brushed her off."

"Oh," she couldn't think of anything useful to say.

"I didn't recognise her…" he shook his head, "I didn't remember anything. It was on my birthday. My eighteenth."

Felicity pursed her lips, she was remembering the girl she saw leave his room. It had been Miranda. She closed her eyes. *The poor girl, that poor girl.*

"Did she have anyone to support her?" Felicity said.

"Rose, her flat mate." Jack rubbed his hand across his forehead.

"So," Felicity held her hands out. "That's why she doesn't want your help. Have you spoken about it?"

"Yeh a bit not much. What is there to say. She said she wanted to have the termination. Her body her choice. But…"

"But?"

"I should have…" He ran his hands through his hair. "A shitty thing mum. I shouldn't have been drunk. I should have remembered that night. It…" he didn't want to say the words, *it meant something to her.*

"She thought I was a fucking hero. She told me. The stuff that happened to her at primary school. I stuck up for her a couple of times. I don't even remember that."

"You took food to school for her," said Felicity.

He did remember that, but it was no big deal, they had plenty of food.

"Yeh but it was nothing."

"I guess it meant a lot to her. She had no friends at school. She had a tough time with that mother of hers."

"Yeh, yeh, I know." He didn't want to remember how the kids had treated her. He hadn't been much better.

"I'm going out mum, I won't be back for dinner." Jack said and he turned and left the room before Felicity could ask him where he was going.

Chapter Thirty-Two

JACK AND MIRANDA

Rose was the one who opened the door to Jack who was standing on the front step, both hands in his pockets, his shoulders hunched, bracing for the rejection. Rose raised her eyebrows at him and forced him to speak first.

"Hi, is Miranda at home?" He tried to make the inquiry casual but it didn't sound like that to Rose's ears. It sounded urgent and demanding. She wondered what was going on in his head.

"Yeh she is, come in." She held the door open and called up the stairs to Miranda.

Miranda had just opened the email from Ancestry and was trying to make sense of the email she had received, someone on Ancestry had a DNA match of 22% with her. *Predicted as an aunt/niece or a cousin.*

She was just trying to process the information when she heard Rose call out to her.

Jack is here?

Miranda closed her laptop. Her heart sped up as though she was about to jump off a cliff. She didn't want to speak to him. She didn't want to see him. She wanted her life back to normal. She didn't need a pretend boyfriend. She could look after herself. She wasn't her mother who always had to have a man around, someone to get drunk or high with.

I don't need him to feel sorry for me. He just feels guilty. Deal with it!

Jack told Rose he would wait for Miranda outside the house. He leant on the wrought iron gate and studied the houses opposite, rehearsing silently what he was going to say. Sorry, he guessed was a start. He noticed that the temperature had suddenly dropped and the wind was kicking up the leaves under the tree on the verge. The pale blue sky had disappeared and a great dirty grey blanket of threatening rain covered the sky. A drop of rain landed on his face. He watched Miranda shut the door behind her and walk towards him.

More rain fell and Miranda hesitated, she didn't want to invite him in the house. She stopped in front of him and folded her arms.

"It's raining," she said.

She wasn't inviting him in, he heard that. "Yeh, can we talk in my car?" He gestured towards his car parked at the kerb.

She had to say yes or get soaked standing there with her arms folded. Rain was dripping off her face by the time she got in the car and she was shivering, her arms were bare.

Jack switched on the engine and twisted the dial on the car's heater. He reached behind him on the back seat where he had thrown his hoodie.

"Here, you can put this on."

Miranda held the blue hoodie on her lap, "It's okay I'm not staying long." *I don't have to explain myself.*

"Okay." He switched off the engine. He angled himself so his back was against the driver's door. It was awkward twisting his body to face her.

"I want to explain myself, okay."

Miranda stared at her hands, she didn't want to look at him. "Free world," she said.

Jack said a silent 'fuck'. It was going to be harder than he thought. All the ground he had covered in getting past that night and what he had done, seemed to have evaporated. He choked back an angry reply.

"Thanks Miranda," he couldn't help laughing.

She stopped studying her hands and turned towards him, her eyebrows raised. The more she frowned at him the more he found it harder to suppress the laughter.

"Sorry," he spluttered. "It just struck me that I'm more afraid of you than I ever was of Stokesy."

"What?"

He shook his head at her. "I know you're pissed off with me, I get that but I've been thinking about how I was going to explain myself all last night and when you didn't text me back, I just had to come here and hope you were home. And now I'm sitting here and you're looking so angry I…" he smiled. "I wasn't laughing at you. I was laughing at myself."

"Stokesy?"

"Footballer, plays for the Bulldogs."

"And I'm more scary than him?" She managed a smile.

Jack put his hands up as though to ward her off, "Way more scary."

Miranda smiled and then looked out of the windscreen and down the street. She didn't wait for Jack to speak. "My mum always had a man in the house. As soon as one left, she'd find another. They would get drunk together or get high on drugs. When a boyfriend moved on, I would beg her not to get another one. They were vile and abusive. They beat her up. Sometimes in front of me. I called the police a couple of times." She touched her lips, "Her boyfriend at the time, gave me a slap for that. Most of the time I just hid."

"You see," she turned and looked at Jack. "She had to have a man. She thought she was nothing without one. I don't want to be like that." That was it, she thought that explained everything.

Jack had a picture in his head he didn't like. "And you think if I help you, in whatever way, you're like your mum?"

"Mm, something like that." She smiled at him. "I've had people being sorry for me all my life. Their help only ever temporarily fixed the problem. A lot of the time it made things worse."

"I hate bullies," Jack said. "Ewan is a bully. He picks on women, girls because he can. That's the only reason I said anything. I know you think I've probably got tickets on myself but I wanted to help, to somehow make up for being a prick." He waited for her to say something and when she didn't, he said, "I just don't think guys like Ewan stop unless they feel threatened. And you didn't want to go to the police."

Miranda shivered and Jack started up the car and turned on the heater. "Just going to take the car around the block. Okay. Heat up the engine."

"Okay."

They drove in silence for a while before Miranda said, "My mum's last boyfriend was a policeman. He beat her up and he tried to strangle her, and the police did nothing."

Jack glanced sideways at Miranda. She looked at him. "My life never got better when the police came to my house. Things always got worse. I think he would have killed her if she hadn't overdosed." She had never told anyone that before. Her mother, her lips blue, the syringe on the floor and the rubber torniquet still around her arm.

"He did kill her," she said, "he supplied the drugs."

"Fuck," said Jack quietly.

He thought of his own experience with the police the night they came to his house. They had been polite, had spoken to him without trying to scare the life out of him. They had helped him.

Miranda looked out of the window, the rain was filling up the gutter, puddles were spreading out into the road. The window wipers were zinging across the windscreen.

She could see they were heading for the beach. The sea was grey and angry, thrashing high against the rocks. Jack pulled the car into the car park and turned off the engine.

"Put it on," he said indicating his sweater.

He waited until she had pulled the hood over her head and he couldn't see her eyes.

"Just before I turned eighteen, I got into trouble with the police. I was being an arse, taking drugs and drinking. I ended up getting involved in a fight. I don't remember anything about it, I was too wasted. The guy I was with, guy from school, beat up someone really badly. He used a bottle. I was there. I didn't do anything. I just watched. They had it on CCTV. At one point, I was actually laughing. They showed it to my mum and me at the police station. She cried… I'd never seen her cry before. I promised her I'd never do drugs or get drunk again."

Miranda pushed back the hood and looked at him.

"But I did, I broke that promise. Not drugs but alcohol that night." *That night we had sex and you got pregnant.*

"I was a dick. Any possible career in football was going down the toilet. I was under age by just a couple of months."

Miranda's expression hadn't changed, she was waiting for the explanation.

"I avoided being charged as an adult. I attended victim mediation through juvenile justice." His voice caught in his throat. He hadn't been able to get the image of the man sitting opposite him in the Justice Department out of his head, his face scarred by the broken bottle that had cut open his forehead. "Mum made me write the apology letter and I waited to see if the victim agreed to meet me and I had to face him. I met him, the guy who got hurt, and I told him I was sorry and I was, really sorry."

It had stopped raining but the sky was still the colour of ash. Jack took a bottle of water from the consul, unscrewed the top and offered it to Miranda. She took the bottle and drank a few mouthfuls and wiped the top with his sweater and handed it to him.

He put the bottle to his mouth and swallowed. She held out the blue bottle cap to him in the palm of her hand. He looked at it for a few seconds his brain refusing to register before he took it carefully as though he was playing a game and his fingertips couldn't touch her skin. He screwed the top back on the water bottle and looked at her. He knew the question she was asking.

"So why did I get drunk that night on my birthday?" He brushed his hand over his face. Miranda looked down at her knees, she didn't want to think about that night. She had been an idiot she'd known he was drunk. The sweet sickly smell, and she hadn't resisted him when he had pulled her onto the bed. She knew the answer to that. The ridiculous fantasy she had carried around in her head for six years. She had wanted him to be her first, that was part of the fantasy.

She didn't want to hear anymore, to have to remember how he had promised to meet her and he put the date in his phone and had taken her number and then she waited for him to call and he never did and when she had gone to find him, he had looked right through her as if she hadn't existed.

She waved her hand in a gesture of dismissal as he started to speak. "I don't need an explanation. It's history now."

"Yeh, I'm sorry. I'm not looking to excuse myself. I guess it sounds like that."

She thought she had got over it but every time she saw him, the flashbacks of him pushing back her hair and running his fingers over her lips, 'beautiful lips,' he said before he kissed her, his hands touching her bare skin and then between her legs and he stopped the delicious touching she wanted and said, "tell me to stop and I will," the silence ringing in her ears, and she said nothing and he didn't stop and she didn't want him to. It had meant something to her. She had been a fool, caught up in the fantasy she had created. She had never wanted to have a baby but she had needed to be sure and when he had looked right through her she knew she was making the right decision.

"It was my dad… that was the reason," Jack said suddenly. "It's a pretty poor excuse, he bought me a car for my birthday and it got delivered on that morning."

"That was it? The reason you…" she couldn't help the surprise creep into her voice.

"Broke my word to my mum? Yeh." She needed more explanation he could see but he was reluctant to give her the reason, that his dad had been a bully, teased him, ridiculed him, called him a sissy when he cried and he cried a lot when he was a kid. It sounded pathetic compared to her life.

"My dad was a bully. He bullied me a lot when I was a kid and then he left when I was eleven and," he shrugged, "hardly saw him after that until the football and now he's back," he swept the space with his open palm. *Just like that he's back.*

He could imagine Ross sitting in the back seat of the car mimicking him in that high whiny voice he used when he was ridiculing him, "Poor diddums your dad was a bully, bought you an Audi." And then his tone changing, hard and harsh. "Grow a pair if you don't want to be a pussy all your life."

Jack looked out of the corner of his eye to the empty back seat of the car. He almost drew a sigh of relief. He hated how much power his father had over him.

He couldn't tell her what he had endured. But she saw the impact of the words. The bleak look in his eyes and the pale blue vein beating in his temple. She understood bullying better than anyone, she could write a PhD thesis on it.

"I know about bullying and what it can do to you," she said quietly. Jack looked at her. In that moment he saw her, the girl with the shorn head and the eyes too big for her face, sitting like a statue at her desk, her eyes fixed on some distant spot.

"It can make you afraid to be yourself," Miranda said quietly. "It can crush you."

"Yeh," she got it. He rubbed at his chest. Just thinking about it was enough to evoke the feeling. He looked at her, she was so vulnerable compared to him but she had mastered it. She had got over it. *How?*

"That's it." Jack said when the silence was filling up the car. "I just wanted you to know that and, yes I wanted to make amends and I overstepped the mark." He gave her a crooked smile. "I don't think I can undo what I said to dick-wad… about you being my girlfriend." He saw the crease between her brows, "the chef guy."

"Okay," she said. She hoped it was. Perhaps Ewan would stop. She shivered and pressed the back of her hand into her teeth.

"Okay then, I'll take you home." There wasn't anything left to say.

"Excuse me," said Jack, his phone had buzzed in his pocket. "I'm expecting a call from my manager." He ducked his head in embarrassment, it sounded so pretentious. "Have to have one," he shrugged his shoulders and pulled his phone from his pocket. He read the message and looked at Miranda. "It's Sam," he hesitated, it was a terrible message but it made Jack want to pump the air with his fist.

"Is it bad?" Miranda couldn't read the weird look on Jack's face.

Is it bad? No, it's fucking brilliant.

"That guy, the chef, he's been in an accident and… he's dead." There was no emotion in Jack's voice. He could have been reading it from the paper about someone they had never heard of. 'Anonymous man speeding on his motorbike killed in accident.' Jack felt nothing for him.

"What?" Miranda mouthed the words. She had no air in her lungs to push the words out.

Jack pressed his lips together and nodded his head at her, "Yeh that's what Sam has texted me." He looked down at his phone and read the message aloud, "Ewan killed last night in a motorbike accident on Orrong Road."

Miranda held her hands to her mouth. She couldn't think, *Ewan dead.* She had wanted him dead, wished him dead. If she could have put pins in a voodoo doll, she would have done that, and now Jack was saying he was dead. No Sam was saying he was dead.

"How does Sam know?"

Jack gave her a blank look. "I'll call him," he said and scrolled through his phone and made the call.

He disconnected the call and held the phone out to Miranda. "Rose told him. Do you want to call Rose? Sam said some guy from the restaurant called you and she answered your phone."

"I left my phone?" Miranda touched the empty pocket of her jeans.

"You, okay?" said Jack.

"It must have been Roger," said Miranda. *He probably called everyone, he wouldn't want to tell people when they got to work. It had to be true.*

"Well that problem's solved," said Jack and he didn't care how callous it made him sound.

Miranda held her hands to her face, she couldn't breathe. Jack wasn't sure how she was taking the news, relieved he guessed and when he saw her shoulders shaking, he thought she was laughing, and then he heard the crying. Her whole body shaking, a keening noise that filled his car. He felt alarm, he wanted to do something, but what?

"Hey," he said tentatively reaching out and putting his hand on her shoulder and squeezing it. He left his hand resting there but she didn't seem to notice his touch. She leant forward, her head on her knees, the crying muffled. He rested his hand on her back and patted it gently a few times and then withdrew it. If it was him crying, he knew he would want to be left alone.

He opened the car door and stepped out onto the wet verge. The car was parked alongside a small green patch of grass around a set of colourful swings and a climbing frame set in a sand patch.

He walked over to it and away from the car until he couldn't hear the muffled sobbing inside. A woman walked between him and the car. She hesitated, looked inside at Miranda and then back at Jack with a look of condemnation. Jack didn't move. He didn't think he had to explain himself.

Miranda wiped her hands across her eyes. Her head was throbbing. She felt as though a dam had burst inside her. She fought to get in control. She was vaguely aware that Jack had left the car but she couldn't stop the tears she had suppressed for so long. Tears that she had never shown to anyone, tears for her childhood, for her mother, for everything that had happened to her. She surrendered to them until she had nothing left. She leant back against the headrest of the car. She felt light as though the air had been sucked out of her.

Jack kicked at one of the metal uprights supporting the swing. It made a hollow sound that made a magpie look up from pecking at the grass and fly up into the air.

He thought he knew what the crying was about, she was relieved he got that, but he didn't get the intensity of it. He walked back to the car, he could see she had stopped crying and was wiping the sleeve of his hoodie across her face.

He opened the car door and ducked his head down, "You, okay? I think there are some tissues in the glove box."

Miranda didn't answer, she reached forward and opened the glove box. He got back in the car, "You, okay?" he said again.

Miranda gave him a watery smile, she didn't think she could talk just yet. She nodded.

"I'll take you home," he said.

Chapter Thirty-Three

MIRANDA

Miranda lay in bed staring at the ceiling, it had been nearly a week since she had heard the news about Ewan. She hadn't heard from Jack after he had dropped her back home. She couldn't remember what he had said when she got out of the car, something inconsequential she thought, like 'See you around.' Was that it?

I should have thanked him. For what? For being understanding while I had a meltdown.

She pushed the covers back, then changed her mind when she remembered that the university semester had finished, she had no assignments, no work at the restaurant and it was Saturday and she had three days off and she and Rose were driving down South to stay at Rose's parents Beach house, that was jokingly referred to as 'the shack'.

Rose took everything she had for granted, the townhouse she lived in rent free, her car, the money her parents gave her, a very generous allowance that came with a proviso. "I have to stay focused on my studies, pass every unit well, or reasonably well. That's the stick to the carrot," she had told Miranda, "and you have to live with me and help me with my studies, no buts." Rose knew how to get what she wanted.

"Hey you still in bed?" Rose pushed open the door and threw herself on Miranda's bed forcing Miranda to roll away before she was crushed.

"Come on let's make an early start, beat the traffic and get to Yallingup by lunch time and spend the day lying on the beach. The three days in Yallingup had been Rose's idea and she had a reason.

They took turns driving. The sky was promising a good day with no rain. They passed fields of cows, paddocks with no trees, new housing estates that seemed to be in the middle of nowhere, towns with familiar names, tourist gift shops and the occasional health food café where they stopped and talked about what they were going to do.

"The chocolate factory?" said Miranda.

"Yes, to that and dinner tonight at a winery," said Rose.

Miranda looked at the huge salad roll she was about to eat. "We haven't stopped eating since we left home, how will we fit in dinner?"

"We can always find room for fine dining," said Rose. "Oh, I am so looking forward to this. The weather is going to be brilliant, hot but we'll get the sea breeze."

Miranda had spent a number of holidays with Rose and her family in Yallingup, the pretty wind-swept beach resort that was a draw card for surfers.

Miranda brushed the crumbs from her lips. She was looking forward to the break from the restaurant and the study. No one at work seemed particularly shocked at Ewan's death. Roger enjoyed the drama thought Miranda. Making sure everyone knew the full details of the accident.

"He was speeding along Riverside Drive, he got pulled over by the police and got a ticket and then he drove through a red light into a truck. No one in the truck was hurt. Ewan died instantly."

"Bloody idiot," said one of the kitchen staff.

"It was bound to happen sooner or later, the way he drove."

"He was a sleezy creep," said Chloe.

Miranda didn't speak, she saw Roger looking at her waiting for some reaction. She turned away before he dismissed them all and went into the staff room. She had nothing to say about Ewan, she didn't want to ever think of him again.

***

They reached the shack at mid-day, stopping first to add to the provisions they had brought in the freezer bag. The shack stood on high ground several streets back from the beach but within walking distance.

To Rose it felt like a second home with familiar furniture that had once been part of the farm house. Rose and Miranda went around the house opening the windows and the blinds. Miranda would have liked to sit on the verandah in the shade and read a book, a novel that she could get lost in, but Rose wasn't wasting a moment. She had checked her phone as soon as she had stopped the car and again while Miranda was occupied getting bags out of the boot, Rose had sent a text to someone.

They had just finished unpacking the provisions when Rose looked at her phone again. "Okay Milly, get your bathers on, we're going to the beach. No, I know what you're going to say." She pushed Miranda back into the bedroom, "Bathers, we are not going to waste a moment of this day."

The sand was warm, the sea turquoise with waves high enough for the surfers to climb. Rose scanned the ocean watching the surfers. She was wearing her bright pink bathers. She walked towards the water until she was close enough to see the surfers. One of them had just guided his board into the shallows and was stepping into the water. He looked up and Rose gave him an imperceptible wave and he jerked his head to indicate someone behind him. Rose smiled to herself and walked back towards Miranda who was putting up the beach shelter and spreading the towels out. Miranda sat down and took the sun cream out of the shared beach bag and started spreading it on her legs.

"Here, "said Rose, taking the pump bottle from Miranda. "I'll put it on your back."

Miranda rolled onto her stomach, rested her head on her folded arms, and closed her eyes. Rose was making circles across Miranda's shoulders when she stopped.

"Oh hello, fancy seeing you here," Rose said and laughed. Miranda opened her eyes and craned her neck. Sam dropped his wet surf board onto the sand and squatted down.

"Hi y'all." He grinned. "Yeh, what a coincidence finding you two here. He gave an awkward cough, "Um, Jack's in the water. We usually hang out. In the break we went cycling, Europe… uh… last year." He was talking too much, he knew that.

Miranda stared hard at Rose. *Jack is here, and it's no coincidence.* Miranda remembered how insistent Rose was that they come away for the weekend.

Miranda rolled onto her back and sat up, "I haven't finished," said Rose shaking the sunscreen bottle. She didn't want to face the accusing look Miranda was giving her.

"Why does this feel like déjà vu?" said Miranda. She raised her eyebrows at Sam, who was looking at Rose for support.

Sam stood up, "Just going to change. We've been here for a couple of hours."

"So Rose, a coincidence, huh?" Miranda could feel her cheeks growing warm at the thought of facing Jack.

"Don't be mad chooky, you know you like him and he likes you." She held out the sunscreen to Miranda, "Here you can do my back." She snatched it back before Miranda could take it, "Second thoughts I'll get Sam to do it. Pity you're all done because Jack could have lathered you all over."

"God Rose, shut up." Miranda felt her stomach tighten. She sat up and looked out towards the surf.

Jack had seen Sam get out of the water but he hadn't watched his trajectory up the beach. He guessed Sam had made his way into the change room. He surfed a last wave and then headed for the change room, cutting through the sand at an angle away from Rose and Miranda. He hadn't looked their way.

Miranda saw him as soon as he got out of the water. *He hasn't seen us. I bet he doesn't know we are here. I'm going to kill Rose.* She stood up and started walking towards Jack.

"Where are you going?" shouted Rose.

Miranda didn't answer. *I'm going to say hello and tell him I didn't know he would be here.*

Jack didn't hear her the first time she called out to him, "Jack," she called again and he stopped and turned around.

"Hey, I didn't know you'd be here." He sounded surprised Miranda thought but he was grinning at her.

"Yeh, well I wanted you to know I didn't know you or Sam would be here."

"You with Rose?" He looked over Miranda's head and saw the familiar blue and white beach shelter and Rose standing under it watching them. Rose gave him a wave and he returned it.

He laughed and shook his head, "I'm going to kill him."

"Let's kill them both," Miranda said.

Jack looked towards the change room, "Okay deal. We can plan it later. After I've got changed."

Miranda wondered what Jack had said to Sam because they were both wearing poker faces as they walked towards the beach shelter.

"Okay whose first?" Jack said to Miranda.

Miranda jerked her thumb at Rose. "She planned it, but he," she nodded at Sam, "was in on it. So, he goes first and she has to watch."

"You were in on it huh?" said Jack throwing his towel on the sand outside the beach tent and raising his eyebrows at Sam.

Sam was kneeling alongside Rose as though he was about to propose. He pursed his lips for a kiss but stopped and furrowed his brow, "What me?" he said leaning forward and planting a kiss on Rose's lips.

"So, you two are here for a few days?" said Sam. "We're heading back tomorrow, Jack's got training?"

"I thought the season had finished," said Rose.

"Yeh, but you have to keep training, it's pre-season training and I'm in a new club," said Jack. "The Eagles, if you missed the news."

"I thought we could have dinner this evening at Blakes's winery," said Rose.

"Yeh good idea," said Sam, "I already reserved a table." Rose touched Sam's knee. Miranda saw it and wondered whether Rose was telling him to keep quiet or praising him.

Rose handed Sam the sunscreen bottle, "Good work," she said turning her back to him and moving over to make room for him beside her. Sam was studying the sunscreen bottle.

"It's a pump," said Rose.

"And I suppose lunch tomorrow at the winery with the lake and the ducks," said Miranda, "that's booked too."

"Yep, you got it," said Sam, "also booked." He pushed himself in between Miranda and Rose. "Only room for two in here, you need to buy a bigger beach tent Rose. You'll have to sit next to the footballer Miranda."

Miranda picked up her towel and looked at Jack, he had one eyebrow raised in a look of innocence as he smoothed the sand next to him. Miranda spread out her towel and folded her legs under her.

"How's your studies going?" Jack said, his eyes fixed on the horizon ahead.

"Good, done for the year. You?" She pulled at a loose thread on her towel. She didn't like the feeling inside her chest, she couldn't tell what it meant.

"Well, no studies, although I guess when the football career is over, I'll need a plan, but everything's cool." He sifted a handful of sand through his fingers.

Rose let out a muffled cry which made both Miranda and Jack look back to the beach tent. "Hey you two get a room," Jack said. "Shall we leave them to it?" He rubbed his hand through his hair. It was almost touching his shoulders. He indicated one of the wooden beach shelters that had just become vacant. "We could sit there." Miranda was already moving, picking up her towel.

Miranda could feel the tension between them, something unsaid that felt like an invisible wall. She waited until they were both sitting under the shade before she spoke, "I'm sorry, I didn't text you to explain the-"

Jack waved away the explanation, "-you didn't have to. I guessed you were just relieved. I didn't read anything else into it."

He felt awkward to say the 'crying', the complete melt down over the death of an arsehole who had made your life miserable, although you never said that. Who had terrified you.

"Why did you pretend you weren't worried?" he said examining the sand he was sifting through his fingers.

She didn't answer, she didn't know how to. He turned his head and looked at her. He wondered if he should have said anything but he wanted to break through the wall of silence that she had thrown up around herself. He didn't think she had heard him. She seemed so still, lost in thought, her face blank. He suddenly remembered her at school the way she seemed to retreat inside herself as though she couldn't see or hear what was going on around her when she was being taunted and bullied by her classmates.

The sky that had been an eye watering blue seemed to suddenly change. A cloud was draping itself across the sun. "Hey," he said, bumping his shoulder against hers, "where are you?"

Miranda blinked, "What?"

"You were ghosting me," he laughed, "and I'm right here."

She blinked again, she could see him clearly before her, his silhouette against the backdrop of the ocean. He had been her hero, the fantasy of him for so long and she'd had to give it up. He was just an ordinary boy and she was an ordinary girl.

"You seem to disappear sometimes," he said.

"Mmm I know." She didn't turn away from him. She wanted him to know. She wasn't sure she could trust him but she wanted to. "It's a coping mechanism. I developed it when I was young." She stopped as a flash back appeared of herself when she was eight trying to sink into the sofa, growing as small as she could, losing herself inside her body, her breath slowing, blocking everything out as her mother fell back against the wall, his hands around her throat until her legs buckled and only then when she was gasping and her eyes were popping out of her head did her boyfriend drop her to the floor.

"It helped, back then when I… and now it's become a part of how I deal with …" she shrugged, "stuff."

He didn't speak but waited, he sensed she wanted to tell him more.

"When I was a kid my mum had a lot of men around, 'a new uncle' every week." She frowned at the memory of those men. Some had been kind, kinder than her mother ever had been. Taking her mother to task, "Hey we shouldn't do this in front of the kid." Whatever 'this' was. "Oh, don't worry she's in a world of her own. Randa go to your room." And she would slip away into her room and wait for the laughing and giggling in the other part of the house to turn to hell.

"There was a lot of violence with some of the men… drugs, alcohol." Miranda looked away from the concern in his eyes. She didn't want that, she hated the pity.

"Sometimes if I couldn't escape to my room, or some other part of the house. I'd escape into myself."

"No one helped you?" said Jack.

Miranda shrugged, she looked out to the surfers, their black shapes floating on the water. People had tried to help, teachers, neighbours who reported her mother to Child Protection or to the police but the outcome often made things worse.

Her mother would be compliant, do as she was told. Attend all the meetings do the drug tests. "We have to jump through the hoops Randa, yes sir, no sir, three bags full. Fucking bitches."

The school would provide regular reports to the case worker assigned the case. School attendance was never a problem, that was her escape. Miranda would have liked to attend school every day. The weekends were a terror waiting to unfold.

"Help?" said Miranda, "Yeh sometimes, for a while we would get some intervention. They helped us get the government house near the last primary school. We'd never lived in such a posh area. Mansions in every street and so close to the beach. We weren't very popular living in one of the government rentals built in the middle of that suburb." She gave Jack a wry smile. "The Department came in and out of my life until… the end." *Until she died and I was free.*

Jack was listening closely, trying to imagine what it would have been like to be in her situation. He wondered if she had been on her own, he hadn't remembered her having siblings at the school.

"You said you were an only child. Do you have any family at all, aunts, uncles?"

"No, just me." She said it brightly as though it was a good thing.

Just me. She was alone, no family, no one. Jack looked at the distant horizon that divided the ocean from the sky. He thought of Felicity and what it would have meant to lose her, it was unthinkable. He didn't ask her about her mother, he knew what had happened to her. He wondered, if despite everything, Miranda had felt close to her mother the way he felt close to Felicity.

Miranda seemed to read his thoughts, "It was difficult with my mother, she was a drug addict…" She lifted her hands up in a gesture of hopelessness. She had never said the words out loud before. She had heard them said about her mother for as long as she could remember. *My mother was a drug addict.*

"Getting drugs was the most important thing in her life." And that was the truth of it thought Miranda. Drugs were more important to her than anything else, they came before caring for Miranda and protecting her. The addiction for drugs consumed her mother, it destroyed her life.

Jack turned to look at her, she had said the words without emotion but behind them he saw what those words meant. Miranda at school searching in the school bin for half eaten food. How many times had she had to do that to survive?

"Did she ever, you know, try to get off the drugs?"

"Yeh a few times when the Department got involved but she never lasted." Miranda eased herself down onto her back.

Jack turned to look at her. She had thrown one arm across her face, the other she held across her bare midriff. He studied her pale pink lips that he had kissed but couldn't remember. He wished he could, he wished he could remember everything about that night. It had meant something to her and nothing to him. He felt a burn in his chest as though he was about to cry. *She's beautiful and fucking amazing.*

Miranda broke the silence that filled the space between them.

"I've tried to find my father. I don't know who he is. I'm not sure my mother even knew."

She sat up and brushed away the sand that still clung to her legs. He imagined himself as a man who had fathered a child he didn't know about. It could have happened so easily.

"I've looked on the Ancestry website. Sent away my DNA." She stopped she was talking too much.

"And, what was the result?"

"Oh, I'm mostly European… Italian," she said, "hence these, I guess." She pointed to her hair and immediately felt embarrassed.

Jack looked at her hair, she had caught it up on top of her head in a mess of curls. She looked at him from under her lashes. He could see her cheeks were flushed.

"It's a nuisance," she mumbled. *Stop being an idiot.* She shrugged her shoulders and wriggled her toes.

"You're beautiful… your hair, I mean it's… beautiful." He could feel the heat in his face. He changed the subject quickly, "I meant did you have any success with finding…" he felt awkward saying the word father as though he was bringing up something painful.

"Oh, with that. You have to hope that someone that's related sends their DNA to the website then you get…" she suddenly remembered the email that she had received and then forgotten. She searched in her bag for her phone as she spoke, "I've just remembered an email from last week." She found her emails and scrolled through them.

"Here, they found a match, not my father," she read out the email, "22% cousin, aunt or niece." She looked up at him, "that means I've matched with someone who could be a cousin or an aunt."

"Cousin or Aunt? And you haven't followed it up?" He could see that if she had matched with a cousin or aunt, that it must lead to her father.

She shrugged her shoulders, "I just got distracted and…" she bit her lip, she knew why she hadn't followed it up, why she had pushed it to the back of her mind.

Her father, the other fantasy in her head she had been nurturing for as long as she could remember. The father who was going to rescue her from her life, but he never came and then there was Jack.

Jack had been her fantasy for so long, the secret fantasy boyfriend. It made her sick with embarrassment to remember how she had nurtured the fantasies of her and Jack, replaying them over and over, tweaking the scenarios to fit her changing circumstances. Jack her first boyfriend, her first kiss, her first… and he had been.

"I guess in my mind I've idolised him, made him my version of what he would be like." She closed her eyes. She wasn't going to cry, she wasn't going to do that in front of Jack again. She opened her eyes and stared at her phone.

"I get that," Jack said and he did at one level. He had wanted Ross to be like other dads he knew. Dads who seemed to like their sons, telling them what a good job they had done at footy, praising them. An image of Ross, hands on hips, berating him for crying when he had taken a blow to his nose when Ross had insisted on teaching him how to box. Jack sighed, when would those images ever disappear.

"Yeh no guarantees, I guess. He could be an arsehole."

Miranda heard something in his voice, she turned to look at him. She saw it at once, the bleak look. He was talking about his father.

"Your dad?" she said.

Jack tipped his head back and laughed to shake off the memory of Ross, "You could say that." He shook his head, "Ancient history," he held the flat of his hand against his chest. Just thinking about Ross brought the tight feeling that threatened his breathing.

"Ancient history," repeated Miranda but the memories didn't leave you. They hid waiting to hijack you without warning. She wondered what kind of father Jack's dad had been. Jack had told her he had been a bully. She remembered seeing Jack's father at the restaurant and remembered the tension at the table. Was there nothing good about him, did he do drugs? Was he an alcoholic? Did he beat up Jack's mother? He'd bought him a car, Jack lived in a mansion, went to a private school.

"He must be proud of you though, what you've achieved?" she said.

Jack nodded his head slowly, these questions were opening up a can of worms and he had to shut them down. Miranda was looking at him, her eyebrows raised, the hopeful look in her eyes, so sure he was going to say yes.

"My life was a bed of roses compared to yours. I had everything money could buy. But he wasn't great, he was a fucking tyrant and he still is. Actually," he took a breath, "I despise him. I wish he was dead." He saw the shocked look on Miranda's face.

He wanted to take the words back as soon as he said them. Did he really wish Ross was dead?

"No, I just wish he would fuck off and leave me alone," he said.

"I'm sorry," Miranda said.

"What for?"

"For making you talk about your dad."

"Nah, that's cool." He gave her a wry grin, "I need to take his advice."

"And what's that?" Miranda looked up to see Rose and Sam were taking down the umbrella, Jack noticed them too and stood up. He held out his hand to Miranda but she was picking up their towels.

Miranda handed Jack his towel, "Thanks," he said and turned away from her to shake off the sand.

"What was the advice?" said Miranda. She was genuinely curious to learn what advice Jack's father had given him. Did his father acknowledge he was a bad father?

Jack threw his towel over his shoulder, the light caught his eyes, they looked darker, as though the iris had expanded. All trace of the wry grin he had given her before had disappeared and now his lips were drawn in a thin line.

Miranda wished she hadn't repeated the question, the easy rapport between them seemed to have gone in an instant.

Miranda watched as Sam and Rose gathered up the bags and towels and began walking towards them. Jack heard Sam call out and began walking towards the wooden steps that led up to the car park at the top of the sand dunes. He turned to Miranda and beckoned with his head, "Let's go," he said, "Sam can manage."

They walked in silence through the sand. When they got to the step, Jack waited for Miranda to go ahead of him. He wanted to snap out of the mood he had put himself in, get back to where he had been before the talk of Ross had brought the black cloud pressing down on him.

"Sorry," he said when Miranda was about to put her bare foot on the second wooden step. Miranda stepped up and turned towards him, her face on the same level as his. She could see the impact that talking about Ross had had on Jack. He didn't need to apologise to her.

"Talking about him," he shook his head. Miranda put her hand on his shoulder and smiled, a sad sort of smile. The sweetness of her gesture made him want to lean forward and kiss her but he grinned instead, his eyes crinkling at the corners. *One day I'll kiss her and she will kiss me back.* He shook his head at himself, *get real.*

"Hey you two get a move on, we've got an hour to get changed for dinner," said Rose.

Chapter Thirty-Four

JACK AND MIRANDA

"Don't you just love this place, Milly?" Rose said twisting in her seat and indicating the lake behind her with her wine glass. She had insisted that Miranda and Jack face the lake which was lit up by the lights that were hung from the trees that surrounded the dark water.

"It's really pretty," said Miranda. She felt as though she was in the spotlight sitting next to Jack. When they had entered the restaurant Miranda had seen the heads turn to track Jack across the room. She had tried to hang back as though she wasn't with him afraid that someone would take a photo of him and she would be the mystery girlfriend.

Jack had picked them up declaring that he was the driver for the night. Sam had got out of the front seat and promptly got in the back with Rose.

"I can be the driver if you like," said Miranda, "I don't drink."

"Me neither," said Jack, "not anymore," he added.

After they had eaten Rose suggested they go down to the lake. "It's well lit," said Rose and it's a beautiful night.

Jack insisted on paying for them all. Miranda hung back and pinched Rose on the arm, "What are you doing?" she said.

"Ouch, Milly," Rose rubbed at her arm, "I'm not doing anything." She gave Miranda a wide-eyed look of innocence.

"Yes, you are," Miranda hissed between her teeth.

At that moment Sam emerged from the cloakroom and threw his arm over Rose's shoulder and walked ahead. Miranda shook her head, she felt awkward waiting for Jack to pay the bill. She walked away from the reception and waited by the restaurant doors. She could see Jack was talking to the girl behind the counter, she was young blonde and pretty. Miranda wondered whether she was a surfer, her bare arms were tanned and she looked fit. Jack was nodding and smiling at something she had said. Miranda saw another girl, one of the waitstaff stop and say something to Jack but he was moving away now, hunching his shoulders.

Miranda stepped back as he reached the door. "Sorry, did I keep you waiting?" Jack said.

Miranda shook her head and smiled, "Can I transfer my share of the meal to you?" she said.

"No, it's on me."

"Thank you, it was really nice."

"Yeh, I've been here before," he said, "with Sam."

"Me too," said Miranda, "with Rose and her family."

"Yeh, Sam said Rose and you are pretty close," said Jack. He pushed open the door for her. Outside the air was heavy with honeysuckle.

"Yeh, pretty close," Miranda said and rubbed her hands down her bare arms. She couldn't see Sam or Rose anywhere.

"You cold?" said Jack. "We don't have to walk, we could wait inside." He turned to look back at the restaurant. "They have a bar the other side of the restaurant."

Miranda shook her head, she preferred to be out in the open and not in some confined space with him where someone was bound to recognise him if they hadn't already.

"No, I'm not cold," she lied.

Jack stepped off the pebbled driveway and onto the grass. The Lake was less than 100 metres from the restaurant and was well lit.

"I don't see those two," he frowned. He knew what Sam and Rose were up to. *Fuck how obvious can you get.* Jack stared into the shadowed areas beyond the lake.

He'd tried to shut down Sam's questioning when they left the beach and were driving back to the Airbnb they were sharing.

"Come on man, you like her, she's nice and she's ordinary," said Sam exasperated when Jack brushed off answering any questions about what he thought of Miranda.

"Ordinary?" said Jack. There was nothing ordinary about Miranda, she was amazing.

"Yeh, not taking photos of herself all the time like your last one," said Sam.

Jack didn't answer, he didn't want to judge Emily. He wasn't taking photos of himself but he wasn't saying no to all the photo shoots he'd been on in the last eighteen months. He was focused on his appearance too. It went with the territory. He'd had to grow his hair and now he had to tie it in a man bun when he played.

"She's nice," he'd said reluctantly, he didn't want Sam and Rose watching his every move. He had enough eyes on him when he went out without those two. "But I'm not looking to step into another relationship right now. I've got to focus on my game and she has to focus on her studies." That wasn't a lie.

Jack turned back towards Miranda, she was studying her phone wondering if she should text Rose but she knew she wouldn't answer. She looked up to find Jack running his fingers through his hair, his jaw set, he was annoyed she could see that. He didn't want to be left on his own with her, forced to spend time with her when he could be with someone more his type.

"You could drop me home," said Miranda. She tried to make her voice light.

Jack frowned, did she want to go home? He couldn't tell but he knew that was not what he wanted. He turned away from her and looked back to the lake hoping to see Sam and Rose somewhere. He was just about to answer her when someone came through the doors behind him and said his name. He froze, he didn't want to turn around, he knew that voice and he wanted to run and get as far away as he could, but it was too late.

Miranda turned and saw who was standing in the doorway, it was Jack's father and the woman trying to hide behind his back was the same blonde woman Jack had brought to dinner at the Bay Restaurant.

Miranda looked back to Jack, he was still, his body tense, she saw him lift his head as though he was looking for escape.

"Jack." Ross Charles' voice snapped the word and Jack turned around, his face unreadable to face his father.

Jack inclined his head and ran his tongue over his dry lips. He was searching for the words, his ears were ringing, he balled his hands into fists and then flexed his fingers. He felt his heartbeat high in his throat.

"Cat got your tongue, or do you need glasses?"

Jack rubbed his hand across his forehead, "You took me by surprise." He took a step back from Ross, the gravel crunched noisily under his feet. "What are you doing here?" His voice sounded thin to his ears.

Ross stepped forward with his hand outstretched. Jack hesitated as though he didn't understand what he should do in response to the outstretched arm. He held out his hand and his father squeezed it hard, grinding the bones of Jack's fingers together. Jack clenched his teeth *you arsehole*. He remembered all the other times his father had insisted that they shake hands and made it into some kind of competition. Jack resisted flexing his fingers and instead thrust his burning hand into his pocket.

"Nice to see you too," said Ross, "I didn't expect to see you here either, shouldn't you be training, making sure you were worth the trade. Making sure you can kick goals?"

Miranda stared hard at Ross, he wasn't joking and Jack was saying nothing.

Ross turned to Nicole, "You remember Nicole?" he said to Jack. Ross didn't wait for an answer. He slid an arm around Nicole's waist and pulled her close. She gave Jack a tight smile that vanished in a second.

Jack nodded, "Yeh, hi," he sounded hesitant as though he was still processing what he had heard. He ducked his head and his hair fell across his face, he raked it back with his fingers.

"Still got the girly locks," said Ross, "You should get it cut."

Miranda heard the mocking tone, a bullying tone that felt familiar, but it wasn't directed at her. She wanted to distance herself, walk away from whatever was happening but something stopped her. She saw the curled lip of Ross and the confident way he held himself. Nicole's eyes danced from Jack's face to Miranda's, she pursed her lips and placed her hand on Ross's chest.

Miranda saw Jack take a step backwards, and in that moment, Miranda saw the boy from school, her hero who had stood up for her when no one else did. She took two quick steps next to Jack, turned to face Ross and said loudly before she could even think about it.

"I like his hair," she looked at Jack and gave him a wicked grin. "I think it's beautiful," she said.

Ross gave a snort, "Beautiful!"

Ross seemed to notice Miranda for the first time, he studied her for a few seconds and then looked at Jack and raised one eyebrow in a question. Jack said nothing, he was waiting for something, a signal. Miranda's bare arm brushed against his, her fingers touching his. He grasped her hand.

"This is Miranda, my girlfriend," he said.

"Oh, really?" said Ross. He could see at a glance she wasn't a model like Jack's last girlfriend, who was a stunner. Jack was a fool to let that one slip through his hands. Blondes were his choice, not dark curls. He couldn't really see her face in the shadows. Someone threw open the restaurant doors and Ross and Nicole moved out of the way and onto the gravel path.

"Why don't you two come back to our room, we're staying here at the winery. We could have a drink," said Ross.

Miranda squeezed Jack's hand. That was a no from Miranda and a definite no from him. Jack looked at his watch, "Sorry, another time, we have to go." Jack was already walking towards the car park.

"Okay, I'll see you when I get back to Perth," Ross called out his voice loud and confident.

Not if I can help it thought Jack. He grinned and glanced at Miranda. She liked his hair, he wanted to laugh. He wasn't a big fan of long hair but it was part of his contract with Prada.

Jack pointed his keys at his car and the lights flashed. He'd got away from Ross and his chest wasn't squeezing.

Miranda reached behind her for the seat belt and Jack leant across her took hold of the seat belt and kissed her quickly, his lips just brushing against hers. He snapped the belt in place and before she could say thank you, he kissed her again. His lips gently pushing at hers, feeling them part until they matched his. Miranda touched his face, she could feel the stubble on his cheek, the prickle of it against her lips. He pulled away and turned on the car engine.

"You're freezing," he said. He smiled at her in the dark, "Your hand feels like a block of ice but I like the cool feel of your lips."

He twisted a knob on the dashboard and Miranda felt a blast of warm air engulf her. She let out a squeak that told him she liked it. "If you like that, wait until you feel this." He said pressing another button that glowed blue in the dark interior.

"What?" She couldn't stop smiling. She could still feel his lips on hers. The only part of her that felt warm. She wanted him to kiss her again and she wanted more than that, she wanted him.

"You'll see," he said, "shall we drive to your place?"

"The Shack? What about Rose and Sam, how will they get home?"

"I'll call Sam, he can figure something out."

"Oh, I can feel it," said Miranda in surprise, "this seat, it's getting warm. Oh, it's delicious."

Jack smiled, "You're like an ice block," he touched his lips.

Miranda pushed her hands under her legs, she had never been in a car with heated seats. "It should be mandatory for every car to have heated seats," she said.

"What like seat belts?" Jack said as he pulled out of the car park and onto the road that led back to Yallingup.

A silence settled over them, an elephant was sitting in the back of the car. Jack twisted his hands on the steering wheel and pushed his shoulder blades together. "So, my dad, now you've met him." He looked at her to see her reaction but there were no lights along the country lane to light up the interior of the car, all Jack could see was her pale profile. The trees along the side of the road flashed emerald green. Jack remembered that this stretch of the road often saw kangaroos jumping out of the bush onto the road. He put his foot on the break and slowed down.

Miranda took her warm hands from under her legs and pressed them together. "Yes," she had been thinking about what she was going to say to Jack about his father. The meeting had been brief but she had seen and heard Ross Charles. There had been no warmth in his voice when he spoke to Jack. He'd been critical and she had seen the change in Jack the moment his father had called out to him. It was as though all the confidence had been drained from him and he was steeling himself for the attack.

"Is it always like that?" she said.

"Like that?" Jack said.

"Well, he didn't seem very…" Miranda was searching for the word, "I guess he didn't sound very fatherly," she said.

"Fatherly," said Jack bitterly. "Yeh that's about it." Jack wiped the bead of perspiration from his top lip. "Do you mind if I turn the fan down now… if you're warm enough?"

"Yes, turn it down, I'm fine," said Miranda.

They lapsed into silence while Jack negotiated a roundabout.

"When did you last see him?" Miranda said.

"That day at the Restaurant. I brought Nicole to distract Ross. I met her the night before at the hotel the team were staying in. She's in property management or something similar and she was interested in meeting Ross when I told her about his money. Seems they got on fine."

The lights of the township came into sight and Jack slowed the car. It was a pretty sight, the dark trees silhouetted against the moonlit ocean. "I didn't have to see him much for the last nine years, but now he's back and he wants…" He knew exactly what Ross wanted, he wanted to be the father of Jack Charles the new player for the Eagles.

"Didn't he want to see you?" said Miranda.

"He and mum got divorced when I was eleven and he moved to New York, remarried, got divorced again. He started to contact me more frequently once I got picked for the Swans, mostly to tell me how I fucked up, but now he's moved back to Perth, says he can work anywhere. I didn't think he'd be here so soon."

Jack sighed, "Every time I speak to him, I want to drink. Did I tell you I used to drink a lot, started when I was thirteen?"

"Thirteen?" said Miranda in a whisper.

Jack looked at her and shook his head. "Yeh, did it in secret. There was always alcohol in the house. Mum liked to drink vodka. I drank that. Used to make me feel okay." He turned to look at her. "I don't drink at all now. Got counselling for it."

"Has he always made you feel like this?" said Miranda.

Jack swallowed; how do you tell the girl who thought you were a hero that you've always been afraid of your father. That he makes you feel physically sick.

"For as long as I can remember," said Jack.

"So, what are you going to do now he's in Perth?"

"Leave the country," Jack said. He sounded serious but Miranda knew he was trying to lighten the mood.

"Or," said Jack I could take the advice he's been giving me since forever."

"What's that?"

"Grow a pair," said Jack. He could see Miranda hadn't understood what he meant. "Grow a pair of balls, man up and tell him to fuck off."

"Oh," said Miranda. She thought about what that meant, standing up to a bully. "Do you think I should have done that and told Ewan to fuck off."

"Nah," said Jack, "Balls aren't a good look on a girl."

Miranda flicked the back of her hand against his arm, "You know what I mean."

"Yeh, no, I don't know. It's like PTSD, that's what the counsellor told me. Something about neural pathways in the brain that get made over time. The counsellor said it was like how a trail gets made, you walk the same trail over and over and you've made a pathway. She said I had to make a new track."

Jack shook his head, they were approaching the driveway to the Shack, he indicated and pulled into the car port as the sensor lit up an old bikes with two flat tyres against one of the walls. Jack turned off the engine. "I have to do it." He shook his head, "I don't want to feel like this," he pressed his hand to his chest. He didn't know what exactly he was going to say to Ross but he felt a determination that he was going to confront Ross and he wouldn't back down.

"I know," said Miranda quietly. "Let's go in. We can sit on the balcony and look at the water."

Miranda made them hot chocolate while Jack talked to Sam on the phone. She could hear Jack's side of the conversation.

"You'll have to find your own way home. I brought Miranda back to the Shack." Jack shook his head and said, "Well this is what you two wanted isn't it?"

Jack laughed at Sam's response and looked over to Miranda who was trying to look as though she wasn't listening at all.

"Yeh, okay, okay. Alright I'll see you when I see you." Jack put his phone in his pocket. "Sorted." He inclined his head and gave Miranda a crooked smile. "They are at the Airbnb," he said.

"Oh," said Miranda. The thought of what that might mean made her face warm. She held up the mugs of hot chocolate and indicated the balcony. She had to get outside, the room seemed too small and Jack was filling up the space with a look in his eyes she remembered from long ago.

Miranda carried the mugs out onto the balcony and put them on the long wooden table that sat in the middle of the space. An assortment of chairs to accommodate all the family when they were on holiday lined the wall of the house, folding dining chairs stacked in two piles against a wall, three deckchairs, and an old leather sofa covered with colourful cushions.

The evening was warm. Jack smiled to himself, he couldn't put his finger on the exact moment when he knew that Miranda was special, perhaps he had always known it. She was the girl who had endured so much and yet she seemed to have shrugged off her past. *Yeh she's special.* He hadn't thought he had a chance with Miranda after what had happened between them but after the way she spoke to Ross, well it made him want to put his arms around her. She was his hero.

He walked over to the balcony railing and looked across the roof tops to the black stretch of ocean. A cool breeze was blowing off the water.

"Feel that breeze, the best thing about being near the ocean," said Jack. He turned to Miranda, he noticed her bare arms, "But you think it's cold." He said and smiled.

Miranda put the mugs down on the table, she wanted to prove him wrong but he was right, she did think it was cold. She smiled back at him, he'd remembered that about her.

"I'm just going to get a sweater." She thought her heart was going to beat out of her chest. Back in her bedroom she stood looking at the few clothes she had brought that were hanging in the wardrobe. She picked up a bright blue sweatshirt and pulled it over her head. Being alone with Jack was making her feel anxious or was it something else? She felt as though she was on the verge of something exciting, a moment in her life that she would remember forever.

"You really do feel the cold," said Jack, "come and sit next to me, I radiate heat." Jack walked over to the leather sofa. Miranda saw his empty mug on the table.

She picked up her drink and took a few sips while she stood next to the table. Jack was sitting with his arm along the back of the sofa. He looked so relaxed as though he had done this a hundred times. All the excitement drained away in that moment.

"What's wrong?" said Jack. He saw the sudden change in her expression. She was retreating, going to that place where no one could get in. He stood up and moved next to her. "Hey, okay. I'm going too fast. Sorry but you make me nervous."

Miranda opened her eyes wide in surprise, "Me? I make you nervous?"

"Yeh, you do. You seem so strong and confident… you're on your own. No family but…"

Miranda tilted her head to one side waiting for the but, Jack rested his hands on her shoulders. "You're amazing."

"No, I'm not," Miranda said, "You're amazing. Aren't you the King of the Kicks?" She walked over to the sofa and Jack followed.

"You know about that?" said Jack. He drew his eyebrows together. He didn't think she knew anything about his football career.

"Yeh, everybody in Perth knows that," said Miranda.

"Only if you read the sports page," said Jack laughing as he stretched his arm along the back of the sofa.

Miranda looked at Jack from under her lashes, "I think Rose told me. I guess that means you've kicked a lot of goals."

"Yeh a fair few and I've missed some, important ones." He thought about what Ross had said, he knew he was referring to the last time he played before the Perth crowd when he had missed an easy goal. No one would remember that miss and remind him of it. Every player had easy shots at goal that they missed. But Ross would remember it to his dying day.

He resisted the urge to let his arm slip around Miranda's shoulders and pull her to him. He wasn't going to pressure her. He liked her too much, he didn't want to spoil the possibility of something real between them. "Hey," he said. "You've got your sweater on inside out and back to front."

Miranda looked down and touched the label at her neck. She tilted her head up to his and smiled. "I guess you make me nervous too," she said.

He pulled her against his chest. "Yeh, can't see why I would make you nervous."

Miranda turned in his arms, she felt the heat in her cheeks. *I'm twenty, I don't have to wait to be kissed. I don't have to wait for him to make the first move.* Jack looked at her, his grey eyes searched hers.

"You can't? Don't worry I'm getting over it," she said and quickly stretched her head up until her lips touched his.

Jack gave her a wry smile. She had kissed him, his heart seemed to expand out of his chest. He felt the heat low in his stomach. He knew what he wanted the kiss to lead to but did she?

He pushed Miranda gently onto her back and she scooted her body up until she could swing her legs onto the sofa. Jack leaned over her, supporting his weight with one arm.

"Is this okay?" he said. He thought she looked afraid of what he was going to do. He wasn't going to do anything unless she said yes.

Miranda nodded her head. He had been a fantasy but now he was real and the real Jack was so much better than the fantasy. He wasn't the invincible hero with the perfect life. He had used alcohol to numb his pain, she had used something else until her mother had died and Jack had seen what that was on his eighteenth birthday. But he didn't remember.

Jack's hair fell forward across his face. *Girly hair.* The words sprang to his lips. He felt a knot of anger flair in his throat, it was a nuisance, he'd shave his head after the photo shoot. He lifted a hand to brush it back. Miranda smiled and caught his hair up in her hands and pushed it back behind his ears. She liked it, it made him look wild. She smiled, and he could hear those words again in the way she looked at him, *it's beautiful.*

Jack kissed her, gently at first but then his tongue found hers and his body turned to liquid. He found the zip on the front of her jeans and pushed it down. He pressed his hand against her stomach feeling for the edge of her panties. He felt her body freeze and he stopped. He lifted his head, her eyes were wide. "What's wrong?" he said, "you want me to stop?"

Miranda held her hand across her eyes, "It's okay," Jack said. "We don't have to do anything." He lifted her hand from her eyes, they were closed but he could see the tears that had pooled in the corners.

"Hey Miranda, it's okay." He meant it too. "Look at me, I mean it." He didn't care how long it took, she was worth waiting for.

"It's just… you don't remember…"

He stopped her, "I know I was drunk and I'm sorry. Really Miranda." What did he have to remember, something she was ashamed of? "What is it? You can tell me."

Miranda bit her lip, and pushed herself up, "I'm the one that should be sorry." She leant her head back against the sofa.

"What? What have you got to be sorry about?" he said.

Miranda pressed her lips together. She had let him take all the blame for not remembering that night but she had to take some responsibility.

"I should have stopped you, I guess. But I wanted you to be my first. You were too drunk to notice the scars."

"Scars?" said Jack.

"You used alcohol to numb your pain, and I..." she shrugged.

"You what?"

"I cut myself."

"You cut yourself?" Jack said.

Miranda could hear the puzzlement in his voice. "Yeh, I started when I was ten and stopped when she died. It made me feel better. A physical pain, it was better than feeling bad."

Jack nodded, he remembered hearing about a boy at school who had done that. He had used a school compass to gouge flesh out of his arms. He wasn't at the school long.

Jack was beginning to understand what she was saying. He must have seen the scars before and she knew he couldn't remember.

"My scars are inside and yours are outside. I get it. You saw some of mine tonight." He tilted his head to the side and gave her a smile. "Only fair you show me yours."

Miranda didn't stop to think, she stood up and faced him and pushed her jeans down until the scars were visible. They were low, close to her pubic bone, four rows of short horizontal scars. They looked neat, deliberate, beautiful in their symmetry.

Jack could see Miranda's hands were trembling. He ran a finger across the raised surface and Miranda sucked in her breath.

He looked up at her and smiled, "Neat," he said, "your scars, just like you." He grabbed her by the hips and pulled her to him and pressed his lips there.

"Okay?" he said standing up. "So, if it's okay with you, can we go into the bedroom. This sofa is way too small."

***

Jack lay on his back, the light from the window was blinding. He wanted to get out of bed and pull the curtains but Miranda was lying on his chest, her dark curls rubbing against his chin. Ross had once said to him, 'they're all the same mate, it's the chase that's the fun part.'

Jack thought about all the girls he had had sex with, too many before he got into trouble with the law. He felt bad about it now, in bed with Miranda. Feeling the connection to her was like nothing he had felt before. She wasn't just another girl, she was Miranda and making love with her… he bit his lip just thinking about being inside her and seeing how he felt reflected in her eyes. I *love her, I fucking love her.*

Jack gently rolled Miranda off his chest, "Mm, what's the time," Miranda lifted her head and squinted against the light.

"My bladder is bursting," said Jack, "and my mouth feels pretty rank." He threw his legs over the side of the bed and stood up, he didn't bother to pull on his pants, he didn't give it a thought. Miranda lay back on the pillow and closed her eyes. It had been a hundred times better than any fantasy she had of them together. It had been real, it had been awkward at times, putting on the condom, but he'd been considerate, gentle, kind, checking with her before he pushed her legs apart and then slowly entering her waiting for her, his face above hers, his eyes reading her every expression. "Okay?" he'd said when he felt her nails on his back. It had been so much better than okay but all she could do was murmur back, okay.

The night had wiped out any memory of the one night she had spent with him before. There had been nothing tender then. It had been over before it had begun. The alcohol on his breath so strong that it had remained with her for days after.

She heard the toilet flush and she sat up pulling the rumpled sheets over her bare breasts. He stood in the open doorway, noticed the sheet clutched to her throat and the shy look she was giving him. He grinned, "Too late, seen it all." He changed the subject quickly when he saw her flushed cheeks. "Hey don't suppose you've got a spare toothbrush?" His mouth tasted bad and he didn't want to think about his breath.

"I think so," she dropped the sheet and put one leg out of the bed and hesitated. She had never been naked with anyone like this before.

"Here," said Jack moving across the room and picking up his shirt, "put this on," he said as he retrieved his boxer shorts from the floor and pulled them on.

He followed her into the bathroom and stood behind her while she searched the bathroom cabinet. The bathroom was large, two matching hand basins set on top of a dark wooden bench with a double mirrored bathroom cabinet above, a large shower and a bath. He was standing too close to her, not giving her the room she needed. He wanted to put his arms around her and feel her dark glossy curls against his bare chest. Miranda closed the cabinet doors and saw him standing behind her his eyes not meeting hers.

She held the toothbrush over her shoulder, he was too close to turn around, she would be pressed against him and she wasn't sure how to behave. Did she mention the night or did she act as if it had never happened, or it had happened and it wasn't important? He took the toothbrush and she stepped to one side and took her toothbrush from the blue painted mug that sat in the middle of the basins.

She handed Jack the toothpaste and waited while he solemnly squeezed the toothpaste onto the brush. He passed it back to her and reached for the tap and ran the toothpaste and brush under the tap and then twisted the tap off.

He looked up at the mirror, toothbrush in his mouth and frowned. Miranda watched as he leant closer to the mirror. Across both shoulders were small red half-moon shapes. He looked puzzled, he twisted his back, more red marks. He knew what they were. He flashed his eyes at Miranda in a bold conspiratorial look that said, 'look what you did last night.'

Miranda bent her head to spit in the basin, she couldn't meet that look but it was going to be okay, it was something, it was real, what they had done together, not something to be ignored.

He rinsed his mouth out quickly and waited for Miranda to do the same.

"Do you want coffee, or something?" said Miranda trying to sound calm as she dropped her toothbrush back into the mug.

Jack smiled and put his arms around her lifting her off her feet, "Not coffee," he said.

Chapter Thirty-Five

Eagles v Dockers

A roar went up from the crowd. Jack Charles, the new kid on the block, had touched the ball and not just touched it, he had marked it, leapt high into the air above every player jostling for a position. Miranda held her fist to her mouth, she knew enough about the game to know that Jack could kick for goal if he took a mark close enough to the posts. Felicity held her breath, *please let him get this, please.* She closed her eyes, she couldn't watch.

It's an easy shot thought Sam, inside fifty, not much of an angle, come on JC you can do this. He watched as Jack slipped his mouth guard into his sock and stepped back five, six paces, tumbling the ball over and over in his hands. He glanced up at the target, stilled the ball between his hands, angled it, turned his wrists down as his fingers spread around the ball. He took a step forward and then another and another.

Miranda jumped to her feet and let out a scream as Felicity opened her eyes to see the ball sail between the goal posts. A tsunami of sound filled the stadium. The Eagles players were surrounding Jack.

Miranda turned to Felicity, her eyes wide, "He scored a goal," she shouted. "He scored a goal," she repeated and then saw that Rose and Sam were looking at her with identical grins. She sat down, she couldn't wipe the smile from her face. She knew how much it meant to Jack to do well. "I just need to play at my best, and I'd really like to kick a goal in my first game." He had wanted her to see him play. He wanted to impress her but he also wanted her in the crowd, someone who wanted him to succeed.

Miranda had known nothing about the game apart from knowing that some people spoke about their team as though it was a religion. When Jack had told her he had been given four tickets by the CEO and would she like to join Felicity, Sam and Rose in a box seat, she had said yes straight away but only if he explained the game to her.

She had made him laugh when she had brought along a note book, "You won't be tested on this," he had told her but she said that was the way she liked to learn new things.

At half time the Dockers were leading by two goals. Jack had missed two goals on the run but he seemed to be everywhere on the field.

"Let's stretch our legs," said Felicity, "we can get a coffee if the queue is not too long."

"I can't believe they are going to play another two quarters," said Miranda, "they look exhausted."

"You mean Jack," said Rose "you haven't noticed anyone else on the field."

Miranda didn't answer, she couldn't deny that she had followed Jack's every move. He'd tied his hair back in a top knot, he was easy to pick out amongst the other players.

"He missed a couple of easy goals, yeh not such a great swap."

Miranda whirled around to face a bald-headed man wearing an Eagles jumper. She glared at him, the words on the tip of her tongue. Rose pinched her arm and pushed her ahead.

"Get used to it Miranda," said Rose.

"Easy to be a critic when you don't play yourself," said Miranda in a voice loud enough for the man behind to hear.

Felicity smiled at Miranda, *good for you, you tell him.* Miranda saw the smile and blushed. She was being an idiot, but it wasn't fair, he was playing hard, and even if she didn't know much about the game, she thought he was one of the best players on the field.

They had only just got served with their coffee when the game began again. The short break seemed to have energised them thought Miranda. They ran back on the field as though the game had just begun.

By the fourth quarter it was the Eagles in the lead by 4 goals. Miranda could see Jack by the Dockers' goal. He darted forward, feigned right, spun on his heel, marked the kick from a midfielder and played on towards the goal. He was close enough to score but the Dockers' defender took him down with a tackle around his waist. Jack went down hard, his head taking the brunt of the fall. He didn't move as the game went on around him.

"He's hurt," said Miranda jumping to her feet.

"He's not moving," said Felicity.

Sam heard the anxiety in both of their voices, "It's okay, probably a bit of concussion, it happens. Look they've stopped the game. The doctor is on the field."

Sam knew that was the end of the game for Jack, they wouldn't let him play on, he would have to get properly checked.

Jack stood up with the assistance of two of the team's physios and was helped off the field. The stadium erupted in cheers and clapping.

Miranda brushed her hand across her eyes. He had played well and now he was hurt. She didn't want to watch the rest

of the game, she didn't care who won, she only cared that
Jack was alright.

***

It was an hour later before Jack could leave the changing
rooms. His team had lost by two goals, he was sorry that he
hadn't been able to finish the game.

Miranda and Felicity were waiting for him in the mem-
bers' lounge. Miranda stood up as he came through the door,
she wanted to run to him but she was deferring to Felicity.
Felicity looked pale, she had seen Jack play many times but
she had never seen him injured. She kept seeing him fall, his
head hitting the ground and his body still.

"I'm okay mum, really." He put his arm around her and
kissed her cheek.

He gave Miranda a crooked smile, he didn't know what
to say. He had wanted her to see him play and now he wondered what she thought of him only getting one goal, missing
some and falling and hitting his head.

Miranda knew exactly what she was going to say, *you were
amazing*. Before she could speak the door opened and Ross
Charles was standing in the doorway.

"Ah there you are. I had a hell of a job getting past the
minders to get in," Ross said. He ignored Miranda and Felicity as if they weren't even present.

Ross thrust his hands in his pockets and studied Jack,
"Well you look okay, I guess no serious damage done." He
turned to Felicity and lifted his head, he looked over at Miranda as she walked and stood next to Jack.

The air seemed to be bristling with tension. Miranda
wanted to run. She swallowed, her mouth was dry, her heart
was beating high in her neck. She reached for Jack's hand

and squeezed it. She stared at Ross, he was going to say something mean and nasty, he was telegraphing it with the curl of his lip and his half-closed eyes.

"Still got that girly hair do," he sneered.

"Shut up," said Miranda, her eyes blazing as though she was on fire. Jack looked at her and grinned, *there goes my hero.*

Jack laughed, "Yeh, shut up Ross, I'm going to keep it too. It prevented a serious head injury the doc said. It's going to be mandatory."

He didn't wait for a response from Ross. He had rehearsed what he was going to say but now he forgot the rehearsed speech. "Hey don't let's do this again, don't bother to contact me again Ross. Mum and I have been doing just fine without you since you left. I don't need you in my life and I don't want you in my life."

Chapter Thirty-Six

TWO MONTHS LATER

ISOBELLE AND MIRANDA

Isobelle Carter moved her chair away from the sun. The girl was late. That's how she thought of her, not as Miranda. She wasn't real yet, just a name. When she had told Brent, her husband that she had matched with someone on ancestry she had said, "some girl, she could be a relative."

Brent was the one who had insisted she not say anything about the family. "Meet her first, find out what she's like. Don't tell her your surname. We don't want her hanging around."

She had waited ten minutes before she had ordered a coffee and now she had drunk that. Something must have happened, she thought. They had spoken on the phone once and had agreed to meet. Isobelle hadn't revealed any details of her family. She had followed Brent's advice. He was always cautious, over protective of their young twin daughters.

She couldn't believe it when she received the email through the Ancestry website. She had been curious about her ancestry and had sent her DNA and now she had matched with someone, who could be a cousin or a niece. A cousin perhaps, that was a distinct possibility. Her father came from a large family, most of them still living in Italy. She didn't know how many Italian cousins she had.

They had agreed to meet at a coffee shop mid distance from where they both lived. That had been Brent's idea, "don't let her know what suburb you live in, don't give too much away."

"Brent she's just a girl, not much older than the twins." He exasperated her sometimes with his caution. "Leave it to me will you. I'm not about to open my arms to her and bring her home." She had used the tone on him that said 'back off' and he did.

'Okay just being-'

'Cautious, I know.'

Isobelle picked up her phone, she was about to send her a text when she glanced up and Miranda was standing at the entrance, a frown on her face, an anxious look in her eyes searching for Isobelle.

Isobelle drew in a breath and stood up, she knew who this girl was, who she had to be. She was family, there was no doubt about that, the similarity was too much. *The same hair, the same eyes.*

"Isobelle?" said Miranda. She touched the table to anchor herself to the ground. She felt disappointed already, she couldn't see any family resemblance between them. Isobelle was tall with short straight hair tied back at the nape of her neck. Her eyes were brown. She looked nothing like Miranda.

"I didn't think you were coming," said Isobelle sitting down. She hadn't been able to keep the note of irritation out of her voice. The least the girl could do was to apologise.

"Oh?" Miranda looked at her phone. She was early. She frowned, this wasn't a good start. "Sorry I thought you texted me 10.30."

Isobelle knew she should have just let it go, but she looked at her phone and Miranda felt her anxiety increase. She couldn't tell Isobelle that she had been early and had waited outside.

Isobelle looked up from the text message she had sent Miranda a week ago, she made an apologetic face and smiled, "My mistake, it was 10.30. I do that sometimes, don't bother to check because I think I've remembered the time. It's nice to meet you, Miranda."

Isobelle couldn't help staring at Miranda, her blue eyes the same colour as his, the curls, she envied and he hated. It wasn't fair that her hair had been dead straight and he had curls.

"Shall we order coffee?" said Isobelle. "I'll order at the counter."

"Thanks, a long black for me," said Miranda.

"You don't drink milk?" said Isobelle.

"Lactose intolerant. I tried drinking it with soy and almond." She made a face and shook her head.

When she returned to the table Isobelle asked Miranda when she discovered she couldn't drink milk.

"Oh, not until I was thirteen. I had a lot of stomach problems when I was younger but it was never picked up until I went to boarding school."

He's lactose intolerant too.

Isobelle stirred her coffee, she knew the question she wanted answered and she wasn't going to wait.

"So, tell me about your parents."

Miranda hadn't touched her coffee, she was glad Isobelle was asking all the questions. She didn't know how to start.

"My mother died when I was twelve…"

"Oh, I'm sorry to hear that," said Isobelle, "your father?"

Miranda shook her head. Isobelle made an 'Oh' sound.

"I don't know who he is. That's what I'm trying to find out."

"Did your mother never tell you… or any of your relatives… grandparents, uncles…?"

"No, not that I know of." Miranda looked at Isobelle and felt her face grow warm. "My mother's parents died in a car crash when she was… twenty. I don't think she ever got on with them. She was an only child too."

"You don't have siblings?"

"No," said Miranda, shaking her head at the same time.

Isobelle leant back in her seat. "Did your mother ever say anything about your father, a clue to who he might be."

"She never wanted to talk about him." Miranda could hear her mother's voice in her head. *He's dead, he doesn't exist.* Miranda smoothed her fingers across her forehead.

"But once not long before she died, she said he didn't know I existed." Miranda hoped that was true.

Isobelle nodded her head. She was building up a picture of Miranda and her mother. She asked more questions, her mother's age when she had Miranda, where she had lived. When she got up to leave, she was almost sure she knew who Miranda's father was.

"Miranda, I have to go. You must have questions for me, but save them until next time." She didn't want to answer any questions until she had talked to Brent.

Miranda couldn't keep the look of dejection from her face. She had questions and she hadn't got to ask one and now Isobelle was leaving.

"Don't worry. I'm going to make some enquiries. I've filed all the information away up here." She tapped her head and smiled at Miranda. "I'm going to get back to you." She paused, "And I'm pretty sure we aren't cousins."

Miranda lifted her head, Isobelle was talking but Miranda wasn't listening, *if we're not cousins*. The email from Ancestry was embedded in her head, 20% cousin, niece, aunt.

Isobelle put her hands on Miranda's shoulders. "Let's hope we get some answers Miranda, and when we do, I'm going to call you. We need to solve this mystery."

Jack was sitting in his car looking at his phone when he saw Miranda coming towards him. She didn't look... he couldn't read the look.

She turned away from him to pull on the seat belt, she wanted him to drive. She struggled to lock the belt in. "Here let me do that," Jack put his hand over hers and took the clip and locked it into place.

He didn't want to ask her how it went, it didn't look good.

He brushed his hand down the back of her head, "You okay?"

She turned her head to face him. Her eyes were glittering and she was smiling.

"Jack, I think... she's my aunt and..." she covered her face with her palms she couldn't say the words.

"She'll know who your father is?" said Jack.

Miranda nodded her head. "She asked me so many questions Jack. How old my mother was when she had me, where we had been living when I was born. So many questions, and I didn't get to ask one!"

He didn't want to put a damper on how she was feeling but he was worried that she'd be disappointed if she didn't get the answer she wanted.

He leant down and turned her face to his and kissed her lips.

"Just be… don't get…"

"It's alright, I've thought about it. He might not want to know me."

Jack clenched his jaw, the thought of Miranda's father not wanting to know her… that couldn't happen, he wouldn't let it. He'd gone quiet already thinking of the confrontation he'd have when he tracked him down.

Miranda, took hold of his hand, "Let me guess what that silence means and that." She pushed her finger into the dimple in his cheek. "Mm the clenched jaw."

Jack put his head back and laughed. "Stop reading my mind. I just…" He put his hands up, "No, no, okay. No looking after you. He gave her a crooked grin, "But I do like being a hero."

"You've been warned about that," she said putting an arm around his neck. He didn't resist the pull and brought his face to rest against hers.

"Mmm, okay, I heard you. Okay gotta get you home and I've got training in an hour.

As soon as Miranda opened the door Rose called out, "In here Milly."

Miranda couldn't keep the smile off her face when she entered the kitchen. Rose was in the middle of emptying the dishwasher. The clean dishes were stacked on the kitchen bench ready to be put away. She held the cutlery rack in one hand as she dealt out the knives and forks into the kitchen drawer.

The ringing noise of metal stopped and Rose looked at Miranda and let out a shriek, "OMG you've found him." She dropped the basket on the bench.

Miranda shook her head but she couldn't keep the smile from lighting up her eyes.

"No?" Rose was puzzled, why was she looking so happy. "Tell me everything from the beginning."

Rose listened until Miranda had repeated Isobelle's words that she was sure they weren't cousins.

"So that means…?"

"She's my aunt, that's what it means. The match was cousins, niece or aunt. She's not my niece, so she must be my aunt."

"Your aunt? Does that mean…"

"Yes, her brother." Miranda opened her eyes wide to emphasise the point. "I've got to wait now and see if he wants to meet me or acknowledge me."

Rose pressed her lips together and picked up the cutlery basket. She didn't want to discuss the alternative with Miranda.

"Be positive Milly," she said over her shoulder as she tipped the basket up and let the cutlery drop in an ear deafening clatter into the drawer.

"Is that the time?" said Miranda looking at the large Ikea clock that dominated the small space above the sink. "I've got to get changed."

"You're not working, are you?" said Rose, her hands on her hips.

"Please Rose, don't give me the look. I've reduced the shifts to just three a week." She pushed out her bottom lip. "And I try and juggle them around so I can spend time with…"

"Your boyfriend?" said Rose.

Miranda smiled, yes, he was her boyfriend.

Rose picked up her phone, "I've got to tell Sam the news." She hesitated before she pressed the call button, "Is that okay?" she called up the stairs.

"Yes, he might already know if he speaks to Jack."

Rose pulled a face, she wanted to be the one telling Sam the outcome of the meeting, not Jack.

***

Isobelle called three days later, she sounded almost apologetic, "Hi Miranda, I've made enquiries and the person I think… it's possible… well he wants to do a DNA test. Your DNA and his get tested." She didn't tell Miranda how adamant he was when she had broached the subject and told him about her interest in finding out their history and how it had matched her with a young girl.

"And you're saying that I'm her father." The volume of his voice had brought his wife to the kitchen window to see her husband and his sister standing next to the pool, she couldn't hear the words but she could read her husband's body language. She wondered what he was saying, his face was so close to Isobelle.

"I'm saying it's a possibility," Isobelle said quietly. "She's a lovely girl. Look," she reached into her pocket, "I asked her to send a photo."

He held both hands up, "I don't need to see a photo. I would know if I'd fathered a child. I'm not an idiot."

Isobelle could see the anger in her brother's blue eyes. "Frank come on. It's possible. Miranda said her mother told her that her father didn't know she existed. Look Frank, I'm not saying you went around getting girls pregnant and left them. I just think it's a possibility. And I've matched with the DNA as her aunt."

Frank thrust his hands in his pockets and hunched his shoulders. He turned when he heard the back door open and Jenny, his wife looking anxiously at them.

"Everything okay?" she said.

"Yeh, it's fine, it's fine." He rubbed at the grass with the toe of his sneaker. The last thing he wanted was this news, that he might have a daughter living in the same city. The papers would make a field day of it. It was common knowledge that Frank Ferrara had no children.

"Frank, please just look at her photo," Isobelle held out the photograph Miranda had sent her. Rose had taken it. She was wearing a pale blue top that Rose had made her wear, 'it makes your eyes even bluer' and 'have your hair out. Stop looking as if you're going to the dentist, that's better, smile.'

Frank didn't want to look at the small photo Isobelle was holding out to him. He didn't want this to be true. No way. "What's that going to prove," said Frank.

"Just look," said Isobelle. She thrust the phone at him.

He took it and stared at the photo. He felt the solid ground he was standing on shift.

"I want a DNA test," he said and handed the phone back to Isobelle and turned and went into the house to tell Jenny.

Isobelle had purchased the DNA kit and she had obtained Miranda's sample and then her brother's. She didn't get any argument from Frank when she asked for the money to pay for it, "You can afford it, everyone in Perth knows your income." Isobelle had said when she'd collected his sample. It was true he could afford it but he hoped not everyone was interested in learning his salary.

Eight days later Frank and Miranda received the results by email. Frank read his email in the morning at breakfast while he was drinking the first of five coffees he would have during the day. He stared at the result, his heart sped up in a way it hadn't for years. He picked up his phone and sent Isobelle a text that read, *positive and now what?* And then he called Jenny over to read… *the probability of being the father is 99.9%.*

Miranda read her email just five minutes later. She had spent the night at Jack's apartment overlooking the Swan River. He had moved in three weeks ago.

She had left him in bed and made herself a coffee with the drip filter coffee maker he'd bought for her as a bribe to get her to stay overnight.

"Come on Rands it's been weeks and we've not spent a night together. I promise I don't snore."

They were lying naked in his bed, she had one leg draped over his, the curtains were open and the night sky filled the floor to ceiling windows. "I've got to go," Miranda had pushed herself up and he'd pulled her back onto his chest.

"You snore, that's it isn't it," he said pulling her onto his body.

Miranda looked down into his grey eyes and shook her head.

"Do you have nightmares and scream?" she said, her eyes wet.

He'd frowned at her, "You do?" He could see that was troubling her, that she would freak him out. "Well, I could just smother you with a pillow." Miranda didn't smile.

"Or I could wake you up and do this." He ran his hand down between her legs. Miranda let out a gasp.

Miranda rubbed her lips across his chest, "I know you, you'd pretend I had a nightmare just so you could wake me up."

She went home that night and the next day he had bought the coffee maker, "You have to try it out. It's got a timer and I'll set it to make the coffee any time you want."

She had stayed that night. But she wasn't moving in. She wanted her independence. He got that, he wasn't pressuring her. She was right, if it was going to happen it would.

"Hey, morning you." He pulled his t-shirt over his head. He wore his boxers, his legs bare. She hadn't heard him pad across the tiled floor to where she sat on the enclosed balcony. The morning sun was casting a wedge of bright light like a sail across the table where Miranda was sitting with her legs up on the balcony, her hands around a coffee mug.

Jack nodded at the mug, "Any good?"

She turned at the sound of his voice, she was getting used to having him in her life and now perhaps someone else in her life, her father. She still didn't know whether he was going to acknowledge her and she still hadn't found out his name. Sam said he could easily track him down if he knew the sister's name. "Just look her up on Facebook." Miranda didn't know her surname and she didn't want Sam or Rose or anyone trying to find out.

"Hey anything wrong? You've got the frown going."

"Have I?" Miranda rubbed between her brows.

Jack sat down next to her and mirrored her by putting his legs up next to hers. She thought hers looked like pathetic sticks next to his.

She tilted her head towards his, "He's my dad," she said over the top of the coffee mug.

Jack let his legs drop to the floor. "Wow, Rands that's good news huh?"

It was good news if he wanted to meet her. "I told Isobelle to give him my number if he wanted to meet me or talk to me."

He wanted to say, 'he will' but who knew whether that was true. His mother had told him about a client she counselled who had been given up for adoption and when as an adult he tried to contact his mother through the Department for Child Protection he was met with hostility and a refusal to see him by his birth mother.

"He's going to text me, I just think he wanted to be a hundred percent sure."

"Or 99.9%," said Jack.

Miranda tried to picture what he was like now that she had met Isobelle. The only image she could create looked like a male version of Isobelle.

Miranda rubbed at her breastbone, now she had to wait. Jack knew she was anxious. He knew about anxiety and he knew what worked for him. "Let's get breakfast out. We'll walk to Santana's."

Miranda made a face, she wasn't keen on being seen in public with him. It was almost impossible to fly under the radar. People looking and whispering. Eyes following them wherever they went.

Jack didn't like it either, but he wasn't about to become a recluse. He'd just had to accept that was part of his life. There was no disguise that worked, someone would always see beyond the cap pulled down over his eyes and the sunglasses.

He knew how Miranda felt about the attention. He kept his distance from her when they were in public. No show of affection that could be caught on a mobile phone. He respected her need for privacy.

"We'll grab a coffee and find a secluded spot." He emphasized the word secluded and raised his eyebrows. "Get your gear on."

Jack could see Miranda was preoccupied. They walked in silence, along the path that skirted the river. The river was like a mill pond, the sky cloudless. They had just reached Santana's when Miranda's phone told her she had a text.

Jack was standing in front of her ordering when he heard the ping of her phone. She reached out and grabbed onto his t-shirt. He took one look at her white face.

"Read it later, when we get outside." He swiped his card across the Eftpos machine and handed Miranda a paper bag with toasted sandwiches. He ignored the eyes of the couple standing by the door, he had got good at reading the body language of someone who had recognised him and he could see the mobile phone the woman was pretending to read but knew she was about to take a photo.

Miranda hadn't stopped clutching his t-shirt. He grabbed hold of her hand and pulled her behind him. He didn't stop walking until they had reached the trees that fringed the riverbank.

"Over there," he indicated a vacant grassed area with a wooden picnic table. He looked at Miranda, and smiled, "Secluded."

She sat opposite him and pulled out her phone and placed it on the table. He looked at her from under his brows. She ran her tongue across her lips and opened the message.

She looked up at him with astonished eyes, and pushed the phone over to him.

Hi Miranda, I got the DNA results today. I think we should talk. Call me if you are free or send me a text when you are available. Frank

Miranda rubbed the perspiration from her top lip. Her chest felt tight and not in a good way.

"That's good news huh?" Jack said.

"I'm not sure. I don't know." She spread both hands across her forehead as if to keep her thoughts from jumping out. She stretched her shoulders and took a long slow breath in. It helped to breathe slowly when she felt like this, worried, confused and the anxiety was just waiting to hijack her.

"Well why don't you talk to him after you've eaten and I'll go for a walk and you can text me when to come back."

She nodded but she knew she couldn't eat. "I'll eat later."

He didn't argue, he got that. "Okay," he picked up his coffee and the uneaten half of his sandwich. "I'm going now. Do it and get it over with."

He walked down to the water and along the sandy river edge. She could see he was heading for the wooden jetty. She turned away from him and picked up the phone and made the call.

Jack watched her from the jetty. She stood up and then sat on the table and looked out to the water. He couldn't tell if she was smiling or not but then she looked up and she was waving to him and he knew it was going to be alright.

As she ran towards him, he could see her grin a mile wide. He understood the tears in her eyes.

"We're going to meet today. He said sorry so many times. He didn't know. His wife knows about me and she wants to meet me too and look he sent a photo so I will recognise him. He said…" she brushed at the tears, "he said I look like him." Jack raised his eyebrows, "well not like him but we have the same hair and eyes."

She held out the photo, "See same hair and eyes."

"What the fuck!" Jack looked aghast, "that's your father. That's the photo he sent. Do you know who that is?"

Miranda felt all the joy drain out of her. "It's okay Rands, it's just unbelievable, fucking unbelievable." He gave a hoot of laughter. "That," he pointed to the photo "is Frank Ferrara."

"Frank Ferrara?" She didn't understand why Jack was looking so incredulous.

"Let me see the photo again," he said holding out his hand. He didn't need to see it again. The man who was her father was even wearing the purple and white guernsey. It was definitely a recent photo.

"Jack, will you stop shaking your head and tell me." Miranda didn't know what to think.

"Your father," Jack said emphasising each word, "is the new CEO of the Fremantle Dockers."

Miranda made a perfect 'O' with her mouth. In the last three months she had learnt a lot about Aussie Rules football. She knew that there were 18 teams playing in the Australian Football League and just two of the teams, the West Coast Eagles and the Fremantle Dockers were in Western Australia.

"You know what this means, don't you?" said Jack. He took her by the shoulders and gave her his intense stare.

"I guess so." Miranda couldn't stop smiling.

"Yes," said Jack in a meaningful way.

She took a step back, grinning at him, "It means you're going to have a girlfriend who votes for the Dockers."

"Votes? Barracks for the Dockers, it's barracks you dope… what? No." He took a step forward and caught her around the waist and lifted her feet off the ground. "You can't Miranda." He kissed her and swung her around.

"I'll barrack for both," she said smiling down at his up-turned face.

Jack shook his head, "I love you Miranda."

Miranda held his face between her hands. He loved her, she thought he had said it once before when they were making love, a whisper in her ear, muffled against her neck.

"And I love you," she gave him a half smile. "Purple doesn't suit me," she said and kissed him again as someone walked past on the grass bank above the sand. Miranda didn't look up and neither did Jack.

Acknowledgements

Thanks to Dylan, Mike and Julie for their footy expertise and to friends and family for support. Thanks to Jo B, Leah, Julie and Mike for reading through my manuscript.

Thanks to Susan as always for her encouragement.

About The Author

Joy Taylor was born in the UK and now lives in Perth, WA.

She's been a high school teacher, teaching English and Maths, and is now a lawyer representing children in the Western Australian Family Court. When she's not writing YA novels she likes to paint, hang out with her family and walk her dog.

9 781923 454163